A THORNE FOR A CROWN

Eva Thorne Book Two

Lorel Clayton

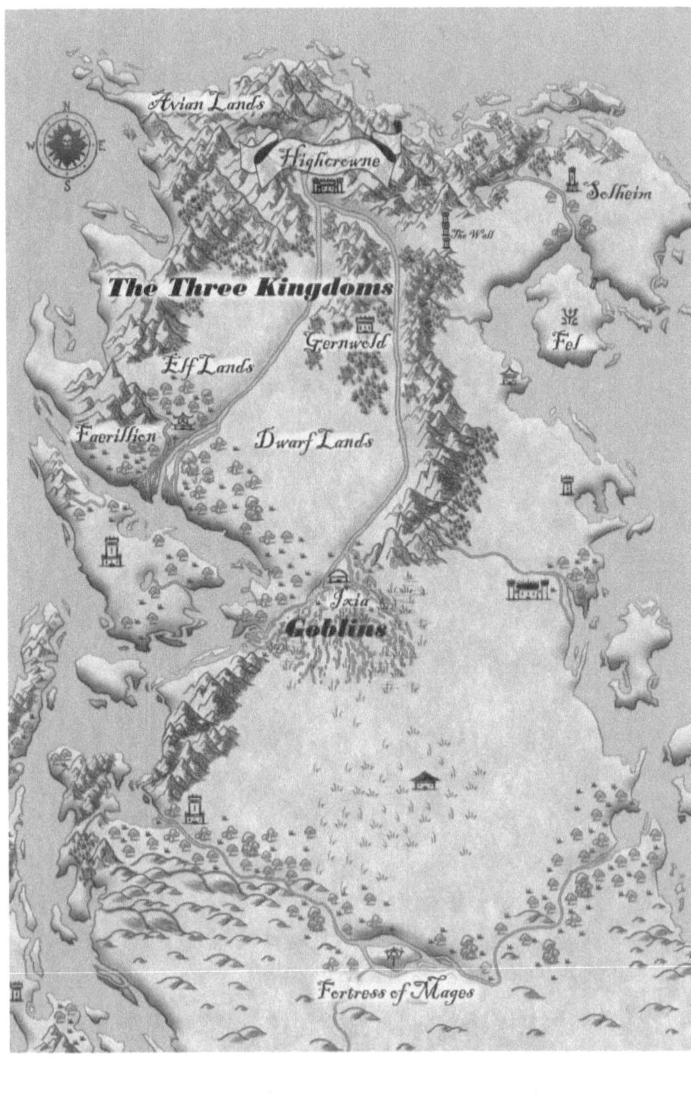

N
W
S
E
Avian Lands
Highcrowne
Solheim
The Wall
The Three Kingdoms
Gernweld
Fel
Elf Lands
Faerillion
Dwarf Lands
Ixia
Goblins
Fortress of Mages

DEDICATION

This is dedicated to our son, Max. You make us laugh, groan, throw up our hands, hug ... and remind us every day 'what is good in life'.

ACKNOWLEDGEMENTS

Thank <u>you</u> for reading...

SOMETHING IN THE AIR

I hate spring. And love. Why did they always seem to be happening at the same time? The flowers spraying us with their pollen, the sneezing, the crying ... and then people were giving you more flowers and asking you to dinner while snot is running everywhere. At least that's how I saw it. Everyone else around me seemed to be having a wonderful time.

"Miss Thorne," the grocer said, giving me a hug and a sloppy kiss on one cheek. "Please take this to Miss Karolyne." He plonked a giant bouquet into my arms, and my nose immediately twitched and tried to crawl away. "I trust this will be to her liking. Have a delightful day, my dear."

He was humming and turned in a circle, arms out to grab his plump wife who was straightening the carrots. He twirled her about the small shop.

"Oh, Carl," the wife said in faux protest as she smiled and danced to unheard music.

Bleh. I had to shut my eyes and start walking. It would have been easier to see where I was going with them open, but the flowers were making them swell shut.

I managed to make out more blurry lovers in the street exchanging gifts and kisses, oblivious to the giant mud puddles they were standing in. Of course, because the streets were cobblestone and lacked gutters or sewers to contain the waste from horses or dumped from windows and lavatories frequented by humans, dwarfs, elves, goblins and every other resident or visitor to the Outskirts of Highcrowne, I highly doubted it was 'mud'.

That was another thing I hated about spring: it thawed the wonderfully clean and unscented snow that usually hid the grime and the stinking pile of garbage that was the Outskirts.

"Out of the way," said a bright green goblin with a mouth of needle-sharp teeth.

He pushed me aside just in time to avoid losing my toes to a street scraper being operated by his friend, an almost identical three-foot-tall green creature with patchy black hair and beady eyes. The friend, not the machine. The scraper was a coughing spluttering contraption of brass and steel and steam that rattled along the bumpy stone road on metal wheels and pushed a wide shovel in front to gather the muck from the spring melt.

I wanted to say 'thanks', but instead said, "What are you doing pushing me around?" My usual anger was heightened at this time of year. I was hoping for a good row as an antidote to the love in the air, and goblins were guaranteed to give me one. "Keep that abominable machine out of my way."

The goblin bared his needle fangs in an impossibly wide mouth, and I happily prepared to drop the bouquet I was carrying and grab the cane strapped to my back.

The 'cane', called an Ashur, was made of carved bone and not a cane so much as a concealed sword with a nasty, serrated blade. I had no intention of drawing it, but the bone sheath would work to block goblin teeth.

"Oh no you don't," the goblin astride the scraping machine warned the one on the ground beside me. "We have a date tonight. No getting yourself locked up by the Guard."

The other one was his girlfriend? Goblins all looked alike to me. There were a few grumbles, but the goblin threatening me hopped onto the machine beside his companion and trundled away.

How disappointing. Sometimes the Guard could be a massive pain. Of course, I'd wanted the Guard and the rule of law just last winter, when I'd been hunting for my brother's murderer and trying to stop rogue slavers who were stealing humans off the street.

Now that the outer wall had been completed, the Outskirts was almost Highcrowne proper. We were enclosed and on the Guard's patrol route, thanks to Conrad, the only human guardsman and one of my more persistent friends.

He'd been pretty persistent on other fronts as well, bringing flowers, until he saw my frightening reaction to them, and then sweets, which I turned away, as I was already putting on too many curves from sitting around in my office all day waiting for a case to show up.

I'd been dodging Conrad—as well as a few other people—because I'm not as easy going about kisses up against a wall as I was before my last lover. The one who tied me up for a dark ritual and nearly stole my soul before I was forced to kill him. Yeah, that did not end well. Best to avoid love. I mean lust. And flowers. *Acht–chu!*

I dodged a string of about ten male dwarfs, arms laden with cloths and jewelry, all trying to woo one female dwarf passing through the neighborhood on her way to the docks. She was coyly not looking at them, while really looking at them out of the corner of her eye, as she marched steadily forward down the street.

Next were the elves in their carriages on their way to the slave quarter to purchase more servants. They didn't have to be in the muck, and their silken clothes blew delicately on the wind. One lady with violet eyes and hair to match let her scarf entangle the elf on the seat beside her to hide their public kiss. I noticed the skin along their arms never touched, staying about three inches apart, a sure sign one or both were using glamour to conceal their true bulk. Elves usually only appeared lovely and waif–like. They tended to sit around more than I did and never said no to any fatty delicacy.

It was wrong to stereotype. Some elves scrupulously avoided glamours and over-indulging, but the more active ones were even worse. Their favorite sport was dragon hunting, which is why you never saw many dragons these days, and when you did, they tended to attack first.

A gang of muscled elves in leather armor, wearing yet more garlands of flowers, had managed to hunt down some poor creature and had its limp corpse strapped to the back of a wagon. The hand-painted sign around its neck said 'dragon' but I was certain it was a baby wyvern. A real dragon, even a baby one, would have taken a few more wagons to move it. And an army to have killed it.

These elves strutted about, showing off the trophy to a handful of elven maidens who had gathered by the fountain to protest the treatment of refugees, or to tell us all to go back home. There seemed to be a couple of different groups with contradictory signs, but most dropped their placards to stroke natural elf muscle and gasp at the 'dangerous' creature they'd defeated.

After that were the humans, who made up the bulk of the population of the Outskirts. They were holding a festival in the main square of the temple district. Flowered garlands everywhere, men and women taking up a ribbon from the festival pole in one hand and dancing in and out of one another's reach as they tied the ribbons tighter and tighter to the pole, until they all converged. Hopeful lovers ending up face to face and a few shy looks away from a festival kiss.

I shut my eyes again. Better to lose a few toes to street scrapers than watch any more.

By the time I reached Karolyne's café, I was ready for whisky-spiked kaffe and a dark corner to hide in until the spring festival was over. Of course, the full festival lasted about three weeks, so I'd need a lot of whisky.

I kicked the café door open with my boot and said, the words half smothered by flowers and my quickly swelling throat, "Someone take these hideous things now!"

"They're beautiful," Karolyne gushed, sweeping in to rescue her precious bouquet.

She took a deep sniff and then added them to the mound of flower garlands, wreaths and other bouquets that had taken over one of the corner tables.

"I may need to make two trips. Eva, can you help get these to the wagon? The ship docks tonight and we can start setting up as soon as it arrives."

"No. They're killing me."

I used a cloth napkin to plug my dripping nostrils and sat myself down, as planned, in the table farthest from the flowers. I had to shout to be heard across the distance. Fortunately, it was a weekday morning and the customers were non-existent this time of day, so I had my pick of tables to hide at.

"When I asked you to be my bridesmaid—" Karolyne began, putting her hand on her hip and tossing back her thick, red hair in a commanding posture I knew all too well from when she used to be my boss.

"—You didn't ask me to be your slave," I said. "Get Reginald or Bert to do it." I indicated the two dwarves setting up tables and drying the freshly washed cutlery as they went.

"I'm no slave either," Reginald grumbled. He gave a butter knife one last polish before setting it on the table with a clank.

"Parallel to the fork," Karolyne reminded him in a voice that was the perfect imitation of our finishing school teacher. "Par-al-lel."

"Kiss-my-a…" Reginald began, but Bert elbowed him in the gut so hard the wind went out of him.

Trust Bert to keep his troublesome brother in line. Or was it second cousin? It was hard to keep dwarf genealogy straight, with polyandry the norm and massive herds of children arising from each union. I knew Bert and Reginald were my friend's, Gypsum's, cousins, but I didn't know if they had the same father.

Whatever their relationship to one another, I was disappointed in Bert always being the goody-two-shoes and stopping Reginald before he could give Karolyne a good comeback. But I suppose that's why I chose Karolyne's as my office. The bickering, and even late-night bar fights, made it far quieter than Nanny's screeching at home.

"Shut up and take them to the wagon," Karolyne said, and Bert hurried to obey, grabbing an armful of flowers.

Reginald moved about one third speed and cursed under his breath as he picked up a single garland between thumb and forefinger, like he was picking up a diseased insect.

Reginald was wearing a red sash tied around his bicep. I'd been seeing those on the most annoying dwarves lately. It was the mark of some new movement that was about male dwarves taking back their power and not listening to women anymore. From my perspective, the movement wasn't making much headway beyond theory.

"And you," Karolyne turned to me, "have a contractual arrangement with this establishment. Window. Now. If you're 'working' instead of being my bridesmaid."

I was pretty sure I was my own boss, but sometimes with Karolyne I forgot.

"Fine." I moved to the table by the window as she'd ordered.

I thought of myself as a reverse scarecrow. I got free kaffe on the house every hour in exchange for luring the customers in. No one visited a tavern, let alone the strange version my friend had created with its 'authentic human food', without seeing some customers inside to demonstrate the cuisine wasn't toxic.

Sure enough, as soon as I sat down and Karolyne reluctantly set a cup of unsweetened kaffe beside me— she still made me pay for the sugar ants—the bell over the front door rang, heralding the arrival of the first customer of the day.

Karolyne's smile of greeting froze when she recognized our friend, Gypsum. Another female dwarf was with her, decked out in fine silks and a veil covering her face like the dwarven matriarchs wore. Of course, Gypsum was dwarf royalty, so the other woman could well be a matriarch.

"What are you doing here?" Karolyne hissed. "Aren't you supposed to be picking up my wedding dress and then the rings and then—"

"—Something came up," Gypsum said matter of fact.

It would have to be important for Gypsum to shirk her Maid of Honor duties. Gypsum was bedrock. I mean solid and reliable, which is why I'm sure Karolyne chose her over me as Maid of Honor.

We'd all been friends at school, and maybe I'd known Karolyne a teensy bit longer than Gypsum had, years actually, and even though Karolyne and I had been roommates, and I'd covered for her all those nights she snuck out, and that one time with the 'accident' as we now called it, and I'd helped her bury ... but we didn't speak of it, and I'm sure none of that was a factor in Karolyne's choice. It was all about who could get the job done. I was not grumpy about not being chosen. No, sir. I didn't want the extra trouble. I ... What was it Gypsum was saying now? I stopped my mental processes and tried to focus.

"We need to speak to Eva in private," Gypsum repeated, pointing her head towards the back stairs.

"Me?" I was slow to start in the mornings. I took a swig of the kaffe to jolt me awake, retched at the lack of sugar and stood up. "Okay."

I ignored Karolyne's crossed arms of curiosity and followed Gypsum and her companion. We went up the stairs to the office. The door was open to my old room across the hall. Bert and Reginald lived there now, the odd couple, with clothes strewn across one half the room and the other as neat and tidy as though someone had drawn a line down the middle and told the Storm God to unleash his might on one side and not the other.

Gypsum knew Karolyne's place almost as well as I did, and she opened the office to let us all in. The room had the expected filing cabinet and solid wood desk, but it also sported a sleeping pallet and a small closet of Karolyne's things. This is where she lived, and I always felt a bit uncomfortable going in here.

I also felt guilty for having moved into the huge house my brother had left me in his will and spending the reward I'd gotten from the Crowns after my first case to make this private investigator gig work, but so far it wasn't going so well. I mostly had requests from old ladies in the neighborhood to find lost pets, to deal with boggle infestations (not my job—I wasn't an exterminator), or to sit and listen to a tirade of what was wrong with the world these days. And since these same little old ladies were from the era of barter, I had few coins left in my purse but plenty of chicken eggs and biscuits for the larder. I might soon be joining Karolyne in sleeping on a cot.

Of course, her fortunes were changing, if the spend on this wedding were any indication. Karolyne's husband-to-be was a windfall for her, and I'm sure money was the primary attractor, as he had few other worthwhile qualities.

"What is it, Gypsum?" I asked, still standing and unwilling to take Karolyne's one chair.

The dwarf in the veil took the seat right away and leaned back, comfortable in her makeshift throne, removing the veil as she did.

"It is I who have requested this meeting, not my sister. I heard you were an amateur sleuth."

"Baroness Syla?"

Syla, Gypsum's sister, had inherited the family title, which meant she was one of the residents of the Central City, with supreme authority over her clan of dwarfs, and a Matriarch on the Council that ruled all of dwarf-kind and had a one-third say over how all of Highcrowne and the Three Kingdoms was governed. She was more important than any client I'd ever had. At least I hoped she'd be my client. This could make my reputation.

"It's professional private investigator. Not amateur. I get paid," I said. I wanted to set the ground rules right away. No more freebies for friends of friends.

"Pardon me, Miss Eva Thorne, 'Private Investigator'. I must admit you don't look like one."

I didn't have the trench coat, cigar and flask of booze in my inner pocket. That was true. I was the tall boots and riding pants sort of gal. Sometimes I wore fur, but this was spring, so I was down to a sky-blue sweater. It was still Highcrowne and mildly freezing. I also wasn't a man or an elf, as most detectives seemed to be in this city. I was quite a bit curvier, with dark hair, cat-shaped pale, pale blue eyes—ok, almost white eyes—and large lips that were red even when I didn't wear lipstick. I looked more like the femme fatale than the detective, and people who got involved with me did tend to get dead, but that didn't mean I wasn't a good detective. Or at least I thought so.

"I'm sure my sister isn't questioning your credentials," Gypsum interjected.

"I'm sure she is," I said, "but that's fine. You wouldn't be here if I weren't your last hope."

"You are not that," Baroness Syla said, decidedly. "I prefer to act immediately and avoid any situation turning desperate. I merely have a small problem, and Gypsum speaks highly of you."

A 'small problem'. I hoped this wasn't another lost pet case. Of course, even one of those for a baroness could be good for business.

"I'm listening. Tell me the Who, What, Where, When, Why and How Much," I prompted.

I wished I had the desk and the lounge chair, so I could lean forward and appraise my would-be client. As it was, Baroness Syla was the one who leaned forward, fingers forming a triangle that she rested her chin on as she looked me up and down with a cold gaze.

"This needs to remain confidential," Syla said. "I remember the affair last winter with the rogue slavers you brought to justice. You were effective but noisy. A commotion like you made over King Fharen's alleged involvement will not do in this situation."

"It wasn't alleged. The Elf King is a slimy racist who organized a round up refugees in order to sell them into slavery."

"Eva," Gypsum hissed a warning. "We agreed this would get us nowhere."

I knew it wasn't healthy accusing kings of anything, but while I'd stopped mentioning Fharen in public, I hadn't forgotten.

"I'm not shouting it from the rooftops. I can be discreet."

"Let's go," Syla said, standing up.

"Wait." I know I sounded too desperate, but I needed the money.

The gold the Crowns had given me after the 'Slaver Affair' was already gone. I'm not entirely sure where, as I'm awful with money, but gone was gone.

"I can keep my mouth shut. I wasn't a private investigator back then, but I am now, and I take my job and my clients seriously. You can rely on me, Baroness."

"Gypsum believes in you," Syla said, sitting back down. "Personally, I don't trust humans, especially Solhans."

I stiffened. The hatred for my people was nothing new. In a city ruled by dwarfs, elves and Avians, human refugees were at the bottom of the pecking order, and Solhans below them. We were the ones who had unleashed the Dead God into the world. By 'we' I meant my family, Thornes, not just Solhans in general, but few knew such details, and I wisely chose not to advertise the fact.

Gods tended to be overachievers. And this one was bent on conquering the world. Our own nation, Solheim, was the first to fall, but others soon followed, and now, years later, humans had few places to hide. Highcrowne was the only refuge, protected by powerful magic and compacts between gods, and so it wouldn't be wise of me to tell Syla, one of the ruling Matriarchs, to go to hell, when I had no place but 'hell' to go to if I were kicked out of the city.

"See, discreet," I told her, happy I'd managed to keep my anger and tongue in check. She must have noticed me struggling.

"I don't trust Solhans," Syla repeated, and I clenched my jaw, barely keeping it shut again. "But," she continued, "I trust men even less, so you're all I have. The only female investigator in this city."

"What about elves?" I asked. "Surely there's a female elf investigator?"

Elves weren't like humans, for all the obvious reasons of pointy ears and height limitations, but they didn't have the sexual inequalities found in other cultures either. Humans tended to keep women restricted to certain jobs and out of the halls of power, while dwarves were the opposite. With a ten to one excess of male dwarves to female, the women had become revered. Their Council of Matriarchs ruled. The elven sexes, in contrast, were equal in power—and rudeness—and you could find a female elf in the Guard or any profession.

"As of late, I trust elves even less than Solhans."

"There must be some female dwarves you could turn to?"

I didn't know why I was trying to talk her out of choosing me, but my curiosity was too strong. I really was the bottom of the barrel.

"No female investigators in my family, and I wouldn't ask any other Matriarch for help. Opposing factions. I don't trust them as far as I can throw them, and they're heavier than me."

"So, you don't trust anyone," I summarized.

"Exactly."

"Welcome to the club." I held out my hand to shake.

"Don't you want to hear the details of the case?"

"Of course, but we might as well seal the deal before the lies start. Clients always lie. On purpose or by omission. I'll find out the truth—and the real case—during the course of my investigation."

Syla shook my hand. "Very good. Alright, on to the lying then. The body of Rutgard has been stolen."

I had my back to the closed door, which was a good thing, as I swayed. This was no 'little problem'. Highcrowne was the capital of the Three Kingdoms, a union of the three major races, and ruled jointly by a royal representative from each. Rutgard was the highest representative of the dwarves.

"The Dwarf King is missing?"

"His Presence remains with the Council. It is merely the body that has been misplaced."

I raised an eyebrow. "The truth is more helpful to me than fiction."

Syla sighed. "Not a word to anyone … And, yes, he's gone, along with the Council's legitimacy."

"I've always been confused by this Council of Matriarchs, King Rutgard thing," I said.

Gypsum stood a little straighter. "Let me explain. King Rutgard was the last dwarven king. He perished about five hundred years ago, but his body was preserved by magic and his soul trapped along with it. One of his last acts as king was to abolish the old, corrupt system that had kept dwarves at war for millennium. He said that it was dwarven women—the precious few who were the mothers of our kind—who should be the wise voice of Council and make the decisions that were best for their sons and daughters. He introduced the Council of Matriarchs to rule when he was gone, as he was gravely ill and knew he was dying. Rutgard's act was not popular among the men, who were the clear majority, thus the Council saw to it that Rutgard was preserved and that his ghost could be turned to for advice. The men were more accepting of the Council's orders when they believed they were relayed directly from the King." Gypsum looked satisfied by her lecture. She'd always considered herself cut out to be a history professor.

"*Believed* to be from the King," I said. "Does the Council really commune with Rutgard's ghost?"

"Gypsum can't and won't answer that," Syla said. "Such things are State secrets and not to be divulged to anyone outside the Matriarchy."

"A likely 'no' then. Alright, so who would want to steal the body? Who has the most to gain?"

"Suffragists," Syla said, a sour tone in her voice.

They certainly would have motive and opportunity. There were dwarf suffragists everywhere. Reginald's red armband downstairs in the café attested to that. But that meant too many suspects.

"I don't suppose you know who the ringleaders of the suffragist movement are?" I asked Syla.

"If I did, they'd be in jail already."

"From what I can tell, they've been peaceful. Irritating, but peaceful in their protests." I couldn't help defending the helpless.

I'd seen a few groups of them around with their signs and chants saying things like, "No more skirts! Stop work and hit them where it hurts!" As a woman, I never got the friendliest looks from them, but I sympathized. Their mothers were always telling them what jobs to take, forcing them to work in the mines or, in Gypsum's case, forcing Bert and Reginald to work at the café. There didn't seem to be much choice for male dwarfs, and I could understand their resentment. I knew the feeling of being trapped. My family had kept me that way until recently. I was loving my new freedom and could understand other people wanting theirs.

"Don't be fooled," Syla said. "They are anarchists. They'd bring the whole system down and plunge us into war again. Menfolk need to be kept out of trouble. All you've seen is their political arm. There's a militant wing that is doing real damage."

"Those cave-ins," I said, suddenly clueing in. "The targets were all dwarven workhouses, matriarch meeting places...."

"Yes, we're keeping the details under wraps, but we know a violent group of suffragists is involved. They are likely the same group who stole the king."

"This really sounds like something the Guard should handle," I said, once more trying to put myself out of a job. Was I scared?

"They are working on finding these militants, but no one can know about Rutgard being gone. No one," Syla warned.

"So, I'm supposed to butt in on a top-secret Guard investigation, find King Rutgard before they do, and return the body to the palace before anyone's the wiser?"

"Exactly."

"There is gold payment involved here? You're not expecting this to be my civic duty or offering chickens in trade or anything?"

"You will be richly rewarded. Plus, Gypsum and I will use all of our influence to discreetly aid you in whatever way we can."

"Can you show me where the body was kept?" I needed to see the scene of the crime, but I was also curious.

"Yes, we had planned to take you there first," Gypsum said.

"What about the wedding?" I remembered. "We're both supposed to be setting up the ship tonight. We leave tomorrow." Dwarf militants weren't as frightening as Karolyne would be when she found out we were ruining her big day.

"I'll take care of it," Syla said. "I'll lend your friend some of my people. I'm sure she won't turn down the assistance of a royal wedding planner. And I suppose this gives you one day to find Rutgard. I like that timeline very much."

I didn't.

"I must go now," the Baroness continued. She stood up and readjusted her veil. I had one last glimpse of eyes a swirling blue like the depths of a crystal-clear stream where a reflection of sky rippled and shimmered with light.

Dwarfs had interesting eyes, probably to make up for uninteresting, squat bodies, muddy skin and hair that was always brown and unable to take any dyes. I figured that's why the matriarchs wore their fancy silks head to toe. Made them look less generic.

"Let me get my sister back to her bodyguards," Gypsum said. I hadn't seen the guards but knew they must be close by. Probably part of the reason the café was still empty of customers, even though I'd done my reverse scarecrow routine. "I'll make arrangements for you to pass into the Central City at the Market Gate and meet you there in an hour?"

I nodded. "See you there."

While the Outskirts had a wall around it these days, we were still a long way away from the Central City, where the nobility dwelled. No human had access, only Citizens, and most of them steered clear, staying confined to dwarven and elven neighborhoods around the periphery of the Central City.

"It was lovely to see you, Baroness Syla." I held out my hand. "Thank you for so few lies."

"Likewise."

We'd made our goodbyes, but I awkwardly continued to follow them downstairs and into the main room. The baronesses' head turned toward Reginald who was back for more flowers and carrying them one at a time, which would take all day. I wished I could see Syla's face through the veil and her reaction to the suffragist-red armband, but I did notice Gypsum's narrowed eyes and tight lips. Reginald must be an embarrassment to her, but neither woman said anything.

At the door, I also refrained from saying anything to anyone, practicing my discretion, and merely held it open for them. As soon as I shut it again, Karolyne was on me like a hovering bee, another springtime infestation that I was allergic to.

"What was that all about?" Karolyne asked, arms crossed again. I had no intention of indulging her curiosity.

"My business. But you should be happy to learn they will be sending over a royal wedding planner to help out."

"Really? Wow. I knew I could count on Gypsum." Karolyne looked giddy.

I was glad to be escaping flower duty, and Reginald must have clued in he would be too, because he dropped the ones he had then and there.

"Pick those up," Karolyne ordered.

"No."

"I can demote you lower than busboy," she threatened. "There's grease an inch thick along the drainpipes I could have you scrubbing out. Not to mention the oven needs scraping, the fryer oil needs replaced, the garbage bins could use a hosing...."

Sounded like spring cleaning time. Once again, I was glad I didn't work here anymore. Of course, I'd only done the fryer once and botched it, and most crap work usually went to goblins and other migratory workers, for which I and everyone else was glad. For while there were pipes to pull nasty things out of the kitchen and lavatories, there were no sewers to hold it, which meant everything went into the alley for the muck-rakers to deal with, which meant garbage bin duty involved clambering over a mountain of waste to even find the bins, as the rakers rarely came by.

"No," Reginald repeated.

Karolyne took a deep breath to start her tirade again, when the bell above the door jangled and her fiancé walked in.

Karo closed her mouth and hurried to take his coat. It was a light tweed with a few real gold threads thrown into the weave. Not as ostentatious a display as the gold chain jewelry hanging from his neck and wrists and the gold rings on every finger. It was difficult to see the person past the sparkle, but there was a flash of white teeth—a few diamond studs in those—skin the color and texture of red clay, short brown hair, and eyes like pools of green seawater.

"...Wouldn't let me in to see my own property," The Jerk said, indignant.

I'm sure he meant the café, which was soon to be his by marriage, but he could mean Karolyne. She was beautiful, and he liked to walk her around on his arm, showing her off like another one of his fancy necklaces.

"The gall of those guardsmen," he huffed. "And what was a Matriarch doing here? They wouldn't let me in until she left."

Not very discrete of Syla, but I supposed it was difficult for royalty to go about unnoticed.

"Gypsum's sister, Dear," Karolyne said sweetly. "She's helping with the wedding. Here, let me hang your coat."

I swear I didn't recognize my old friend when The Jerk was near. Reginald seemed to be enjoying the change, because he sat down at a table, rolled a cigarette, and leaned back in a puff of smoke.

"I have to be going," I said, trying to inch towards the exit, but Karolyne's fiancé was twice as wide as me and blocking my route.

He too was sporting a red armband, but that was no surprise. I'd heard him proselytizing to Reginald almost every day.

I still couldn't believe Karolyne was marrying a dwarf. I'm not species-ist but.... Okay, even thinking 'but' meant I was a little. But I'd dislike this dwarf no matter what race he was, so maybe it wasn't his being a dwarf which repulsed me so much as his overall sleaziness.

"Won't you have breakfast with Wade and me?" Karolyne asked.

Oh, yeah, Wade was The Jerk's name. I'm sure Karolyne only wanted me there so she'd have an excuse to stay seated and chat with me rather than be forced to hurry back and forth to the kitchen to fulfill Wade's every need.

"No," Wade pronounced before I could say anything. "I've been reading the old texts, and they state men and women should sup at separate tables. We'll be instituting that mandate right here at this very café from now on."

"Of course, Dear," Karolyne said. "It's amazing how much lost wisdom there is for anyone willing to read those dusty old tomes."

The Jerk puffed his chest out when she agreed so readily. Most dwarves didn't get to order women around, and Wade was clearly enjoying it.

"And that's another thing," Wade added. "No more women reading. It gives them ideas and words to spew back like serpent's venom to their husbands and fathers, those whom they should be showing due respect."

Karolyne nodded quickly, like a chicken pecking up kernels, her eyes wide and entranced. She could not possibly believe this idiocy? I knew she had a stack of books in a suitcase beneath her sleeping pallet. Was she planning on burning them next?

She was clearly suffering from greed-poisoning, but I didn't understand how she thought this could work in the long run. Karolyne was not the sort to be a meek little wife. Ask Bert and Reginald. If she were Solhan, I'd say she was planning a honeymoon murder, but most humans weren't as bloodthirsty as my people, so I didn't know what her plan was. She certainly wouldn't be outliving him, as he was in his prime and dwarves lived twice as long as humans anyway. The way her eyes shone ... could she actually love him? I felt ill.

"Well, I don't have any husbands or fathers," I said. "Looks like I have to rely on my own perfectly functioning brain. You know, Karolyne is far cleverer than anyone in this room. She runs a successful business and balances the books, and she started from nothing."

"Eva." She gave me a warning jab with her elbow.

"I would not call this hole in the Outskirts a 'success'," Wade said, his nose wrinkled with distaste. "The lack of male supervision explains much about you."

"And all that gold you wear makes me curious about you. I thought women controlled dwarven wealth? What kind of mother would let you leave the house looking like a thief's dream?" I asked.

"His mother is dead," Karolyne whispered, trying to make me feel bad.

"I'm not afraid of thieves," Wade said. "I'm not a weak woman."

"Neither am I." I gave him one of my good glares.

The remaining flower arrangements at Reginald's table were making my tongue thicken and my throat swell shut, else I would have had a thing or two more to say to Wade. Instead, I shoved him aside and darted out the door.

I breathed in the stink of smoke and pollen and coughed and sneezed all at once. After wiping my face, I looked up and stopped cold when I saw the tax collector coming toward me.

I glanced back but decided I would rather be drawn and quartered than go inside and listen to anymore of Wade's nonsense.

"Miss Thorne, you are difficult to track down," the elf said.

He was immaculately dressed in a black suit that wouldn't look out of place on a mortician. He was older and thinner than any elf I'd seen, his skin wrinkled and sagging around his jowls, hair pure white and tied up in a bun he kept concealed beneath a black hat.

Most elves used natural glamours to appear eternally young and beautiful—and to hide the fatty flesh put on by their hedonistic lifestyle. They still lived much longer than humans, but they did not age as gracefully as they wanted everyone to think. This elf seemed not to care about hiding his true appearance. Tax collectors were scary enough, but one that lacked vanity was even more frightening.

"I keep odd hours," I explained, hastily. "Investigation keeps me busy. Lots of lost pets. Usually they end up in a goblin's stew, but tracking down the others often involves climbing through back alleys, and most cats and dogs are nocturnal. Fenurian flying fish only flit about at sunrise and sundown, and pet bats are difficult to catch until about midday when they're roosting and deep asleep. As you can see, I need to be in odd places at odd times." I fidgeted.

"So that's why you dashed out of your brother's bookshop the other day, took off down the alleyway and vanished?"

"I spotted Missus Henderson's pet snake. It's been missing since last fall. Must have come out of hibernation with the spring thaw."

"Uh hum."

He opened his fan-fold briefcase and pulled out a document packed with tiny elvish characters. I read and spoke elvish fluently, most everyone in Highcrowne did, as elves tended to be the ones running everything, especially the civil service, but this writing was difficult to make out because of the dense jargon and lawyer-ese. I was reading it at an odd angle, which didn't help, but I was hoping to catch sight of the final tax amount owing, so I'd know if I needed to start running again.

2 NOT THE USUAL SUSPECTS

I hadn't realized we were under attack until the screams and giggles from the spring festival activities down the lane turned into real screams. The crowd broke up, paired lovers clutching each other, or parents scooping up children, people running off in all directions. There was a central point they were running from, and I set my sights on that.

"Stay here," I told the tax collector, but he wasn't about to let me out of his sight again. He was at my heels as I waded into frightened throngs of people.

I smelled cinnamon.

I pulled my sword. I used to keep the Ashur's blade sheathed until I was in a situation so deep my life was at stake. Drawing steel tended to ensure a bloody outcome and it was best to avoid that. But if I was right about this situation, bloodshed was inevitable and even finely-honed, Solhan steel wouldn't help much.

Something stirred inside me, a jolt more powerful than kaffe could hope to achieve, and my fingertips tingled. A green glow emanated from my palms. I wrapped both hands tightly around the bone handle of the Ashur and tried hard to ignore the magic building in me.

Magic was my family inheritance, or so Uncle Ulric said, but it wasn't rainbows and sparkles—more the evil kind that involved necromancy and playing with souls like children played with marbles.

It was also the kind of power that drew the attention of dark gods. The Dead God to be specific. He seemed to have an interest in Thornes, after my parents and Uncle helped summon Him into the world, and a special interest in me. I didn't need that kind of attention. Magic brought out the worst in me and could do worse things than a blade, so I fought it down and focused on the walking corpse headed toward me.

Usually the term 'corpse' conjured images of rot and worms and a shambling gait if one happened to be moving about still, which really wasn't he norm. But since the Dead God stepped into the world, He'd been calling the dead to Him as soldiers in His war of conquest. He wanted His soldiers a bit more ship shape than they were at the time of death and transformed them over three days into creatures of deadly beauty.

The first one I'd encountered face-to-face had skin as hard and fair as alabaster, a grip like stone, plus speed and ferocity I'd only seen matched by a snow leopard.

This corpse did not disappoint. Even though it had been an old man, his wrinkled skin was now like the marble replica of some ancient statesman immortalized for future generations to marvel at. Blood coated his hands, and a fine spray of red droplets covered the rest of him. Combined with his nakedness, it made him look painted for some primitive war. He walked more smoothly and swiftly than he must have managed for decades, and he came right up to me.

"Eva," a hollow voice said. The man's mouth was open, but a god was speaking from it.

I ignored the voice and whatever it planned to say next. Instead, I took a huge swing with my sword, narrowly avoiding the tax collector hiding behind me, and cut into the creature's neck. The metal barely scratched the surface, but I kept cutting, taking advantage of the Ashur's serrated edge to dig in deeper.

I was an idiot for taking on a walking corpse. I knew it, but the blood on its hands meant at least one person was already dead, and I couldn't let it take anyone else with it to Solheim. I was a good distraction.

The corpse clawed at me, and I danced aside. It kept reaching for the tax collector, and I had to give him a shove out of the way. It was hard enough trying to keep myself alive.

"Get out of here," I told the elf again. He listened this time and hurried back towards Karolyne's. I breathed a sigh. A walking corpse wasn't nearly as terrifying as taxes.

I dodged another swipe for my throat. Yes, keep up the funny, Eva. I'd be laughing in the Halls of the Dead soon. Where was the Guard? Then I heard them—finally!—clanking down the street.

"Positions!" the Guard leader, a dwarf with a massive wiry mustache, cried.

The soldiers surrounded me, or the corpse I was fighting, but I felt fairly surrounded.

"Out of the way, Eva." It was Conrad, and he shoved me back.

My usual impulse was to push into the fray again, but we were fighting one of the Risen dead, and I was happy to take a back seat.

The soldiers were methodical in their methods. Hack, shift, hack ... shift position again, raise shields, and climb up again after the corpse knocked them down. My bet would have been on the corpse, if the Guard weren't so relentless. They were like a self-repairing machine, replacing one wounded soldier with another fresh one as soon as the first fell, pushing in and chipping away as though they were demolishing a structure.

In the end, it worked. They hacked the thing to bits. Nothing but twitching, bloodless, body parts remained when they were done. A guardsman came forward and bagged the pieces using large metal tongs. He carried the shifting sack of debris over one shoulder and marched off, leaving the square and the festival to recover as though nothing had happened.

"Move along," a dwarven soldier told the few remaining bystanders. "Nothing to see."

There certainly had been something to see a few moments ago. I'd heard of the rare corpse run amok. Usually, humans were aware of the danger and burned their dead long before the three-day time limit came up, but sometimes people were missed. This though, in the center of the temple district, was odd. And the Guard's practiced response even more suspicious.

"This is not your first corpse," I accused Conrad.

The last time I'd seen him, he'd been offering chocolate and flowers to which I'd responded with a resounding 'No, I will not go out with you.' This was probably not the best segue back into a more comfortable conversational topic, but I wasn't well known for my tact.

"It's our third today," Conrad said, his hands shaking.

He looked gleaming and immaculate in his white, shining armor, but apparently, he was still human. The only human in the Guard to be precise, which tended to be composed of elves and dwarves, with the odd goblin thrown in when they were understaffed. He was a representative for our species, with a lot on his shoulders, and I often wanted desperately to lean on those broad shoulders myself, but I resisted. Conrad was too good for me.

"Three in one day? How can that be?"

Conrad went quiet, and I knew when he was hiding something.

"This was deliberate," I reasoned. "Someone secreted a few dead people around town, someplace where no one would smell them in the spring heat, and now they've all woken up at once. This was a planned attack. By suffragists."

"How do you know that?" Conrad goggled.

I was good, but this was all too easy to figure out after I had Baroness Syla's information. Still, I liked him being bewildered by me.

"A hunch. Now ... tell me the details. I can help with these militants."

Conrad took a cautious step backwards. He knew I wouldn't be happy with whatever he had to say. "You know I can't. I have orders." He turned away, falling into step with the rest of his squad, but he glanced back and said, "It was good to see you, Eva."

"You too." I meant it.

I loved looking at Conrad with his golden good looks and gleaming armor. He was what every girl dreamed of—except me. I dreamed of dark gods whispering into my ear of power and eternity. I was

Solhan, and Conrad was human. Most people in High-crowne saw no difference between our people, but I knew better. We might as well be milk and blood.

I watched Conrad disappear with his squad, and I knew I'd be seeing him again. Even if the Matriarch hadn't hired me to butt into what was happening, I'd be nosing in anyway. Let Conrad have a breather after the battle. I'd be hitting him hard soon enough.

The tax collector frantically washed his gloved hands with a rag.

"The dead. Walking," he said with a shudder, before washing his gloves harder, even though he hadn't touched a thing. Well, there may have been some splatter. "I can't imagine anything more unhygienic."

He eventually composed himself and resumed his bored, yet relentless, bureaucratic body language. "As I was saying, Miss Thorne, I discovered something most irregular when I was reviewing your brother's tax records."

I took off running.

With no snow in the cobbles and my good boots on, I made it a full block before I got winded. Running was not my forte. The soldiers were way ahead of me, but that was okay. All that mattered was that I'd lost the tax collector. Seemed he disdained running even more than I did. I veered left and started climbing steps towards the Market District. Gypsum would soon be waiting to escort me into the Central City.

I hated all the stairs in Highcrowne, but they were better than long, switch-backed roads that took forever to scale. The city was like a layer cake. The best parts, including the Central City where the nobility dwelled, were in the center, high on the mountain that looked down on the muck that made up the rest of the city. Most neighborhoods like the Market District, Goldsmiths Sector, and Red Precinct were well-to-do and inhabited by dwarf clans or snooty elves. The Outskirts surrounded everything, a nest of rats fleeing the wars in the human lands to cower against the base of the city for protection.

The Outskirts had its own, less gaudy Temple District and Market, but they were pale imitations of the grand affairs found in the central parts of the city. The Outskirts was like a grimy ring of scum around the edge of a pond: full of interesting lifeforms, but not very nice to look at—or sniff.

Still, with the war against the Dead God heating up, we'd been brought to the bosom of the city, given an outer wall to protect us and a Guard patrol available to hack up misplaced corpses as well. As Karolyne liked to say, things were looking up every day. I was far more cynical than my old friend, and far more right of course. I knew Highcrowne proper saw the Outskirts as nothing more than a convenient killing field, a buffer between them and the bad guys should the war come calling here.

While I could pass freely into the Market District, where elves and their slaves busily shopped for perfumes, fine clothes, and their daily fare, the entrance to the Central City was not so easy to bypass.

I made my way to the giant, barred gates. They were gilt gold and designed with curling motifs of vines and flowers, but a few inches behind was another layer made of solid steel. They seemed fused shut. There wasn't even a knocker or bell for me to get the guards' attention. Where were they, and where was Gypsum?

I stood there tapping my boot and almost wished I had one of those ridiculous timepieces everyone was buying these days. Sure, the sundial beside the neighborhood well was useless all winter long, and the Central Clock only chimed the hour, but they were precise. The timepieces from the south depended on cogs and wheels that could break, and on people to manually wind them up. And everyone forgot. Not to mention the *tick-tick*-ticking all the time. Still, people were continually looking at them and shaking their heads like I was the one who was late. I had a great internal sense of time. I trusted it before I trusted a machine. But if I had one now, I could be the one checking it and shaking my head when Gypsum showed up a half hour late.

"Sorry," she said. "I needed to organize access to the palace. That's a whole level of paperwork above and beyond our regular catch ups for tea."

I was no fresh-faced visitor to the Central City. Gypsum did invite me in from time to time, but we never went past the rose gardens where her favorite tea shop could be found. I'd become a kaffe addict of late, so our tea chats weren't doing it for me, and I usually invited her to Karolyne's these days. Still, I swear last time I'd been here there had been handles on the gates and gate guards. Gypsum hadn't even passed through them: she'd sneaked up beside me using a small hidden door in the wall.

"What's with the sealed gates?" I asked. I added in a whisper, "It's not because of Rutgard is it?"

"No. That information is not widely known. It's part of the extra precautions."

"Like the outer wall? What's happening? Did Fharen's antics disturb the Compact?" I whispered that last bit too.

Sometimes Highcrowne was too sheltering and made you forget there was an outside world where nations were collapsing like dominos. I hadn't thought much about the war until my encounter last winter with a shadow servant of the Dead God and with the Slaver Affair that had been orchestrated by the Elf King.

Gypsum seemed surprised when I mentioned the Compact, a bargain that called for human sacrifice to keep the Dead God from advancing on the Three Kingdoms. If she was surprised, that meant she already knew about it and had never told me.

"How do you…?" she started. "Never mind. It doesn't matter how. Your tenacity and ability to find the truth is what made me recommend you to my sister. Discretion, however, is still something you need to work on." She made a show of eyeing the passerby in the market district. None of them had been close enough to hear my whispers, but I knew keeping my mouth shut was second only to running on my list of non-abilities.

I kept it shut for a whole minute—as judged by my reliable internal clock—while we made our way into the Central City.

Gypsum used a key to go back through her hidden door, but then we were up against a pair of stern, elven guards in a black uniform I had never seen before, capped by black berets: The opposite of the City Guard's white.

"Who are they?" I asked, examining them as I would some strange bug that had crossed my path.

"Elven Elite Protectorate," Gypsum said.

"EEP?"

"Why do you have to make everything an acronym?"

"Only when it's funny. Where's the Guard?"

"The recent attacks have them pretty busy and the royals pretty twitchy, so the Crowns have been calling in their elite forces to increase security around the Central City."

"Do the Avian's have elite forces?"

"Not that I know of," Gypsum said. "They can take care of themselves as far as I'm aware. So, I should say it is King Fharen and the Council of Matriarchs who are feeling vulnerable."

Our little conversation in the dark tunnel was obviously irritating the EEP soldiers, as judged by the way they twitched and failed to hold a good solid guard pose. Finally, one stepped forward.

"Papers," he commanded. Gypsum produced them, but the elf continued to eye me warily.

The other one did more than eye me. She pushed me against the wall. I almost pushed back, but Gypsum cleared her throat in warning, so I played nice and stood there while the EEP soldier searched me.

"Hey!" I said, finally breaking my silence when she took my Ashur. "That's a family heirloom."

"It's also a weapon." She pulled a few inches of the serrated blade, and it gleamed in the light from the oil lamps. "You can have it back when you return in one hour. You have only one hour, Human."

"You have a stopwatch or something, so I can keep time?" I asked, mocking, wondering if they too were using those hideous timepieces.

The other elf guard produced an hourglass. Oh, right. The traditional way. It was about a foot high, made of wood and glass, and he turned it over before shoving it into my grip. The sand was crystal and glowed with a faint blue light.

"If you do not return it to us to be reset within an hour," the guard warned, "you will not enjoy the consequences."

"Got it." I also noted it had stuck itself to my palms, so I basically had no hands. This was some tight security. "Let's get going," I told Gypsum.

She led me out of the winding tunnel that ran through the massive central wall and out into daylight again. I sneezed and sent a passing butterfly wobbling away into the flower bushes. I raised my arm awkwardly to wipe my nose with the inside of my elbow. The blue cloth of my sleeve looked wet and slimy now. Just great.

"How did anyone sneak something as big as a body past those soldiers?" I asked.

"Security isn't as tight going out. Or for non-humans."

"So, we're probably not looking at human suspects." I sniffed and raised my running nose to keep the goop in my sinuses, but it turned out to be a fair imitation of the elves who passed me with their noses in the air. They clearly didn't like seeing my kind in the Central City. A lot of it was vast gardens, so I'd prefer not to be there either.

"What else do you know about King Fharen's activities?" Gypsum asked, when we were alone on the path.

"Not as much as I'd like."

"Well, the Compact is intact. Fharen would be a fool to disturb it. No, these precautions are against humans only. We dwarves have no fear of being out-numbered, and the Avians insist on continuing to offer sanctuary, but the elves see your kind as a potential danger to our way of life and say we are taking in too many refugees."

"So, they want us contained. Just as I thought."

"You know I don't feel that way." Gypsum touched my shoulder.

"I know."

"But the elves are gaining political strength, and the loss of Rutgard will give them even more opportunity to take power. The dwarves will be in turmoil and unable to marshal arguments against whatever new policies they seek to impose. The Council of Matriarchs must remain intact and unques-tioned if we are to keep this city together."

"Do you think the Elf King is behind Rutgard's kidnapping?" I asked, happy to blame my favorite villain.

"Nice of you to call it a 'kidnapping'. I know you don't believe Syla's explanation of governance by ghosts."

"Hey, I'm a Solhan. We perform necromancy for breakfast. I believe in ghosts, but I also know people—even dwarf people—and no one will repeat verbatim a ghost's orders when their own will do much better."

"True. But I think that is exactly what Rutgard wanted from the start. He wanted the Matriarchs to rule, with their wisdom, not his. Not the wisdom of a king who had kept the dwarf nation at war for centuries."

"Who were the dwarves fighting all that time?" I asked, curious. I was no historian, but I liked to know things.

"Everyone. We were essentially mercenaries for a greater empire, fighting the wars of others."

"I can see how that would get old, but it explains why Reginald looks like he's holding a battle-axe when he's sweeping. It's in his blood. Your men want to fight. Maybe that's your answer for the suffragists: direct that pent up energy elsewhere."

"Like against the Dead God? No thank you. As much as I'd love to restore the human lands and help your people, Eva, the Dead God is ... well, death. I love my husbands and sons too much."

"I get it. I don't like to fight unless my back is up against a wall, but we may yet get there, and you still haven't answered me. Is Fharen likely to be involved? Will you unleash me to question him?"

"No and no. I don't want to see you killed either. Crossing the Elf King, even with proof, is suicide. You need real power on your side to do that, and none of us have that right now."

"Let me guess? Syla might if I help her find Rutgard and take up a position of dominance among the Matriarchs. Isn't that right?"

"You do know how I think. If you succeed, we can help my sister, my clan, and you can get a powerful benefactor on your side. I know you will try to butt heads with Fharen again someday. But not today," she warned again.

"How do I find the body if I can't go after Fharen?"

"Find it. That's all that matters, not the culprit. Getting it back is what's important."

"I hate being less than thorough."

"Really?"

"Ok, as an investigator. I was never very thorough as a waitress or student because I didn't care. Can we hurry up and get there? I'm afraid this hourglass is going to blow up before I have a decent chance to look around."

"It won't blow up, but it will entangle you in a web that roots you in place and makes you deathly afraid until a mage can restore you."

"Sounds even less fun. Lead the way." I sneezed again.

I wanted to get away from flowers, but they seemed to be everywhere. At least the center of the city was a barren mountain. The peak rose above us, raw and un-cultivated. The top was still covered in snow, and I could make out the black dots of distant caves where the Avians lived. Few ever saw them, as they were so reclusive, but as we were headed for the palace, I hoped to catch a glimpse of one.

The palace was as massive as I expected a building that contained the royalty of three kingdoms to be. Doubled. I was glad Gypsum was leading the way, because I was lost just looking at it. She led me up a narrow section of steps on the eastern side of the structure and into a gallery of open rooms and pillars that seemed deserted. No Avians then.

The place would be freezing in winter, but this was the Central City and magic was not spared. I felt it when we crossed the threshold and warmer air surrounded us. The area was surprisingly empty, except for marble floors, pillars and busts of famous dwarves as far as the eye could see. I supposed the Matriarchs did not encourage visitors to see Rutgard, so there wasn't much point in having couches or tables in what was essentially a giant mausoleum.

As we walked, the open galleries closed up, and a pair of solid bronze doors greeted us at the end. A single dwarf stood at a desk with an open book on the table before him and a quill pen in his hand. He didn't look up until we were right in front of him and then it was merely a glance over the top of his spectacles.

Where had he gotten those contraptions? Bell had pointed them out once in a catalog she'd been drooling over, but I'd never seen them in real life. Who wanted to go around looking through a foggy window all day long? If your eyes were failing, save up and buy an enchantment to correct them. It's not like it took a great mage to do the spell. Even Old Nanny could do a fair approximation using Solhan necromancy and a pair of pig's eyes. Of course, I'd never recommend her to anyone, as there was no telling what cost to your soul, or that she'd use pig eyes.

"Excuse us," Gypsum said. "I'm here on Baroness Syla's orders."

"Need to sign the ledger first, Mistress Gypsum." The dwarf handed over the feather pen, and Gypsum signed with a flourish.

I looked for an inkwell, and when I couldn't spot one, I realized it was one of the new pens with a supply of ink stored inside the quill. I had no idea how they got it in there, but it was yet another Southern invention busying up the place. As my hands were stuck to the hourglass, I signed with my mouth and a bit of help from Gypsum. She handed the strange pen back after a moment's inspection. She noted my look of displeasure.

"You were born in the same century I was, Eva. Technology is not black magic."

"If it were, I'd understand it better," I said.

I asked the dwarf behind the desk, "Where did you get the pen? And the spectacles?"

He straightened them, seemingly uncomfortable with the questions. "Gifts, my lady." He withdrew a large iron key from his pocket and did not elaborate. "Now if you'd like to step this way."

Gypsum followed him, but I hung back and looked at the ledger. Each page was a different date, and I noted that for the last two days there had been only six visitors, two of them Gypsum and Syla. Three names didn't look dwarvish: a Doctor Ghunnan, a Miss Student, and a Miss Kissel. The doctor's name was connected to Miss Student's by a dotted line, which looked peculiar. Were they married? Strange thing to note in the visitor's ledger.

I flicked the pages with the tip of my nose and noted the same connection and the same three names going back for several weeks, all at the top of the list, with a few variable names listed below theirs. Looked like Rutgard had some friends who liked to come by regularly. I mentally moved them to the top of my 'to question' list.

"Uh hum," the dwarf cleared his throat to get my attention.

I guiltily pushed the ledger back with my elbow and hurried after him and Gypsum. I shouldn't feel guilty; this was my case, but I also didn't know how much the dwarf knew, so I had to be careful not to look suspicious. Syla had said to tell no one.

"Who are Ghunnan, Student, and Kissel?" I asked, before my brain could come up with an excuse for asking. As it was, the question came out like an interrogation.

"And who is 'Miss Thorne'?" the dwarf asked snootily.

"My friend," Gypsum said. "Now give me the key and run along back to your desk." Her tone of command was undeniable, and the dwarf obeyed. Male dwarves often deferred to their women, but Gypsum was more than a regular dwarf, and her stance shouted he would regret having angered the baroness's sister.

Gypsum wrestled with the lock on the giant set of doors before us. Her voice lost its regal edge and slipped back into the tone I was more familiar with: frustrated, with the most impolite curses whispered under her breath. It was usually either that or outright screaming, all directed at a swarm of her children. It had been a long time since I'd heard her use her civilized voice.

"Come to think of it," I said, "where are your little ones, Gypsum? I haven't seen you without at least half a dozen of them since your last wedding two years ago."

Dwarf women were outnumbered by men, but they compensated by taking several husbands and giving birth to litters of children. It was how the race not only survived but thrived, and the dwarf race ... well 'dwarfed' every other race in the Three Kingdoms.

Since we'd returned to Highcrowne after school, Gypsum had become a mother many times over, while I was still unsure about keeping myself alive let alone a tiny person. I couldn't even keep a rat alive. I knew because I'd had to rescue one last week from an alley, only to accidentally drop it when I saw it was pure black—not a lucky color—and so Mrs. Hirst's pet rat ended up in a rusty trap. I managed to return its silver collar, but that was one more case I didn't get paid for.

"I'd like to say 'with my husbands', but my men, like Reginald, have taken to wearing those red arm-bands and standing on street corners with placards all day instead of being fathers. It's an embarrassment to say the least, and an annoyance. I've sent the children off to visit their grandparents in Gernwold. My hands are full as it is helping with Karolyne's wedding, and I need to be unencumbered to deal with all of this." She pushed the doors wide and spread her arms in a theatrical gesture.

All I saw was darkness that sounded cathedral-like. In the spill of light from the open doors, Gypsum found an oil lamp and lit it with only a touch to the fire rune etched into the ceramic surface. The lamp's hood was frosted glass and decorated with tiny golden flowers painted across its surface. It glowed brightly, but it didn't do much to push back the gloom. She closed the large doors behind us; they were heavy and pulled out of her grip, booming shut. I winced at the noise in the otherwise quiet tomb.

"This way," Gypsum said, hurrying off with the lamp. Her small legs were fast, even with the full dress she wore, and I struggled to keep up.

My hip hit something hard and I cried, "Ouch! Slow down."

When Gypsum came back, I had enough firelight to see I'd run into a giant sarcophagus. The lid was on the ground and leaning against the side of the sarcophagus. The top of the lid was adorned with a life-sized, stone replica of a dwarf warrior wearing a crowned helmet.

"Is this Rutgard's coffin?" I asked, a little creeped out by running into it this way.

"His coffin is actually a magical substance entombing and preserving him for all eternity. This was the box we kept him in. Let's keep going."

"But this is what I came to see. I'm looking for...." I didn't really know what I was looking for. I'd recently read one of Conrad's procedural books that talked about 'clues' and 'deductions', but I had no idea what any of it meant. "I'm looking to see if someone left their calling card or something obvious. Maybe they borrowed him for cleaning?"

"Very funny. No, I have something much more useful than a calling card to show you." Gypsum grabbed my arm and dragged me after her in a most unladylike fashion.

Soon we were at the other end of the massive chamber, and through another set of doors that led to a smaller chamber. This room didn't echo as much and seemed to have been made for the living, with couches and lots of oil lamps. It took my eyes a moment to adjust, not only to the suddenly bright light but to the incomprehensible nature of the scene.

Several dwarven soldiers wearing real gold chest plates emblazoned with the symbol of a crown stood there, hands on their sword hilts as though I'd interrupted something I shouldn't have, something which would get me killed. When they saw Gypsum, they relaxed and turned their attention back to the thing in the center of the room. At first, I thought it was a deformed troll. Then I made out the component pieces: There was a large human woman strapped to a chair, and strapped to her was what looked like another, smaller chair resting on her shoulders. Atop it sat a small green man with flyaway hair, brass spectacles and lips like shriveled limes. He was tied up with a gag in his mouth. The human woman was also gagged.

"What is all this?" I asked Gypsum, warily.

"Something better than a calling card. Witnesses. Or suspects. I'm not up on your detective terminology. When they wouldn't answer our questions, we chose not to alert the royal torturer, as he's an elf. Syla ordered the King's Guard here to keep watch over them until we found you. We reasoned you'd be up on all the latest torture tactics, being Solhan and all."

"Thanks," I said, not meaning it. People commonly mistook me for an average Solhan, which could be useful when intimidation was needed, but I had hoped my best friend at least would think better of me. "When did you capture them?"

"Early this morning. Syla and I found them here and the body missing, but they deny seeing anything. Now, you can question them properly and solve the case."

3   Too Much Information

Gypsum asked the gold-plated soldiers to untie the suspects.

"I'm sure you three King's Guardsmen can handle a girl and a goblin," she said when they hesitated, eying me. I think it was due more to distrust of the newcomer than any fear on their part.

"I could handle both of them and their cousins all by myself, Aunt Gypsum," one of the dwarves with ochre skin and hair the color of red clay said.

I believed him. He was probably the most muscled non-grall I'd ever seen. He had muscles on top of muscles, and the gold breastplate he wore barely covered his chest. His arms bulged so much there was no way to strap any other armor around them, so he wore leather in most places and didn't look as shiny as his compatriots.

"Is this the detective you and my mother went to fetch?" he asked, eying me up and down. I've been eyed before, so I knew the feeling of being mentally undressed.

"Yes. The detainees are Eva's to question as she sees fit. Be a dear boy, Malcolm, and remove the gags as well." Gypsum made it sound like she was asking him to pour her some tea. She didn't seem to find the situation as disturbing as I did.

It was strange having captives—I was usually the one tied up—but this was State business, so they were 'detainees' according to her, not that I understood the distinction.

"What's a goblin doing here?" I asked.

"There were two here yesterday. The other was an assistant of Doctor Ghunnan's," Gypsum said.

"Two goblins. They didn't eat the body?" It would explain why it was missing.

"They are goblin researchers," Gypsum pointed out.

"They're less hungry than regular goblins, are they?"

"They are most irregular goblins. Speak to the doctor and you'll see." She rubbed her hands together. "Let's get this interrogation going."

"I'm not employing hot pokers or anything."

"Oh. Well do what you do." Gypsum sounded a little disappointed.

"And who are these King's Guardsmen? I thought Syla said to trust no one?" Now I was the one eying them distrustfully.

"That's Malcolm, Syla's son," Gypsum pointed to the redhead with all the muscles who had managed to untie the human woman but was having difficulty with the knots on the goblin. He paused to wink at me.

"That's my older brother, Alum." She indicated a muddy brown dwarf who looked like a male version of herself and scowled at the doors behind us, as though daring anyone else to come through and cause trouble,

"And that's Verdis." She pointed to a sand-colored dwarf whose nose ran almost as badly as mine. He had a kerchief stuck in the top of his gold breastplate to catch the drips, leaving his hands free for weapons. "He's simple. No offense, Verdis."

Verdis sniffed and stared at me blankly.

"He likes you," Alum said, not shifting his gaze an inch. "He rarely likes anyone. It's a sign you're trustworthy."

"All of these men are virtuous dwarves, pledged to protect Rutgard, and un-swayed by Suffragist nonsense. They are utterly reliable," Gypsum said.

"I thought you couldn't even rely on your own husbands?" Despite Gypsum's assurances, I didn't trust anyone's loyalties.

"Blood kin is different, and Verdis doesn't count. He never speaks."

"As loud as the Suffragists are, they are a minority," Alum said. "My sister isn't the only student of history in my family. I know the terrible things we men can do when we have power. I'm fully aware of the horrible things I often dream of."

"I have more sex dreams," Malcolm interjected. "Don't get me wrong, there's plenty of fighting too, and blood, battlefields littered with my enemies, the wind in my hair as I raise my dripping sword and shout triumphantly ... but mostly sex." I wasn't sure how Muscles, I mean Malcolm, could tell the difference between war dreams and sex dreams from the sound of it.

"Malcolm's father was from the line of Blood Axe, a very old clan with a fierce history, as you can judge by the name," Gypsum said, clearly uncomfortable with his over sharing. "That's why he is one of our warriors. They are a necessary evil to keep the borders of the Kingdoms safe. As suitable as others, like Reginald, might be for the profession as well, more dwarf warriors would only mean trouble. We prefer to teach them the benefits of peace and protection, rather than aggression."

"Were you all here 'protecting' the body when it was stolen?" I asked Malcolm and the others.

Alum pursed his lips. "Well..." he began. Malcolm looked away sheepishly, while Verdis continued to stare at me. "...King's Guard is an honorary title. We're soldiers."

"Dwarven Elite soldiers," Gypsum said proudly. "Those elf EEPs wouldn't stand a chance against them."

Alum raised an eyebrow. "EEPs?"

"It's annoyingly catchy," Gypsum told me.

"We're usually posted outside the city," Alum continued when it was clear Gypsum wasn't going to elaborate on the origin of the acronym, "in order to honor the Three Kingdom's treaty, which mandates the capital be protected by the City Guard, who are unaligned with any of the kingdoms. No one expects Rutgard to actually be watched all day long. He's not going anywhere. Or so we thought. We happened to be in the Central City because my sister called us in for extra protection. The elves having their elite soldiers here makes the Baroness even more nervous than these suffragists do."

"My mom's not nervous," Malcolm said, "she's smart. Can't let these elves strut around in their black uniforms when we look so much better in ours."

"These three were with Syla and me when we discovered the body was missing," Gypsum clarified. "We left them here while we went to fetch you and come up with a plan. So far, you are the only plan, and your hourglass is running out. Please hurry it along, Eva."

I had an audience. Great. It was a bit unnerving. I looked at my captives and kept thinking, goblins? Not the usual suspects for a devious caper that didn't involve bloodshed. I supposed there was a first time for everything. Even more perplexing was the woman Doctor Ghunnan was riding everywhere like a horse. I stepped past the dwarf soldiers, so I was close enough to look the goblin in his beady black eyes as his gag was removed.

"Now that you're more comfortable, I have a few questions," I began.

"Who are you?" the goblin asked, picking at some fluff left on his impossibly long tongue.

"A private investigator."

"Interesting. Female?"

"You think we're all chattel?" I asked, indicating the girl with the seat contraption and goblin strapped to her.

"What is your name?" I asked her, trying to treat her like a person rather than furniture.

"She's just a med student," the goblin said, waving his hand dismissively. "Don't mind her."

"Miss Student?"

"A med student. The idiot at the desk heard me wrong as well."

I think he was calling me an idiot by inference. This questioning was not getting off to a good start. "Does she speak?"

"Not if I don't tell her to."

"Well tell her to. You're not a slave?" I asked her. I didn't spot any marks or brands on her arms, but magical enslavement would explain her muteness. I didn't like seeing people kept against their will, although that's pretty much what I was doing to them right now.

The goblin sighed. "Of course, she is not a slave. Students are indentured for the course of their study. It's not a permanent state of servitude, merely a temporary paying of dues, so to speak. Student, tell this detective that you are here of your own free will."

"I'm here of my own free will," she said in an unexpectedly clear and confident voice.

"Repeating your master's words isn't reassuring," I said.

"Doctor Ghunnan is not a mere Master. He's one of the most distinguished research physicians in the unconquered world. If not the most distinguished," she gushed. "He's Chair of the Society for Reanimation Studies, Dean of the School of Historical Reformation, and his work on 'Physical Properties of Light and Psychosocial Explanations of Primitivistic Notions of Magic' is one of the most highly cited and exciting works of the last century. I've read it twenty times, and it's the basis for my thesis, which I'll begin writing as soon as I finish my medical residency with Doctor Ghunnan. He's a surgeon as well, if you can believe it!"

Now I knew why they had kept her gagged.

"You don't mind carrying him on your back?" I asked, hesitantly, worried another incomprehensible soliloquy would follow.

"It's an honor."

"And a necessity," the doctor added. "You see, despite my mental prowess and accomplishments, I suffered severe spinal injuries during my rather rambunctious youth and require an extra set of legs as it were. Now, can we ignore the student and move on to more important matters, such as when you plan to release me?"

"Why should I do that? You were the last people to be alone with Rutgard, and now the body is missing." Time to get some answers. I looked at the hourglass I was holding and noted it was three quarters gone already. "How come you didn't get an hourglass?" I asked, losing the train of my questioning already.

"We have a special pass," the goblin said.

"To do what?"

"It's confidential. I can't be blathering about it until the data is published. I have competitors."

"Either tell me where the body is, or we can seal you in here until you feel like talking," I threatened. "Your competitors should enjoy that."

"Are you sure you don't need me to fetch some hot pokers?" Gypsum asked.

"You have those lying around?"

"The elves must have some. Or there may be some ancient torture implements around here." She took a few steps away and examined the walls more closely. There were some faded tapestries and rusting, ancient battle-axes hung there. She reached for an axe.

"No need for such barbaric measures," the goblin said, baring his needle teeth. "I'm happy to help in any way I can. I need that body returned as well. My assistant, Miss Kissel, was the last one to be with it. She stayed behind yesterday evening to finish off an experiment for me."

"What kind of experiment?" I asked.

Glancing nervously at Gypsum, he whispered, "We were sampling ancient tissues for an early form of the current plague, in order to develop a vaccine."

"A what-cine?"

"A vaccine," he said loudly, as though I were deaf. "A medicine, if you understand that better."

"This isn't like one of those 'fabulous' cure-all medicines charlatans are peddling on the streets these days?" I asked, suspicious. As much as I hated magic, I knew it worked, and I doubted the efficacy of cure-alls that smelled like turpentine and castor oil.

"No, nothing like it. But I am saddened by your mistrust of modern medicine. Rest assured that I, at least, have invented an effective cure-all, a colloidal tincture of iodide. Med Student, give the lady a sample."

The woman felt around in the bags that dangled from the contraption she wore and pulled out a small glass vial. It was filled with something red brown in color.

"Take one drop in a glass of water each morning to keep illness away," she said. "A more concentrated formulation is very effective for sore throats and mouth ulcers."

"I don't get those." My hands were full, so I couldn't take the vial she held out, not that I had any desire to do so in the first place. "You go ahead and hold on to that for me."

"I'll take it," Malcolm said, snatching the vial and giving it a sniff. He passed it to Verdis who gulped the whole thing and smiled.

To the goblin I said, "Stay on topic. Tell me more about this vaccine you mentioned."

"I thought the discussion of modern medicine very topical. Topical. Get it?" He chuckled and so did the student.

I did not get the joke, so I turned on my dangerous glare, which I'd been trying to keep in check on this case, and got instant results. The smiles faded.

Doctor Ghunnan coughed into a kerchief and then put it away in a pocket, straightening his waistcoat as he did so. When he had collected himself, he went on. "The vaccine would prevent any more human people from being overtaken by this abhorrent plague of madness that causes them to walk around like risen corpses and attack everyone with their bare hands."

"They're not 'like' risen corpses. They are Risen corpses, empowered by the magic of the Dead God," I said.

"Nonsense. No such thing as magic or gods. These people aren't dead. They only seem to be, their heart rate and breathing slowed, so uneducated people such as yourself might be fooled."

"I'm not uneducated." Admittedly, finishing school was not a place where you'd find a Dean of Snooty Talk, but we did crack a book now and then. "And I've seen plenty of magic." Not to mention the Dead God himself. Sort of.

"Such rampant ignorance continues to astonish me. It seems an insurmountable task to change people's thinking." The goblin shook his head, and so did the med student, which, since they were out of sync, made me a bit dizzy to watch.

"Let's move on," I said. I didn't feel entirely in charge of this interrogation. "What do you mean by 'sampling ancient tissues'? What were you doing to Rutgard?"

The doctor glanced nervously at Gypsum again. "Nothing. We were, of course, merely doing an external examination as we awaited the Council's final approval to extract a piece of the body."

"You were planning to take a piece of the Dwarf King, like a souvenir?" I asked, incredulous.

"Not if Syla and I could stop it," Gypsum said. "This quack has most of the Council convinced it's worth desecrating Rutgard if there's a chance of stopping the human dead from rising, but we don't see how Rutgard's remains would be of any use. It is nonsense."

"You do not understand," the goblin said pointedly, "but I do. To date, the older races have shown no susceptibility to this plague, which suggests to me they may have encountered an ancient and less virulent form of it, to which they gained resistance. If I can isolate the older, weaker strain, then we can transfer this resistance to the humans as well. The way the king's body was preserved makes that glad outcome highly probable."

"Not all the older races are immune," I said. "I've seen a half-elf, half-Solhan woman rise." It was something I'd like to forget, but those things tend to stick with you. I was also the one who had stabbed her in the heart and killed her and could verify she'd been dead for three days. I was pretty sure this plaque was not a mundane disease.

"Half-Solhan?" the doctor leaned forward. "That is a worry. Tell me more."

I thought he would be more worried about the half-elf part, but I didn't allow myself to get distracted this time. "No. You tell me more. You're the suspects.

"Where would your assistant have taken the body and why? Was she tired of waiting for Council approval and decided to hack it up herself? How did she get it past the guards?"

There had been no 'King's Guard' around, and the dwarf at the desk with his key and ledger wasn't much protection, but the elves manning the gates to the Central City certainly weren't pushovers.

"My assistant is innocent," the doctor proclaimed. "She has to be. Otherwise, this incident could be disastrous. There is an unfriendly history between dwarf and goblin kind. When the dwarfs stopped warring with everyone else, they kept up their enmity for us."

"You keep pushing into our lands, eating cattle, eating our citizens, burning crops...." Gypsum said heatedly.

"Yes, our young warriors get quite overexcited. I'm afraid they are what most members of the Three Kingdoms think of when they think of goblins. But we have our own kingdom, now ruled by an elected parliament to check the Emperor's impulses, and I daresay we are more forward thinking than your society. It has been quite some time since we've invaded dwarf lands, and we have firm control over our military now. We are trying to repair relations, and I don't want this incident to spark another war."

"Maybe your missing assistant, Miss Kissel, isn't so peace-loving. Maybe she wants a war," I said.

"Well, I shan't let her have one if I can do anything about it," Doctor Ghunnan promised. "I will help you find the body."

"I thought you didn't know where it was?"

"I don't. Nor do I know where Miss Kissel is. But I can track them."

"Are goblins like bloodhounds?" I asked.

"Oh, no. Nothing so animalistic or simple. This is science. I have a sample of the resin the body was encased in—"

"You what?" Gypsum looked angrier than I'd ever seen her, so I stepped between her and the goblin/student.

"Let him speak," I said. "How will the resin help? Can you smell it?"

"We are not bloodhounds! Well, yes, the substance is a bit smelly, but no. This will take complex modern methods to devise a means of detecting the unique particles emanating from the resin at a distance. I believe I can configure directionality into the emulsion...."

"You don't have a detector," I said.

"Not yet," he admitted.

"Find me when you do," I told him.

I turned to Gypsum. "Do you think we can trust this doctor? He does seem different from other goblins."

"Older goblins tend to be more sensible," Gypsum said. "They usually don't survive to be older, however, due to the hazards of being eaten by fellow goblins. I don't trust him—he's a grave robber—but I don't think he's physically capable of stealing a body. I did meet Miss Kissel, and she seemed resourceful enough to cause some trouble. You should focus on her."

"I was thinking something else," I said. "This science experiment will likely lead nowhere, and I can't stay. My hourglass is running out. I need to follow up on the suffragists before the wedding, as I'm starting to agree with Syla that they are the most likely culprits."

"Really? We can cancel the wedding if we need to," Gypsum pointed out.

"And tell Karolyne what? Best not to let on that anything is amiss. Plus, I'm not going through all of this again. The way I've been eating, my dress won't fit if we delay the ceremony. Can your King's Guard friends keep the other Matriarchs out of this chamber for long? Too many people already know the body is missing."

"Matriarchs never come here unless it's the required time of Conferral. Only Syla and I have chosen to keep tabs on Doctor Ghunnan and his assistants, so no one else is likely to visit in the next few days."

"Good. We need to find the body sooner rather than later anyway. The longer we wait, the farther away it gets. Do what you can to help the goblin set up his Rutgard-detector. As unlikely as it is to work, we might as well try."

The hourglass seemed to be running down more quickly, so I left Gypsum and the King's Guard to deal with the detainees, while I hurried back to the market gate on my own.

I felt exposed without a dwarf escort, and I was slowed down stopping to sneeze in the gardens. I made it just in time. The EEPs tried to shove me out of the Central City as quickly as possible, but I made sure they remembered to give me back my Ashur. I slung it across my shoulders and sighed as I stepped into the slightly less hostile elvish Market District.

Both dwarves and elves were bringing in private armies to the Central City. Not good. The Three Kingdoms had been in peaceful alliance for centuries, but any peace could be broken by enough people hammering at it.

This case was already creating a hammering sensation behind my eyeballs. As detailed as the entry log to Rutgard's chamber was, it was useless. The clerk outside the mausoleum had spectacles suspiciously like the goblin doctor's, and I was certain that wasn't the first 'gift' he'd accepted from his visitors. Yes, the goblins were up to something, as were the elves, but as Gypsum pointed out, it didn't matter who was responsible, only that I find the body.

Elves would have been noticed visiting the dwarf section of the palace and Rutgard's tomb, while goblins would have been noticed sneaking a large package past the gate guards. The EEPs could have helped the goblin assistant with the theft, theoretically, but someone in the Central City would have raised the alarm at seeing a goblin with something so large. Goblins were often hired for household cleaning, and while needed, they were not respected. Miss Kissel would have been turned in on suspicion of being a thieving servant.

Dwarves, however, could come and go both places as they pleased. That meant the dwarf suffragists, whether they were working on their own or as unwitting dupes of the Elf King or goblin warmongers, could most easily have gotten the body out. I needed to find their mastermind and question him. Preferably before lunch.

4 Clues

Baroness Syla had told me to nose in on the City Guard's investigation of the suffragist attacks, but that was easier said than done. Especially since it seemed the baroness hadn't yet gotten the memo out.

"Like I said, she wants me to see if any of her husbands are suffragists and what they might be involved in. She hired me to be her eyes." That was my cover story anyway. "Send a messenger to the Baroness if you don't believe me," I told the desk sergeant at the Market Guardhouse for the tenth time.

"Busy right now," the dwarf said.

I checked his arm for a suffragist armband, but that affiliation would not be something he advertised here.

The Guard had been cracking down on suffragists, kicking them off street corners and imprisoning those who resisted. I figured he must be a sympathizer—until I caught sight of a sheet of paper hung among the wanted posters. It had a drawing of me and said, 'Crazy human lady: Ignore'.

Great.

I'd obviously earned that reputation during the Slaver Affair, when I was harassing every authority I could get my hands on. That left only one person I could talk to. Conrad would not be happy to see me twice in one day.

"Miss Thorne."

I recognized the voice and froze. It was the elf captain who ran this Guardhouse. I'd been jailed here for several days once, and he'd been my interrogator. Good times.

"Nice to see you again, Captain...? I'm sorry I never got your name when I was hung up by very uncomfortable manacles and threatened, after days without food. It's difficult to remember little courtesies at a time like that," I said.

"My name is Uanal."

"You didn't say...?"

"No, I did not. I shall pronounce it slowly. You-a-null."

"Even lovelier. As much as I'd like to stay and chat, I best get going." I had little fondness for elves of late, and less than the usual for this one.

"I thought you wanted to join our investigation?" he said, a mocking lilt in his voice. "The suffragists have bombed a warehouse at Cliff's Edge." He made it sound like he was tempting me with a sweet dessert.

Of course, I wanted to go along, but I was wary. "I thought I was only a crazy lady to you?"

Captain Uanal noticed my gaze and stepped behind the desk sergeant. He tore down the sheet of paper and crumpled it. "A little joke of mine. I'm known for such things around here, aren't I, Sergeant?"

"Yes, indeed," the dwarf said. "The Captain's a right prankster he is."

"This invitation isn't another prank is it?" I asked.

"The Baroness spoke to me herself. Come. Join us." He gestured to some of his men, who were arming themselves, adjusting sword belts, and making sure their white Guard tunics were straight. They headed out the door, and then Captain Uanal held it for me. I followed the marching soldiers, and the elf fell into step beside me.

"The attacks are escalating," he said. "We've had bombings for weeks, deliberately stashed human corpses for the last several days, and now three corpses and a bombing on the same day. I would very much like to know what they have planned for their finale—and what they want in the end."

The elf captain was giving me information without coaxing or threats? Such helpfulness was more unnerving than torture.

"I thought the suffragists wanted representation on the Council of Matriarchs? At least that's what their placards say. I haven't read their manifesto or anything, but I don't see these attacks fitting with their agenda. This is killing their own people, men, women and children. This is pure chaos," I pointed out.

"Correct. But militants are rarely logical. While most suffragists are starving themselves or stopping work, there are always splinter groups with more violent tactics and a different agenda. Usually power, infamy, or a simple thirst for blood."

"I've lived in this city my whole life," I said, "and I've never seen this kind of thing before. Where else have you dealt with militants and splinter groups?"

"There are elf lands and cities beyond Highcrowne. I come from Velerax, on the border of the Western Mountains, near dwarf lands."

"So, you've encountered dwarf militants who are what? Wanting less elves around?" I could understand that.

"No. Human militants fighting slavery and backed by dwarven arms buyers. Abolitionists. Your sort of people," he said distastefully.

Now this sounded like the elf I knew. "I see. You've acquiesced to Baroness Syla's request to have me around so you can see if I'm a suffragist. In case you haven't noticed, I'm a woman."

"As I mentioned, militants are seldom logical. Also, I believe human women and dwarf men share common problems among their own people."

"Well, I haven't joined the club, and I'm certainly not bombing things. I don't know the first thing about magic, let alone creating firebombs. That's warlock work, and as far as I've heard they're all dead or fighting on the front.

"This is why the Guard is so ineffective. You spend all your time questioning 'dissidents' and 'undesirables' rather than tracking down real criminals. Baroness Syla must have sent me here to show you how to do your job." I was proud of my little speech, but there had been a flaw in it: I might not be a warlock, but I knew more about magic than I wanted to.

I hurried ahead of the elf, which wasn't hard as my legs were longer than his, and I walked beside the other soldiers. Not too close, as I didn't want people in the Outskirts noticing the company I was keeping, but close enough I could follow them to the scene.

We had to pass through the Outskirts to reach Cliff's Edge, and I saw that the streets in the temple district were still deserted, the spring festival abandoned after the morning's attack. As horrible as that had been, the devastation around the bombed warehouse was worse.

Cliff's Edge was a neighborhood literally on the edge of the cliff. Below it was the river and the docks, which most commerce in Highcrowne depended upon.

The river was huge and had tributaries going in every direction, which aided the flow of goods and people, but the bank of the river was narrow, and there was little room for more than the docks, so most warehouses were at the top of the cliff. I couldn't tell what this one had stored, because it was a blackened ruin. A fire still burned, and the locals, covered in soot, some bleeding from being hit by shrapnel, had formed a bucket brigade to extinguish the flames.

As soon as we reached the scene, Captain Uanal stepped forward and raised an arm, as though he were reaching for the fire. He squeezed his hand, and I felt a wall of air rush by me. It hit the flames, momentarily giving them more life, before it smothered them completely. The captain was a weather mage? That explained why he'd never used his spells on me when I'd been his prisoner. Not a lot of weather indoors.

I squeezed my fists, trying to smother the green glow emanating from my palms the same way the elf had smothered the fire. As hard as I was trying to avoid magic, it was trying harder to get my attention. The power within me seemed to flare to life whenever magic was being wielded around me. Like a sympathetic reaction. I blamed my twin sister. All of this had started after I'd accidentally stolen a part of her soul, but that was another story.

"Odd," Uanal said.

"What?" I asked. Hoping he didn't mean the green glow I was trying to hide.

"I sense a few bogle- and rat-expelling runes, a protection spell on the doorway … but there is no trace of a fire rune or a plasma bomb like the ones warlocks are mass producing for the war. I can't detect anything that could have destroyed this building."

He sensed magic too? Great, I wasn't hiding anything from the elf by covering my palms.

"Something must have," I said. "Buildings don't spontaneously explode."

"No, they do not. Your deductions are already astounding me, Miss Thorne. I see now why you were assigned to this case."

And I was back to hating him again.

I took a few steps away from the captain and watched the squad of guardsmen I'd come with spread out through the wind-cooled wreckage. They found a few bodies but no survivors. My nose and eyes were running worse than with the flowers. All I could smell was smoke and burned hair.

I grabbed the arm of a man on the bucket brigade. He was human. "Did you see what happened?" I asked.

"I heard it. There was a loud 'boom' that shattered the window." He looked at his arm where I was holding him and seemed to notice the tiny cuts up and down the length for the first time. "I heard screams then. I came to investigate, saw the fire and joined in to help. My warehouse could have caught next."

"What can you tell me about the warehouse that burned? Did you see anyone go in?"

"I wasn't watching, but only a few people work there. It's long-term storage. Fur coats and other things waiting for winter to come back again."

That explained the stench of burnt hair.

"Thank you," I said.

The man looked dazed, so I left him standing there and went into the wreckage. I kicked at burnt wood and piles of what must once have been coats and fabrics, now fused together, edges black, but the insides still looking like material. The windows had melted, and droplets of brown glass were everywhere. The fire must have burned hot. There were piles of charcoal and ash taller than me, and I had no idea where to start. What did a clue look like?

I made my way back to the cobblestone street, where two bodies had been laid out by soldiers and covered with blankets. I raised the edge of one blanket and saw an arm that looked like charred meat. I felt something too, the soul, still tethered to the body. It was like electricity shooting through my nerves, sending goosebumps along my arms and making the hairs on the back of my neck stand up. It called to me. I knew instinctively that I could reach out to the soul. I could—but I wouldn't. Performing illegal necromancy, and any necromancy involving non-animal souls was now illegal, in front of the Guard's magic-detecting Captain would be very stupid. Even worse, it might draw the attention of the God of Death. As much as the soul's power called to me, I didn't want to take the risk. It would be far too easy to become lost in the dark. I ignored the lingering ghost and focused on the flesh.

I held my breath and peeled the entire blanket away, the fabric sticking in some places and leaving threads behind. I didn't want to look, but I had to. The body's build was short and broad-shouldered, a dwarf. Adding to my theory that if these militants were suffragists, they were crazy. That was Captain Uanal's theory, actually, and I was starting to believe it. Who could do this to another person? Fire was a terrible way to die.

I looked closer and noted huge cuts on the dwarf's chest, three parallel gashes that went all the way through the breastbone. I didn't see how fire could have done that, so maybe he hadn't been killed by it after all. Maybe he'd been killed by a blade, and the fire was meant to cover it up? Or the fire was meant to destroy something in the warehouse and this dwarf had merely gotten in the way? I checked the other body, another dwarf, and saw that it too had been gashed. The marks looked like they were made by one of the claws that pit fighters used. A strange choice of murder weapon.

I heard a familiar voice say, "Stop. What are you doing?" It was Conrad. He had arrived with another detachment of guards. The crime scene was getting crowded.

"She's helping with my investigation," Captain Uanal said, coming to my defense.

"Captain." Conrad stood at attention. "I must, respectfully, ask you to secure the area and hand this investigation over to me. I'm on special assignment." He handed the elf captain a sheaf of papers. Uanal perused them and grunted in a manner better suited to gralls than elves.

"Very well, Special Detective. You can have the scene. But you get her as well." He pushed me forward. "By order of Baroness Syla."

"Eva? Why?"

"Don't sound so incredulous, 'Special Detective'. We're in the same line of work now," I said.

"I'm the Guard, Eva, sanctioned by our lawful rulers. You're...."

"What?" I crossed my arms, ready to shred whatever he had to say next.

"Good day," Captain Uanal said as he turned to leave. He leaned in and, in a whisper, told me, "Let me know what this idiot uncovers so real guardsmen can follow up."

"Oh, yes. I'm certain to do that," I said sarcastically. I kept my arms crossed and didn't take my gaze off Conrad.

"You can't be here, Eva. A lady shouldn't see these sorts of things." Conrad snatched another blanket and covered the nearest body.

"I'm not a lady," I told him. "You should know that by now. I am Solhan and ten times tougher than you are." I took the blanket off again. "There are wounds on these bodies. I want to know what made them."

"Claws," he said with a resigned sigh. "We've seen these marks before."

"The gladiatorial kind?"

"No. The large, natural kind of claws you might find on a troll or a grall."

"My grall did not to do this," I said quickly.

Jorg wasn't technically 'my' grall. He just lived in my basement, but I'd felt responsible for him ever since he saved my life. He was also the only grall in the city. They were considered dangerous and only allowed in if they had a patron to watch over and vouch for them.

"I didn't say he had. We have other leads."

"Is there a troll assassin in the city or something?"

"Or something."

I'd never seen Conrad so tight lipped. He was usually talking my ear off, but that had been when he was still hoping we'd be 'friends'. I hadn't entirely given up the notion of friendship, or even something more. But right now, I was wary of love, for good reason, and I had no desire to feel guilty for my cautiousness. I chose to ignore his attitude.

"Syla told me she believed suffragists were responsible for these attacks," I said. "I don't see what they have to gain."

"This warehouse was owned by a powerful Matriarch."

He'd done his homework already, and the ashes weren't yet cold. Very good. I was happy he'd made Special Detective. I still remembered the gung-ho recruit I'd first met guarding the dyer's vats in the Red Precinct. I'd sensed he would go far, but I had no idea how quickly. Especially with him burdened by the disadvantage of being human.

"Why kill other male dwarfs?" I asked, warming my usually frosty tone a bit to acknowledge his competence. "I guess a troll assassin would be difficult to control, but why employ one in the first place? Maybe these militant attacks and the suffragist movement are totally unrelated?" I didn't like that idea, as it would make solving the crime today more difficult. Maybe I was being a bit ambitious.

"They are related. Somehow. Look, Eva. If you really want to learn what's going on, come with me tonight. I could use your help."

Tonight? That was a whole day wasted. "Why can't you tell me everything you know now? Why does it have to wait until tonight?"

"I'll tell you everything, even give you the files to read as soon as you want, but this evening I'm meeting the suffragist leaders, and you can come with me. As my wife."

"Wife?"

"I need one for my cover. I've been infiltrating their group for weeks, and tonight is a social gathering. I was going to take one of the elf guards, but a human wife will be much more believable."

"Why would dwarves let a human into their group? Especially a guardsman?"

"I'm a man. That's more important to them. Plus, they think humans have it all figured out, the way we keep our women down. They think I can impart great wisdom."

5   Lunch is the Most Important Meal

Conrad brought me to the Smiths' Quarter Guardhouse where he was stationed and left me alone with his files, while he went back and finished sifting through the debris at Cliff's Edge.

There wasn't much to read, but it was enough to give me plenty of questions in addition to the ones I already had. Such as, how can a bomb blow up an entire warehouse without leaving magical imprints behind?

My stomach was rumbling something fierce by the time I returned Conrad's files to the desk sergeant, so I went out for a walk to digest my learnings ... and to find some food to digest that might quiet my tummy, if not my mind.

I didn't have enough spare coins to afford lunch at a local tavern or bake house, not even crow pie, which was cheaper since the dead began wandering off to Solheim and the birds got thinner and stringier. The glares I got from dwarfs and elves walking the streets convinced me the Smiths' District was not friendly towards humans, even if I were a paying customer. I didn't know how Conrad managed coming here every day. Maybe the Guard uniform made a difference, or maybe he simply brought his own lunch. I headed back to the Outskirts where I felt more welcome.

The Jerk was probably still at Karolyne's. I didn't want to go there anyway, as all I could afford was the free kaffe before being roped into bridesmaid duties. The thought of home and Nanny's cooking gave me a shudder. I decided to stop by Bell's new place, which I'd helped fund—it's where most of my misspent gold had gone, I remembered—and rummage around in her kitchen. Besides, she might be just the person to ask about bombs.

Bell lived in a junk heap. It was the way she liked it; lots of materials around to prospect through for creative nuggets. I thought her end creations were junk too, things like locomotive garbage scrapers and server automatons, but I hated anything inspired by the human lands. Inefficient clocks and wasteful contraptions that still required magic to power them in most cases. To me it was a sign that humans did not have the chops to face down the Dead God. Power would be needed to stop Him. All this technology made me feel more and more like humans were doomed.

Of course, none of that had kept me from investing in a new workshop for Bell. I felt guilty after blowing her last one up. We'd used dynamite for that, which is why I thought she might know how the warehouse had been destroyed. I was working on the theory it was a combination of someone circumventing the magical wards on the door and then others carrying in enough crates of dynamite to turn a massive building into ash. I was hoping Bell could tell me how to detect dynamite residue and validate my theory. That would show Captain Uanal.

I navigated through a maze of twisted scrap metal to reach the new workshop. When it was built, the scrap was moved aside, only to have Bell move it all back again. The maze was part of her protections. There was also a massive steel door. I banged on it.

"It's Eva," I shouted. "Get the kettle on."

I'd bought her a new kettle too, along with a new kitchen and a proper living space. Not to mention shiny new tools and gadgets beyond my comprehension. In exchange, I got a share of the profits. There weren't any at this point, but Bell and Kali were working on a deal with the city to upgrade their sanitary services.

The door opened with a screech of metal—no one was sneaking in here—and I saw Duane looking at me. Great. He must be here to claim his share of the non-existent profits too.

Duane was a gangster, meaning he operated gangs across the Outskirts, Slave District, and Docks. He was moving up in the criminal ranks faster than Conrad was advancing in the Guard. Sometimes I forgot Bell was one of his flunkies. I should have scouted the place out before knocking. Duane must have a few more goons out in the street watching his back. I hadn't spotted them, but I hadn't been looking. Some of them I might not have spotted even if I had.

"Eva," Duane said with a lopsided smile. "You're in time for lunch."

I wanted to turn around and go back to wandering the streets, starving and grumpy, but the smell of spring vegetable soup, spiced with lemon and rose-mary, enticed me inside. Living with a fantastic cook like Jorg the grall had taught me how to smell, taste and explore good food. Of course, Jorg did most of his cooking at Karolyne's, where he worked, but some-times he cooked over the crude hearth in my basement. No one was allowed upstairs to use Nanny's kitchen but her. I knew this was Jorg's cooking even before I spotted him beside the long table ladling soup into Little Viktor's bowl.

"Hi Eva!" my nephew, Vikky, waved enthusiastically. He was five, soon to be six, and everything was done enthusiastically.

Bell, perky blonde pigtails waving above her head like the eyestalks of some bizarre creature, sat next to Kali. Kali was a complimentary opposite, with shiny black skin and straight black hair that hung down her back so far it touched the floor when she was seated. They were whispering to one another and exchanging spoonfuls of soup, as though either bowl was different. Kali and Bell started kissing, and it seemed their lunch, and the audience, was entirely forgotten. Spring fever had hit even here, and there was no escaping the plague of love in the air.

Little Viktor noticed my annoyed gaze and piped up, saying, "I have a girlfriend too! Uncle 'uane is taking me to buy flowers after this, and I'll leave them on her doorstep. With a note. See," he held up a colorful stick figure drawing of a girl with a dress kissing a stick figure boy holding flowers. "That way she'll know it's from me."

"You'll need to sign it," I said, sitting wearily and the day only half done. "I'm sure a lot of boys want to give her flowers and kiss her."

At least that was my usual experience. Until I glared and shouted at them and drove them all away of course. Killing usually worked to get rid of men too.

"Here." Jorg placed a bowl in front of me. It looked like a thimble in his massive hands. I noted Jorg didn't even have claws, because he kept his nails cut short. They were flaking, yellow and generally not pretty, but at least they were manicured.

"Thanks," I said, giving his muscled gray arm a squeeze, like I was hugging a cat. One that wasn't trying to scratch me and escape down an alleyway. It felt good. I was also glad I could eliminate Jorg as a suspect.

"Do I get a hug?" Duane asked.

"No." I looked at him more closely and realized he was wearing a suit.

Duane usually went shirtless, even in winter. His muscled bronze skin emanated heat, which you could feel standing a yard away from him. It was strange to see him so properly dressed. The silk waistcoat he wore matched the jade green of his eyes, and the jacket was dark gray with white pinstripes, the dark suit just the right shade to make clear the demarcation between his shoulders and his long, dark hair. He looked uncomfortable. He kept trying to take the jacket off but stopped himself and stuck his hands in his pockets instead.

"Why are you all dolled up?" I asked. "You think you need to look like that to talk to an elf?"

I had my spies in Duane's court. Well, Kali, and she'd told me Duane was always going into the Market District to meet with elf businessmen. Seemed his ambitions involved joining the truly evil criminals: The ones who bought and sold humans, who helped shape the laws saying it was ok; the people who wanted everyone in the Outskirts they didn't own kicked out to face war and starvation alone. The government. True criminals. Duane would be right at home. If only he could switch species.

And Duane was not Vikky's uncle. He was his godfather. He was so beloved because he had ill-gotten money to burn on taking Vikky to do fun things. I'd taken my nephew on a boat ride when I had some spare coins, but Duane had already done that, and it was Duane's trip Vikky had talked about the entire time.

Still, I was glad Duane had brought him here today. I almost never saw my nephew unless I ran into him on one of Duane's outings. I was avoiding my uncle's place, because he was even eviler than Duane, and because my sister, Ilsa, lived there, and she wanted to kill me and take back the piece of her soul I'd stolen. The house I'd grown up in was not a good place to be if I could avoid it.

"What have you been up to?" I asked Vikky.

"Drawing." He brought out a stack of papers marked with colored wax and held them up for me to see. They kept wiggling and flapping, so it was hard to make anything out, not that they looked much like anything.

"That's great," I praised. Then one of the drawings in black caught my eye, and I reached across the table for it. "What's this one supposed to be?"

"A werewolf," Vikky said in a spooky voice.

"Why are you drawing werewolves?"

"Because they howl at night and wake me up, and Morgan says the house is warded so we're safe and need to go back to sleep."

"But werewolves aren't real," I said carefully. I didn't want to disillusion my poor nephew.

"Oh yes they are," Duane and Bell said at the same time.

"We saw one the night before last," Bell said. "A great hunched shadow, with a howl to chill your bones."

"I live in the same neighborhood as all of you, and I haven't heard any howling," I said. Of course, I slept like the dead and wouldn't hear someone shouting in my ear.

"Ask Nanny," Kali said. "She's heard it too. We all have."

Jorg nodded.

"I try not to ask Nanny too much these days, or go home too often because of the tax collector," I said.

"That's why I'm here too," Kali said. "He keeps going through the accounts at the bookshop and asking me things I can't answer."

I could have commiserated with Kali for hours about the tax collector, but I didn't want to lose the topic.

"Tell me more about the wolf," I said.

The werewolf story fit with Conrad's report, the one I'd read at the Watch house earlier, which talked about the claw marks found in previous victims of the militant attacks and how magical analysis indicated they were made by 'no known creature'. Werewolves fit that description. They were legend, which made them unknown. Of course, gods weren't known to normally walk the land either, so there was precedent for legends coming to life.

"What do you want to know?" Bell said. "It was a werewolf, not a wolf, by the way."

"So, where did you see this creepy shadow of a 'werewolf'?" I asked. I was studiously ignoring Duane, as I usually tried to do.

"Near the docks," Bell said. "We saw its shadow up on the cliff and heard the howl. We've all heard the howls now and then of late, and everyone's been thinking its timber wolves been chased out of the forest for some reason, but when we saw that shadow, standing up like a person, we knew better."

"Scary," Jorg said. This was coming from a mountain of muscle, with tusks and the capability to grow impressive claws that could be mistaken for a werewolf's. I obviously wasn't up on all the legends.

"What makes werewolves worse than trolls?" I asked. "Or dragons for that matter?"

"Dragons don't kill you without good reason," Duane said. "Stay away from them, they stay away from you. Trolls too, but everyone knows they make good hired killers, if you're not looking for brains. Trolls can be dangerously stupid sometimes. I worked with one once. Never again."

"So, werewolves have brains and a penchant for unprovoked killing?" I deduced from Duane's meandering answer. "That's all?"

"Their touch is poison, their gaze is the gaze of Death, and when your dearest brother is turned, he becomes your direst enemy," Jorg said in a poetic lilt.

"What's that from?" Kali asked. "I haven't read it before, and I've read everything." Kali had been reading all she could get her hands on since Bell and I had taught her elvish script, but not even she could have read everything in our bookshop.

"A story my people used to say across the fire, whenever the mountain wolves howled." Jorg looked momentarily homesick.

"Well, they can't be that bad," I said. "Else they wouldn't be so near extinction that no one has seen them before now."

"Unless they're not creatures that go extinct but more like those that are summoned. Like demons and shadows from the Void. Like gods," Duane said.

The thought had occurred to me. The Dead God already had corpses for his army, who knew what else He had up His sleeve?

More worrisome was why they were in Highcrowne, rather than on the battlefield. Highcrowne was supposed to have a Compact, a deal. I really hoped

Fharen hadn't screwed it up somehow. Not that I condoned human sacrifice, but I'd grown used to High-crowne being the one safe place for humanity—me included. If that was no longer the case, then there would be a whole lot more people slaughtered than the few chosen for sacrifice. And I supposed that was the whole point of the sordid bargain: a lesser evil.

"You have eyes everywhere," I told Duane. "Can't you find out where this werewolf has been seen? Track it?"

"What for?" Bell asked. "We don't want to fight a werewolf."

"What if it's in town to cause chaos? Best to deal with it before the Guard clamps down hard on every-one."

"What makes you say that?" Duane looked to be clueing in. I didn't want to reveal my current job, so I stopped talking.

"Never mind," I said. I had a network of spies I could draw on without involving him. It would be use-ful to know where the werewolf had been sighted and determine if it corresponded with the sites of militant attacks. Now, where was a bogle when you needed one? They were always too good at hiding.

After lunch, Vikky insisted he and Duane go to buy his girlfriend flowers already. The plague of love was unstoppable.

Jorg headed to Karolyne's for the afternoon shift, saying, "I want to be punctual. I'm taking over the restaurant while she's away on honeymoon." He looked proud.

"Congratulations. Karolyne doesn't trust her life to just anyone, and that café is her life." Of course, now that she was marrying mister rich jerk, who knew what her life would be like? Would she even be Karolyne anymore?

Bell and Kali cozied up together on an old lounge chair in one corner of the living area. Their relationship had confused me at first; I thought Bell had been in love with my brother. When I'd asked her about it, she'd said, "He's gone, but I'm still here, and I want to be in love with someone."

On the hunt for bogles, I flipped the lights on to the main workshop and winced at the metal sounds and clanking that started. Bell had built an automatic shop for building more automatic machines. It was a night-mare. I quickly tried to find the lever to turn off the building machines but leave the lights on.

"Need help?" Bell asked when she came up for a gulp of air.

"No. I'm fine." I got the confusing levers and dials figured out. It was a matter of adjusting the path of the magical green goo that powered everything, so it went to the lights but not the workshop floor.

I went inside and found a dark corner—bogles were always hiding in them—and opened the napkin full of biscuits I'd saved from lunch.

"I have food," I called. "I want make bargain."

I knew I sounded and looked ridiculous. Fortunately, no one human was paying attention.

A blur streaked by me, grabbed a biscuit, and vanished in a cloud of crumbs. I closed the napkin again and waited.

"Come out. I won't hurt you. There's plenty more."

I felt something tugging at the napkin, but I held tight.

"Open," a frustrated little voice ordered.

"I'll give you more than I have here, much more, if we make a bargain. It's simple. No danger. Just a listen and look around. You do that all the time, anyway, don't you?"

"Much more food?" the invisible creature asked.

"Lots more. Every single meal over the next moon that Nanny cooks and I don't eat, and that's all of them, you can have."

"What wrong with them?"

Uh oh. This one was smarter than I thought. I knew bogles ate from garbage in the sewers, so I decided on the truth. "It's usually Solhan, month-old stew made of necromancy-preserved offal."

"Oh. Okay. But also give biscuits now."

"Bargain first." I held out my hand to shake.

The bogle dropped its camouflage. It was a foot tall, its leathery skin brown instead of gray like most I'd seen—well the five or six I'd seen; they weren't known for being noticed—and it had bulbous eyes reminiscent of overripe black cherries. It sniffed with a pointed, rat-like snout, and it was hard not to cringe as its nose brushed my fingers. It leaned back on two legs, floppy ears waving. The pointed ears were so large it looked like it might fly around the room with them. The rest of its body was skinny, ribs showing, and its four, tiny hands and feet were all identical, with thumbs and three fingers. It held out a hand and shook my finger.

"Bargain," it said. "Me looksee around, and you give all food."

"I give you all the food Nanny serves me for a little while, not forever. I'll leave it out the backdoor of my house. I'll show you where that is. Clear?"

"Clear. We have bargain."

"Good. Now, I hear there has been a wolf howling in the city. A werewolf some think. Are you able to track where it's been sighted? Ask other bogles what they've seen and heard?"

"Werewolf?" It shivered. "You no make nice bargain. You is mean lady."

"That's true, but you shouldn't be in any danger. You hide good." Now I was talking like them again. I forced myself to use more elaborate sentences. "Your camouflage ability should make you impossible to spot, and you're so fast I'm sure you can get away before the werewolf even notices you around. In fact, you don't even need to get close to it. Ask the other bogles; they're bound to have spotted it. If it exists."

"Me hear it too. I find for you."

"Here you go." I gave it the remaining biscuits, which it gulped down. "I'm heading home after this, and you can follow me there, so you know where to report in for food."

"Home. Food. Got it." And the little guy vanished.

"Wait. I have to show you the way."

It didn't reappear. Just wonderful.

It probably hadn't understood a word I said besides 'food'. Here I was thinking bogles were the perfect informants—at least I knew they could be from past experience as the one informed on—but I supposed it only worked if you were a grandmaster necromancer.

Back to the original plan.

First step was to extract Bell from Kali. They were like fused creatures since they started seeing each other. That had to wear off eventually. At least I hoped, because I needed Kali in the bookshop. She managed it for me and was the only one bringing in income of late. Of course, getting the bookshop running again would first require appeasing the tax collector and his audit. Like most things, I was trying to ignore him and hope he went away. I was good at stubbornly ignoring things, and I could keep it up for a long time. Problem was, we had no shop while I was ignoring him, so I might have to grit my teeth and hear the price. Back taxes sounded painful.

Maybe I'd wait until this case was over and I had some money again. That was if Baroness Syla handed over the gold. I found the aristocracy could be stingy, which was why they were so rich. They held on tight to what I too quickly gave away to people like Bell on stupid ventures like this.

I took note of all the new machines in her workshop. Even more than last time I was here. The army of mechanoids was armed with shovels, rakes, scrapers, hammers, serving trays ... a tool for every profession almost. A few I'd seen on previous visits were gone, so she must be selling some. I hoped for a profit. I think I had agreed to a percentage when I handed over the capital for her new venture, but it was a bit fuzzy. Percentages didn't stay in my head, and gold didn't stay in my hands. I was terrible that way. At least Kali was always telling me so.

I poked one of the brass machines that looked like a dwarf with wheels for feet and a pick and shovel for arms. Sad the little guys—they were half my height, so I couldn't stop calling them little—were stereotyped this way. Surely, other people mined?

I'd seen dwarf fathers covered in children like beekeepers smothered in bees, and I'd seen grumpy servers like Reginald carry heaped platters of dirty dishes that must way a ton, while others like Bert made the most delicate frilly drinks for the after-church crowd, adorned with cherries, flowers, and miniature umbrellas. Dwarfs did a lot of things besides mine. And I guess that was the problem. They did everything and had no freedom to choose their role or what they enjoyed most. That's why the suffragists had come to be. If they were only happy little miners, like the smiling machine in front of me, then there wouldn't be all the chaos we were seeing in the city.

Before I lost my train of thought yet again, I went up to Bell and Kali, wedged my hands between their collarbones and pushed them apart. There was a very audible sound of lips losing suction and deep breaths.

"What do you want?" Kali asked, annoyed.

"To speak to my newest business partner for a moment. Besides, don't you need to do something else?"

"No."

"Find something to occupy you for five minutes." I turned my attention to Bell. "I need your expert opinion on a sensitive Guard investigation."

Bell extracted herself from Kali and stood up. "Sounds exciting. Tell me."

Kali crossed her arms grumpily and wandered off, singing a song in her native Lallalokan that I couldn't understand, but it didn't sound like a love song.

"Did you hear that a warehouse at Cliff's Edge was burnt to the ground this morning?" I asked.

"Duane mentioned something."

"It was deliberately destroyed. The Guard sent their bomb-sniffing elven mage out there, and he couldn't detect any magic. Not even a tampered fire rune. To me, that suggests dynamite. The non-magical bombs you're an expert in."

"Hey. I didn't do it. Just because I work for Duane doesn't mean I go around destroying warehouses for no good reason."

"You destroy them for good reasons then?"

"Well ... when we were taking over the docks, a few demonstrations were required, but I never blew up a whole building. I don't have anything that strong. It would take a wagon-load of dynamite, and people tend to notice."

"Not if it looks like cargo to be stored in a warehouse. I think it would be very easy. What I need from you is a test to show that dynamite was used. Can you do that?"

"A test? Like ask the warehouse questions?"

"I don't know how you do it without magic, but with magic, yes, it is usually a matter of asking the energy of the place to reveal itself."

"Well it doesn't work that way with dynamite. It don't talk. It's just chemicals packed into wood and paper. I suppose ... those chemicals are not easy to get in great batches. I could do some asking for you. See if any has gone missing. Also, I've heard of gas chromatography used to check the purity of samples, so it might detect residue at that warehouse. I'll have to ask around on that too, as it's not my area."

"Please do that. And soon. We don't have long. The attacks are escalating, and something worse could happen."

"Escalating? There have been other attacks?"

I didn't want to reveal too much, but Bell's curious nature was what was useful about her. If I wanted her help, I had to let her in on some of the secrets, so I told her about the militants. I left out the missing Dwarf King though.

"We should lock them all up," Kali said. She'd obviously been listening in.

"Lock who up? We don't know who's doing it."

"Lock up all those dwarves wearing red armbands. It's got to be one of them."

"They can take them off," I pointed out.

"Then lock up all the dwarfs."

"You were a slave. How horrible was it being locked in a cage? And you're proposing we lock up all dwarfs, guilty or innocent?"

"Not forever. Only until the bad ones confess. I saw that body in the square this morning," she said. "I saw that old man killing people. And now you say dwarves are blowing up buildings? More than dwarves live here in Highcrowne, and we all need to be safe. I need to be safe."

She squeezed Bell's hand, and I understood the source of Kali's fear. She *had* felt safe, for once in her life, and now that was in jeopardy. Once you have a taste of something, you'll fight hard to hold on to it, sometimes too hard.

"Dwarves are Citizens and we're not," I pointed out, "so I don't think we have much say in the matter. Even so, Gypsum and others are helping me, dwarves are helping, so we'll find the culprits soon. Don't worry."

I turned to go and heard a smack. I looked back to see Bell lip-locking Kali again.

"No," I told her. "Stop that. Go talk to your bomb and gas people, whatever you were saying. That's better than kisses to help make this city safe for Kali."

Bell swung on a light jacket and preceded me out the door. We split up after we were through the junk maze. She headed for her people, and I headed for mine. I should check in on Nanny, as unpleasant as it sounded, and make sure she was staying indoors while these attacks were happening.

As I walked, I kept thinking about the militants. How did a werewolf fit in? Rare and unlikely assassins. Deadly for sure, but all that howling was too noticeable, unless it was part of the plan? They wanted people to be afraid.

Using dynamite would indicate the militants didn't have magic at their disposal, or money enough to hire a powerful mage. Most human mages were on the frontlines, but Highcrowne was neutral, and so it had some mages who could be bought. Still, magical bombs were the work of warlocks, and they had all been drafted into the war. There might be a few elves and possibly Avians capable of it, if they had learned the skill. Although from what I understood, the Avians hidden away in the Central City were making magical creations for their own amusement or for the benefit of the Three Kingdoms, such as the green goo that powered the lights, and didn't hire themselves out like lowly mercenaries. Almost every Avian was a noble.

Elf mages could be bought, but they were generally bastions of law and paperwork and not prone to random violence. Unless they were following the Elf King's orders? Dwarves didn't seem to produce wizards with showy magic: theirs was all to do with earth, shifting of soil, constructing golems, bringing mountains down on your head.... The cave-ins I'd heard about could be blamed on a dwarf mage, but fire magic wasn't their thing. Maybe that's why they had to use dynamite at Cliff's Edge?

None of the puzzle pieces were fitting together, and by the time I reached my house, I hadn't yet been able to see how a missing Rutgard, suffragists, and werewolves were all linked.

I wondered if I'd bitten off more than I could chew and should tell Gypsum to hand over the Rutgard investigation to the Watch. Who was I kidding? I was a wannabe detective who couldn't find lost pets most of the time. I should learn to run my brother's bookshop, pay my taxes, and leave Kingdom-shattering crime to people more skilled than me.

I'd been so lost in thought I'd forgotten to keep an eye out for the tax collector and had a moment of panic before I realized he was nowhere nearby. I noted the 'closed' sign on the bookstore that made up the ground floor of my house. I could go in and turn the sign around. It would make my life simpler.

But as much as I was tempted by the apparent ease of a normal life, I wasn't normal. I'd learned that when I killed the man I'd thought I loved—albeit an evil necromancer who had murdered my brother—and was able to go on without too much regret.

I ignored the shop and climbed the staircase to the second level. I used my key to open the door and narrowly dodged a large, black frying pan aimed at my head.

This was more like it.

The Beginnings of a Plan

"Nanny," I shrieked. "Stop trying to kill me."

"Stop breaking into my house, Ilsa."

"It's Eva. Eva!"

Old Nanny was always confusing me with my twin. I raised an arm to block the next blow, and green fire arced from my palm to the iron and sent it flying out of Nanny's wrinkled fingers and across the wooden floor.

"Interesting," Nanny said. "Ilsa couldn't do that. Come in and have some soup."

"I had lunch already." For which I was extremely grateful. Nanny's soup was barely distinguishable from her homemade rat poison. "I stopped by to warn you."

"Of what? That you're going to continue to deny your power, continue to turn your back on your people, on those who raised and cared for you, all so you can behave like some ordinary wench who works in a tavern?"

"I'm a detective now."

"As though that's any more important than being a slave? You are a Thorne, Eva. A Thorne."

I knew as much as I needed to about being a Thorne, and I knew I didn't want any of it. I also didn't want to have this argument with Nanny again.

"I came to warn you about the militant attacks. They seem to be getting worse, so stay inside and don't go to the well for the next few days. Jorg can bring you anything you need."

"I will not eat that creature's cooking. It's all pretty smells and colors and no substance."

"You don't have to eat it, but let him fetch what you need."

"I can take care of myself."

"Not as well as a grall can. Listen to me for once, will you?"

"Not until you have some stew. You're skin and bones."

I was trying to fit in a dress that was made a size too small deliberately.

"Fine," I said, if only to quiet Nanny down.

She ladled the noxious stuff into my bowl, and I tried not to gag. She'd found sheep's brains somewhere. At least I hoped it was sheep.

"What's this about werewolves howling at night?" I asked, trying to distract her while I emptied the bowl into an oiled leather bag normally used for holding leftover animal fat. It was empty, meaning Nanny had either been frying breakfast with it or dumped it into the stew. That would explain the gelatinous chunks.

"Such sweet music," she said. "Keeps waking that Kali up, though. I hear her whimpering, and it spoils the symphony."

"I think I've heard a similar line about 'sweet music' and wolves somewhere," I said.

"I don't know where. I made it up. Werewolves, you say? I do miss the sounds of Solheim. Our city was wondrous, you know. In the white karst, the sounds of the owls and the wolves carried, echoing. We had none of these horrible machines with their clanking and sputtering all day and night. Abominations."

I agreed with her on that point.

"How's the stew?" she asked.

I quickly made a slurping sound and hid the bag. "All done."

"Have some more then." I tried to cover the bowl, but she had no compunctions about scalding me, and I moved my fingers just in time.

No one from Solheim spoke about the place since it fell to the Dead God. Nanny was being strangely talkative, so I asked, "What else do you remember about Solheim?"

"The Hall of Glory. The achievements of our kind remembered in bas relief carvings on basalt walls that stretched across the city from one end to the other. The Hall was straight and long and led to the Chamber of Inner Seeing. But when we looked inward, we touched the divine, and the world outside withered and fell apart without our guiding hand. All that remains of our worldly achievements were in the Hall. Gone now too, I suppose." She stared at something I couldn't see.

"What about my mother and father? Were they in the Hall when you last saw them? The Chamber?"

"Don't be asking after such as them. No good can come of it. No good. I think this stew needs something." She rummaged through the cupboards for yet another disgusting preserved body part.

As I suspected, my questions about Solheim were quickly nipped in the bud. I took advantage of her distraction to dump the second bowl of soup in the bag. I stood up before she could reach for the ladle again.

"Well, I need to get going. Remember what I said about staying inside."

"I'm always inside," she said distantly.

"Right."

I headed for the back door, but a knock on it made me pause with hand outstretched for the little brass knob. The tax collector was annoying beyond belief.

I heard Nanny readying another cast iron skillet and was debating whether to stop her or let her loose on the tax man, when a cold feeling swept over me. I sensed something monstrous on the other side, dark and deadly.

Green magic arced from my palms and up my arms, moving across my chest, as if coating me in protective armor. I drew my Ashur and debated once more about opening the door or running away in terror. Even when facing death, I'd never been more terrified in my life. Something not right was out there.

"Finally, being sensible when people come knocking," Nanny said, hefting her frying pan higher.

"Hello?" A high, girl's voice drifted from the other side of the door. "Is Miss Thorne there?" the voice asked, followed by another delicate knock. "Nanny Wight? It's Olyve. You knew my grandmother?"

"Olyve? It's been years," Nanny said, packing away the frying pan. "Put that sword away," she told me, as she shifted me aside and opened the door. I wanted to stop her, but I felt rooted to the spot.

A young girl barely past puberty stood there. The dingy alley with its greasy, soot-stained bricks was a contrast to her pink summer dress, lace gloves and straw hat. I didn't think Highcrowne weather, even in midsummer, allowed for such airy dresses, but the girl didn't seem to be cold. She had golden blonde hair, pale golden skin, and eyes the color of sweet honey wine. With coloring like that, it was no surprise she was an elf, her long ears sticking up through holes in her straw hat.

"You haven't aged a day!" Nanny exclaimed. "But it's been so long since we went rat hunting through the karst together. I was a child, and you still are. Amazing. I've rat stew now if you want some."

Rat stew? I shuddered, glad I'd been smart enough not to take a bite.

"That was my grandmother you remember," Olyve said, calmly. "Can I come in? It's freezing out here." At least she felt the cold, even if she didn't show it.

The girl waved her hand in front of my face, and I suddenly felt self-conscious, covered in green magic and brandishing my Ashur. I put the sword away, and the magic vanished as soon as I did. I must really be on edge to have reacted worse than Nanny to someone knocking on the door.

"You're not my Olyve? I could have sworn...." Nanny said.

"It's her granddaughter, Nanny," I repeated. She could get confused at the best of times.

Although, I was quite interested to know how Nanny could have befriended an elf in Solheim. Solhans weren't friendly to foreigners. Of course, now we were the foreigners everywhere we went. Even more curious was why the elf was asking after me.

Nanny finally opened the door wide enough to be inviting, and the girl took a seat at the kitchen table. I noted Nanny kept the back door ajar, as though planning to shove the elf out at a moment's notice. Perhaps she and Olyve's grandmother hadn't been the greatest of friends.

"Here's some stew, Dearie," Nanny said, ladling a bowl for her. I wasn't sure if that were meant as a friendly gesture or a threat.

"Thank you kindly." The girl swallowed a spoonful without gagging, and said, "Delicious, if a bit over-cooked." She then turned to me. "Miss Thorne?"

"Yes?" I said, suspicious.

"I'm so glad I found you. I've asked all around Highcrowne, been to taverns, cafes and every place in between. Finally, someone mentioned this was your house."

"It's my house," Nanny insisted. "She's an unwelcome guest."

"How did your grandmother come to know Nanny? Miss Wight, I mean?" I tried to sound conversational, but it came out like an interrogation. I was getting a lot of practice with them lately.

"My grandmother knew your mother also. She was a frequent guest of the Solhan court."

"I thought Solhans didn't like anyone, let alone elves?"

"Olyve's grandmother wasn't an elf," Nanny said with a snort. "She was human I think." Either Nanny was confused, as usual, or there had been an elf grafted onto the girl's family tree since Olyve the elder had been to Solheim.

"Even so, how did your grandmother know my mother?" I was always dying to hear more about my past, as Nanny, Uncle, and even Morgan, were tight-lipped about my parents.

"Many races were once subject to the rule of Solheim," the girl said. "Pilgrimages and tributes were made, even in my grandmother's day, despite the loss of interest from Solheim in worldly affairs. I know much of your mother and her power. It is for that reason, and because word has travelled of your actions against slavery, your apparent concern for others, that I have sought you out."

"You've found me. Now what do you want?" I said, not falling for the flattery.

"Why, I want you to come with me to Faellion, My Dear." The way the child said 'My Dear' sent a chill scuttling down my spine.

"Faellion is the other side of the Kingdoms, and deep into elf lands. Not a friendly place for a human to visit," I pointed out. "Can't you find a detective closer to home?"

"I need you, Miss Thorne," the girl insisted. "There's nothing to fear there. I can protect you in the Elf Lands. There are many things that will interest you in fact. I can tell you more of your mother, Lili," she said, temptingly.

I was so terribly attracted by the bait, but I was also wary of the hook. "There's something to fear, else you wouldn't be trying to hire me. You are offering to pay, right?"

"I have gold."

"Good. But no. I can't go." I had a missing king to find and militants to stop. Besides, how much would Olyve's grandmother really have told her about my mother? She'd probably only known her as an infant.

If any word this child said could be believed.

I got the distinct sense that she, and her story, were a lie—almost. There was enough truth to tempt me, but my strange meter was now off the charts, and I couldn't ignore it. If she had been a darkly handsome man with a dangerous past and bad intentions, I might have succumbed. I know my weaknesses, and this wasn't one of them. My mother had left me behind in Solheim to die. I wanted to know why, but not enough to risk the life Morgan had saved when he took me from there.

"You must come with me," she repeated.

Her golden-eyed gaze was intense, even as she playfully twirled her pink parasol. She wouldn't part with any more details and seemed to be relying on her sincere insistence to convince me. The strange thing was it almost worked. I felt a bit woozy, like I had my head underwater and no sense of balance.

I shook off the fuzziness and said, "I'm on a case, one I can't drop. I should go and work on it now." I took a step toward the exit.

"You must come with me. Lives depend on it."

"And the lives of people I know and care about are depending on me right here in Highcrowne," I said.

Through the open back door, I spotted a blur that knocked into a trashcan.

"I have to go," I repeated. I dashed out and set the bag of stew down in the middle of the alley. The moment I did, the bogle appeared.

"Followed you, followed you," it said.

"You can have the stew, even if you don't have any information."

"Me have knowing. Me see the others. All saying they see what you want."

I'm sure it meant the werewolf. There wasn't anything else I wanted at that moment. "Where?" I asked.

"Here and there. Smell like strange. Then smell go away. Snap!" It snapped its fingers. "But howling things pop up again by docks, by gates, by here, there and everywhere."

"Not helpful. Was the werewolf smell at the warehouse that burned?" I asked, debating which was more difficult to deal with, the strange girl or the barely intelligible bogle.

"Oh yes, smell was there and all along the cliff."

"What about by the caverns that collapsed last week?"

"There too." It nodded emphatically, and I wondered if it were humoring me. It had somehow polled every bogle in Highcrowne in less than an hour.

"And the temple district? Did the werewolf plant those bodies that rose this morning?"

"Not sure. But many, many places."

At least there was one place it had missed, which made me trust the rest of its information more.

"Looks like the werewolf could be behind the militant attacks. How come only Bell and Duane have spotted it?" I wondered aloud.

The bogle shrugged. "Others see, but maybe they no wants to see? Bogles hide. Maybe humans too?"

Humans were pretty good at hiding their eyes from what they didn't want to see, but Solhans were even better at it.

"Thanks," I told it as I handed over the bag of stew. "Keep on the lookout for anything else strange. Plenty more of this whenever you want it."

The bogle sniffed the soup and cringed, but then it covered its nose and started slurping.

"Miss Thorne," Olyve said, carefully lifting her skirts as she climbed down the few steps to the alley. "You must take my case."

I was tired of her already. "I told you: I'm on another job. Besides, Faellion is too far away. I know Highcrowne, so I stick to Highcrowne." My tone was final.

The girl appraised me with her honey-colored eyes, eyes that seemed far older than the girl she appeared to be, but I crossed my arms in a stance that clearly showed I would not budge.

"Very well. Remember, I offered you this opportunity." The elf girl raised her pink parasol and marched off, nose in the air.

"Olyve?" Nanny called from the stoop.

"Farewell, Miss Wight," she called back. "Let us chase rats some time." She rounded the corner and vanished.

Nanny glared at me. "Can't be civil for three seconds."

"I can't be civil? You're the one always threatening to make Jorg into stew rather than let him cook the stew, so it's edible for once. All I did was turn down a case. It's not my fault she didn't want to stay for a chat."

"You met her at the door with a sword and then paid more attention to vermin than you did to her kind offer of employment. You don't have enough of that to be turning anyone away, Missy. At least she liked my soup. I see you fed yours to that creature." The bogle was noisily slurping away, wincing when it encountered a particularly chewy bit. "Disgraceful."

I didn't want to argue. "Goodbye, Nanny. Be seeing you."

"You'll be seeing the backside of my griddle next time you come barging in whenever you feel like it," she threatened. "This isn't a public house!"

"No, it's my house!" I'd started yelling. She always drove me to it. I was trying to avoid yelling; it made my temples hurt.

I sighed and followed the alley out to the main street. It was nice having multiple exits through which to escape Nanny's lectures.

I looked back at the house, expecting to see her glaring at me through the window as she often did, but instead I spotted Gypsum and Doctor Ghunnan. The goblin was astride his med student like a gentleman astride his steed, headed up the stairs for the front door. Malcolm, the King's Guardsman, followed behind, conspicuous in gold armor, and now there was a dog with them; one of the huge hairy hounds the Watch used to track down fugitives and escaped slaves. It looked like the circus was visiting.

It would not be good if Gypsum, sister to Matriarch Baroness Syla, was whopped upside the head with a frying pan. I also doubted the guardsman would stand idly by and let it happen without a bit of bloodshed.

I hurried up the steps after them, calling out, "Stop! Here I am."

"Can we go inside?" Gypsum asked. "You know we can't talk about this on the street."

All these strange visitors would stir up gossip in the neighborhood, so we needed to get inside for that reason alone.

"Let me go first." I went in and dodged the frying pan again. I managed to get it away from Nanny without revealing the green magic in front of everyone. Doctor Ghunnan would probably think it some parlor trick, but Gypsum would know something was wrong with me. We'd become fast friends in boarding school and knew everything about each other. She wouldn't like it that I was keeping this a secret. But you couldn't ignore something if you started talking about it to everyone.

"Nanny, can you get some tea for our guests?" I asked, essentially shooing her out of the room so we could talk.

"They're not my guests. You frightened away my only real guest in years," she grumbled, but she headed off to the kitchen anyway.

"Don't drink the tea when she brings it," I warned them. "It's probably eyeball-flavored."

"Mm, sounds good," the goblin said.

I indicated he should take a seat. There was room for everyone. Our parlor had several couches, chairs, tables, and divans, not to mention vases, armoires and settees, but all of it was in decay. The upholstery was threadbare, the vases cracked, even the faded wood furniture had a few chips missing. Just about all of it had been in pieces at one time or another—detecting was not popular—but I'd had all of it mended with magic when I had the funds. Nanny seemed to love her furniture and wouldn't part with it to make way for anything new. I might have inherited the house, and Nanny, from my brother, but it didn't mean I had any say in the place.

"Allow me," Malcolm said to the med student, as he helped her maneuver into the soft cushions, the seat contraption still strapped to her back. He 'accidentally' brushed her breast in the process, a crooked smile on his face. "Apologies."

"None taken." She blushed at the dwarf's lascivious look.

It was immediately clear when the tall human sat down with the goblin on her shoulders, no one was comfortable. I felt I needed to stand up again to look the goblin in the eye. Gypsum was a dwarf, so standing was no help, and when she sat down she got lost in the cushions, her legs wiggling futilely, while the dwarf guardsman couldn't even bend in his gaudy armor, so he stood stiffly beside the couch, the dog sniffing at his boots. In public houses and in the Central City there were chairs around for every race. We only had Solhan stuff.

"You have beautiful hair," Malcolm told the student.

"Thank you." She blushed again. I thought her hair an ordinary, red brown, but compared to dwarfish mud brown it was probably stunning. Oh no, no more spring fever please.

"What have you found?" I asked, choosing to sit down across from Gypsum and crane my neck to see the goblin. "The body?" It would make my job easier, but if the goblin found it all by himself, I might not get paid.

"He says he has the detector working—almost." Gypsum's words were a bit muffled by a throw cushion that was getting in her way.

"Why are you here then?" I asked. Not that I expected the goblin's contraption to work, but it was supposed to be keeping them out of my way while I investigated the suffragists.

"It is functioning, I assure you," Dr. Ghunnan said. "I can detect the resin sample in my possession. I'm simply working on boosting the range, and I'm finding line of sight to be the difficulty. Large stone mountains tend to interfere. We have even, reluctantly on my part, attempted to use the bloodhound to get around the problem." He indicated the tall, hairy mutt that was now snuffling its way across the floor and stirring up dust as it went.

"The doctor gave Jake some resin to sniff. He is the best tracker in the Dwarf Lands," Malcolm said, grabbing hold of the dog and giving it a wrestle. He ruffled its ears and patted it roughly, before pushing it away as it gave him a huge doggy kiss. "Stop that. I only kiss beautiful women."

Gypsum's over muscled and over sexed nephew winked at the med student, and she blushed again.

"The creature hasn't smelled anything useful," the goblin said. "I do not believe the animal will be much help. I understand you are embarking on a voyage tomorrow?"

"For Karolyne's wedding," I said, not happy about it.

"I would like to bring my detector along. Getting away from Highcrowne's mountain will make detection simpler, and it will allow us to survey the length of the river, as it is highly likely whoever stole the body will be trying to remove it from the city by ship."

"Why would you think that?" I asked suspiciously. "If it is dwarven suffragists, they have plenty of caverns right here in town to hide things. Seems like they'd be well hidden from your detector as well. Perhaps you are looking for a convenient way to leave town and escape custody? Or perhaps you know where your assistant is taking the body, and you want to appear the hero when you recover it?"

"Miss Kissel is innocent, and I am without ulterior motive." He made everything he said sound like an indisputable fact. "Perhaps you surmise correctly, and the body is hidden within the city. In which case, if the voyage reveals nothing, we can always return and leave it to your Guard and this hound to mundanely search each cavern and potential hiding place."

That didn't sound fun. Although, I agreed we should bring the Guard in on the search, even if we couldn't tell them about Rutgard. At least not all of them.

"Conrad is reliable," I told Gypsum. "He should know about the missing body. He's running some Special Investigation and all his people are hunting for militants already. When one finds the King's body in a suffragist hideout, Conrad can swoop in and get it back to the Matriarchs before anyone else hears a thing. That way we can be sure we're searching everywhere possible."

Gypsum sighed. "I fear you're right, and we must engage the Guard in some capacity. Conrad may be the best means, as you suggest. I will talk to Syla and ask for her permission. In the meantime, if this goblin's methods have any chance of working, I'd like to try. It would be so much simpler and discrete. I've left my brother, Alum, and Verdis behind to make sure no one discovers the tomb is empty, so we have some time."

"*The Mathésis* is a fancy new ship with a showy launch party planned. It will be packed," I said. "Which is probably why Karolyne wanted her wedding there—lots of guests she didn't have to buy drinks for. You'll never get a ticket for the goblin and his student."

"I will manage it," Gypsum said.

I eyed the goblin. Malcolm seemed like a competent guard, but maybe we should manacle the doctor to the ship to ensure he didn't get away when we were out of the city.

"Fine," I told Gypsum. "We do it your way. Everything for the wedding is being loaded tonight, and if the doctor's contraption is large, it's best to get it aboard this evening, before all the passengers and their baggage show up in the morning."

"The detector is not large, but there are specialized chemicals involved. I should return to my laboratory and pack them carefully," the goblin said.

"After I arrange things." Gypsum stood up. "Can I leave Doctor Ghunnan and Malcolm with you? I need only a few hours."

"With me?"

I planned to spend my afternoon questioning suffragists on street corners, joining in and holding a few signs if needed, until I heard whispers that might be useful. If Captain Uanal thought I was their natural ally they might too. I squirmed at the thought of playing nursemaid and dog watcher, or leaving them with Nanny. The beast was already starting to gnaw on a cushion.

"I don't...." I stopped mid-sentence, as the furniture rattled, and a loud boom shook the glass windows in their panes.

I hurried to the front door and swung it open. There was a billowing gray cloud one tier above us.

"It's the Market District," I said.

I forgot about Gypsum and the goblin and took off running toward the site of the explosion. It wasn't the Outskirts, where I knew almost everyone, but I wasn't thinking about differences between dwarfs and elves and humans at that moment. I wanted to do whatever I could to help. I took the stairs up to the Market District two at a time.

When I got there, the smoke made it almost impossible to see. The stench of charred wood and hair was becoming a too-familiar scent. This was no abandoned warehouse, though. Market stalls and wooden carts burned, cooking the apples, carrots and other food inside them. I saw something bright, like a light in a fog and went toward it.

My foot encountered something soft, so I got down on my hands and knees where it was easier to breathe and see. The softness was a dead stall owner. I saw the tether of light holding his soul snap as I watched. It was a paler green than the light that burned in my palms, but it tasted similar. At least according to that strange second sense I had developed for souls and magic. My hands wanted to catch the soul as it fled, pull it back. Bend it to my will. I let the soul flee.

I spotted more lights through the smoke, some souls close to their bodies, others barely tethered, and some drifting away, as though carried on a gentle breeze. They were all around me, and their power tingled along my nerves. Despite the run here, I felt strong and refreshed. Was I stealing power from these ghosts without realizing it? That was wrong. So wrong.

There was no wind, but I heard something like the rustling of dry leaves.

A whisper that carried the scent of cinnamon said, "Eva. My Eva. So many souls are coming to me this day, so many shining and bright, but none burn as brightly as you. Come to me...."

The voice stirred inside me, dredging up a longing for something I couldn't explain. It was alluring, a cocktail of rich power and sweet ecstasy that was almost irresistible. The sweet taste of poison. I stopped listening.

I swatted at the smoke around me, trying to clear it, and staggered to my feet. I stumbled through the chaos with my eyes closed, able to see the souls more easily without my regular sight to confuse me. I searched for one with the tether still strong.

I found an elf woman breathing, so I hoisted her half-way over my shoulder and dragged her to the edge of the square. She wasn't as light as she looked. I went into the smoke again and found another survivor, before stumbling upon a makeshift medical station past where the silk merchant's stall used to be. The souls there burned so strongly, I had to open my eyes or be blind. There were plenty of living, but so much blood and pain as well. For a moment, I worried about my old friend Ahsaed, the cloth merchant, but there was no sign of him. Instead, I saw something that put my heart in my throat.

"Kali."

I laid down the elf I was helping and hurried over to where Kali lay. Someone had used a roll of silk to prop her head up. She was breathing, but there were splinters of wood sticking out of her everywhere, the largest ones oozing blood.

"Eva?" It wasn't Kali who spoke. She was still unconscious, but I recognized the voice and turned with dread.

I spotted him deeper into the makeshift hospital. Duane. He was holding Little Viktor.

The world seemed to drop, and a cold panic froze me in place.

"No," I whispered, when I was finally able to make my mouth move again.

Duane's new suit was a mess, and he looked at me with such guilt. "We went to get flowers..." he said.

I couldn't look at Viktor. He was only five. No.

"Eva?" A small voice whispered. "Uncle 'ane?"

Tears washed the soot out of my eyes. He was alive. I kissed Viktor's baby cheeks in a flurry, but he groaned in pain, and I saw the massive splinter of wood sticking through his leg. Duane had bandaged around it, holding it in place, but there was too much blood.

"I'll get my uncle," I said.

I hadn't spoken to him in months. He was evil, but Vikky was his heir, and I knew Uncle Ulric would do everything in his power to help.

Duane nodded. "Get him."

I ran into Doctor Ghunnan, Malcolm, and Gypsum on my way back. I mentioned the makeshift hospital, and the doctor said he would help.

"No." I told him. "Those people need magic, not your nonsense."

The goblin and his student ignored me and continued toward the wounded. All that mattered was I reach Uncle, so I kept running. I was amazed at the speed I managed, the cobbles blurring beneath my feet. There had been power in the marketplace, and it still coursed through me. I wasn't even breathing heavily when I reached the front door. I knocked, and Morgan answered.

Morgan was a father to me. He'd taught me everything worth knowing, saved me from Solheim as an infant, but he wasn't my father. He was Uncle's bodyguard and manservant. Still, it was comforting to see his wide shoulders, his strong, sinewy hands holding the door open, and a stern expression on his face that put my glares to shame.

I fell into his arms. They were huge, and I suddenly remembered them picking me up as a child. I had been clumsy or simply not paying attention, because I fell down a lot.

"Viktor..." I began.

"I heard the explosion. I'll get Ulric." Morgan was in motion, darting towards my uncle's office, and I was left standing, feeling dazed now that I'd gotten help, and still needing someone to hold me.

"Seems like wishes do come true," Ilsa said.

I stiffened at the sound of my sister's voice, my voice.

"I thought you were the type to rely on dark spells rather than wishes," I said. "Or have you begun dynamiting innocent people now too?"

"I was referring to having you—and my missing soul—so near to me again, Sugar. The chaos outside is none of my doing. Although, it will be interesting to see what comes of it in the end. How weak the current rulers are beginning to seem, and surely the Crowns will agree on some measures to restore order? It is unfortunate that our poor Little Viktor has been affected by politics and war and things so far beyond his control."

I didn't believe her regret over Vikky's injuries for a moment. Eliminating Uncle's heir would be a wish come true for her indeed. That way she could inherit the family business, which as far as I could tell was dark magic, crime, and power brokering. Duane practically worked for my uncle, as did many of the slavers and other nefarious cartels. No one in the Outskirts, whether priest or gangster, did business without his consent. What I did believe was that Ilsa was happy to have me within reach again. Not for long if I could help it. I backed toward the door.

Ilsa stepped toward me with speed and grace. She wasn't wearing shoes, and her small feet tapped across the marble floor with no more sound than a butterfly tiptoeing. She wore a delicate dress made of sheer white fabric, her black hair and red lips a violent contrast. Only her pale, pale eyes matched. Is that what I really looked like? I asked myself the same question whenever I saw my twin.

She reached for my hand, and I noted the many bracelets around her wrists: bone charms etched with runes, glass and metal beads in the shapes of various people and creatures, bits of charred wood.... I didn't want her to touch me, but I couldn't back up anymore.

"None of that now," Uncle Ulric said in his powerful voice, which always boomed like thunder no matter if he were speaking to a single person in his office or a crowd at a funeral. He pushed Ilsa aside. "Let us past. You two girls can continue your squabbles another day."

I didn't consider Ilsa continually threatening my life a 'squabble', but in Uncle's mind it might be. I let him lead the way, Morgan following us both. I was relieved when Ilsa stayed behind.

I showed my uncle where the makeshift hospital was. There were more bodies than before, some moaning or crying, and too many others not moving at all.

Doctor Ghunnan was no longer astride his student, but instead stood on wobbly legs with her support. He wiped Kali's brow. Then he took something from a black leather satchel he had with him, a vial of clear liquid, and placed it against her lips.

"Stop that," I said. I wasn't close enough to intervene with the doctor, and too many bodies were between us.

"Do not fear," the goblin told me. "It is a simple restorative."

That's what I was afraid of. Turpentine and iodine were no good for anyone.

Kali stirred, opening her eyes and moving an arm to knock the vial aside. "Keep it away," she said. Maybe the restorative worked by tasting so horrible the body preferred to be conscious and in pain rather than taste any more of it.

My uncle and Morgan had spotted Little Viktor and were beside him already. I joined them.

Duane was reluctant to let go of the boy. "Careful," he said.

Morgan cradled Viktor in his huge arms, so he looked like a baby and even more fragile. Ulric pulled a large, silk handkerchief from his pocket and draped it over the wound. He grabbed the large splinter of wood through the cloth and pulled. I thought I saw a flash of green light, but it was too quick for me to register. My own hands began to tingle, so I knew magic had been used.

Vikky screamed. Duane and I winced, reaching out for him, but Morgan stayed calm as he held Viktor tightly, preventing the boy from thrashing about too much. My uncle touched Vikky's forehead, and in an instant my nephew was asleep. Ulric folded up the kerchief, and I noted that the wound was no longer bleeding.

"Take him home," Ulric commanded. Morgan nodded and carried Little Viktor off.

"I suggest you curtail your excursions with my heir until the city is safe once more," Ulric told Duane.

"I have a right to visit my godson. You promised me that."

"Visit him all you like, but it will be within my home and walls where I can keep him safe. Understood?"

Duane frowned but nodded ever so slightly.

Ulric walked away without a word to me. He hadn't even noticed all the other wounded in need of help.

I stood awkwardly for a moment, the shock of it all beginning to set in.

Then I summoned my anger.

Dwarves fighting one another was one thing, but when people I cared about…. I wanted these militants stopped. It wasn't what I'd been hired for, but I was making it my job. The militants were now my number one priority. If finding Rutgard's body helped catch them, fine. Otherwise, the centuries old corpse could wait a bit longer before being hidden away in the palace again.

"What did you see?" I asked Duane. "How did this happen?"

"A little assistance?"

He held out a hand, and I reluctantly helped him stagger over to a low wall that bounded a garden bed. The plants and flowers were covered in soot. He coughed and hacked for a while, before spitting up a few gobs of soot himself. I felt somewhat sorry for him. Somewhat.

"Did you see anything or not?" I asked again, impatient. I could move on to other witnesses if need be.

"I saw something. You know me." He picked a few splinters from his bleeding arms.

Duane was smarter than he looked, but I'd never admit he was better than me at the observation game we used to play as kids.

"Spit it out," I said.

He spat out another gob of sooty phlegm.

"Very funny."

"I was in an explosion. A little sympathy?"

"This is me you're talking to."

"Sometimes, it might as well be Ilsa."

That stung. I was a little insensitive, a little angry, and far too tempted by magic, but I kept my dark side in check. She embraced it. I folded my arms and waited. When he realized he wasn't going to get a reaction from me, he finally talked.

"I didn't see the wagon go into the shop. It was one of the stone buildings built into the mountainside, the artisan cabinetmaker's place. I went in there once to get a wardrobe made—"

"—for all your new suits, I suppose?"

"Very funny yourself." He looked down at his ruined suit with a frown. "As I was saying, I've been in there before and the place is vast. It goes into the mountain a bit. You can feel the damp on the walls. I'm sure the back offices connect to old tunnels from when the shop was owned by dwarves. The cabinetmaker was an elf though. He told me how he'd learned from a dwarf master and bought the place when he retired. I remembered, because I thought it odd an elf ever admitting it was worth learning something from another race.

"That's not important, though. The main point is the explosion was so big because it wasn't about getting these little stalls and carts or the people in the market square. It was about destroying that shop. We were all collateral damage. The shop must be buried in rubble now. Maybe even the tier above has collapsed a bit. Yes, I think it has." He peered through the smoke at the mountain above us.

I noted the sagging stone structures. That was inside the Central City proper. No wonder there was no Guard here yet, despite an elven district being hit.

They'd be focusing on the damage done to the noble's houses. Maybe one of them had been the real target? Was there a dwarven matriarch up there somewhere? I'd have to ask Gypsum.

"Did you see anything else?" I asked, taking a step away.

He grabbed my arm, and I clenched my fist. My hands were still tingling, and I'm sure a bit of green light was showing. I'd have to do something about that soon, if only to hide it better. Problem was, I didn't know who to ask. Not Ilsa or Ulric for certain. Nanny too seemed unwilling to help, so who did that leave? Maybe Morgan.

Duane had seen. He saw everything, but he didn't comment on the sure sign of dark magic he always knew I'd fall prey to. He looked into my eyes instead, and I saw how hard the jade color of them was at that moment. He wanted someone to die for what had happened.

"Vikky and I were walking by," he said. "The wide doors were open for loading and unloading furniture, and there was a carriage parked inside. It was too small to carry any large cabinets, so I presumed it was picking up a chest or something similar. But then I saw the wolf step out of the carriage's side door. It was on two legs and wore a hat and vest like some civilized person.

"Vikky thought it was funny and pointed. The creature looked at us with yellow eyes that glowed, and its lips turned up in a smile. You know the way dog's smile? But there was nothing friendly about it. It looked like it wished it could stay and watch what happened next. But it didn't stay. It dropped to all fours and bounded back into the depths of the shop so fast I could have believed I imagined the whole thing. It must have escaped out the back tunnels, if it did escape. We were fortunate. I hurried Vikky away up the street. As much as I wanted to go in and follow the werewolf, I knew I had to get the boy someplace safe first. If we'd stayed there a minute longer, we'd have been hit by the full blast."

"Thank you for watching out for Little Viktor." I couldn't believe I'd said that to Duane of all people, but I was grateful my nephew was alive. "I will get that wolf. I promise. Now get someone to help you pick those splinters out and find a bandage or two. You're leaking everywhere."

I walked away as dispassionately as my uncle had.

"You're not going to do it?" he shouted after me.

"I'm not as good at stopping pain as I am at causing it," I called back.

The wolf would learn that too soon enough. I had the beginnings of a plan, one that would leave the creature and whoever else was responsible with nowhere to hide.

7 UNDERCOVER

I made sure Kali was alright. She had gone back to sleep, and the goblin doctor had moved on to other patients. Gypsum was buzzing about, helping everyone within reach as best she could. I took her by the shoulders and made her focus on me for the moment.

"Go organize the doctor's ticket for the ship," I said. "And get me the guest list for this maiden voyage. I want to know how many matriarchs besides your sister will be onboard. If there are only a few, get tickets for more. Make them come, no matter what excuse you or Syla need to give them."

"But these people...?"

"Send the Guard to help the wounded. You have more important things to do. If we want to catch those responsible, if we want to catch a wolf, we need to set a trap."

"You want the militants to attack the ship?" Gypsum asked, incredulous. "I can't put matriarchs in danger. I can't allow you to put yourself and Karolyne in danger like that either."

"We have to stop them. That means drawing them out into a place of our choosing. The maiden voyage of *The Mathésis*, dignitaries and matriarchs galore? They won't be able to resist. They may already be planning to attack it. I can make sure they don't get a bomb onboard. At least I think I can. Their only choice will be to send some of their people to sink it, and then we'll grab them, hurt them, and find out who else is responsible for all of this." I gestured at the destruction around us, and I had to close my eyes. I couldn't look at it all. But when I closed my eyes, I saw Little Viktor's face in pain, so I opened them again.

"Sink it? You do realize it's..." Gypsum began. "Never mind. I think it can work—if we have enough security in place, and if we know how to spot a militant when we find one?"

"I'm working on that too."

"But how does this help us find ... the body?"

"When we catch the bad guys, we can ask them where they put it. Some things are more important than preserving the political status quo, don't you think? People are dying."

Gypsum looked at the blood smeared up her arms from the injured she'd been nursing. "I know that. And you're right, Eva. You're right. I'll go now and make arrangements." She wiped her hands on her dress and turned to leave, but she stopped and asked, "What about the good Doctor Ghunnan?"

"I'll handle him."

As soon as Gypsum was gone, I went to the goblin. He was trying to get his reddish-colored cure all down the throat of a reluctant victim.

"Go back to your laboratory," I told him. "Get your detector ready and meet me at the ship tonight. Malcolm, escort him."

The dwarf guardsman was nearby, his golden armor now a dusty gray. He was trying to keep the massive hound with him from putting its snout in someone's wound. He nodded.

"But, my patients?" the goblin said.

I took the vial out of his hand, for which the elderly elf he was trying to 'treat' looked extremely grateful and said, "I think they'll be fine.

"I thought you were uncertain about Lady Gypsum's idea of using the ship?"

"I'm trusting you. Something I don't do very often, so don't take it lightly. You were with me when the Market District blew up, and I have a witness who spotted the likely culprit. You may or may not have been involved in the king's abduction, but I don't give a damn about kings and Crowns right now. Especially when they don't give a damn about me and those I care about. That—and getting paid—can wait. I have more important things to do, but if you can get your locator to work, I won't hold you back. Actually, I was wondering if you had any other types of locators. Such as one that detects wolves?"

"Wolves?" The goblin's green brow wrinkled deeply.

"Yes. Werewolves. The Guard has samples of hair on file if that will help."

The goblin chortled. "I doubt dog hair, as they've likely found, will work to locate a mythical and nonexistent creature. Perhaps you should try that bloodhound over there, or better yet, ask a fairy for help? I believe they can be found in dew drops and flower tufts and are attracted to gifts of honey and milk. If you believe other children's stories."

"Don't you dare mock the Unmentionables. They are everywhere and not friendly. Not friendly at all. I'm going to have to leave an offering of milk now to apologize for listening to you talk about them. Go get your detector ready, and I'll see you tonight." I walked away.

The ignorance of the goblin. I felt an itch between my shoulder blades that was intolerable. I grabbed a handful of salt from a bag that had fallen from a destroyed merchant stall and tossed it over my shoulder. That was better. Superstitions existed for a reason. I already had enough dark odds stacked against me as a Thorne and a Solhan I couldn't afford to ignore traditions.

When I reached Bell's place, no one was home. As co-owner, I had a key, and after digging around for it among the thick ring of keys I kept tied to my belt, I let myself in.

I stole some milk from her icebox. I was surprised to see it was literally a wooden box with a half-melted ice block fetched from above the snow line. She used Avian magic in her mechanoid creations; why couldn't she use a decent Avian-enchanted ice box like other civilized people? The stubbornness of that girl.

I left a good dollop of cream along with the milk in a dish outside. I spotted Bell worming her way through the labyrinth of junk and held the door for her. I kept her from stepping on the milk.

"You are incredibly superstitious, Eva."

"If you'd grown up on Solhan bedtime stories, you would be too. Did you find a way to detect dynamite?" I asked, impatient.

"Did you hear what happened to the Market District? Wild."

"I was there, and it was brutal. Bell … Kali was there."

"What? Why didn't you tell me?" She turned to leave, and I grabbed her. I had to pin her arms to keep her from fighting free. It helped that I was taller and longer limbed, but she was tough.

"Stop fighting," I insisted. "Kali is fine. I checked on her. You can go to her after you tell me what you learned. If you want to keep this from happening again, you have to help me. I need you, Bell. Focus."

I loosened my grip and she pulled free, panting. She went into her workshop and started pulling bits and pieces off shelves, even removing a few parts from already built mechanoids. She did everything forcefully, and her lips were set with anger.

"Talk to me," I said.

"No one is missing any dynamite, or the chemicals to make it. Few can do it but me anyway. I know the others in town, and they know Duane. None of them would dare cross him or lie to me about what they know. If these militants are using dynamite, then it's imported."

"Can we detect it then? I don't want to get on a ship that could blow up and have no way of knowing."

"What are you up to?"

"I'm using the launch of *The Mathésis* as a trap for the militants."

"And your own friend's wedding is part of the bait? You are cold, Eva."

"I'm part of the bait too. So is Gypsum and her sister and everyone else aboard. All our lives are at risk in Highcrowne anyway. No one knows where they will strike next. We need to do something decisive to stop them."

"Alright." I was surprised Bell didn't argue more. "Take this."

She handed over the thing she had built in front of me. It was a funnel, connected by translucent tubing to a series of glass vials, which were screwed into a metal casing. I spotted thin lines of glowing green goo running along the wire wrapped around the tubing and the glass cylinders, so it was powered by Avian magic at least.

"What is it?"

"A portable gas chromatograph to detect the key chemicals in explosives. When all three glass tubes glow green, you can be sure you've found dynamite."

"What if only one glows?"

"Either you're getting closer, or you've found mechanoid propellant instead, only one ingredient."

"Okay." I wasn't about to complain about abominable technology this time. It could save my life and the lives of everyone boarding the ship in the morning. "You're sure it works?"

She dug around in her ice box and came back with a greased leather bag like the one Nanny stored lard inside. Bell pulled out a stick of dynamite and waved it in front of the funnel end of the detector. All three glass cylinders glowed bright green.

"It works," she said, a satisfied smile momentarily replacing the concern on her features.

"You had dynamite in the ice box?" I said.

"It's more stable at low temperatures."

"This is Highcrowne. It's freezing all year round."

"I get nervous when the snow melts. Better safe than sorry." She wrapped up the dynamite again and put it back. I wouldn't be stealing any more milk from her ice box.

"I don't want to bust this thing," I said, awkwardly handling the detector. "I'm bad with technology. Can you come tonight and help me search the ship? Please?" I begged.

"I want to take care of Kali."

"Do that, but then come find me tonight. I could use your help."

"I'll think about it. You hold it like this." She corrected my grip. "This whole thing is your plan. I don't want the responsibility. This is all on you."

She left me there and went to look for Kali.

I eyed the detector and groaned at the idiocy of my idea. This is what happened when I thought angry. Now my more rational mind would have to work out the details. I was still angry though, which helped me keep going. I hiked back home to Nanny, waving the detector about, so I could get a feel for it as I walked.

No glass tubes lit up along the way, which was good, but I wasn't sure if I was using it properly. How close to dynamite did I need to be?

If only I could detect the werewolf too. Magic couldn't track it; else the Guard would have done so already. They had hair samples, which is all you needed to make a charm. Werewolves were myth, but I remembered a few stories said the creatures were immune to enchantments. At least, all the good witches in the stories ended up using ingenuity to beat the wolf, like dressing as a vulnerable granddaughter going through the woods at night. Werewolves must be immune to detection spells. That could also explain why they used dynamite instead of fire runes. Maybe being immune to magic also meant they were unable to use it?

Still, they changed form from wolf to man and back again. That wasn't normal. I'd like to know how it worked. Not that I liked knowing more about dangerous magic than I did already, but curiosity always got the better of me.

There had to be some way to track the wolf. There was the bloodhound ... or the bogles. The one I'd fed had scented something that kept vanishing. Perhaps I could get the bogle to search the ship with me? That sounded like a plan.

When I got home, Conrad was waiting in the parlor. Nanny had let him of all people in for some reason. He was out of uniform and wearing a simple suit with black pants and white shirt, the sleeves rolled up, but no jacket. He looked very good this way as well, but he didn't say anything to me, so I didn't say anything to him. This whole excursion was business, not the date he'd kept asking me for. I sometimes regretted not giving in. I also wondered why he hadn't been more persistent. Maybe he was smarter than I thought?

I set Bell's contraption on an end table and screamed to Nanny, who must be somewhere in the house, telling her not to touch it, not that she even knew what I was talking about.

"What is it?" Conrad asked. I was already halfway up the stairs, headed to my room to change.

"Dynamite detector. I have a plan, and I'm going to need you and your Special Investigation team to help make it work. You think you can get onboard *The Mathésis* tomorrow? Undercover and looking like that? What am I supposed to wear to this Suffragist party tonight anyway? Chains and a burlap bag, or is a dress allowed?"

"A dress." He never used to be so stingy with his words. Of course, he became more interesting when he stopped talking to me.

"How about pants? Can I bring my Ashur?"

"No. To both. Try to look like a lady."

"I don't like you when you talk like that." I'd made it to the second-floor landing, so I had to lean over the bannister and shout to make sure he heard me. Maybe he had stopped speaking to me because we'd run out of nice things to say to one another.

I went into my room and kicked through the mess, trying to find something to wear. I had my bridesmaid dress laid out on the bed and was tempted to get an extra wearing out of it but decided not to risk it. I might end up visiting another explosion tonight the way things were going, and soot got into everything.

I drew a bath and peeled off my blackened clothes. When I was in there, I heard a quiet knock on the door. It had to be Conrad. Nanny would never knock.

"Come in."

"Aren't you taking a bath?" he asked.

"Yes."

"I'll stay out here. What's this about *The Mathésis*, and why do you need me?"

"I'm making your job easy," I said. "The militants are going to try and kill everyone onboard."

"How do you know that? What information do you have?" He always got more excited whenever I made it sound like danger was imminent.

"I know they won't be able to resist when Baroness Syla and her matriarch friends are onboard."

He opened the door and stuck his head in, his eyes closed. "No. You cannot endanger royals like that. We've been keeping the VIP guests on that launch quiet and security high so that it won't be a target."

"You keep the royals safe but allow the militants to run rampant and bomb the city? It's fine for ordinary citizens to be in danger?"

"You're not even a Citizen, Eva."

"Neither are you. How does that work with the Guard? How do you get to be a Special Investigator when you don't even rank as high as the lowest dwarf?"

"I'm a special case. I've been given special papers...."

"Special, special, I don't care about special. I care about the people at the spring festival today who can't celebrate without a corpse killing everyone in sight. I'm talking about Kali and Vikky and Duane, even, who can't go to the market in safety. As much as I'm looking forward to this civilized evening with suffragist leaders that you've organized, I'd prefer you got off your butt, got your people onto *The Mathésis*, and set a trap to catch the bad guys once and for all."

"Your idea will get everyone on that ship killed."

"I have a dynamite detector. And a werewolf detector too. I just need to find the bogle and feed him again. This can work, and I'm doing it whether you like it or not. I have special orders too, from Baroness Syla."

Of course, her orders weren't specifically about the militants, but I could convince her this was the only way to find the body as well. Oh yeah, I had a body detector too, but I wasn't cleared to speak to Conrad about that yet. All these secrets could get confusing.

"You can detect the werewolf?" He sounded impressed. I must have been right, and the Guard had already tried every magical detection spell known.

"Bogles can smell him, when he's in wolf form that is. We can search that ship head to toe before it launches, make sure there's no dynamite or fire runes, and the militants will be forced to send their killer wolf aboard to do their dirty work with claws alone. Then we can catch him.”

The bath was relaxing my tired muscles. They weren’t nearly as tired as they should be after all the running I did today, and I knew the souls of the dead had fed me. I didn’t like that. I didn’t like there being dead people and souls laying around for me to run into. Everything was wrong in my city lately, and I was going to make it right.

Conrad had been quiet for a while. His eyes were still closed. Such a gallant.

“Alright,” he said. “I have to be a part of this if it’s going to work. As much as I believe you have a dynamite detector, I want Guardsmen searching that ship as well.”

“I wouldn’t have it any other way.”

“And not too many matriarchs. We don’t want it to look like an obvious trap.”

“Sounds like you’re getting excited,” I said.

“It’s too dangerous ... but it could work. Although, we may not need any of it after tonight.”

“You think the suffragists will simply tell you their evil plans?”

“I’m being initiated, made one of them. I hope to learn a lot.”

“Don’t they know you’re a Guardsman? Are they stupid?”

“There are more Guardsmen among them already than I like. They are feeling pretty confident that their movement has almost universal support among the male dwarves."

"The King's Guard says otherwise. So, why do they need to blow people up if they already have so much support?"

"I don't know. That's what I want to find out."

"Then let's get going. Hand me a towel."

He had to open his eyes to find one, but he closed them again and dashed out of the room before I could stand up.

Damn. I might not want a lover right now, but I wouldn't mind having some male wrapped around my finger. That sounded like the bit of Ilsa inside me talking, the part of me I didn't like.

Conrad and I were quite the married couple when we reached the suffragist meeting place, barely talking to one another.

It was an abandoned temple on Craftsman Terrace, at the foot of the Central City. The temple had been converted to a workshop of some kind. Contraptions clanked and spluttered, spitting out ink and paper. One huge machine seemed to place writing on the paper rather than having a scribe do it, and all the papers it produced looked the same, spouting suffragist slogans. So, this was how they made those pamphlets they were handing out to everyone? It looked less heartfelt when I realized a machine had printed them.

You could see the remnants of the temple from the shape of the windows, the elaborate carved doorways, and the altar where the speaker stood. We hadn't missed anything. The dwarf was flipping through a sheaf of notes as he readied himself.

I didn't recognize him. He looked like any dwarf you might see working at carpentry or rug making, long gray beard and balding head, ochre skin, wearing plain, undyed clothes and boots, and a leather apron he hadn't bothered to remove. The apron was smeared with black ink, so the writing machines were probably his.

I did, however, recognize quite a few people in the gathering crowd. I had expected a secret knock to get into the place, but there'd only been a grumpy dwarf at the door waving people inside. He had paused at sight of me, but then seemed to recognize Conrad and grunted for us to go in. We towered above the dwarves around us, so I directed Conrad to a bench on one side where we could sit. It was still easy enough to see over the heads of those standing. They were all males, of course, some wearing red armbands, some not.

Cups of watered mead and plates of bread and cheese were on the sideboard near us, so I grabbed a drink and a few bites. I couldn't resist cheese, and while I feared putting on fat before wearing the bridesmaid dress tomorrow, everyone knew food eaten after sunset didn't count.

I spotted Reginald from the café—and Bert. That was a surprise. I'd thought Bert the more levelheaded of the two. Had Reginald forced him to come along? Near them was Gypsum's brother, Alum, who I thought was guarding the King's tomb. She would not be happy to hear that her blood kin were as untrustworthy as her husbands. I noted Karolyne's husband-to-be at the back, but that was not a shock in the slightest. Wade, The Jerk, probably wrote the speeches, or wished he did.

"Welcome fellow dwarfs, men ... suffragists..." the speaker began.

"You're not sufferin'!" someone heckled from the crowd.

"We are all suffering and do not know it. Did you choose your profession?" The presenter pointed at someone in the crowd. It could have been the heckler, but I couldn't tell.

"I'm a baker, same as my fathers before me. I'm proud to be a baker."

"Proud. What other choice do you have but to be proud of the lot you've been given? You haven't even dreamed of anything else. Well, I've dreamed, and you can see my dream here. The printing press. I heard tell of this wondrous invention, and my mother would have nothing to do with it. She's near in the grave, and she forbade me, a grown man who has lived more than half a lifetime. She forbade me to even speak of it. Well, I did more than that. I built one. And now it speaks for me, spreading my words far and wide for all to read."

"In elvish," someone else pointed out. "If you're so concerned for ye fellow dwarves, why not use the mother tongue?"

"And shame on you!" Another person called. "Shame on you for disrespecting your poor, bearded mother."

"Mother-hater!" another person called.

"Settle down now." The speaker raised his arms and lowered them as though indicating they should sit, but there was no place for most of them.

I stayed quiet and hidden behind the cheese wheel, feeling very out of place at this gathering. Conrad squeezed my hand, and I jumped. I didn't know what to make of that. Was he warning me to settle down as well? I hadn't even begun to get riled up. I was saving that for later.

"Dwarvish is our mothers' tongue," the speaker said, "so I chose elvish as a symbol of the reality of today. We all speak elvish. We all care what the elves say, but no one cares what dwarves say. Let's speak in a tongue people respect. Better yet, let's create a new language of our own. Join me...."

"A new language? Printing presses?" a dwarf in the crowd guffawed. "How does this keep me poor, dear nephew from being sent to the mines just 'cause he loves to throw a punch or two? You need think of the common dwarf ye do, standing up there on yer pedestal. What can a common dwarf do to change his mum's mind? His matriarch's? The whole council? What can we do?"

"We can stop work! We can refuse to eat or lift a finger. We can say 'no', until they say 'yes' to our demands."

"Me's kinda like to eat," a hefty dwarf said. "And me work isn't so bad. It's only the bad ones they send to the mines."

"The mines chew men up and spit them out as bones," the dwarf with the brawler for a nephew said. "No one deserves to go there. And who says they're trouble? Your mum? She wants us all knitting tea cozies and playing nice together over Parcheesi."

"I won't hear no more of this disrespecting of mothers," one of the earlier hecklers said. "I'll hear no more of it! And none of you others should either. Leave this mother-hater to his hunger strikes and elvish blather. I'll be getting on with getting on I will!" The dwarf pushed his way out the door, and about half the room joined him.

Well, that left the true suffragists behind. Not quite the groundswell movement Conrad made it seem, but there were enough, about fifty people left, who could cause trouble. Plenty of suspects.

"Thank you, brothers, for seeing sense," the speaker said to the ones who remained. "You see the difficulties we must overcome? When our comrades do not even recognize their suffering. That's why we must suffer publicly, make the Matriarchs suffer, to understand our pain."

Make the Matriarchs suffer? That made me stiffen, and Conrad held my hand even tighter.

"Excuse me," I told him, extracting my fingers. I stood up and wormed my way around the crowd to where Bert was standing.

The speaker was launching into a tirade about unfair work practices, and the duty to resist, but I'd stopped listening.

"Bert," I said in his ear. "What will your aunt Gypsum say about you being here?"

He started when he saw me. He seemed to have been entranced by the speeches.

"Hush, Eva." He glanced nervously at Reginald, but the other dwarf hadn't spotted me. Bert took my elbow and led me to the back of the crowd. I let him. Otherwise, he wouldn't have been able to get me to go anywhere.

"What do you know about the attacks on the Matriarchs?" I asked him.

"Nothing," Bert whispered. "I didn't know ... The marketplace. Wasn't that an attack against elves?"

"No. Everything's been about the dwarfs. The suffragists want to make the Matriarchs suffer—didn't you hear the same words as me?"

"I'm not one of them."

"Then what are you doing here?"

"What are you doing here?"

"I'm the one asking the questions."

"I'm here..." he looked around to make sure no one was near, and his whisper dropped down to an imperceptible mumble in my ear.

"What?"

"I said..." This time the mumble was a little clearer, and I made out the word "spy."

"You're spying?"

"Shhh." He made a hushing gesture. "I'm doing want Aunt Gypsum told me to do."

That made sense. Gypsum would want to know what Reginald was up to, so Bert made the obvious informer. Thing was, could I trust him? I could verify his story with Gypsum, but that didn't mean he hadn't been swayed by the rhetoric in the air.

"Make sure you remember why you're here. Whomever bombed the marketplace won't survive me, so if your leader up there is responsible, he won't be around much longer, and you don't want to end up the same way."

Bert gulped.

I gave him a last warning glare, before I moved on to the next person I knew.

"Alum," I said. "The tomb still empty?"

The dwarf jumped slightly. I think I must be as stealthy as Ilsa. "I ... yes." He said. "Verdis is guarding it."

"He didn't seem able to function independently."

"He'll be fine. He's capable of blocking doorways and not letting anyone in without an explanation."

"You know this puts you at the top of my suspect list?" I said. "A King's Guard with access to the tomb, to the Central City … and a suffragist as well?"

"I'm not a suffragist," he hissed a bit too loudly. "They are pathetic. I'm not pathetic. No, Gypsum asked me…"

"…to spy for her," I finished in a more discrete tone of voice. "I'm starting to see a pattern."

I left him to it and made my way to the back. I thought I'd managed to stay out of the line of sight of Karolyne's fiancé, but when I went around a stone pillar he was there.

"You trying to defile the sanctity of this place with your harlot's ways?" Wade asked.

"Dwarves aren't my type," I said. "But, yeah, this huge stone pillar is kind of sexy. Yeah, this might do." I rubbed it lasciviously, which made The Jerk turn red.

"Leave," he told me.

"No, you leave. I'm here with a date to do some defiling." I indicated Conrad across the room. Conrad was Karolyne's cousin and Wade had to know he was a Guardsman. I didn't want to ruin Conrad's 'brilliant' undercover work, but The Jerk made any social situation unbearable. "Wouldn't do for you to miss your wedding tomorrow, on account of being tossed into jail for messing up our date. Although the official charge might be 'illegal assembly of an unauthorized civilian organization'."

I did sometimes read the laws, mostly so I wouldn't do anything that would get myself arrested.

"Things will change around here after the wedding," he said, pointing a finger at me. "Mark my words. Things will change." He turned and left, walking slowly to hide his fear of the Guard or maybe because he was so furious; either way it looked like he had to go to the bathroom.

With the Jerk gone, I was free to mingle. I made my way around the room, scouring my memory of visits to the Market Guard house and the Smiths' Watch house. Yes, there were lots of dwarves I recognized, and the few I pulled aside for a threatening chat all revealed they were with Conrad or spying for Gypsum or Syla or some other matriarch. From my little survey, I estimated three quarters of the room were there to spy on the suffragists. Maybe more. Supposedly. It really was impossible to trust anyone. Maybe that was the excuse they all gave their mothers when they left home—I'm off to spy on the suffragists for you. When really, they sympathized. Who could tell?

Eventually, the interminable lecturing eased up, and everyone was invited to share some bread and mead and get to know one another. I cornered the few dwarves who might be genuine suffragists and said, "I wish you could see my bridesmaid dress. It will be a proper dwarf wedding in red. Beautiful. On *The Mathésis* too. I'm so lucky to be going to such a fancy wedding with so many fancy matriarchs attending...."

"What are you doing?" Conrad asked.

I hurriedly went to his side and tried to act like Karolyne would. "Nothing, Dear. Just telling them about the wedding on *The Mathésis*. If only everyone could be there. With the matriarchs."

"I know what you're doing." He pulled me aside.

"I hope so. We have to bait the trap somehow. Not that I think it matters much. Most of the dwarfs here say they're spies, and most of them are from your Special Investigation unit."

"They told you that?"

"They know I'm with you. Besides, I can be persuasive."

"Threatening, you mean."

"Same thing. Now, I'm heading off to search the ship. Join me when you're done comparing spy notes and want to do some real investigating. This is going nowhere."

"Eva..." Conrad looked like he was trying to come up with another excuse to stop me from turning Karolyne's wedding ship into a trap, and part of me wanted him to have a better plan that didn't mean putting more people I cared about in danger, but then the big doors behind the altar opened.

The speaker raised his voice to get everyone's attention once more. "Some of you are here to commit to be a Suffragist. To wear the red proudly and to be a voice for the voiceless. You know who you are. Step forward now."

"I've got to go," Conrad said.

"So, this is where that speaker guy is going to bring you in on the secret militant group?" I mocked as best I could in a whisper.

"That speaker guy is Matriarch Kyln's son, and my chief suspect. This is my first chance to get close, so don't tease me until you've given me a chance to do my job."

"Sorry." I did mean it. "Good luck."

I turned to go but a whiff of cinnamon made me turn back. There was something in the darkened chamber I couldn't make out, an old statue from the building's time as a temple that seemed to be looking at me. But what made me grab Conrad's wrist was the banners I noticed hanging inside the entrance, curtaining most of the room beyond from view. There was a red skull on the white banners. The symbol of the Dead God.

"That's supposed to be banned." I said.

I knew, because my uncle no longer dared keep symbols of the god at home. Solhans were hated enough without risking having some evidence found of our connection to the enemy of humanity. The red looked to be painted according to proper ritual, with blood. Probably animal blood, but if it were a traditional Solhan religious symbol it wouldn't be.

"What are dwarfs doing worshiping a Solhan god?" I asked.

"I told you there was plenty here to see," Conrad said. "They call it 'Equality in Death', and I'm not sure they know it is Solhan. Lots of places beyond the Three Kingdoms are bending knee to the Dead God. Better that than being forced to serve Him after death. The Guard fears such beliefs are coming here, despite Highcrowne's safe zone, and despite the Crowns' specific ban. I'll find the answers, Eva. Trust me."

And he walked into that room.

I stood there until the doors closed, sealing the red skull banners and Conrad inside. There were a few non-committed suffragists milling around, finishing off the mead and food, including Bert and Reginald.

"What you are doing here?" Reginald asked me.

"Spying, of course," I said.

I wanted to go in after Conrad, but what could I do? This was his investigation, and he was a big boy. The suffragists were playing with dangerous symbols, but nothing I'd seen of them so far indicated any of them were dangerous. Even Wade, who could be sent scurrying by the mere threat of Conrad. The Jerk was the only one I'd met with extreme views, while it seemed most suffragists had a legitimate complaint. I only hoped they weren't involved with the militants. That would dirty the suffragist cause, no matter how justified it was.

"How about you walk me back to the Outskirts?" I asked Bert.

"Sure," he said, and he took my arm.

I wasn't usually the sort who asked for an escort, but I wanted to get Bert and Reginald out of there and out of trouble. They were supposed to be helping Karolyne load the wedding supplies on the ship tonight, and so was I, so I might as well make sure they got where they were supposed to go.

8 THE MATHÉSIS

The walk home increased my knowledge of suffragists more than the endless lecture about printing presses and work stoppages ever could. Bert had no overt affiliations, but Reginald wore his red armband proudly, and that meant we had a lot of manure thrown our way. While crossing Craftsman's Terrace, Reginald was struck twice; once full in the chest, and the next time it looked to be aimed at the armband alone. That projectile splattered Bert and I too, which did not make me happy.

Reginald—the most hot-headed dwarf I knew, who quit work regularly whenever he thought he wasn't being respected—stood there and took the abuse without saying a word.

When the splatter hit me, I raised my fist at the dwarf responsible, a leatherworker who was wearing gloves and pulling the manure out of a small barrel. Looked like he kept it around for these occasions.

"Knock it off, or I'll…" I began, but then I remembered Conrad had made me leave my Ashur at home, so I had nothing to clonk him over the head with. "Just stop being so rude," was all I managed. I elbowed Reginald. "Aren't you going to say something?"

"A suffragist suffers in order to open others' eyes to the suffering all around them, to their own unrecognized suffering," he quoted.

"There was a lot of suffering in that sentence. I don't think that dwarf cares," I said.

"He will one day, when he tastes freedom. He doesn't know what it is yet. It's a good sign I anger him so much. It means I make him uncomfortable in the world he knows. One day, he will start questioning that world instead of this armband."

"I had no idea you were intelligent," I told Reginald. "I mean it. Most of the time you sit around smoking and grunt angrily whenever I try to talk to you at the cafe."

"Most of the time you sit around drinking kaffe and grunt angrily whenever anyone speaks to you. I'm still not convinced you're intelligent," he retorted.

"Good point. You only ever see me when I'm kaffe-deprived, and I only see you when you're working at a job you hate."

"I hadn't thought you noticed."

"This private investigator would be pretty blind not to. Why don't you hate your job, Bert?" I asked the dwarf on my other arm. Gypsum's insights as a royal weren't applicable to most, and hers was the only side I knew.

"I like the people," Bert says. "The tavern, I mean café, is always interesting, with new people to meet, and the drinks I serve make them happy. It's certainly better than I imagine the mines would be."

"That's the thing," Reginald said. "The specter of the mines hangs over us all. Banishment. For what? Not being what we're supposed to be? Not doing the job assigned us?"

"If you could do anything, what would it be?" I asked.

"I like my job," Bert said.

"I'd like to try anything else," Reginald said. "I'd just like to be free to try."

I gave him a hug. We were both already smelly and gross anyway. "I used to feel the same, Reginald, and it feels great to try whatever I want. It feels amazing and frightening to have the chance of failing. I want you to have that opportunity too, but I want to stop these militants. You've probably guessed that."

"I have," Reginald said.

"I'm not against the suffragists. I believe you deserve freedom and a voice on the Council. It's only fair. But we had better stop the militants soon. They haven't claimed to be fighting for your cause yet, but the minute they do, this city will tear every one of you apart and you'll never have a chance to be free. You know that?"

"I know. That's why I let this little spy, Bert, tag along tonight, so he can see everything is kosher and report back to Aunt Gypsum. If I knew anything about these militants, I'd put a stop to them."

"Glad to hear it." I had to trust people or go crazy, but it was tough when anyone could be on the side of the bad guys. "I need to make a detour. I'll meet you at the docks and help set up the wedding decorations later."

Bert and Reginald headed for the ship without me, not without a grumbled complaint from Reginald along the lines of me being lazier than a noble-born elf on holiday, but I didn't plan to be too far behind them.

It was full dark by the time I got home. Nanny was asleep, her snores making the paintings rattle on the walls. After another quick bath to wash off the manure, I grabbed the dynamite detector, the bridesmaid dress, and my one small bag of luggage and set off for the docks.

I'm glad I stopped to read the sign at the top of the gorge. It gave the berth numbers for all ships currently docked on the river below. Normally, I would have headed down the steep and chaotic route to the river and asked questions later, but I was feeling particularly thorough with my detector in hand and unwilling to drag my dress and suitcase further than needed. It was a major effort to keep the hem of the dress out of the muck on the street. There was no listing for *The Mathésis.* Had it not made port yet?

I went hunting until I found an elvish bureaucrat overseeing the customs searches on a load of goods, which had been brought up from the riverboats on a miniature locomotive run by goblins.

The elf pointed towards Cliff's Edge, further along the top of the gorge. "*The Mathésis* is there."

All I saw was the airdock and a giant white balloon where he was pointing. It was probably the largest dirigible I'd ever seen. "That's the..." I began. Oh, no. *The Mathésis* wasn't an airship was it?

I had never been on an airship, and as much as I liked to look at them from a distance, I never wanted to be on one. Ever. It was unnatural. If a boat sank, you could swim. You can't swim in air.

I didn't thank the elf, but instead walked toward the dirigible as though mesmerized. I walked for a while, and it continued to grow bigger as I got nearer.

The balloon section was the most prominent, but it had an impressive vessel suspended beneath it, shaped like one of the massive war galleys I'd seen in books but never in real life, because not even a river as wide and deep as the Serpent's Ribbon could accommodate them. Such ships were usually only found on the open ocean. It wasn't no scow either, its wood finely polished and stained. Brass gleamed around every porthole and window, and it shouted 'rich' from hundreds of feet away.

When I finally reached the airdock, I stared up at the huge white cloud of cloth and wood and metal and air that blocked out the sky. I must have looked like a country grall new to town, because Reginald and Bert chuckled.

"Didn't know it was an airship, did ye?" Reginald said.

"She kept talking about life vests and sinking when we were packing the other day," Bert said. "I didn't have the heart to tell her there are no life vests."

Maybe this was not a good plan. Then again, the wolf would have nowhere to go once we were in the air. Neither would we.

I dropped my bag and dress on top of Karolyne's pile of luggage. "Where is she?" I asked.

"Inside with the 'royal' wedding planner," Reginald said. "I can't believe she'll be joinin' me clan."

"The Jer– I mean Wade is your clan? I thought the mother's lineage determined clan. He said his mother is dead, so that means it can't be Gypsum or Syla."

"Clans are huge," Bert explained. "Think 'city' instead of small family gathering. Wade's mother was one of Aunt Gypsum's second cousins twice removed."

"How come he inherited then? If there are so many other women in the extended family? I thought dwarf law required a woman to tend the finances?"

"An unjust law," Reginald said. "Tis how they keep us slavin' our entire lives." He picked up one small bag and carried it inside.

"Wade is a strange case," Bert said. "One that has a lot of dwarves nervous. By rights, his Nan should now control the money since his mother's gone, but she's old and lets him do anything he wants. She gave him his entire inheritance. And you see how he wears it about. There's a reason we listen to our mums. I see what Reginald and you are saying about freedom, but how much is too much?" Bert's arms were full of wedding decorations, but he grabbed my suitcase with his pinky finger and carried it inside too.

Through marrying Wade, Karolyne would be distantly related to Gypsum and Baroness Syla? Very diluted royalty, but she would love that. If I looked at a dwarf genealogy chart my head would explode. This entire marriage didn't seem real, more like a strange dream. I knew dwarves and elves could interbreed— that's where those strange gnomes came from—and humans and dwarves produced tall dwarves, but it wasn't common. I shook my head and took up the dynamite detector.

I ran it over my dress and Karolyne's luggage. Nothing lit up. I next waved it over a pile of crates full of lettuce and other vegetables meant for the galley. Still nothing.

"You're doing it all wrong," Bell said behind me.

"How's Kali?" I asked.

"Fine. Shaken up but fine. She's resting in my bed for fear of going home to Nanny's remedies. Give me that thing." She took the detector from me and wound up some gizmo I hadn't even noticed on the side. It began to make a crackling noise. She then took the funnel and moved it back and forth across the crates in a careful grid pattern. Nothing lit up.

"That's how you do it," she told me.

"How can we be absolutely certain it's working?" A lot of things, like me and my friends' lives, depended on this.

"I brought a control." She swung off her backpack and added it to the pile of Karolyne's possessions. When she swung the detector past it, all three glass tubes lit up brightly and the crackling turned into a whine.

"You did what? Get that dynamite out of here," I told her.

"Calm down. It will be fine. Now we know it's working, how about I keep sweeping the cargo and you take it back for me?"

"I'm not carrying dynamite through the city. For many reasons, chief among them an unwillingness to blow myself up."

Bell whistled, and two of my favorite goons stepped out of the darkness to join us: Grim and Gormless. Grim was small and twitchy, and very unlucky. I took a step away from him. Gormless was tall, fat and muscled at the same time, and very lucky, at the expense of others, so I took another step back.

"You're not still following me?" I asked them.

"Not all the time," Gormless said. "What ya need, Bell?"

She pulled the stick of dynamite out of her bag and handed it to him. "Take this to my house and put it in the fridge."

"Sure thing." Gormless set off into the night, Grim trailing behind, and Bell tossed her pack onto the pile again.

"You didn't even tell him to be careful. Or what it was," I said.

"You know Gormless; he'll be fine. Now let's get back to work."

Bell had taken over the dynamite detection job and was doing it far better than me, so I went hunting for my 'werewolf detector' behind a pile of cargo.

"Little bogle man?" I called. "I have more foods. Better foods." I'd stopped by a tavern on the way to the docks and spent my last coin on crow pie. I was full from the suffragist shindig, so I wasn't too tempted to eat it. I had saved the whole thing for now.

No bogle showed.

"Come little bogle. Lots of food for one small bargain."

"What kind of bargain?" a gruff voice called from the dark.

Must be a new bogle. I could always strike a fresh bargain. "Come here and I'll tell you."

A mound of what I thought was broken wood crates, ropes, and sailing cloth twisted and stood up with a pained groan, like an old man, but this thing was no man. It was walking junk as far as I could tell, but then the pile of stuff shifted and twisted as if each piece were alive, and a face appeared. Its skin was oiled canvas, its lips made of rope, and its eyes the darkness between.

The ropes parted as it spoke, revealing more darkness and that same gruff voice. "Do you want me to come closer? Most do not."

"What are you?"

All sorts came through Highcrowne from the Three Kingdoms and the vast lands beyond, some to trade, some to take advantage of a safe harbor in the storm of war, some to hide ... but I had never even heard of a creature like this.

"A traveler. I am No-Thing," it said.

"I wasn't calling you a thing, just a bit surprised to run across something like you. I mean, are you from around here? You're not a demon, are you?"

Demons were basically earth spirits that dwelled in rock and stone and mud. The most infamous were those that came from volcanoes and had fiery eyes and a sulfurous smell and went about striking bargains like bogles, but always with a trick in mind to cheat the one bargained out of their magic or very soul. I'd never heard of one made of objects, but I was wary. Who knew what was beneath that pile of junk?

"I am not a daemon."

"A demon would say that."

"I am No-Thing, not flesh or stone or spirit or metal or magic."

"What does that leave?"

"No–"

"Nothing. Got it. Well, sorry to disturb your nap. I'll let you get back to it." I edged away.

"I was not sleeping, merely waiting for my vessel to depart."

"You're getting on *The Mathésis*? I don't think so." The last thing this plan needed was an unnatural creature running about doing who knew what.

"My kind enjoy travelling from place to place, and I have been waiting a long time for a vessel as fast and far reaching as this one. I move ever so slowly on my own."

He had only managed a few 'steps', if you called wooden crates creaking and bending forward 'walking'.

"There are more of you?" I asked, curious despite my hairs being on end with a very sensible feeling of fear and distrust.

"We are everywhere, but few. I am the only one in this city, and I believe it has been nearly a century since one of my kind last passed through here. I heard stories, but these lands are much changed from what I expected. The harmony of the three races is always a wonder to be remarked upon, but the exclusion of others, such as the humans as I have seen, is not cause for joy."

"It's also a lot smellier and noisier than it must have been a century ago, thanks to annoying machines like this one." While not clanking and spitting out black smoke as most of the scrapers and miniature locomotives did, a mechanical pump was loudly inflating the dirigible with more of whatever made it fly.

"Such creations are fleeting wonders, for which the humans should be proud."

"I'm not proud," I said.

"You are not human."

"Solhans are close enough in everyone's mind for us to be pushed to the Outskirts like the others."

"Solhans are very different. A far older race than any but the Avians."

"Really?"

"Yes, your history is a glorious tale of a people who rose quickly and effortlessly to power and conquered all, before empire gave way to pursuits beyond mortal desire, pursuits which brought a great nemesis into the world. Inward gazing oft reveals a darkness to be purified, I find. Yours is a story that is still being told, and I eagerly await its conclusion."

"You find this war against the Dead God an entertainment?"

"All is story, but story is more than entertainment. It is my breath, my blood, my soul, as you would call it."

"So, you don't want to eat this pie?" I was still holding it out.

"No. Save it for your bogle friend. He may come once I am gone, as they are sensitive to the Void."

"You're the Void?" That did not sound good, but I supposed that's what No-Thing meant.

"The Void is vast and beyond reckoning. It is not No-Thing, but instead the potential for all things. Still, I am close enough to it that it makes the little ones nervous."

Had he just read my mind?

"Well, I need those bogles to do some sniffing around for me, so if you could skedaddle and stop making them nervous, please?"

Should I be shooing off a creature from the Void, of the Void, near the Void ... whatever? I should probably ask it more questions, but I was focused right now, and there was something about it that made me not want to ask things. It got my 'wrong detector' lighting up better than dynamite or little girls with cream-colored eyes, because this thing had no soul as far as I could tell. It wasn't there, but it was. I had an overpowering desire to not see it, to believe it was nothing but crates and rope.

"I am aware of your wolf hunt," he said, "for I have seen inside your mind. You have not laid eyes on such creatures yourself. It is still a story to you. When it is made real, you may not be so eager in your seeking."

"What do you know about the werewolf?"

"Only that your stories shall collide, but you will find that out soon enough. I am more curious about the keys for a door that swings both ways. Are the two still needed for it to work, or have they been melted into one? And which key are you? The key that turns left ... or right ... or the one the lock shall swallow whole as is foretold?"

"What are you saying?" It was babbling nonsense, but I instinctively knew what it meant. "By two keys do you mean Ilsa and I?"

"I see that I am interfering," the creature said. "I will go now, so you can continue your story. I wish to watch it unfold rather than affect the outcome."

"Wait. You have to tell me...." But the creature vanished. The pile of canvas and rope collapsed into the crates and lay unmoving. I inched forward and kicked around. Nothing stirred. I thought he had said he couldn't move fast.

"Are you planning on eating that pie?" The voice made me jump. I turned to see the goblin had spoken. He sat astride his student, Malcolm and Gypsum on either side.

"It's for someone else. You're only getting here now? I thought you'd be inside setting up already," I said.

"It was harder to arrange passage for everyone than I expected," Gypsum said. "You're going to have to bunk with my nephew and our detainees here."

"What? I already have a private cabin that Karolyne arranged."

"It's not private anymore. You're sharing. There was absolutely nothing available."

"What about your cabin?"

"I gave it to Matriarch Kyln—you wanted more bait, and she's all I could find—so I'm sharing with the wedding planner and with Bert and Reginald. It will not be comfortable. You have far fewer in your room, so don't complain."

"But two of us are twice as tall." I gestured to the med student. What was her name? I should ask if we'd soon be sharing a bunk.

"That's your fault for growing so uselessly big," Gypsum said. "I'm taking Doctor Ghunnan and his detector inside." She gestured to a small wagon they had brought with them; there was a single chest nestled within a mountain of cushions to keep it from bouncing about.

"That stuff isn't going to explode?" I asked. "No point doing the militants' job for them."

"The chemicals are benign, I assure you," the goblin said. "I merely want to maintain the uniformity of the silver emulsion layer, which I spent many painstaking hours adjusting."

"I have no idea what you said, but I'll leave Gypsum and Malcolm to look over your shoulder and keep you out of trouble as you set up."

The goblin threw up his hands. "How many times must I assure you I am helping out of my own deep desire to do so?"

"I'm not the sort that relies on assurances. Help me, and then I'll believe it," I said.

"Aren't you coming in with us?" Gypsum asked. "The ship leaves at dawn; we might as well settle in for the night."

"I'll be a little while longer. I'm waiting for Conrad. He promised to help make sure it was safe before we took off."

"You're talking to him then?" Gypsum smiled.

"Sort of. I wasn't the one who stopped talking. I simply said I don't want flowers or chocolates or anything that resembles flirtation with the opposite sex for a while. I think he took that the wrong way."

"What way did you want him to take it?"

Malcolm and the med student were listening intently. I didn't want to be the evening's entertainment.

"I'll tell you how I'm feeling later, when I know myself. See you inside."

I wiggled past luggage and crates to make my way around to the main ramp, where there was still no sign of Conrad. It had been more than an hour already. How long did rebel initiations take?

"No dynamite out here," Bell said. "I'm heading inside."

"See you later."

"Are you going to eat that pie?" Bell asked. Who knew crow pie was so popular?

"No, but neither are you. If you're hungry, go find the galley."

"I'm not a passenger, and I need you to get me onboard. And to gain access to the kitchen."

"Haven't you ever stowed away on a ship before? Surely you can get inside."

"Oh, you expect me to skulk about like a common thief?" Bell said, affronted.

"Yes, because you have training in that area or you wouldn't be working for Duane, and because I need you to search every hatch and every locked room. The ship's crew won't let me any further than the common areas, so I'm relying on you to get into the areas that are off limits."

"Sounds like I'm pretty integral to this plan of yours working. How come you didn't invite me along?" Bell said.

"Because I make up my plans as I go, and because I figured you'd come if you're anywhere near as pissed off about the Marketplace bombing as I am. I had the Guard as a backup in case I was wrong."

"Looks like your backup is late, so you're lucky I'm so predictable. Ok, here goes. If they catch me and toss me out a porthole into thin air, I am coming back as a risen corpse to get you."

"I know. So, don't get caught, for both our sakes."

When Bell was gone, I stood there in the dark, listening to the cursing of the longshoreman as they loaded the airship by lantern light, and the occasional complaint from Bert and Reginald about me not helping with Karolyne's luggage, but I ignored it all. I really needed Conrad to show. Even more than that I needed....

"Are you going to eat that?" a small voice called from the dark.

A bogle!

"It's for you, if you do another job for me," I said, my hopes soaring. A werewolf detector was also crucial to this plan.

"Another job? I unemployed," the bogle said. "Never seens you before. But I is civilized and like to ask before taking yummy, scrummy smelling pie that is just sitting there and not being eatens."

"Well, if you make a little bargain with me, I'll give you this pie now and a few more, or something else yummy, tomorrow."

"A bargain? You know about bargains?"

"Quite well."

"You a demon?"

"No," I said, chuckling. I'd asked the same thing earlier and suddenly wondered how strange humans—or Solhans—seemed to bogles.

"That mad laugh not reassuring," the bogle said.

"I don't have a mad laugh! I ... I'll get to the point. The bargain is this: I give you food for three days, the length of this voyage, and you come along on the ship and let me know as soon as you smell something strange."

"I smell lots of strange now. Strange smokes, strange pee on the wind from the sailor who did his business over the cliff, strange oils on cloth, strange you...."

"A strange werewolf is what I mean."

"Oh. I smelled one of those before. Is you's Jig's friend who was asking earlier today?"

"Jig is another bogle? The brown one?" I had no idea what color this bogle was because he chose to remain camouflaged, so I was speaking to a disembodied voice. I was getting awful comfortable with such conversations of late.

"Yes, Jig is brown. Me Swert. She made bargain for food? Little tellsies and me get food? That's all?"

"That's all. Tell me when you smell the wolf on the ship and where, so I can catch it."

"Done!" it snatched the pie and gobbled it down until there were only a few crumbs on the ground. And then they too vanished with the sounds of licking.

"I'd feel more comfortable with this bargain if we could shake," I said.

A little, invisible hand grabbed my thumb and yanked it up and down. "Bargain is official. Pie yums. Me stick close to you and do sniffins. Maybe more pie tonight?"

"Maybe. We'll check out the galley later. I want to wait a little bit longer."

Now that I knew the bogle was there, I could hear it skittering about as it hunted rats on the dock. It was so dark, I wouldn't have seen the bogle even if it weren't camouflaged, but, eventually, the first moon rose, coming around the mountain, and the white cloth of *The Mathésis'* giant balloon practically glowed in the moonlight.

I turned around to go inside, when I heard the clatter of horse's hooves. Usually only merchant wagons or elven nobility took horses around town, as they tended to get in everyone's way, but Conrad in his white guardsman's uniform sat astride this one. The horse was white too, so he glowed in the moonlight like some shining knight, and I was reminded of the first day I saw him, standing beside the dyer's vats, all golden and perfect.

A squad of guardsmen marched behind him in formation. He gestured and called, "Spread out," setting them loose on the ship.

Some began opening the few remaining containers, while the rest marched inside, pushing past the crewman who was guarding the entrance from the gang-plank.

"I thought I said 'undercover'," I told Conrad, crossing my arms and feeling huffy at this jackbooted intrusion.

He swung down off his horse, his gaze settling on me with such intensity I felt rooted to the spot. He crossed to me in two long strides. "Eva."

"It's been hours, Conrad. What took you so long?"

He looked at me like I was the only person in the world, but it didn't seem as though he'd heard my question. He reached out hesitantly, touching my face.

"It is good to see you." The timbre of his voice was lower than usual, vibrating through me with a hunger, a need, I could sense. He desired me, and I suddenly desired him back.

My skin tingled where he touched me. That and the moonlight made it feel as if some force was pulling at me with its gravity. I desperately hoped spring fever wasn't hitting me too. I resisted.

"Explain," I said, coldly, taking a step back. "Where were you?"

He reached out to me again, but when I took another step back, he gestured for me to stand beside one of the great mooring ropes that held the airship down. It didn't seem like a more secluded spot than any other, but it was easier to move into its shadow than endure the moonlight a moment longer if that's what was making me feel strange. Conrad had never affected me like this before. Maybe it was the white horse and shining armor? Those things should come with a warning label.

"I imprisoned the suffragist leader," he said.

"You did what? That guy with the endless speeches? Matriarch Kyln's son? The matriarch was supposed to be on this voyage. She might not come now."

"You catch hold of little things and ignore the obvious ones." There was amusement in his tone, which I didn't like one bit.

"Are you calling me oblivious? Doesn't imprisoning the suffragist figurehead make it harder to find the militants? Don't we want them feeling untouchable, complacent, so we can draw them out? I think I'm pretty focused on the important stuff."

"And so certain of yourself. I like that about you. That man irritated me," Conrad said.

"They make you a Special Detective for one week and suddenly you imprison anyone who irritates you? I better start fixing up my old cell in the Market Guardhouse, because I irritate you more than anyone."

"You do. Nothing but Northcliff prison will hold you, perhaps not even that. I'll send word and make certain they arm themselves appropriately." He was smiling wider than before, and the playful glint in his eye made me suddenly wonder why I was hiding from the moonlight.

"I'm serious," I said, trying to be anyway.

"Here is reasoning that may placate you, Eva." The way he said my name made me shiver, but I blamed it on the moonlight again, and the cold. "When I was initiated," he continued, "I learned many things. For one, the militants are not controlled by the suffragists."

"What?"

"They are enemy agents meant to disrupt Highcrowne's political stability."

"Enemy agents? Working for who?"

"They could be agents of one of the surviving human nations. I hear humans are jealous of Highcrowne's apparent safety—and neutrality." He was smiling again, and I didn't know what he thought was so funny.

"And where did you hear that? That kind of talk will get the humans in the Outskirts treated even worse than they are already. We could be expelled from the city if anyone believed we were behind these attacks," I said, suddenly wondering if I should add a few humans to my list of suspects. There were plenty as unhappy with the status quo as the suffragists were.

"Elves say such things as justification for bringing their elite soldiers into the Central City. The point is, curtailing the suffragists will not hinder the militants in the least, and so it is of no import that I imprisoned Matriarch Kyln's son. With the guardsmen I've brought here, the militants will know we are vigilant and must send their wolf against us instead of relying on bombs to destroy this ship." He seemed pleased with his roundabout argument.

He'd probably acted without thinking. All excited about being in the suffragist inner sanctum, he had reached for the manacles without pausing to remember what I'd told him. If he'd even been listening in the first place.

"Or they might not attack the ship at all because it looks too risky. You are ruining my plan," I said angrily.

"Trust me. We will find your wolf." Either hanging out with the male suffragists or being a Special Detective had made Conrad pretty certain of himself. Not that he'd been hesitant before, but now he spoke with strength and authority and absolutely no doubt.

"You sound pretty confident with nothing to back it up. That's usually my department," I said, a bit of warmth creeping into my voice despite my best efforts. I wanted to be mad at him, but the beautiful night and his smell—gods, he smelled good—was conspiring against me, as were my hormones. I'd had a deplorable man addiction my entire adult life, and I was trying to kick the habit. I was failing.

The more I thought about it, while Conrad's plan had as many holes as one of my plans, it did make sense to let the militants know that if they wanted to take down *The Mathésis* they'd have to work for it.

"I am very confident," Conrad said, placing his hand on the rope, which was the width of a wagon, and leaning toward me so that I felt hemmed in with the rope at my back, him in front, and the moonlight on either side. "Do you know what I saw in their initiation chamber?"

"A creepy statue with wings?" I remembered it looking at me.

"Creepy? The little things again." He frowned. "No, their initiation involved invoking the Dead God."

"Really?" Old symbols and statues was one thing, but they knew invocations too?

"Worship of the banned god was enough reason for me to arrest the leader. What's more, I learned this religion is spreading. Merchants and travelers fleeing the war zone are telling stories of the Dead God performing miracles, of penitents leaving Solheim alive. Belief in Him is growing. What do you think about that?"

"Oh, I believe in Him already. I just don't like Him. That is very dangerous talk, but very seductive. It's hard to beat a real god walking around answering prayers."

"The other gods have been distant and powerless for too long," he noted. His voice was even deeper than before, and I wondered if he was getting a cold. That would be right, stuck on an airship with sickness running rampant alongside militants and a werewolf.

It was easier to focus on those 'little things', as Conrad kept saying, rather than the big bogeyman whose shadow was cast over Highcrowne and all the world.

"Do you plan to arrest everyone found worshipping the Dead God?" I asked, wondering if Ilsa and my uncle would be on that list. I wondered if I'd be. As soon as the wrong people caught sight of the green fire I couldn't control, I'd be labelled a necromancer.

"That is the latest command of The Crowns, at least of King Fharen, but the other rulers do not contradict the order. Any such worship is to be treated as treason. Highcrowne is no longer neutral in this conflict but openly in opposition. Perhaps the militants' job is already done?" Conrad seemed to want my opinion for once, and I thought for a moment.

"No longer neutral?" That was scary. "It could be humans responsible for the attacks," I mused, "or the Dead God's servants. Either would win. The humans have a forced ally, the god another victim. As soon as Highcrowne sticks its neck out it will get its head cut off."

People were so stupid. Elves especially. The Compact was supposed to keep the Dead God from outright war on Highcrowne, but now that Highcrowne had declared sides, the Compact could be forfeit. Even if it wasn't, and the Dead God's armies were still barred from the Three Kingdoms, it meant we had His attention.

I doubted the Compact said a secret war was against the rules, so destabilizing the dwarves, building up hatred of the humans even more ... all of this could be playing right into the Dead God's hands. All of it could actually be His design.

9   Close Quarters

I was about to tell Conrad how stupid it was for the Crowns to openly take sides in this war, and grumble at him again for usurping my plan, but then I saw an apparition in the moonlight that made me freeze.

"It can't be," I said.

"What is it?" Conrad turned to look, and he saw it too—the tax collector. Here.

"I have to go. Don't let him on this ship no matter what documents he shows you or laws he cites. I'll see you onboard." I grabbed my bag and dashed up the gangplank. The ship's crewman was still off balance from all the guardsmen pushing past him, so I made it inside without being stopped.

That was a close one.

I really needed to deal with things and stop avoiding them. I knew it, and I had no problem facing a bad guy, going toe to toe, but they were physical, flesh and blood encounters. Tax laws—and magic—were different. They were ephemeral things, mysterious, and frightening. I couldn't hold them in my hands and shake sense into them or glare at them from afar to make them keep their distance.

Even though I knew magic was something that came from me, I didn't feel in control of it. Even when I knew how to invoke a spell—and Morgan had taught me a few things growing up—whenever I touched that power, I changed. I wasn't me anymore. I was the power. It whispered to me of sweet death, seduced me with thoughts of bending all the world to my will, and I forgot about whatever I had set out to do. It felt so damn good. I didn't know how to handle the temptation except to avoid it. But this was about the tax collector ... him I only had to avoid until I got paid.

Once inside the dirigible, I stopped and stared again like the worst country yokel. The main entrance had crystal chandeliers aglow with Avian-fueled magic and parquet floors so polished you could see your reflection in them. There was a concierge and baggage collection counter to one side, unmanned at this time of night, and a massive cloak room, all made of rich wood with brass handles and rails. That was just the entrance.

Past that was a series of arched doorways, separated by what looked like marble columns. I had no idea how the dirigible could carry such weight. And past the archways was a ballroom. The room was as wide as the massive ship, and distant mountains were visible through its floor-to-ceiling glass windows. These weren't the usual hand-blown sort of glass either, with their swirls of distortion, but perfectly clear. I had no idea how they were made if not by magic, and even then, it would have to be an artisan to craft physical materials so perfectly. More crystal chandeliers dangled from the high ceiling; some I swear floating unsuspended. Wood paneled corridors led off in four different directions from the ballroom, and several wide, spiral staircases of solid brass led to the levels above and below.

I expected to see Karolyne taking over the ballroom, but it was empty, which made it all the more stunning. I was perplexed. I inched my way back to the crewman at the entrance, keeping against the wall so the tax collector outside wouldn't spot me and said, "Where is everyone?"

The man jumped. He looked out of place among the elegant surroundings with his grizzled beard, swarthy skin and skullcap, like some pirate sailor. "You with the wedding party?" he asked, his language more cultivated than the rest of him.

"Yes. Where are the others? And where did all the guardsmen go?"

"The guardsmen are likely everywhere, peering into everything, like rats, and as difficult to get rid of. You know what they're looking for?"

"No," I lied.

"Well, it is probably only the start of the security checks, as I expect more tomorrow ahead of the dignitaries arriving."

Matriarchs and elf royals usually put up a fuss everywhere they went, as though most people would have even noticed them if it weren't for all the soldiers and bodyguards making them stand out.

"The wedding party?" I reminded him.

I could hear Conrad talking to the tax collector. I couldn't make out what he was saying, but whatever it was wasn't working because he hadn't scared the elf off yet.

"They are down in the lower ballroom."

There was another ballroom? "Thanks. I'll find my way."

I picked one of the staircases at random and headed down. The main entrance was in the middle of the ship, and I passed three floors before I found the ballroom at the bottom. Everything in between had been corridors and rows of wooden doors which must lead to passenger cabins. The lower ballroom was smaller than the one above but impressive in its own way.

The floor was glass, and I could see all the way down to the river far below. I felt dizzy and grabbed the wall for balance.

I made my way to Karolyne and the royal wedding planner, who was the fattest dwarf I'd ever seen. He had rich clothing of silk and brocade, but his waistcoat looked like a doll's on him, his huge round belly sticking out so far that it kept bumping Karolyne every time he leaned in to speak to her. They didn't notice me.

"I think the flower garlands should hang straight down from the ceiling, like jungle vines," the planner said.

"I've never seen jungle vines," Karolyne pointed out, "so I'll take your word for it. Won't that obstruct people's view of the ceremony? That's what they've come to see."

They were probably coming for the food, but I knew Karolyne's wedding dress and the ring were sure to impress as well.

She was really going to do this. Tie herself to a loathsome, insecure misogynist who was perfectly happy to take her freedoms while he was fighting for his own. The Jerk was a contradiction, but I doubted even Karolyne could change him, especially as she didn't seem inclined to try. The café would now be unendurable, women seated separately from men, with no reading allowed. Looked like I'd have to set up office back in my office. *If* I could placate the tax collector. *If* I could finish this case and get paid.

Bert was hard at work setting up rows of chairs on the glass floor. It seemed he was standing on nothing,

which was disturbing, so I looked up at the chandeliers. I caught sight of Reginald perched on a high
ladder, rolling a smoke and not working too hard.
There were garlands draped over his shoulders and a
hammer on his lap as he awaited a decision from
Karolyne and the wedding planner.

Was it wise to smoke in a dirigible? Or to be using
a hammer when standing on glass? I was completely
unnoticed, so I decided to find my cabin before I was
roped into helping and forced to face more danger than
I'd already signed up for.

I dug the ticket out of my bag and saw I was Level
3, Room B60. While there were little brass signs
everywhere, none of them were useful, so I began
wandering around until I found 'B' at least.

As I made my way down the nearest corridor, with
door after door lacking the numbers I was looking for,
I began hating my plan.

This ship was too big. How was Bell going to find
anything with her detector? Even if Conrad's people
searched every room tonight, as soon as more
passengers came onboard it would be chaos trying to
check all the new luggage.... Maybe I should ask the
guards to stay? Of course, I had no idea where we'd
put them. I supposed they could camp in one of the
ballrooms.

I heard a rhythmic, throbbing sound that carried
through the walls and floor and realized I must be near

the mechanical engine. With nowhere else to go, I headed toward the source of the sound.

Then I spotted my room and whipped my head around, trying to remember the route I'd taken to get here and mark some reference points in my memory, so I could find my way back again. The only noteworthy feature was the fire extinguisher, which was nothing more than a large bottle of water with a hose attached.

Fire. I had a very claustrophobic moment, imagining being trapped on this ship after an explosion, fires everywhere.... I darted into my room, fought the fastenings on the porthole and swung it open to take a big gulp of air. At least I had a porthole. It seemed most cabins were internal, window-less, coffin-like. I tried to turn my thoughts from such morbid directions, but I was starting to panic.

I locked the door and lay down on the bed. I stared at the ceiling, nauseated, because I could feel the gen-tle swaying of the ship in the wind as it shifted against the cables that suspended it beneath the balloon. I pulled out the commode, a cabinet door that swung open to reveal a toilet, and vomited. Great. I was air-sick already.

I lay back on the bed and closed my eyes. I hadn't been tired after the marketplace, but I was feeling it now. I must have passed out, because it took a lot of banging on the door to wake me some time later.

"What!" I asked, groggily unbolting the cabin door.

Malcolm stood there, gaudy King's Guard armor replaced with an everyday tunic and breeches. Even that outfit didn't hold his bulging muscles, however, as the front was unlaced and the seams at the shoulders coming apart. His head was about chest height on the med student who stood behind him. The goblin doctor was on her shoulders, hunched over so as not to hit his head on the low ceiling.

"Can I bring my prisoners in now?" Malcolm asked, obviously uncomfortable in the corridor. The cabin wasn't much wider, so he wouldn't be getting any more comfortable unless he lost some muscle mass in the next few minutes.

"Come on in," I said, standing aside to let them all pass. The bloodhound came bounding in from the hallway, did a few loops around the room, and then curled up at the foot of the bed.

"It smells like sick in here," the med student noted.

"Very astute olfactory sense you have," the goblin praised his protégé. "The scent has been quite diluted by fresh air and dog odor. Are you ill, Miss Thorne? I have a restorative—"

"No thanks. I'll be fine."

"Aunt Gypsum was looking for you. I'm glad I found you first." Malcolm was eying my disheveled neckline, where a bit too much skin was showing.

I covered myself and scowled. He winked, which made the med student scowl. Surely, she didn't think Malcolm was the monogamous sort?

"I'll find Gypsum later. First," I turned to face Doctor Ghunnan, "please tell me your Rutgard detector is working?"

I was hoping it would lead the goblin and his entourage off the ship, so I'd have the cabin to myself again. There was only one bed, a compact sink hidden in the cabinets along with the commode, as well as a closet, but nothing else. That meant two small people could have the bed—not that I thought Malcolm and the doctor would like to share—or one on the bed, one on the floor, and one in the closet who would have to sleep standing up with a dog at his feet. That wasn't even counting me. There was absolutely no place for me to sleep.

"I have setup the detector on level four, in a storage room above the crew section. My jailor, Mister Malcolm here, was able to secure the proper authorization from the captain for me. I told him it was for atmospheric experiments to aid dirigible navigation in future. It was complete drivel, but the captain believed my hackneyed explanation."

"Is it working?" I asked again.

"I have calibrated the coordinate system to accommodate the shifting position of the dirigible. You see, normally the detector is stationary, and we aim to detect a moving sample of the resin, while in this case we are moving and hope the resin sample—more accurately, the preserved body—is stationary. It could easily be in motion as well, requiring some further recalibration, but it's too early to determine if those adjustments are needed."

"Too early? Meaning you haven't found anything?" I said.

"He hasn't," Malcolm confirmed. "It's drawing a blank."

"We are still too near the mountain," the goblin said, bristling. "Once we gain altitude, I have every confidence in the detector."

It made sense. I think. My head was a bit fuzzy from airsickness, but it's not what I wanted to hear. I wanted this case to get easier. I was already missing The Hunt for Miss Larson's Pet Crocodile; he had been extremely easy to track by screams alone.

"I've had a rest, so I think I'll wander around a bit more," I said, feeling claustrophobic. "You three can work out who gets the bed."

"I do, of course," the doctor said. "I'm the Elder here."

"But Miss Katherine is the tallest and most in need of it as a lady," Malcolm said. So, Katherine was the student's name. I'd have to remember that. "A most striking lady, I should add. I find tall women very attractive." He was looking the student in the eyes as her cheeks flushed bright red.

"Looks like you get the floor—or the commode," I told the doctor. "See you in the morning." I'd rather curl up in the hallway than jam myself in with the circus.

I set out with no idea where to go, so I followed the sounds of the engine again. They led me to the crew section, which was sealed off by a locked door. I nearly broke the handle off, pressing down on it with all my strength, but it held. I gave it a kick and grunted with frustration.

"What is behind that door?" Conrad asked.

I started. Somehow, he'd snuck up behind me. Even more amazing, he'd found me in the vast ship when I hadn't even told him which cabin I was staying in. Maybe he'd been smart and asked Gypsum or Karolyn. If I'd been smart, I'd have asked them too. I was feeling far from smart.

"I have no idea. I hate being shut in. This whole place feels shut in. Sure, there are vast ballrooms and scary glass floors with a great view of where we could easily fall to our deaths, but there are too many doors and corridors and tiny rooms with secret cabinets. There are too many places to hide a bomb, and there's no way we can stop the militants. They will blow this ship up, or at least a sizable portion of it, and the rest of us will be trying to put out fires with those stupid water bottles they have for extinguishers—where are the water runes or other devices, when they feel so free with spending magic on perfect glass and floating chandeliers?—and we'll all burn to death or bleed out from shrapnel or go splat hundreds of feet down on the ground. This was a stupid, stupid plan, and I want to call it all off. Let's ground the ship, tell everyone to go home, no matriarchs aboard, no dignitaries, let's all just go home … and then be killed when we go to market, or stop at the rose gardens for tea. Only, we can't get into the rose gardens for tea thanks to the new elf soldiers in the Central City—not that I like going to the gardens in spring with all the nasty flowers, but they are nice in winter with the curling vines and thorns—so there's no point going home either. We're all going to die, and there's nothing we can do." I finished, gasping for breath.

I felt tears springing up at the corners of my eyes but quickly wiped them away with the back of my hand. I was shaking. I blamed it on my upset stomach. The whole weak, stupid outburst had probably been airsickness talking. All I knew was I felt sick to my core and completely out of my depth.

Conrad looked at me with that new, intense gaze of his. It made me feel chilled and feverish all at once. There was no moonlight to blame for my reaction this time.

"You mentioned death and dying many times," he said. "The way you face danger, I had no idea you were so concerned by it. All you can do is live while you live and surrender to death with dignity."

"You think I don't have any dignity? That I'm frightened of dying? Of course, I am! I'm not going around in fifty-pound armor like you or a 'Special Detective' with squads of guards at my beck and call. I'm just Eva, and my stupid, stupid ideas are going to get more than me killed. They're going to get everyone I care about killed as well. Sure, I'm frightened of dying and facing the Dead God and whatever sick plans he has for a corrupt Solhan like me, but what frightens me more is taking everyone else with me."

The tears threatened to come again, so I turned and faced the wall to wipe them away. Maybe it was the Solhan in me, but I hated showing such weakness to another person. I hated being weak in the first place. If only I could be hard and cruel and certain of everything, like Ilsa.

Conrad's arms enfolded me, and I stiffened.

"Eva," he whispered into my hair, and it sounded like a hungry growl, low and deep, reaching into me and sending vibrations to the core of my being. "Beautiful, Eva. You are more powerful than you think, stronger than you know. I have seen you face Guard Captains and slavers and necromancers. I have seen you face Ulric and the gangsters who rule the edges of this city with no more fear than you face a runaway cat. I have watched you fight yourself, and that is the most formidable adversary I have ever seen. I do not think you are without dignity, and I do not ridicule your fear, for fear, and love, propels you to do great things."

I turned around, still encircled by his arms, and closed my eyes, letting his amazing scent and strong arms wrap me up like I used to wrap myself in a blanket to hide as a child. I didn't feel claustrophobic or trapped, only safe. Loved.

That was a terrifying word.

He kissed me, and heat tingled through every nerve, from my loins to my fingertips, to my toes and back up to my sensitive lips again. His kiss was gentle, not asking for more, but I wanted more. I kissed him back deeply, tasted his sweet tongue, and wanted more still.

I pulled away. "I'm sorry," I said. "You're not helping."

I tried the door again, and this time green light arced from my palm to the handle and it clicked open. I stepped through and closed the door behind me.

By the gods, I had not expected a kiss like that from Conrad. I'd never kissed anyone like that before or felt so in need of more than physical touch. I wanted to climb inside and wrap my soul around his. I wanted it too much, and that frightened me.

I was already feeling weak and out of control. He had said I was battling myself, and it was true. I couldn't afford to give ground, be vulnerable, or I'd lose the war. More than ever, I needed to get away from Conrad. Surrender was not what I needed right now. I needed to face these militants like I would any bad guy. They were much more straightforward than magic or taxes—or love.

I swayed when I took my next step and blamed it once again on airsickness, although Conrad had left me even more off balance.

Conrad Falconbridge with his golden looks and boyish smile, his white armor and gleaming goodness.... I had never thought he could be the one for me. Maybe I was wrong?

I kept following the sounds of the engine. I hated engines and mechanical things and didn't understand them, so I had no idea what good it would do me when I got there, but it was something to focus on. When I reached the engine room, the floating cloud feeling I had hit the hard, grimy reality and shook me out of my dazed state, for which I was grateful.

The engine filled a room almost as large as the lower ballroom, and it was loud. It was part hissing, clanking steam engine with boilers and release valves leaking clouds of steam and part magical monstrosity, covered in veins of glowing green Avian fluid used to animate mechanical parts. It was hideous, but even more disgusting was the glob of black tobacco Bell spit on the floor not a foot away from me.

"Hey there," she said, holding out a pouch with more dried black tobacco leaves inside. "Want some chaw?"

"Obviously, no. What are you doing with that disgusting stuff?"

"Making friends." She gestured behind her with her chin, and I spotted two dwarves I didn't know in stained overalls. "Hey, Kob and Vin, this is my friend, Eva."

"Glad to meet you, friend of Bell's," they called back before returning their attention to the pipes they were fitting.

"They're helping me with my dynamite detector," Bell said. "Brilliant engineers, but not comfortable with girly girls. Put some chaw in your mouth and talk slow and they'll feel more comfortable." She held out the chaw again.

"I'm at no risk of being mistaken for a girly girl." I grabbed the Ashur strapped to my back and showed her the intricately carved sheath. "This is made from the thighbone of one of my Solhan ancestors, and I know how to use it."

"Suit yourself. I'm at a disadvantage because those two dwarves only have about six fingers left intact between them—machinery like this can be hazardous— while I've got all mine and can do base ten math when they're stuck with base six, if it even exists. Makes them distrustful, so I've had to work hard to show them I'm not some fancy mathematician but a grease and machine-guts worker like them. They've nearly finished, and then I can crank this new 'tector up. Want ta watch?" Bell couldn't speak well through the chaw, which she spit at my feet. Again.

"What do you mean by new detector? Was the other one not working? Do you have to wave it over all the cargo again?"

"No, no, that way is too inefficient. I realized it as soon as I stepped onboard and saw how crazy opulent this place is. Course, this is the most advanced dirigible ever built, a joint Dwarf-Avian project, influenced by a brilliant human engineer who fled the war zone to avoid being drafted and who is holed up in the palace designing things for the Crowns, or so Kob tells me. Could be urban legend. What that means though, is they have advanced air circulation and heating systems, for the higher altitudes, that pumps atmosphere from every crewman's quarter, passenger cabin, and storage room through here. All I needed to do was splice my chromatography system, with boosted sensitivity that was no simple feat to work out, into their air system and voila, as the elves say, I can detect dynamite anywhere on this ship."

While long and convoluted, that explanation wasn't nearly as technical as Bell's usually were; that or I was scarily starting to understand what she was saying.

"So, you can detect if there's dynamite on the ship," I said. "What about where on the ship? That's kind of important to know, so we can find the dynamite and disarm it before it blows up. We can disarm it right?"

"If you mean toss it out a porthole or extinguish the fuse with water, sure no problem. As for detecting where, that's the beauty of this system. I can close valves on the pipes leading from the air systems to the detector in order to exclude sections of the ship and narrow down where the dynamite chemical traces are coming from. Easy as crow pie. Do you still have that pie by any chance? I'm starving."

"No, it's been claimed by a new bogle friend of mine who should, hopefully, let us know if he scents a werewolf onboard."

Bell gulped. "I'd rather dynamite than a werewolf any day."

"True. They can't be tossed out a porthole as easily, but the wolf is our real prey. Catch him and we'll catch who's behind all of this."

"Only a Solhan like you would consider a werewolf as 'prey'."

"A dark, evil Solhan like me, you mean?"

"I didn't say that. But Solhan magic, necromancy, all that stuff is scary. I'm happy for you to deal with that kind of thing and leave me to the straightforward mundane world of pipes and valves."

"You work with Avian magic. What's the difference?"

"I try to think of the Avian goo as something like oil and forget it's magic. Plus, there's ways around using it. Plus, it don't make people rise from the dead."

"I can't do that either, and I don't know that much about necromancy, believe me."

"Right."

"I mean it."

"I've seen your hands glowing green. Duane's seen it. Little Viktor, Kali ... we've all seen it and been wondering what the hell that's all about."

So much for me thinking I'd managed to hide it.

"I don't know, but when this is all over, I'm going to see Morgan and get it under control. All it's good for is annoying me."

Although, it had been useful for that locked door and blocking a blow to the head from Nanny's frying pan, so it might not be entirely bad.

"If you say so. Let us know if we need to start avoiding you the same way we avoid Ilsa."

"Your lack of faith in me hurts, Bell."

"No, it don't. You're tougher than that." She was the second person today to call me tough. I suppose I'd best live up to the reputation.

I tried to smother all the queasy self-doubt that had thrown me into a kiss with Conrad of all people and said, "Okay, show me your new dynamite detector."

Bell and the dwarf engineers fired it up. She smiled when only one of the glass cylinders glowed.

"What does that mean?" I asked.

"Means we're detecting the accelerant they store for when the engine starts getting cold or needs a boost, but we're not detecting the full cocktail that would mean we have to worry. It means there's no dynamite onboard."

"For now. Keep a watch on it, and I'll get Bert or Reginald in here to act as a runner. They can let me know if we need to act."

"There are speaking tubes," Bell said, grabbing a thing off the wall that looked like a cow's horn with a wire attached and lit up with Avian magic. "No runner needed. I can call any of the crew on the ship with this as well as the main suites. Gypsum's in a suite, so I can get her if need be."

"Okay." Not all technology was bad, I supposed, same as not all magic.

"I'm starved. Let's head to the mess, Kob and Vin. You coming?" she asked me.

"Don't they realize you're a stowaway?" I whispered.

"Naw. I came in with the Guards who went searching through here. They think I'm a Special Detective like Conrad. Least I led them to think so. All's good. So, you comin'?"

I spotted a double decker cot in one corner of the room, probably where the two dwarf engineers slept. I felt the weight of the day pressing in on me, from EEP soldiers and hourglasses, to rampaging corpses and bombings, to Conrad and the suffragists and Conrad... "No. I think I'll stay here and go to sleep. It's an early start tomorrow."

"Don't you have your own cabin? Karolyne paid for your ticket, unlike some of us."

I wouldn't let her make me feel guilty. "Let's just say it's been usurped by a travelling circus act, so I'm homeless. Kob or Vin can kick me out later if they need to, and I'll sleep in the hall."

Bell spat again, shook her head, and went off to the crew galley with the dwarves. I lay down on the bottom bunk and covered up with a blanket that smelled like oil and rust. I fell asleep almost as soon as I closed my eyes and began to dream of a golden smile, but the dream was soon swallowed by the scent of cinnamon smoke.

10 An Anti–Social

Gathering

lven Elite Protectorate soldiers woke me, and rudely. They rolled me onto the hard metal floor and ripped the oily blanket off. I blinked awake and looked into the frown of a young elf whose perfect golden skin clashed horribly with his pink and silver irises and his sheared green hair. If he had his glamour on, he had it set to bad taste.

"What are you doing here, human?" he said, curling his lip. "Show me your papers."

"I'm a passenger. And I don't have 'papers'."

"Show me your ticket then." He held out his hand and waited.

I felt in my belt pouch and realized I'd left it in my bag in the cabin. I told him as much, and he lifted me roughly by the elbow and stood me on my feet with surprising strength. I almost stomped on his instep and shoved the elbow he'd grabbed down his throat, happily playing the scene out in my mind, but I refrained from acting. I was on a case. I noted other EEPs scouring the engine room, but there was no sign of Bell or the dwarf engineers to back up my story.

"Tell me where your cabin is, and if you have no ticket, you will be arrested, vagrant."

"I'm no vagrant. I have a house," I pointed out lamely.

"All humans are squatters and vagrants in a land that does not want them. Those houses should belong to Citizens."

This is why I usually stayed in the Outskirts, where I didn't have to listen to idiot elves.

"You certainly have a lot of opinions for a public servant. Last I heard it was the Crowns who set policy, for which I'm grateful."

"You won't be for long. Keep moving." He gave me a shove, and I almost followed through with my earlier fight fantasy, but I bit my lip and walked.

I managed to find my way back to the cabin without getting lost. Anger had focused me. Plus, my airsickness vanished: another bonus. I knocked and was relieved when Malcolm opened the door. I would have preferred him wearing his gold armor in this situation, but I was still happy to see the dwarf.

"Can you please tell this thug to get his hands of me," I said.

I pulled free without waiting for the elf to comply and hurried into the room. The goblin was in the bed and the med student on the floor, I noted. That meant Malcolm and the dog had shared the closet ... or hadn't slept. I could hear the dog's waffled snores and whimpered dream-speak coming from there, so maybe it was only Malcolm who had suffered. I stepped over the student to find my bag in the corner of the room and rummaged for my ticket.

"Not a step further," Malcolm said, holding his hand against the elf's chest. "This is King's Guard business."

"You don't look like King's Guard, ruffian," the EEP soldier sneered. Sneering was not something you normally saw unless you were human, so I was used to the laughably dramatic expression, while Malcolm seemed a bit surprised by it.

"Well he is, and the son of Matriarch Syla to boot, so why don't you get lost," I said, waving the passenger ticket at him. "I have more right to be here than you do."

"I will search this cabin for fire runes or other dangerous magic artifacts," the EEP insisted.

"Already done," Malcolm said, staring him in the eye.

I think the staring contest would have lasted all day if Conrad hadn't showed up with half a dozen guardsmen behind him, all dwarves who didn't like sneering elves any more than Malcolm did, judging by the sound of cracked knuckles.

What was Conrad still doing in uniform? Had he no concept of the word 'undercover'?

"This section was already searched," Conrad said dangerously. He looked at the elf with distaste. "Captain Uanal has cleared this entire ship of magical threats. You may join him on the entrance level for a full report."

"Don't talk down to me, human."

"And don't see me as a human, elf." A new staring contest began, and I was amazed at what good glare Conrad could summon. I hadn't known he was capable of being scary-eyed. I remembered our kiss and blushed like an idiot girl.

"I am a Special Detective in the City Guard," Conrad continued, "with full legal authority in Highcrowne and with responsibility for this ship and its passengers. You are nothing more than a private bodyguard in this jurisdiction. Move along."

The elf twitched with fury, but he looked away from Conrad. Staring contest victory for my side. The elf pushed past him and marched off down the corridor.

"What was that all about? Who was that EEP?" I asked Malcolm.

"A nothing bodyguard who should not have been harassing you," Conrad said.

"Actually, the Elf King's personal guard," Malcolm pointed out. "I heard they'd be here for the launch ceremony."

"Fharen is coming?" That news made me twitchy.

I'd never seen the Elf King, but what I knew of him made him enemy number one of the Outskirts and humanity in my mind. Well, enemy number two after the Dead God, but it was a close second.

Gypsum had warned me I'd not get within fifty feet of him to speak my accusation that he had orchestrated the illegal enslavement of thousands of people. If he was going to be here, I might get my chance to call him a pig to his face after all.

If I weren't on a job.

Damn. Being a professional investigator had major down sides. Also, the Elf King being here—if he was behind the militant attacks and Rutgard's kidnapping as part of a plan to destabilize the dwarf Matriarchy and assume more power—meant this whole thing might not work at all. There might be no attack planned for us to thwart, no wolf to trap. Double damn.

"I hate Fharen," I said aloud.

"It's not safe to talk about a Crown like that," Malcolm said, "but he is an ass, and that's an insult to asses. He thinks only elves know what's best for the Three Kingdoms."

"I would be surprised if anyone in Highcrowne knows," Conrad said. He looked at Malcolm in his street garb. "Eva has asked you to be here undercover as well?"

Seemed Conrad and Malcolm knew each other already, which made sense as Gypsum had been Conrad's patron. She had helped Conrad get his first position in the Guard. I'm glad someone had offered a helping hand to a human, but I wasn't surprised it was Gypsum. Natural kindness was only one reason she was my best friend.

"Yes, I'm watching this goblin who has a detector for ... something that is missing," Malcolm said, barely remembering to keep the theft of Rutgard's body a secret. I had planned to tell Conrad and enlist his help, but it seemed every time we were alone other things happened.

"At least someone remembered to blend in," I told Conrad, eying his uniform and the very noticeable Guard detachment with him.

"It is better to blend in as Security," Conrad said, "and much easier to keep tabs on what's happening throughout the ship with more resources at my command. I'll leave you to catch the wolf, Eva."

The way he said my name made me feel all tingly again. I could not focus with him around.

"You're right. Better you do what you do, and I can mingle with the guests." I wanted desperately to do a very different sort of mingling right then, but I shook off the feeling. "Now, can I have some privacy to change clothes in my own cabin? I'll be playing the bridesmaid in this little charade."

I shooed Conrad off but couldn't help standing at the doorway to watch as he walked away. The guards marching behind him looked orderly and disciplined, while his gait was relaxed and confident. He looked back at me and smiled as he rounded the corner, and I knew I'd been caught. Caught bad.

Malcolm woke the goblin, and I helped the student to her feet. "You can have the cabin first," I told her. "It must feel good to be free of the doctor for a while."

"I did get a neck cramp at first," she said, "but I'm used to it now. I won't need long to get ready."

When everyone was ready, the goblin once more strapped to the student's shoulders, I told them, "We'll launch after sunrise, and hopefully your detector will work this time, Doctor. Please find that body. Something has to go right for once."

My hopes of catching the wolf with Fharen aboard were diminished, but if we could find the Dwarf King, then the trip wouldn't be a complete waste.

"I want to do more than babysit," Malcolm said.

"I may be small, but I am not a baby by any stretch of the imagination," Doctor Ghunnan said. "I've lived twice as long as you and survived a youth with wild goblins who would frighten you to your core. I am perfectly capable of conducting this experiment on my own. You can go off and play soldier if you like."

"Don't even think about ditching your watcher," I told the goblin. "You, or your missing assistant, have plenty of motive for stealing Rutgard. Until you find that body for me, you are still a suspect."

To Malcolm, I said, "You're my backup. If a wolf does spring this trap, and as soon as my bogle tells me where he is, I'll need you and Conrad and every soldier I can get my hands on." I noted he only had a dagger on his belt with the civilian attire. "You do have your sword handy?"

"It's in the closet. Jake's guarding it." He indicated the space from which dog snores emanated.

"Good. I'll find you before the wedding starts."

When everyone had gone and left me the cabin, I looked at the traditional red bridesmaid's dress—traditional in the sense it was meant to look bad, so the bride would look better—and while it appeared beautiful, this one was cunningly cut so I'd look fat no matter how much I starved myself. I groaned at sight of all the lacings on the bodice. I should have kept someone around to help. What was worse was the lack of practicality. There were pleats and trailing fabric, not to mention huge sleeves to get entangled in, but nothing that shouted this dress would work in a sword fight. I donned it anyway and strung the Ashur over my shoulder, so it dangled in back to hide the undone bodice. Then I went looking for a little help.

I found Gypsum's cabin by some miracle. The corridors had come to life, bustling with ship's crew, porters, and arriving guests, and either people or luggage blocked my way at every turn. The first thing I noticed when I got there was that Gypsum's dress fit her better.

"How come yours isn't trailing all over the floor like mine?" I asked. "You can walk in that."

"Did you go to the tailor to have it fitted as I reminded you ten times?" she asked in that annoyingly justified mother tone of hers.

"Oh. Well … can you do me up at least? And not too tight. I want to be able to breathe and fight if need be." I took off my sword and turned around.

She deftly started pulling and tightening. "Too tight!" I warned her a few times, and then it was done. I tested it out but still couldn't bend as much as I'd like. Being a bridesmaid would get me killed.

"I could barely tie that thing," Gypsum complained. "Are you sure you ordered the right size?"

"I'm not familiar with dwarven dress sizes, so I guessed. If it's made for dwarves, how come it's so long?"

"Because they make clothes for other species as well. I think you ordered an Avian size. Look, there's even slits here on the sides for wings."

That would explain why it was so damn tall and skinny. I'd thought I was getting fat. And the slits explained why I was cold.

"By the way, there will be an Avian at the launch party," Gypsum said. "You should wear that feather the Crown gave you. It would be polite."

"Right."

After solving the Slaver Affair, I'd been rewarded with gold from the dwarves, nothing from the elves, and a strangely inscribed feather from the Avians. I think the Avians would have kept the barter system if they could, as they tended to value odd things like feathers, sticks, and shiny stones and apparently had no care for gold. I usually kept the feather with my purse, hoping I'd learn how to spend it.

I promised to meet Gypsum at the launch party and trudged back to my cabin to get the feather. Once I had it, I had no idea where to put it, so I stuck it in my hair like a wild grall. Looking in the mirror, I thought it wasn't bad, white against my black hair. If only the dress weren't such a deep red. It made me even paler by comparison.

I turned to leave and noted the bloodhound was awake. Malcolm had left him behind in the cabin, and now he was on full alert, body stiff, tail stretched behind him, lips raised in a low growl.

"What is it, Jake?" I asked.

Of course, dogs didn't speak, which I'd learned after many vain attempts to coax runaways out of alleys using logic and appeals to their better nature. A smelly river fish spoke to them louder than words. I hadn't grown up with pets—Nanny classified anything not sentient as foodstuff, and probably even some sentient species if she could—so I hadn't known much about dogs until the last few months as a pet detective. I supposed hunting a wolf now meant I still was one. The wolf had to be someone's pet.

"Do you smell something big and hairy that walks on two legs and has sharp teeth?" I asked the dog.

No reply except for a longer growl.

Jake was looking at the door, and I decided to pull my Ashur before opening it. There was very little space even for my short sword, and I decided I should find a kitchen knife to wield at the earliest opportunity, not that I had any place to hide it in the dress.

"Who's there?" I called.

The door swung open and I swung the sword, catching it on the doorframe. Fortunately, there was nothing on the other side. Leathery bogle hands grabbed my ankle. I jumped. It was under my dress.

"Smelled the strange," it said. "Smelled the strange!"

"Where?"

I thought the bloodhound would switch its attention to the camouflaged bogle, which I'm sure it could smell as dogs were used as rat catchers and bogle hunters, but it stayed focused on the corridor, which was unnervingly free of passerby at the moment.

I could stand there forever or do something, and I wasn't known for patience, so I edged toward the open door. I heard breathing and the wet sound of a large mouth opening. Every hair on my body stood up, and I swung the Ashur.

I'm glad I was already in mid-swing, because a flash of yellow eyes, white teeth and black fur filled the doorway. The wolf was so fast I got no more than that glimpse before it ducked low and hit me in the chest. I went flying across the small cabin. I thought the pain of the wind being knocked out of me and the blow to my gut was bad until my back slammed into the brass fastenings around the port hole.

Jake the dog was barking furiously, but I still couldn't see the creature clearly as it tore open the closet in a rain of wood splinters and then upended the bed I had slumped onto. I fell back into the corner, wedged between the wood slats the bed rested on and the wall, down feathers flying everywhere. The mattress was shredded in seconds, followed by the wooden bed frame.

Then there was nothing but barking and the gentle rain of white fluff and wood splinters. The wolf had gone.

I kept stepping on the dress and fowling it up, so I had to roll across the wreckage before I found enough space to stand. I rushed to the doorway but saw no sign of a wolf. Another ship's porter was coming down the hall with an armful of baggage, and he said, "Can you please quiet your animal?"

"Did you see a man-sized wolf run through here?" I asked.

He peeked from behind the luggage. "I cannot see a thing, my lady. Perhaps you should rest a bit longer."

I wanted to tell him that would be difficult with the bed in splinters, but I decided I might be blamed for the destruction.

I'd been right there with the wolf and lost him. Triple damn! I stroked Jake to soothe him and fumed at my incompetence. Then I saw my Ashur laying on the floor and the blood staining the blade. I had got him. The wolf could bleed.

I wiped the blood onto a torn bit of bedclothes and held it for Jake to sniff. The dog whimpered and growled in alternating concession. My invisible bogle climbed my hand. I held still when the tiny claws scratched against my skin, and I heard it sniffing as well.

"That is the strange," it said. It leaped off my hand in a flurry of more sniffing. From the corridor, the bogle called, "But the strange vanish here. All gone now."

As I learned from my first bogle informant, the wolf changed its scent when it changed forms, and now it seemed it could change forms almost instantly. This was an impossible job I'd set myself. At least I knew two very important things: the werewolf was onboard, and it could bleed.

I put the Ashur back in its sheath, locked Jake in the room, and hurried off in search of Conrad. I passed one of the talking contraptions that looked like a cow's horn and stopped.

I went back to it and held it to my ear as Bell had done. "Hello? Is there anyone there?"

"This is the bridge, and this line is not to be used by passengers."

"I'm with the Guard," I said, being deliberately vague. I didn't say I was a member of the Guard, only with them, and Jake was a Guard dog, and I had been with him a moment ago. "I need to speak to Special Detective Conrad ... Wait, first get me the engine room."

I wanted to know if Bell's detector had caught a whiff of explosives. The wolf could have come aboard to set them and vanished, hoping his job was done. Although, that didn't explain why it had torn up my quarters.

There was a resigned sigh on the line. The ship's crew must be annoyed by all the security checks. I highly doubted we would make the dawn takeoff scheduled, as the city outside my window had been lighting up in shades of silver when last I looked.

"Very well," the voice said. There was a click and a buzzer sounded repeatedly. I held the horn away from my ear.

After a few moments, a gruff voice said, "Engine room."

"Is Bell there?" I asked.

"Minute."

It was really only three seconds before Bell spoke. "Eva? Is that you?"

"I saw the werewolf," I said. "What's your dynamite detector showing?"

"Nothing."

"Are you certain?"

"Just a second." She went silent for several minutes, and I shook the horn-thing, wondering if it had stopped working. Eventually, her voice came back, saying, "I've double checked everything. The ship is clear."

"Good. That means we can focus on finding the wolf. Can I call Conrad with this?"

"Where is he?"

"I don't know? The ballroom? Never mind. I'll go there myself. It will be quicker."

"Okay, but I'll call the other guardsmen," she said. "They're on the bridge, I think. Let's get your prey before it gets away."

I set the horn back on the hook I'd taken it from, not knowing if that was all I needed to do to shut it off.

"Bogle?" I said. "You there?"

"Yes," the invisible voice answered. I felt like I was on the speaking horn all over again.

"Can't you show yourself to me? I hate talking to empty air. I'm sure you're not that hideous."

"Not hideous. Scared."

"The wolf completely ignored you. It ignored all of us. It was looking for something, so I don't think you have to worry."

I peeked around at some of the nearby cabins whose doors were open and noted their bedding and furniture was all intact.

"In fact, I think it was looking specifically for something in my cabin."

Was it the goblin? There was far more to him than he let on.

Or had word spread that I was on the case? Maybe they were trying to send me a warning? They didn't seem to care about killing, though, and it would have been easier to slash open my throat than the bed. So, it hadn't been me the wolf was after, which was kind of disappointing. I wasn't a famous detective certain to crack the case and spoil his plans. I was a non-entity, as invisible as the bogle.

The bogle suddenly materialized in front of me and said, "I is not ugly."

He was right. He was an iridescent pink, purple, and green with a bit of gold thrown in. The body shape was the same as every other bogle, all ears and nose with beady eyes, but this one's eyes were a bright green, as though it had been infused with Avian goo.

"I'd say. You're the prettiest bogle I've ever seen. Why do you look so different?"

"Me male."

"The others I've spoken to are all female?"

"Yes. Jig is my mate. I battled many to win her. She is brown skin and special."

"Don't you feel the ladies are a bit bland after you look in the mirror?"

"No, I like brown. If bogle sparkly like me, it means bad male trying to steal from me."

"Okay, got it. You're pretty to attract females and scare other males away. I wonder if that's why men wear armor. Interesting. I'm off to tell Conrad about this wolf sighting, but I need you to stay close and tell me the instant you smell the wolf again."

The bogle vanished.

"You'll do that, right? I'll feed you under the table at the wedding feast. I promise."

"Okay, okay. But me will be hiding."

"That's fine. Let's go."

I headed up the stairs to the main ballroom and hoped the bogle was following. When we found the wolf again, the bogle needed to warn me sooner, I needed to fight better than last time, and we both needed a whole squad of Conrad's guards to back us up.

The main ballroom was empty no longer. Groups of elves, dwarves and a few humans, all dressed in some of the finest suits and gowns I'd ever seen, drifted about like swarms of wealthy gnats. I thought my bridesmaid dress would do for the formals of the voyage, but I looked downright plain in comparison.

I edged through the crowd, saying, "Excuse me. Pardon me."

The humans were all a head taller than the tallest elves, but I didn't spot anyone I knew, and there was no sign of Conrad. I caught a glimpse of Captain Uanal near the cloakroom. With his silver hair and white uniform, he was a striking contrast to the contingent of black-garbed EEPs around him. Despite being an elf, he didn't look happy to have their company.

"Captain." I waved, trying to get his attention.

He saw me. Then he frowned and looked away. How rude.

I needed to tell someone about the wolf, so I pushed closer. I was stopped by a black-gloved hand on my chest.

"Where are you going, human?" The EEP who stopped me was a female, her yellow hair tied back in a severe bun, and her large, pointed ears twitched from the din of the crowd.

"I don't see how that's your business."

"What is your name?" she demanded.

"Eva Thorne." I stood straighter, hoping the name would set things right. Surely Captain Uanal had mentioned I was working with the Guard.

She took out a small notebook and wrote something. "We'll be watching you. Now step back, clear the entry way. Make room for your betters."

She gave me a shove, and I grabbed her wrist. There was another moment where I matched gazes with her and so very much wanted to knock her on her ass, but I stopped myself. For the sake of the job, I let go of her and stepped back.

Just then a pair of heralds marched inside the main doors and blew long, brass trumpets. The noise quieted everyone down, and the EEPs spread out in a large semicircle, acting as a barrier between the main entrance and the guests in the ballroom.

After the heralds came a cadre of courtiers, even more lavishly dressed than the other guests, who quickly and efficiently swept the floor and tidied the path, before laying down a roll of purple carpet. They vanished into the wings of the cloakroom and—after a long, dramatic pause that had me wondering if that was it—three figures stepped forward, the outside light silhouetting them in the open doorway. A dwarf, an elf, and an Avian, judging by their outlines.

When they stepped onto the carpet and into the full light of the ballroom, I clenched my fists and hoped Captain Uanal did not detect the surge of magic that rose up in me alongside anger and adrenaline. The Elf King had arrived.

11   Unwelcome Guests

I'd never seen King Fharen in person before. He was not what I expected a human-enslaving, power hungry, and downright evil excuse for a living being to look like.

In fact, I couldn't see his face at all. It was covered by a porcelain mask painted with delicate gold and pink flowers. His suit was modern—long jacket with tails, white bowtie and top hat—and not the usual robes you'd see the hoity-toity elves wearing around town. Of course, the suit wasn't black like a wealthy dwarf might wear, but instead made in the floral, silken fabrics elves preferred, embroidered with gold and silver threads. Fharen was nothing like the somberly dressed EEPs around him, but he had the same superior posture, hands behind his back, stiff neck, and nose in the air.

I stopped glaring at my nemesis—as he probably didn't even know or care that I existed—and took note of the other two royals.

At first, I thought the Avian might be Queen Calka, but then I remembered my school textbooks and realized it was a 'he'. He stood a step behind Fharen, another sign it was a noble and not the Avian Crown. The plumes on his head stuck up like a bad hair day and were patterned in grey and white. His beak was black and sharp, his eyes large and glistening like a mountain eagle's watching everything from a great distance. His tall, thin body was covered in more grey-speckled feathers, at least from what I could see poking out of his well-tailored suit, wings trailing on the floor like a long cloak. His scaly talons were clasped in front of him in a calm pose. The Avian was not anywhere near the peacock the elf was. He would have looked shabby in comparison if it weren't for his serene demeanor and the ring of black fluff around his neck that gave him a regal appearance.

The dwarf was a matriarch, of course, but she was veiled and gowned head to toe, so I couldn't tell if it was Baroness Syla or someone else. Whoever it was must have been chosen as the dwarf representative, because she was standing as an equal next to Fharen. Dwarves in golden armor stood behind her—more

King's Guard like Malcolm. In fact, I recognized Alum and Verdis, so it probably was Syla.

"*The Mathésis* is a great achievement, as it represents the might and ingenuity of the Three Kingdoms," King Fharen began without preamble. "It is a symbol of our superiority over the lesser lands who continue to succumb to the Dead God and know nothing but defeat. We and *The Mathésis* are about triumph. We soar, like Avians, above the war ... ignoring it, relishing our frivolity—"

The Avian put a hand on the Elf King's shoulder, cutting him off without a word. Fharen stiffened. He gestured angrily, and a courtier stepped forward and handed Baroness Syla a golden bell.

She rang it and said, "Let the voyage begin."

The royals stepped further into the ballroom, a dozen EEPs and the two King's Guardsmen encircling them.

More courtiers came aboard, chatting and taking little notice of where they were. One of them, dressed in cream-colored silk and covered head to toe in a lace veil, caught my attention. There was something familiar about her outline, the dark hair barely visible through the veil, and the hairs along my arms stood on end at sight of her.

She paused, as though seeing me as well, but her face was invisible. She joined the throng of courtiers around the Elf King, and I tried to shake off my dread. I'd already encountered a creature of the Void and a werewolf on this trip, and now something truly evil had crossed my path. Had my sister snuck aboard to steal back her soul when I wasn't looking? Even so, I didn't see how things could get any stranger.

The procession ended with the arrival of another matriarch, carried on an ornate and cushioned pallet by servants. The extra bait Gypsum had roped into joining the guest list at the last minute. Matriarch Kyln. Her son had been arrested for open worship of the Dead God, and I wondered if she'd been told yet. Or did she have too many sons to care what they were up to? She was here to make the ship a more tempting target, but I'd already seen the wolf, so the extra temptation hadn't been necessary.

I saw Captain Uanal and the soldiers with him take their leave. They weren't coming with us? The doors closed behind the guardsmen, sealing off the golden light of dawn and trapping everyone inside the monstrous airship. My heartrate sped up.

I sneezed from the elf perfume all around and from the florets in every male dwarf and elf's lapel. Did I mention I hate spring?

Fortunately, the first planned stop on the voyage was the old dwarf capital, Gernwold, which was built on a mountain much broader and taller than Highcrowne's peak and well above the snow line. I might not love the snow, but it would be a relief. Maybe I could solve the case on the way and stay there until summer came and the flowers in Highcrowne all shriveled up in the heat and died. The tax collector would be sure to be gone by the time I came home too. Sounded like a plan.

If it weren't for Nanny and Little Viktor, I'd seriously consider it. Maybe even stay in Gernwold permanently. It's where I'd gone to boarding school, where I'd met Gypsum, and I still had friends there. I'd only left because Uncle Ulric ordered me back to Highcrowne for my 'coming of age' celebration. It had been a traditional Solhan thing with lots of midnight chanting and drinking of noxious substances I'd rather not remember. Back then I'd been more afraid of Uncle and more willing to obey. I was glad I'd grown past that stage; otherwise, I'd still be as frustrated as the dwarf suffragists were. At least now, I was free.

Free to mess this case up royally.

I finally managed to calm myself, but then I spotted something that made me choke worse than the scent of unwashed elves covered in cloying perfume. There was Duane, face still covered in cuts and bruises from yesterday's market bombing, wearing another fancy suit and with his hand on the arm of a beautiful elf woman—and he was making her laugh.

I went over to him, put my hands on my hips and raised my eyebrows, waiting to be noticed. The elf woman wasn't as smelly as most or perfumed. She was thin and tall for her species, with pure black hair tied up in an intricate weave of braids, her golden skin almost as pale as mine. I'd say she had more than a trace of something non-elf in her lineage, but it could be a glamour. Her face was certainly too perfect, with large topaz-colored eyes, red lips, and a perky nose.

I cleared my throat. "Interesting seeing you here, Duane." I was happy when he finally noticed me, and his smile faded.

"Eva."

"Won't you introduce us?" the elf said. She held out her hand to me, the wrist encircled by half a dozen gold and diamond bracelets that sparkled in the lamplight. Now I knew why Duane was draped all over her.

"Eva Thorne," I said, politely, not bothering to shake or kiss her hand, whatever she had expected.

Duane frowned. He knew my polite tone was usually a prelude to me being very dangerous.

Surely, he'd heard I'd be here for Karolyne's wedding. Bell probably even told him all about our dynamite-sniffer and the trap we were setting. Yet, here he was, right in the middle of everything and … carousing!

"I'm Hilja," she said putting her hand away. "How do you know Mister Rose?"

"Mister Rose? Duane is an old friend of the family," I said.

Another alias. It was even worse than The Adder, but I supposed it might be more appealing to elves if he called himself a noxious flower while trying to wheedle his way into their company, and wealth. I wondered if he aimed to simply rob her, or was he working on a longer-term plan, such as getting her to invest in one of his illegitimate businesses?

Duane had recovered from my appearance and took my hand, kissing it like a gentleman. Now I was the one who froze in shock.

"Yes, I've known little Eva since she was a child," he said. "Her brother was my best friend." Little Eva? Before I could retort, he continued, "She is like a sister to me, always following me around."

Sister? Following him around? I spluttered and pulled my hand away.

He took the elf's delicate hand instead and entwined his fingers with hers. "I'm glad you finally get a chance to meet. You see, Eva only knows me from the streets and my time as a criminal. I'd like her to see how you've changed me, beautiful Hilja."

"Last time I checked, you still were a criminal," I blurted out.

"I know all about his past—and present," Hilja said seriously. "I'm not ashamed of him. I have no comprehension of what it must be like for humans who come here, lost and alone, their homelands and families ripped from them. I'm an elf of fortunate birth, so I cannot know, but I do know that I won't be one of those who continues the madness, who forces brilliant men like Mister Rose to turn to crime because there is no other hope of advancement for them. My father may see him as a useful pawn and value his criminal connections for his plots and plans, but I value 'Duane' for who he is. I am not ashamed to hold his hand, no matter what my father thinks or how much the Elite Protectorate disapproves."

"Who is your father?" I asked, suddenly dreading the answer.

"Don't you know?" Hilja said. "I thought everyone knew, for there is no greater scandal whispered at court of late than the Elf King's daughter in the company of a human."

Duane had really done it this time. I knew men would date anything with breasts, but King Fharen's daughter? Was he suicidal? Actually, I was surprised he wasn't dead already.

What sort of plots was Duane helping Fharen with? And all the times I ranted about slavery, all the times I raged about Fharen, Duane never said a word or mentioned he was working for him.

How long had this been going on? Had he helped Fharen and my uncle's slaver friends—and my sister— round up humans and ship them off to the wall? I'd always thought Duane a harmless bad guy, no worse than the average Solhan at heart, but maybe I was wrong. Maybe he was one of the real villains.

Duane must have noticed something shift behind my eyes. He told Hilja, "Give us a moment, please."

She nodded and stepped aside, merging with a nearby circle of elvish businessmen who seemed happily surprised by her company.

Duane stepped closer and took my arm. I yanked it away, but I couldn't escape fast enough, and he managed to pull me closer to him, whispering, "Don't judge, Eva. Not all elves are like Fharen, and definitely not Hilja."

"She's slumming, don't you realize? She's trying to get daddy's goat by being with you. And it's not her I'm judging—it's you. What the hell do you think you're doing playing with elves and a Crown at that? What the hell are you into?"

"You think I'm not worthy of associating with Hilja or the King? You think I'm worthless? You know absolutely nothing about me then. You've spent your whole life being a princess in my eyes, rebelling against your uncle like Hilja rebels against her father, but unlike her, you still stick your nose up at me. Well guess what, Eva, a real princess and not some finishing school dropout is interested in me, and I'm worth being interested in." He let go of my arm and moved away with that powerful, cat-like grace of his. He stood next to Hilja and put his arm around her waist.

Finishing school dropout! I'd graduated.... As furious as I was at Duane at that moment, a worse feeling crept over me. It felt like a cold lump of ice in my gut that was slowly working its way up to my heart and into my throat. I didn't know what to think about Duane, to hate him or suspect him, but I knew it felt awful having him turn his back on me like that.

All our fights and arguments over the years … none of them had felt like that. None of them had hurt.

"Truthspeaker?" a high voice chirped in my ear.

I whipped around, feeling shaky and off balance. I saw grey feathers and black fluff and looked up, and up, at the Avian. Its beak appeared even sharper this close, and its black-eyed gaze bored right into me.

"Your grace," I bowed quickly.

I'd never seen, let alone spoken, to an Avian before. All I knew about them came from books. While the elves and dwarves had nobility and rank within the Three Kingdoms, there was something about the Avian nobles that made them feel worthier of their titles. Perhaps it was because Highcrowne was within their ancient domain, or because the Avian's themselves were ancient. They were said to be immortal. The Avian before me could well have remembered when the first primitive elf, dressed in spider's silk and painted with fairy dust, wandered, grunting onto their lands.

I couldn't help but bow. It also gave me an excuse to conceal the tears welling up from the argument with Duane. Ever since I'd learned about my brother's death, ever since I'd learned Viktor's darkest secrets and knew that no one could escape the Thorne legacy, my emotions had been too close to the surface. I missed the days when I could bury them deep and give the world a baleful and dry-eyed glare. Instead, I stared at the parquet floor and the Avian's scaly feet, sporting three massive talons and a hind claw bigger than the rest, and let a tear stain the wood. I had no idea what to say.

I felt a touch on my head and looked up to see the Avian had taken the white feather out of my hair. I stood straighter and wiped my eyes. "That's mine," I said.

"I know, for this is the one Calka bestowed before all of us. I remember she had little to say over the whispers carrying Fharen's name, but the fact she granted this spoke more loudly than whispers. Our Queen favors you," the Avian said.

"Really? She might not if she met me."

"We see much, and we see far from our mountains. Most is like the play of leaves over the ground in a wind, entertaining to watch for a moment but quickly forgotten. Some things, however, are like the crack in the face of a mountain. Much time and stormy weather may have worn it down and set the conditions, but that first crack that carries deep into the stone is of note. It heralds an avalanche not far behind, a reshaping of the landscape."

"Uh huh." I suppose it made sense Avians would be interested in geology. They must have the patience for it. "You're the third enigmatic creature I've spoken to recently, and I think I'm growing use to slanted words. Tell me more of this crack. Do you mean the war? The Dead God?"

"He is the shadow within it, brought about by happenstance into this world. The crack was formed by the eldest of the elder race of Solheim, and their blood will flow into the darkness, turning the crack into a wound on the mountain. Or perhaps the wound is but a necessary tool for the creation of something new? The mountain must be torn apart sometimes to create a valley where those without wings can dwell in peace and prosperity. For a time. Time is ultimately unforgiving and balances joy and sorrow in equal measure, so we never know too much of one above the other. If there were naught but light, the universe itself would cease to be from the imbalance."

"Okay." Now the geological analogies were entering territory beyond my comprehension. I knew the Avian was wise and smart and telling me something extremely important, but couldn't he dumb it down a little bit? I was also hyperaware he'd mentioned the bloodlines of Solheim. "Is there something about my blood that's important?" I asked.

"Blood is but a metaphor, child. Souls are what matter. But that is more within your expertise than ours. We enjoy the power of a pebble falling, we feel the shifts in its potential as the ground pulls at it, and we enjoy distilling and creating wondrous new things, such as this ship. That is the kind of magic native to our kind."

"Green goo and city lights?"

"Amusing and helpful at times are they not? What purpose life without play? Yes, that is the magic best left to me and my kind, the magic of the world. Your magic is that which traverses worlds and shapes them anew. We do not seek to play such dangerous games."

"I'm not trying to play anyone's game, and I certainly don't have one of my own. I just want those I care about to be safe. I want the city to be safe."

"And the lands beyond? The sheltering nest is never safe while the storm still rages. Best to quiet the storm."

"Not in my power that. All I can do is..." I paused and glanced side to side, but no one was in earshot. The guests were keeping a distance from the Avian. I also noted he had no EEPs around him and no personal guard. The bird wasn't afraid of anyone here, but everyone here was afraid of him. "...All I can do is catch a wolf, and that job alone seems far too big."

"Then you will certainly need this." He held the feather out, and I took it. The talons that were his hands were tiny and delicate, the claws almost non-existent. They were hands meant for art and crafting. "Truthspeaker it is, and it will help you see the truth."

"How?" I said, thinking I was handling this strange conversation well. No-things and Avians shared the inability to speak plainly.

"If ever you suspect something is not right as seen by your eyes, if ever you doubt what stands before you, then close your eyes and see through the feather. Say its name and it will speak truth to you when no one else does."

"Really? Let me try." I closed my eyes and held the feather to my eyelids, saying, "Truthspeaker," before opening them again.

The Avian was gone.

I spotted him headed for the main doors. He spoke a moment to the crewman there, who bowed and opened the door. But we were in flight!

Wind tore through the cabin when the hatch opened, messing up all the finely coiffed hairdos, and the Avian leapt out. I saw it rise up again, arms outstretched and a cry on the wind that was bird-like and decidedly joyful. It would be nice to be able to jump out of an airship without worry of falling. The crewman pushed the door shut again and sealed it.

Typical. The Avian had gotten my hopes up about the feather, but he left before I could tell him it was broken. As I was putting it back in my hair, I noticed the golden Avian script on the feather's shaft. Maybe I needed to say the incantation in Avian? I'd have to ask Gypsum what their word for 'Truthspeaker' was. She knew a bit of the language. Languages hadn't been my thing in school. Or much of anything else. I looked at Duane, who still had his back to me, and set off in search of Conrad instead. I had a job to do.

I circled the room but didn't spot any white Guard uniforms in the crowd. It was all colorful finery or severe EEP uniforms. I didn't even see Baroness Syla and the King's Guard; they must have gone to their cabin. King Fharen and his retinue, including the woman in white, had vanished as well.

I paused by the giant windows at one end of the ballroom and held the wooden frame to steady myself. I felt a bit woozy looking at the river below. I could see barges and small sailing vessels, steamships and paddlewheels, but they were like toys they were so far away. The city was on the opposite side of the ship, so I couldn't see it at all.

What I could see was the horizon aglow with morning light. Jagged mountains painted black and limned in yellow, green plains glinting with golden puddles that must be lakes and ponds and streams. The sunlight and the sight of that vast landscape buoyed me. My troubles, and Highcrowne's, seemed as small and toy-like as those ships in comparison. This must be how Avian's always saw the world.

I noted a shadow flying above the nearest lake and froze, for it had a golden, lizard-like body and massive wings. A dragon. I let out a breath when it turned and flew away from us. Always best if a dragon were flying away rather than toward.

The ship rose higher, the clouds a fluffy layer of down blanket over our heads. The undersides of the clouds were puffy and bright in the sunlight, and beneath them drifted huge, pink creatures shaped like paper lanterns with long tentacles hanging below. A few floated down to window height, and I could make them out more clearly.

Jollups were a favored food of the elves, and I often saw chunks of them for sale in the market. They had stretchy pink and purple skin with the texture of a catfish or frog, same with the tentacles, but their bodies were mostly blubber. The white, fatty globules were always squished flat at market, but when living they held air, much like the balloon that held up *The Mathésis.* Jollups were more beautiful than I'd imagined, floating gracefully, especially these younger ones with their pale pink and white flesh. It was the older ones, purple and plump with fat from the birds and flying creatures they ate, that lost their air sacks and drifted close enough to the ground for elves, or their slaves, to catch.

"Hungry?"

The word me made me jump. I'd been entranced by the view out the window and hadn't noticed Malcolm.

"Not for those. Elf food is disgusting. What are you doing here? Where's the goblin doctor?"

"Messing with his detector. He's found something. Want to see?"

"Yes, but I found something too. I saw the werewolf," I said the last in a whisper, although it felt like old news now.

"Where is it?"

"I've no idea, but it's on this ship somewhere. Keep your eyes open."

"They're always open. So, you coming?"

Of course. I was tired of standing around looking for help when there was none to be had. "Lead the way."

Malcolm was almost as wide as he was tall, and he walked straight through the crowd with his broad, muscled shoulders knocking aside anyone who got in his way. It was much easier to get around with the dwarf than it had been on my own.

When we were down the stairs and headed toward the crew section, he said, "I hope she's missed me."

"The student, Katherine? You like her?"

"Yes. She's beautiful with that red hair and pale skin of hers. And so tall. I like tall. You're tall too. How about a tumble?"

I spluttered. When I recovered, I said, "I thought you liked Katherine?"

"It's only a tumble. It's not like I want to marry you."

"No thanks."

"But look at my muscles. My ass muscles have muscles."

"Nice ass," I had to admit, "but no."

"You're loss." He shrugged and kept walking.

As annoyingly oversexed as Malcolm was, he was nicer than Karolyne's husband to be—of course a baby-devouring troll would probably be nicer than The Jerk—and he was also better looking than most dwarves I'd met.

I knew it was wrong to dismiss a man because he was shorter than me, but facial hair was a huge put off too, and most dwarves had it. Whether it was weird curling mustaches or beards that hit their knees. Malcolm and the other King's Guardsmen were refreshingly clean-shaven, and so I could see he had a strong jaw and smooth skin. His eyes were striking as well, and eyes always got my attention.

Not that I was interested in 'a tumble'. I had enough complications in my life. But I was wondering if it weren't too late to talk some sense into Karolyne. If she was attracted to dwarves, here was a far better one I'd found. Of course, I hadn't spoken to her since I set foot on the ship and the wedding was in two hours, so if I were to get her to fall in love with a different dwarf I'd have to act quickly.

We'd reached the crew section. Malcolm opened a hatch and led me into a small, dark room.

I instinctively reached for the Ashur on my back. Damn, I'd forgotten to find myself a dagger or small knife for such close quarters.

Malcolm put a soothing had on my shoulder. "Calm down. It's supposed to be dark in here for the detector to work."

My eyes adjusted quickly. Solhans saw in the dark as well as dwarves. In the center of the room was an open crate with a faint glow coming from inside. The goblin leaned over it intently, Katherine crouched behind him and looking over his shoulder.

"Yes, I see," she said. "How do we compensate, Doctor?"

"Compensate for what?" I asked.

"For all these signals," the goblin said, shaking his head.

The box they were staring at was filled with a silvery liquid. A large, swirling circle of it sparkled and glowed like moonlight.

"How in all the hells is that not magic?" I asked.

"It is science," the goblin insisted. "The resin in which the Dwarf King is encased puts off invisible particles that interact with this tincture, passing energy to the colloidal suspension and causing the colloids to glow. The invisible particles are unable to penetrate lead, so when I place a piece of it so...." He took a small lead plate and inserted it into the middle of the box. It stopped the mixture from swirling the same direction, and now there were two separate sides of silvery liquid, both aglow. "It should block the signal." He turned the box around slowly, but there was no change in the glowing light pattern.

"What does it mean?" the med student asked.

"We're detecting a signal from all around. It's everywhere," the goblin told her.

"Invisible particles? Coming from everywhere?" I said. "Your magical detector is broken."

"It is not," the goblin insisted, but the sound of a buzzer cut off whatever he was about to say next to explain away his failure.

The buzzer repeated, and Malcolm went to the horn on the wall. He picked it up and held it to his ear.

"Yes?" There was a long pause as he listened. "She's here. I'll tell her."

"What is it?" I asked.

Malcolm put the horn back and said, "They've found a body."

"Our body? Rutgard's?" I asked hopefully.

"No. A fresh one."

12 Everyone is Acting Strangely

Malcolm's expression was furious. "Verdis is dead."

Verdis was the quiet King's Guardsman I remembered. The sandy-colored one whom I'd met when first questioning the goblin in the mausoleum. Alum was Gypsum's brother and Malcolm was her nephew, but I didn't remember them saying who Verdis was related to.

"I'm sorry," I told him. "Was he a friend?"

"Like a brother to me. I would have gone into battle with him without a moment's hesitation. I want to see him."

I looked at the goblin and the student, still peering at their contraption and oblivious to our conversation. "You two stay here," I told them. "Call on the horn if you find anything useful."

To Malcolm, I said, "Let's go." I locked the goblin doctor and his protégé inside as an added precaution. Not only did I want to keep them from escaping, I wanted to keep them safe. They wouldn't notice if someone snuck up on them.

Malcolm led the way to a luxurious cabin section on our current level. Conrad stood in the doorway of a stateroom, waiting for us.

He looked at Malcolm and said, "A werewolf killed him."

I wasn't surprised. The wolf wouldn't be onboard if it didn't plan to cause some pain.

Conrad stepped aside to reveal the body in the middle of the floor. The place was a wreck, torn up like my cabin had been, claw marks everywhere and blood sprayed across the walls. Verdis had claw marks on him too. I noted a set of black veils on a stand, now decorated with glistening beads of blood.

"Is this Baroness Syla's room?" I asked, curious.

I had not been so blasé at my first murder scene, which had been where my brother died. I'd seen more death since then, and sadly, I was getting used to it.

"Yes," Conrad said. "I've had word she is with the wedding party and safe."

"Good." Syla was my paycheck. Plus, I kind of liked her. "What was the wolf looking for do you think?"

"Looking for?" Conrad scrunched his brow in thought. "What makes you say that?"

"Because my cabin was trashed like this, while I was in it, not half an hour ago. The wolf came in and searched the place, barely noticing me and Jake the dog."

"Did you see what color the wolf was?" Malcolm asked intently. "What did it look like?"

"I don't know. It was more a blur of claws and fur. Black, I think. I couldn't see so well after I'd been flattened against the wall."

Malcolm looked at Conrad. "I'm going to hunt it down." The dwarf pushed past us.

"How do you think you're going to find it?" I called after him, but the dwarf ignored me and disappeared around a corner.

I'd had no luck finding the wolf with bloodhound or bogle. In fact, the bogle hadn't made a peep when the wolf was killing Verdis, which had to have been recently, so either my invisible friend was hiding somewhere, or he'd jumped ship while the nobles were arriving. Some good he was.

"You're lucky to be alive," Conrad said, taking my hand.

I froze, feeling a chill. I thought it might be the ghost of Verdis, but I could see his soul was gone already, the body on the floor nothing but a body. Another guardsman was in the room, examining the scene.

"Do you know what happened?" I asked Conrad.

I wanted to pull my hand away, but the chill I'd felt was being pushed back by the warmth of his touch. The warmth seemed to flow along my fingers and arm, all the way to my chest, pushing out the cold lump Duane had placed there.

"Verdis was supposed to be watching the Baroness. I don't know why he was here alone."

"We should question Syla."

"Yes, we should." He stepped closer to me. "You ... are a bad influence on me, Eva. I can think of nothing but you. When you said how close you'd come to the wolf, I felt…. I'm glad you're safe." His voice made me feverish again. He seemed to notice my reaction and smiled. "Still, I'm surprised you did not take the creature's head and bring it to me as a trophy," he added teasingly.

"Rub it in. I was pathetic, tripping over this monstrosity of a dress, my Ashur nearly useless in such a tight space."

"Then take this." He undid his belt sheath and handed it to me. The dagger inside was pure silver and serrated like my longer blade.

"This doesn't look like standard Guard issue," I noted.

"It isn't. It will be more useful here. Werewolves can be cut by most anything, but they heal quickly. Only silver will wound permanently."

"Thanks." He had given me his only weapon without hesitation, and I suddenly felt bad for keeping secrets from him. "Can we step outside for a minute?" The guardsman examining the room seemed intent on his work; still, I couldn't share Syla's secret in front of a dwarf.

Conrad followed me down the corridor. No one was in earshot, but I moved close to him anyway. That feverish feeling came over me again as I leaned in and whispered, "I want to stop the wolf more than anything, but I'm here on another case. I was hoping you could help me?"

"Whatever you desire, it will be done."

"Still that confident? How about you stop the bombings and catch the wolf for me then?"

"Then I shall."

I smiled at the cocky grin on his face.

"In the meantime," I said, "can you keep an eye out for a missing person I'm looking for?"

"Who is missing?"

"The Dwarf King. His body was stolen, and Malcolm is helping me find it. If you hear anything, let me know. I think this theft, abduction, whatever, is all part of some plan to throw Highcrowne into turmoil, and we can't let that happen."

At that moment an EEP came down the corridor, her very footsteps angry and demanding.

"Why was I not informed of this immediately?"

She was tall for an elf, or maybe it was the heel on her high boots that gave her the extra few inches. She was golden haired and golden skinned, but it all stopped at her eyes, which were a cruel red.

"I'm Special Detective Faulconbridge," Conrad said, "and this is none of your concern, Commandant Rhen."

"The Elf King's safety is my paramount concern. What's happened, and why are you two filthy humans here?"

Conrad turned his back on the elf and said to me, "This might take a while. Best you go now. Good fortune on your hunt, and may you be carrying the black wolf's head when next I see you. Although, Malcolm might beat you to it." He smiled and turned back to the EEP, giving me a window of escape. I took it. I did not want to be caught up in a dispute over jurisdiction.

I was halfway back to the ballroom before I realized I had no plan. Conrad was showing uncharacteristic faith in me, probably to boost my spirits after my embarrassing breakdown last night, but I really had no idea what to do. I should find Syla, but she probably didn't know why the wolf had been in her room any more than I knew why my room had been searched. My Rutgard detector wasn't working, and Bell's dynamite detector was, thankfully, not sniffing out anything, while my supposed werewolf detector was missing.

Perhaps an incentive would lure the bogle out and make him work harder? I headed for the dining section. It was past time for breakfast anyway.

When I got to the dining room, everyone was acting strangely. There were whispers across menus, which were raised like shields to hide people's faces, and not a lot of eating going on. Then I set eyes on the main attraction: a dwarf suffragist dressed head to toe in red had chained himself to the massive terrarium that took up one wall. He stood there silently glaring at everyone. I did a double take when I realized it was The Jerk.

I felt self-conscious, maneuvering along the narrow path between tables, until I reached him. When I was close enough, I hissed, "Wade, what are you doing here? Aren't you supposed to be getting married at midday? Where's Karolyne? This would mortify her."

"I care not what my woman thinks, or you, trollop. When I saw this injustice, I had to act."

"Injustice?" Then I noticed what was in the terrarium behind him. It wasn't sand crabs as I'd assumed, but pixies.

The ship had clearly been stocked with elf culinary tastes in mind. Pixies looked like miniature humans with wings—no relation to the Unmentionables as some people assumed—and their female queens were as intelligent as humans too. The males, however, were drones, like worker ants, with no willpower or brain of their own. I could see how Wade might draw a parallel with dwarf males. I'd seen pixies caged like this when I was a child; they'd been in the black market section of the Outskirts where Duane once roamed. While an elven delicacy, *yuck*, the eating of pixies was banned in Highcrowne. The rule didn't extend beyond the city limits, apparently.

The dining room was filled with elves, so I didn't think Wade would find much sympathy here. I had the most peculiar lack of hatred for him at the moment.

I didn't like seeing pixies caged and earmarked for deep frying either. It was disgusting. Only, I knew it was better to sneak back in the middle of the night and set them free when no one was looking, rather than make a spectacle in front of an uncaring crowd. I knew, because I had managed to convince Duane to take me back to the market later to set the pixies free. Duane used to do anything for me. Once again, I felt a congestion in my chest, thinking about how different he had become. Or was it me who was different?

As I suspected, EEPs quickly arrived to handle the Wade situation. I knew better than to stand too close and had my back against the wall while he was battered in the gut and on the back of his neck until he dropped to the ground. They searched him and dragged him off, one EEP remaining behind long enough to survey the crowd with his steely gaze.

The soldier noticed me—the only human and in a red dress to boot—and stepped closer. "Come with me."

"No, thanks."

"That was not a request."

The table beside me had an assortment of uneaten food, mostly globs of jollup fat or meat and tubers burnt to charcoal, but there was a fruit and cheese platter. I grabbed the wheel of cheese and took off before the EEP could manage a sneer. He remained frozen in surprise long enough for me to get myself through the crowd and out the door, despite my trailing skirts.

"Stop!" he called.

I didn't look back, and the clanging sound his boots made on the metal deck receded.

When I reached the lower ballroom, I flung open the doors with one hand, while clutching the cheese wheel with the other. But the EEP had caught up, and he stepped on the train of my dress. I jerked to a stop and tumbled to the side, the cheese wheel cushioning my fall. There had been the sound of cloth tearing, and I cringed.

"What do you think you are doing?" Baroness Syla's voice had a needle sharpness to it.

My gamble had paid off. Syla, Gypsum, and the wedding planner were all there with Karolyne, who was in rehearsal with Reginald standing in for the groom and Bert holding the ring. They stared, and while some of the shock was directed at me, most was reserved for the EEP soldier.

"Matriarch," the EEP said, noting the veil Syla had automatically dropped back into place as soon as we showed up. I thought I'd spotted a jagged cut on her cheek before she hid her face, but I couldn't be sure. "This is Protectorate business, and I demand you stand aside."

"This is my business, and Miss Thorne is under my protection. I don't care what she's done...." She paused and asked me, "You didn't kill the Elf King or anything that stupid, did you?"

"No."

"Then this woman is under my protection," she finished. "Go now or face the fury of the Council."

I thought that threat would have sent him scurrying, but the self-important thug stood there and waited for backup. Soon we had a gaggle of goons, or was it a flock? They blocked the doorway in a very orderly V-shaped formation. When their leader arrived—elf woman who had been harassing Conrad last I saw—they parted enough to let her through and then closed ranks again.

"Matriarch Syla, you are wanted for questioning in the death of a King's Guardsman and for harboring this human, who was associating with an anarchist only moments ago. Another dwarf. I don't normally concern myself with dead dwarf soldiers and suffragists coming between elves and a delicious feast of pixies, but King Fharen is on this ship, and I will not tolerate such disrespect," she said.

"So Verdis being dead somehow disrespects Fharen?" I shot out before I could stop myself. I'd regained my feet and stood between Syla and Gypsum, hugging my cheese wheel.

"The presence of so many inferiors disrespects the King," the commandant said, curling her lip at me far better than her rude flunky had managed. "Disorder disrespects the King. Impurity of thought is disrespect. Impurity of body, impurity of...."

"I get it. We're impure and generally messy. That is no crime, and King Fharen doesn't get to make laws willy-nilly. Tell them, Syla."

"Actually, they can question me," Syla said.

The elf woman smiled. "No single matriarch, or in fact the Council, is equal to King Fharen. Only King Rutgard holds a position that can save you from me, and I don't see him here."

Oh yeah. The Dwarf King. I really needed to find him.

"Technically," Gypsum interjected, "you are not King Fharen and cannot wield his authority. The Elite Protectorate has no formal role within Highcrowne."

"We're not in Highcrowne any longer. Seize them," the woman ordered.

The squad of elves in black uniforms surrounded us. Karolyne said, "Hey! What about my wedding?"

"Don't worry," I told my friend. "Show a bit more impurity and they can lock you up with us. Wade's already in jail. We can have the ceremony there."

"Stand down," Conrad's voice rang out, and the EEPs obeyed, taking a step back. A warning look from their commandant stopped them from retreating further.

Conrad marched in with his own flock of soldiers, swords drawn and pointing at the ceiling, which helped the dwarves appear a bit taller. There were more of them at least.

"I told you before, Commandant. I will not cede authority. Return to your King's side where you belong," Conrad ordered.

It looked like the jurisdictional argument continued.

The elf woman was too furious for words. She raised her arm, and the EEPs drew their weapons.

The dwarves stopped pointing their swords at the ceiling.

"This is madness," Syla said, cutting through the thick silence. "We all have the best interests of the Three Kingdoms at heart. I will answer the Protectorate's questions if it will ease their minds."

"This ship is Highcrowne's no matter what sky it passes through," Conrad argued.

"And I will answer the Guard's questions after I've finished with the Commandant's," Syla continued reasonably. "Eva is guilty of nothing but being human. Leave her be."

"That is crime enough," Commandant Rhen said. She didn't send her goons after me, though. They surrounded Syla, and the Baroness let them lead her away.

Syla called back to me, "Keep working. I'll be free soon enough."

I wished I could be so sure. Those EEP thugs didn't look too inclined to let anyone free once they had them under their power.

Conrad's guards followed the EEPs out, and I told him, "Help Syla."

"After I find out what she knows." He marched out with the soldiers, leaving silence behind.

I was still hugging the cheese wheel, but I wasn't hungry anymore. I handed it to Bert who stood between Reginald and the wedding planner, looking stunned.

"Come on," Gypsum told Karolyne. "Let's make sure we finish this wedding before the situation grows even more chaotic."

"What is so important about the wedding?" I cried, wondering what Gypsum was thinking. "A werewolf killed Verdis. Your sister, not to mention the groom, are in jail. There are more urgent things."

Karolyne frowned. "You don't understand …. Wait a minute. Wade is in trouble? And who is Verdis?"

"Long story," Gypsum said, clearly not wanting to reveal more about the King's Guardsman. "I heard when you said Verdis was dead, Eva. It's not good, but it doesn't change things. Do what you have to do, and we'll do what we have to. Syla's only being held for questioning, and I've learned a few things about lawyering from my husband, Markham, that will enable me to extract her and Wade from the elves and leave them trembling in their boots. I have a plan."

I wished I did. "Aren't you frightened of the wolf running loose?"

"Not any more than I was at home. This was what you hoped for, wasn't it? A chance to trap it?" Gypsum said.

"Yes." I wasn't sure what I'd hoped for, but she was right. I needed to find a way to take advantage of the wolf being stuck onboard with us. Somehow.

"And I have to finish trapping Wade," Karolyne said, turning to Gypsum. "Unless you think the EEPs won't release him?'

"Even in prison, he'd be able to get messages to his friends and to his mother of course," Gypsum said.

"Wait a minute. I'm missing something here." I hated not knowing what was going on.

Gypsum glanced at the three other dwarves. The wedding planner and Bert were now straightening the mess an invading squad of soldiers had made, but Reginald was watching us with narrowed eyes. "Let's go across the hall."

Gypsum led me and Karolyne to the reception area, another massive room that boggled my mind. The tables were already set, crystal and silver glistening in the candlelight.

"It was her idea," Gypsum said, pushing Karolyne forward, as though expecting me to be angry.

"I can do more than wait tables," Karolyne began. "Running a café, I see and hear a lot of things and meet a lot of people. I'd noticed Wade and Reginald and the other suffragists meeting in there. I'd seen the gold exchanging hands. Wade was funding all of it as far as I could tell. I told Gypsum about it and offered to help in any way I could. She introduced me to Syla, and that's when the marriage idea came up."

"You're a spy?" I asked, incredulous. "Do I even know you?"

"Don't be so dramatic," Karolyne chastised. "I'm only helping out."

"Going so far as to marry Wade is a lot more than helping. That's some dedicated spy craft," I said.

"Wade isn't so bad," Karolyne blushed. "He has his good points. I did a lot of thinking after the Baroness suggested the marriage; she's obsessed with stopping the suffragists and very persuasive. I never planned to marry anyone."

"Then how come you're always trying to get me hitched to Conrad and every other man with prospects who comes through the door?"

"I was living vicariously. I don't want marriage, and so this is my only chance at the fancy dress and big ceremony. I want a wedding, not a husband."

"Well you're getting a woman-hating, poorly dressed, insufferable excuse for a husband," I pointed out.

"He is to be imprisoned," Gypsum said. "There is already ample evidence against him. Wade's female relatives have proved ineffectual at controlling him, however, so an essential part of the plan is for Karolyne to exert her rightful say over the finances, according to dwarven law, to shut Wade down and possibly a good portion of the suffragists too. The Jerk, as you call him, will soon be out of the picture."

I was impressed, and a bit disturbed by the cold ruthlessness of it. "You'd make a good Solhan," I told Karolyne.

"It was for the good of the city," she said, obviously not pleased with my sideways compliment. "Now you know our plan, don't you have something to do? A werewolf on the loose sounds dangerous. Although I'm not sure I believe it—are you sure it's not a troll?"

"I'm sure. I'll figure out what to do next. See you both later," I said, moving towards the exit.

I felt somewhat sorry for the suffragists. For the Reginalds at least, if not the Wades. They wouldn't stand a chance with the likes of Karolyne, Gypsum, and Syla against them.

I stopped halfway out the door. "Oh, one more thing. How do you say 'truth speaker' in Avian?"

Gypsum thought for a moment. "*Yusha Kalal.* Why?"

"I want to try something." I was deliberately vague, as I had no idea what would happen.

I thought about mending my torn dress. My plans for sewing and mending never got past the 'thinking about it' stage, though. Instead, I found something to eat in steerage, where you'd never spot an elf, only dwarves down there. I also didn't spot the bogle, even though I was on the hunt for him. He was no longer essential to my plan anyway. City guardsmen were elusive too, all holed up wherever Conrad and the EEPs were.

I checked in with Bell, dutifully babysitting her detector, who said she'd alerted the bridge to the werewolf, but from her tone I got the distinct feeling nobody in charge believed me. Verdis' death was much more simply, and reassuringly, explained by an assassin with Baroness Syla in his sights. Not that it didn't worry people; only they weren't as worried as I'd have liked.

Seemed it was up to me to fix that.

I climbed up the main stairs, alone, no guardsmen behind me as I'd hoped, and soon reached the upper ballroom, where only a few stragglers remained from the morning's celebration. They chatted away, nursing their wine as though it might last the whole voyage.

Damn, I needed more people. I supposed I could test it at least.

I put the feather over my eyes and spoke the words Gypsum had told me, crossing my fingers and hoping I'd remembered them correctly. I heard gasps and looked up to see that most of the elves in the room were suddenly years older, their hair and skin coloring completely different, and wobbling around in layers of fat hidden by unfitted sacks of clothing.

I smiled wickedly. Seeing past glamours could be useful.

A girlish laugh caught my attention, and I spotted Princess Hilja in the distance. The circle of admirers around her had grown bigger, most of the elvish businessmen wider of girth yet shorter of height. Hilja, however, looked as beautiful as before. That soured my mood.

Hilja politely covered her smile with a fan while the elves summoned their glamour again.

"Causing trouble?"

I jumped. Duane had snuck up on me.

"I'm trying to hunt down the wolf who nearly got Little Viktor killed, instead of trying to schmooze despicable elvish courtiers." I kept thinking about what Duane had said earlier, how he had turned his back on me, and I couldn't blunt the anger in my voice.

"I'm not schmoozing. I'm here for Hilja and for ... I want to catch the wolf too," he added lamely.

"I'd never have guessed."

Duane glanced behind me, venom in his gaze, and I whipped around in case I was about to be attacked. It was Conrad, not clattering around but moving silently for once. He wore only a white tunic and breeches now.

"What are you doing out of armor?" I asked, worried. "The wolf is on the loose. You need all the protection you can get."

"I can move faster this way. Baroness Syla says she knows nothing about Verdis' death, and Gypsum is with her now. I thought you might need me." He looked at Duane without expression. There was usually a bit of tension between the guardsman and the gangster, but Conrad was hiding whatever he was thinking well. Duane not so much.

"You've seen the werewolf?" Duane asked, fear in his voice, something I'd never heard before. It seemed he too disliked the sound, and he frowned even harder at Conrad. "Did it kill one of your guards? The wolf show you who the real enemy is? Did it remind you guards and soldiers bleed same as us thieves?"

Conrad didn't answer Duane right away, but from both their expressions I guessed there was plenty not said. I'd like to think they were fighting over me, but they were natural enemies. I wasn't even the excuse.

Finally, Conrad said, "Not everyone bleeds the same, and not everyone dies the same. Some fight it like a lifelong enemy, while others embrace it as a welcome friend. The question is not when death comes but how, and that is predicated by the life you've lived. Soldiers and thieves throw themselves equally against the blade, the only difference being whether it is an enemy's or an executioner's."

Duane eyed him closely. "You seem different."

"In a good way, I hope." He smiled at me.

Even seeing Conrad smile was different. He was usually so tense, almost unsure of himself and the role he'd taken on, but since he'd arrested the suffragist leader, he had changed. I had noticed it too. I liked it.

"If that werewolf is here, I'll help you stop it. I owe it one." Duane indicated the scabbed wounds across his cheek and brow.

"I have an idea," I said. I could best use the Avian feather to reveal the wolf among the sheep if I could get more sheep gathered. "Can you ask Princess Hilja to command everyone back into this ballroom?"

She glanced my way when she heard me say her name, pausing her conversation with the crowd of admirers around her. Duane looked at her intently, and she raised an eyebrow questioningly.

"No," Duane told me.

"No?"

"I won't endanger Hilja. If you've seen the wolf, she needs to get off this ship before we try anything."

"We don't need the Princess. I can make an announcement on the intercom in the name of the Guard," Conrad said. "But why?"

"You'll see. Let's get Doctor Ghunnan first. He won't hear the intercom." I took off for the stairs again, Conrad close behind, and I paused to see what Duane would do.

He'd said he wanted to help, but he was looking back and forth between us and his elf. He stood straighter, head up, decision made, and moved forward to touch Hilja's shoulder. He whispered into her ear, and she pulled him into her circle, their backs to me again.

I thoroughly hated her. She seemed so sweet and even good for Duane, and hating her felt as bad as hating a kitten—what kind of monster hates kittens?—but I hated her anyway.

Duane accused me of following him around, but the reality was he had always been eager to follow at my heels. To always be there. For Viktor. For me. Now all that history we shared wasn't enough. I didn't believe it should be, but sometimes it was hard to let go of the past and grow up. Hard for me at least.

I made it halfway down to the next level before I stopped. Conrad noticed my hesitation on the stair. "It is painful being alone."

"You think that's why he's with her?"

"I was speaking of myself and of you." He took my hand. I'd been squeezing the railing so hard my knuckles were white. He was so delicate with me, admiring my palm as though he had never seen it before or was seeking to tell my fortune. "I see how you look at him from afar, and I wish you would look at me like that."

"No, you don't," I said. "I look at him with disappointment, for what might have been, for what's become of him, of me. I feel my Solhan blood racing when I'm near him, but there's always a chill undercurrent to it, ice water, that keeps me from feeling what I want to feel."

"Is this where the ice runs?" he asked, tracing a blue vein along the heel of my thumb. The chill chased along my spine and sent a shiver through me that turned once more into that feverish heat he'd first brought out in the moonlight.

"It's not so cold near you," I said. I remembered Erick and how he had chased away the chill too, made me forget about it at least, although not so well as Conrad was managing now.

But Erick had turned out to be even more cold-blooded than me, which must have been why I was drawn to him. I'd loved him in my way, but it was the shallowest of loves, like you might love a sunrise or a warm cup of kaffe on a winter's morning. It wasn't anywhere near as strong as the familial love I had for Little Viktor, or even for Gypsum and Karolyne. It wasn't even friendship, only ... a desire to feel heat.

"What's wrong with you, Conrad? Why do you want me when I can't stand myself most days?" I asked. I didn't even try to flirt or play the coquette. I wanted to know.

"Because I want to fill the void inside me. I want to be complete." He kept looking at my hand with an aching vulnerability that was such a contradiction to all his earlier confidence, like he was afraid to let me see his eyes and the truth behind them.

He kissed my fingertips with a soft brush of his lips. Feverish heat washed over me from fingers to elbow, to neck and lips, and straight down between my legs. I really didn't care about truth at that moment or much of anything. I opened my mouth with the smallest breath of pleasure, and then he was covering it with his lips.

With a hungry growl of desire, he tugged me down the stairs to the next landing, where he took me by the waist and pulled me to him.

He kissed my neck, intertwining his fingers with mine. He wore no cologne, but his scent was beautiful and like nothing I'd smelled before. I breathed deep. I stroked his hair, his neck, his strong shoulders, and felt his chest muscles pressing against me through his shirt. I liked him being out of his hard armor for once, and I pressed myself against him. He was hard where it mattered.

With another hungry growl, he picked me up and wrapped my legs around his waist and kissed me. His tongue penetrating my lips, pushing past my teeth and pressing against my tongue as though trying to subdue an opponent in wrestling.

He gasped for breath and said, "I need you, Eva. I have always needed you. You make me feel … un-alone."

"I hate being alone too," I said.

I surrounded myself with people all day, friends and café patrons, even family and Nanny when I had to, but I knew what he meant about being alone. That ache for someone to sit beside me at a table and hold my leg or hold my hand as I walked down the street … or to kiss me on a stairwell when I was feeling lousy.

There was something I'd been planning on doing, but at that moment I pushed it aside and kissed him back, hungrier for the taste of him than he had been for me.

He pressed me against the wall and fumbled for the edge of my dress. There was a lot of fabric, but he kept pulling it up until he found my thigh. His hand began to move slowly upward, and I gasped.

"Excuse me," someone said.

I ignored whoever it was, barely registering the voice through the hot fog of desire I was feeling.

"For gods' sake, Eva, get a room." That was Bell, and I suddenly realized I had an audience.

"Sorry," I told Conrad, as I pulled away and hastily tucked things back where they should be. I looked down at my dress and made sure everything important was covered before I scowled at my voyeurs.

Bell was there, along with the goblin and his student. The goblin would have had a good view of my cleavage from above, even if half of it hadn't been hanging out before. The student had one hand over her eyes, and I blushed.

"I'm a doctor," the goblin said when he noted my blush. "I've seen female parts like yours before."

"Can I open my eyes now?" the student asked.

"Yes," the goblin told her. "We've managed to successfully interrupt the mating ritual."

"Why are you here?" Conrad demanded, a little angry. I felt the same, but Bell was right. I should have found a room, and I still wanted to.

"Thought you should know—" Bell began.

"—I've found King Rutgard," the goblin cut in.

That splashed cold water on my desire. "Where?"

"Follow us," the doctor ordered.

13 UNEXPECTED TURN

My head was still a fog of hormones from my encounter with Conrad, who I was a bit embarrassed to look at right now. I felt him beside me, listening, but I think his mind was on other things as well.

"This bossy goblin got me on the horn, and he seemed to know everything about everything already. More," Bell said. "When were you going to tell me about the real case you were working on? I thought we were partners?"

"That blabber mouth," I said, glaring at the goblin's back. "My client made me promise not to mention the missing king. Besides, I thought we were only business partners?"

"I'm here helping you hunt down dynamite and a werewolf, aren't I? I want to know what's happening."

"Fine. Next time I'll enlist your help from the start. If there is a next time. This might be my first real case and my last one too."

"You giving up being a detective already?" she asked, disappointed.

"No. Because we might be dead soon."

"Oh. By the way, your friend, Karolyne, told me to tell you the wedding is happening now. And to make sure you show up. The Elven Protectorate won't let her announce it over the speaker as it's reserved for emergencies, so she's spreading the word by all and sundry other means available. Yet another thing I wasn't invited to. I need to stop answering the horn," Bell grumbled.

"Well, I'm going to be late," I pointed out.

Either Karolyne was willing to plow on ahead oblivious to reality, or the The Jerk had been cleared of the heinous crime of defending helpless pixies. That was fast. I wondered if bribes had been involved.

The goblin and his med student stood mid-way down the stairs, waiting. "This way," he prompted. "You are annoyingly slow for one who has functioning legs."

"We're coming," I told him. I lifted my skirts as best I could to avoid tumbling down the steps and followed the goblin and his student to one of the middle levels, which seemed to be entirely composed of passenger cabins.

"What's Rutgard's body doing here?" I wondered aloud.

"Resting quietly," the doctor said, gesturing to a door, which the student opened.

I stepped inside and there was indeed a king on a third-class passenger cot. The blanket that had been covering him now lay on the floor, and there was no sign of suffragists, wolves, or any other bad guy around. Just a body.

It looked like it was cocooned in pale amber. When they said he'd been preserved, I'd been picturing a glass coffin like dwarves often used to display their loved ones on funeral barges. This was something else. The resin the goblin had been talking about was like ancient tree sap hardened to stone, but it wasn't natural amber as I first assumed. It was too perfect, no bubbles or imperfections in the yellow brown material. I touched it, and it was warm.

I peered at King Rutgard. He was short and stout like any dwarf, clean-shaven though, same as the King's Guardsmen. He wore intricate chainmail, an equally well-crafted sword clutched to his chest, and a silver crown rested on his gray-haired head. I could see every detail through the resin, down to the carvings in the crown; a wolf's head dominated. That was interesting.

"How did you find him?" Conrad asked the doctor. The same thing I wanted to know.

"It was merely a matter of refining the scale and purpose of the emulsion chamber; in particular, making it deeper and incorporating latticed three-dimensional grids for the silver particles to adhere to. As well as making it more portable." The goblin proudly indicated the detector, which he'd left on the floor in the far corner of the cabin. It now looked like a wooden shoebox filled with metal mesh and liquid. "Eventually, the colloidal silver formed a crystalline structure pointing in the direction of the body, which was very odd. It should merely react to the invisible particles emitted by the resin, not physically move in response to them. It explains much of the difficulty I was experiencing, as the colloidal particles of the detector itself were shifting and coming out of solution, attracted to it. But not the resin sample I had tested. Only the presence of the fully encased body was making them behave strangely."

"Yes, go on," Bell encouraged.

I would have told the doctor to get it over with it by now, but I found it interesting his detector relied on silver. Silver was supposed to affect the Unmentionables as well, or was it iron? That part of the legends was a bit confusing. I did know that, in most magical practices, silver was used as a material of purification. Out of curiosity, I drew the dagger

Conrad had given me and held it out to the king's body. I felt a strong pull.

"Once I realized the body was on this ship," the goblin continued, "and that was why the signal seemed to be coming from everywhere, I was able to take advantage of the curious reaction from my silver emulsion, as I mentioned. Then it was simply a matter of following the silver arrow as it were. It led us here," he concluded, a satisfied tone in his voice.

"How did you get out of that locked room and into this one?" I asked as I sheathed the knife.

"I'm good with mechanical things, locks among them," the doctor said, adjusting his spectacles nervously.

How many locked doors had he bypassed for less reputable reasons in his life? At least he had lived up to his word about finding the body.

"Conrad," I said, not daring to turn to him. I felt a heat between us that was hard to ignore. "Are you and your guards able to keep an eye on this room for a while? I'd like to take the king back to Highcrowne, but I've a wolf to catch first."

"You don't trust me, but you'll trust your boyfriend's soldiers?" Bell said.

I still couldn't look Conrad in the eye. "He is not my boyfriend."

"Kissing and groping buddy then, whatever you want to call him. All I know is that something is not right. I can feel it in the ship." Bell stroked the bulkhead with a worried frown, like a stable master stroking a prized horse in need of soothing.

"Feel what?"

"I don't know, exactly, but isn't it a bit strange the body was just sittin' here? Now that I know everything, it feels an awful lot like cheese in a bogle trap."

I could use one of those about now. The bogle was hiding too well for cheese alone to draw him out, however. I'd tried that.

"You're being paranoid," I told her. "The wolf who stole the body is probably busy causing trouble elsewhere. All the more reason to find it."

"If it will allay your worries, Eva, I'll remain here and keep watch over the King. I needn't let my men know about it," Conrad said.

"Eva's worries? Hello, I exist," Bell said, waving her hand.

I ignored her, because I was thinking a few steps ahead for once. Bell's mention of bogle traps had given me an idea.

"We've got bait for a wolf trap right here," I said. "Someone has gone to a lot of trouble to retrieve Rutgard, and I doubt they'll leave their prize unguarded for long."

It was a better plan than the feather. Would the werewolf in disguise really come to the ballroom, especially if the mass assembly was ordered by the Guard? I'm sure it would just go deeper into hiding.

Bell's gaze shifted uncomfortably towards the door, seemingly wondering if a werewolf was about to burst through it. "How are we supposed to kill it?" she asked.

The goblin and his student were examining the resin encasing the king's body, oblivious to the discussion.

"We need more silver weapons," I said. I knew where there would be a reception hall full of them. "Come with me, Bell. I need help carrying the wedding cutlery, and I'm hoping your engineering friends have something like a forge so we can make a better weapon. This dagger feels like a toothpick."

"There's a workshop and tools galore down there. I'll figure something out," she said, eager to go now that she realized she was in a wolf trap.

"You two." I raised my voice to get the attention of the goblin and the student. "Go back to my cabin until it's safe."

"I shall not leave the specimen," the doctor insisted.

"Our work is too important," Katherine added.

"Don't be stupid," I began, but I could tell from their unyielding expressions that they would be. "Then if the werewolf comes..." The goblin snickered at the term. "...if the wolf comes, throw your silver liquid in its eyes and run away."

I pushed Bell out the doorway and turned back to look at Conrad.

"Same for you," I said more gently. "Take your dagger back, protect yourself, but run if you need to. The wolf has already killed too many people. And hurt those I care about." I held out the weapon.

He touched my hand, brushing his thumb against mine, and I shivered. He tightened my grip on the handle. "Keep it. I won't take back what I've already given away."

I wanted to kiss him again, instead I said, "I'm trusting you."

I didn't say those words lightly. Ever since Erick tried to kill me, I'd had a hard time trusting anyone. My heart tended to betray me. I think it has a death wish.

I desperately hoped Conrad was not a wolf in disguise, or an evil necromancer in his spare time, or working with the suffragists, or a dozen other things my distrustful imagination could come up with, because I was feeling something ... different with him. I felt like I was hanging off the edge of a cliff, and he was holding me. He could pull me up or let me drop, and I didn't care either way, as long as he came with me.

He nodded and shut the door. I heard the lock click and relaxed. Not that I thought it would keep a were-wolf out, but because he was taking this seriously and trusting me. Before today, it felt as though Conrad had never truly believed in me, like he was humoring me to get down my knickers. I'm sure he still wanted to. I wanted him to. But there was more.

Of course, I wasn't sure the wolf was responsible for stealing the king. The two could be unrelated, and this wouldn't work at all.

I also didn't intend to leave him to defend the room alone. A trap needed bite. Bell and I would get the weapons, but we needed more people to wield them.

I spotted one of those speaking horns with a sign above it saying, 'for crew use only'. I picked it up, claimed I was with the Guard again, and asked the bridge to get me Baroness Syla's retinue. I waited while they transferred me around, and I finally heard Alum's voice over the tinny speaker.

"Where are you?" I asked.

"Outside the lower ballroom."

"What about Malcolm?"

"Not sure," he said, sounding like he didn't really care.

The over-muscled dwarf must still be wandering around, wolf hunting on his own. He was going to end up like Verdis, if he hadn't already, and I felt a pang. I liked him.

"Get up here and help Conrad," I ordered. Pretending to be a guardsman so much made me forget I wasn't. "We've found what we're looking for." I gave him directions.

"On my way."

Bell was waiting at the end of the corridor. I hurried to catch up and spotted Alum coming up the stairs. "Conrad can explain the plan. We'll be back as soon as we can," I said.

When Bell and I reached the lower level, the sound of wedding music cut through the worried haze of wolf thoughts in my head. I was very late.

The lower ballroom was full of guests. I spotted Karolyne's parents in the front row. Most of the audience were dwarves I didn't know, but there were plenty I did, like Gypsum, Bert, Reginald ... and Wade. There were two EEP soldiers to the side behind him, and I noted the manacles around his wrists. It looked like they'd released him from the brig temporarily. The Jerk's red suit was dwarven traditional wedding garb. Gypsum was in her red dress, like mine, and Karolyne's wedding dress was red as well, but more opulent with layers of skirts and rubies. My vision had a sudden overlay of Syla's stateroom, and it seemed there was blood everywhere with all the red in sight, but no. Everyone was standing happily in their places as the ceremony began. Syla was there, free and un-manacled, wearing golden robes and holding the dwarven holy book. She began officiating.

"Bell," I said. "Can you get started on the silver? There's something I have to do."

"Sheesh. Is it really so important to be a bridesmaid? Of course, no one's ever asked me..." she grumbled, as she began opening doors looking for the reception room.

This wasn't about being a bridesmaid. Not really. It was about having a room full of people and another chance to try out the feather. The Avian had sounded so convincing, like it would solve all my problems.

"I'll help." Duane had snuck up behind me, and I jumped.

"Boss," Bell said, shooting him a relieved look. I was relieved too, because if my feather worked, it would be three people against one werewolf. Slightly better odds. Slightly.

"Why do you need the wedding silver?" Duane asked. He must have been skulking nearby and listening in. He tended to do that.

"Bad guys," Bell explained succinctly.

"Where's your elf?" I asked. I couldn't keep the accusation out of my voice. Working with the Elf King—and courting his daughter!

"Where's your guardsman?" he shot back, as though Conrad were as out of my league as a princess was out of his. Maybe he was right.

"He's helping me with my case. Besides, he's not 'mine', and he's not working with one of the Crowns to enslave humans. Plus, Conrad can take care of himself," I added.

"And neither Hilja nor I are working with Fharen to enslave humans. She too can take care of herself, especially with a squad of Elite Protectorate around her right now. Everyone's heard about the death of the King's Guardsman earlier, but no one believes it's a werewolf. There's talk of evacuating the Elf King and his retinue anyway," Duane said.

"Once they see the werewolf, they'll wish they'd left yesterday," I said. "Now, I need to crash a wedding."

Duane and Bell shared a look—one that asked what's the crazy Solhan up to now?—before they ducked into the room Bell had finally located.

It wasn't technically crashing, as I was supposed to be here, but everyone glanced my way when I hurried up the aisle to Gypsum's side, almost pushing Karolyne aside to get there.

Syla did not pause in her recitation from the holy book.

"How did the Baroness get free?" I whispered in Gypsum's ear. "Conrad had no luck." He'd been distracted by helping me I remembered. And other things.

"I told you I'd picked up some things from Markham."

Karolyne gave us a look that seemed to say, 'I've been through untold hell to make this wedding happen and you are not going to ruin it for me', so I kept quiet and tried to be a good bridesmaid. It seemed all I had to do was stand there and look pretty, but I had already failed, as my hair was a mess and the hem of my dress torn by the EEP who'd been chasing me.

I spotted my stolen cheese wheel; Bert had tucked it behind some drapery. I shifted over to pick it up, just in case I could find the bogle again, and got more glares from Karolyne.

Baroness Syla was not unscathed from her ordeal. There was a long wound across her forearm, which I could see through the gold lace of her sleeve. I continued my observations, sweeping my gaze across the crowd. Reginald's head was tilted back, sleeping, while Bert kept pinching him to no effect.

Mister and Missus Frost, Karolyne's parents, beamed, clearly overjoyed. I noted their once fine clothes were tatty and unkempt, the mother's neckline bare of any jewelry. They'd looked very different when first we met years ago, but from what Karolyne said, both were to blame for their current poverty: her mother for bad investments and her father for gambling in a vain hope to regain their wealth.

Karolyne's parents were the only humans in the seats; the rest were filled with dwarves a head shorter and …. I froze for I'd spotted familiar golden ears and white hair. A white kerchief appeared, and an elaborate ritual of hand wiping began. It was the tax collector. He was onboard. I gulped. He must have seen me.

I felt twitchy and whispered in Gypsum's ear once more. "What's the Avian word for 'truth' again?"

I'd forgotten a syllable: was it *sha* or *ska*?

"*Yusha*," Gypsum shot back, barely moving her lips. She was holding the crystal tray with the wedding rings and trying not to let them slide off.

"And 'speaker'?"

"*Kalal*," she said, before giving me a kick to the shin to shut me up.

The ceremony was supposed to be short. Dwarves preferred to get on with the drinking as soon as possible at these occasions, so I stood as patiently as I could, my gaze shifting nervously to the tax collector and then darting away whenever he looked me in the eyes.

I hoped Bell and Duane were alright. If they'd encountered any problems, I'm sure I would have heard screams or, more likely, the sound of an explosion, thanks to Bell's pocket bombs. I looked for a window to see if I could gauge the time of day and then remembered where the windows were in this room. The entire ballroom floor was one large piece of glass.

I looked down at my feet and saw only empty air, white cloud with the occasional gap showing brown land and golden ribbons of river far, far below. We'd been gaining altitude. Wonderful. I looked up quickly, afraid I'd get airsick again. Something niggled for my attention, and I dared another look down.

It was past midday. The shadows cast by mountain peaks were shifting, and I could clearly tell which direction was which. We were supposed to be headed south—instead we were going east.

Solheim was in the east.

I set down the cheese wheel. There was no sign of the bogle anyway.

I reached up and felt my hair, glad to find the Avian's feather still tied into it after the acrobatics I'd performed with Conrad earlier. I undid it as discretely as possible but got a warning elbow from Gypsum in the process.

It sounded as though the ceremony was concluding at last, with a few dwarvish words of agreement spoken by first Karolyne and then Wade. Gypsum took a step forward to present the rings.

Karolyne had done it, gone and married a man she didn't love—one most of us hated—all for a pretty wedding and to achieve some lofty goal I wasn't even sure was right in the first place. What was wrong with giving dwarf men representation on the Council? What was wrong with protecting pixies? Of course, Wade's version of dwarf freedom meant enslavement of women. He wanted the tables turned, not equality. Still, should all suffragists be judged badly because of him? It was hard enough being a Thorne, fighting against my nature, my family, trying to do the right thing ... when too often it wasn't clear what 'right' was.

We were headed east. A deep dread was building in my gut.

Solheim. The Dead God was involved in all of this somehow. This was more than suffragists, or elf politics. If the God of Death wanted King Rutgard, it meant He wanted Highcrowne in chaos. It meant He would be coming for us, and no place was safe.

Karolyne and Wade kissed briefly, before the EEPs dragged him away. Syla closed her holy book with a thud of finality and handed it to Gypsum. The crowd stood up, ready to make their way to the reception lunch in the dining room. This was my chance.

"Excuse me for a moment," I called out. "Can you stay where you are?"

"What are you up to?" Gypsum asked.

I ignored her and continued with my plan. "As some of you may have heard, a dwarf guardsman was killed in a stateroom about an hour ago." There were a few gasps at that, including Karolyne's parents, who must not have heard about it before. "And all of you know of the bombing of the Market District yesterday. These events are not unrelated but part of a plot by Highcrowne's enemy, the very enemy who has now set this ship on a course towards Solheim."

More people gasped and put hands to their mouths. The tax collector seemed to be handling my revelations calmly, but he'd faced a risen corpse with me yesterday, so he was probably well past shock.

"You're going to cause a panic," Baroness Syla warned.

"I'm trying to find a murderer," I said dramatically, loud enough for everyone to hear, thoroughly enjoying the mass interrogation scene. My favorite had been in *Murder on the Troll Road* where it turned out every suspect was guilty. I didn't have any real suspects yet, but that was about to change.

At that moment, Commandant Rhen appeared with two more EEPs. They took up positions around Wade, ready to escort the 'dangerous' suffragist back to the brig or wherever they intended to hold him; probably indefinitely and without trial.

I didn't want them to get away, so I hurried my speech. "Another thing you may not be aware of is that the culprit responsible for the crimes I described could be in this very room, at least on this very ship. I saw it this morning. I saw the werewolf."

Karolyne's mother fainted, and Karo went to her, giving me a look of reproach. Okay, maybe I was enjoying myself a bit too much.

"Look to the person beside you, to the person behind and in front. Do you know who it is?" While I had everyone distracted, eyeing each other distrustfully, I raised the feather to my eyes.

"What's that supposed to do?" Gypsum asked.

"Stop her!" Syla ordered.

"*Yusha Kalal,*" I said in my best imitation of the Avian's high-pitched accent.

The bogle suddenly appeared. "Strange is here!" he said, voice trembling, before he grabbed the cheese wheel and darted beneath my skirts. He must have been hiding nearby the whole time.

The strange was indeed here, but it took me a moment to register what it was. The whole room seemed to be enveloped in fog. Half the dwarves vanished, their shapes outlined in white mist.

A werewolf suddenly shot through the door behind the EEPs who were closest to the exit. The light in the lower ballroom was better than my cabin had been, and I saw gray fur, glowing eyes and lots of white teeth. It ran around the room so fast it seemed to run across the walls, tearing down floral streamers as it went.

The EEP soldier next to Syla had his throat torn out before he could even draw his short sword. The spray of blood was the same color as my dress, I thought distantly.

"Kill it," Commandant Rhen shouted as she drew her own sword. She slashed but hit only air on the wolf's next pass, the creature ripping the EEP leader's sword away—and her arm along with it.

I was not the sort to remain paralyzed with shock for long, so I drew the silver dagger Conrad had given me and on the next pass slashed, drawing wolf blood. The wound boiled and steamed where the dagger struck. The creature growled. The sound poured liquid fear into my veins, and I took an involuntary step back.

Between one eye blink and the next, the wolf became a cloud of white mist. Baroness Syla did too. They both vanished in a white blur.

The mist was some kind of magic. Wolves and matriarchs can't simply disappear. But for once, the green glow did not come, my own magic did not stir. I felt incredibly vulnerable and exposed. That growl left me covered in gooseflesh.

The bogle under my dress clutched my leg with tiny claws. The pain of it helped me shake off preternatural fear, and I pulled him loose.

Then other dwarves besides Syla turned into mist. It was the feather, I realized. The mist was the truth of them. It was....

Gypsum reached out to me. She became a ghostly, transparent white, like the clouds visible through the glass floor. Her dwarf-shaped cloud shifted from that of the person I recognized into a new shape, like clouds often did in the wind. But this shape turned solid again, starting with glowing yellow eyes and white fangs.

A moment later, Gypsum was standing in front of me on her hind paws, all fur and ears and claws. All wolf. Half the room was now occupied by werewolves. That's when the screams started.

14   SOME OF MY FAVORITE PEOPLE

Dwarf werewolves were just as scary as the regular kind, not that I could compare. For all I knew these were the regular kind. Gypsum certainly looked like the wolf I'd seen earlier, except ... her eye color was a bit different, coat color too. She was the closest to me, and I could smell her musky aroma. Her yellow claws twitched as she reached for me.

I stepped back and raised a shielding arm. What looked like arcs of green lightning erupted from my palm and formed something in the shape of an actual shield around me. Gypsum's claws touched the surface, and she jerked away, howling in pain.

The howl sent ice water down my back, but it had an even stranger effect on the other wolves. They joined their howls with hers in a hair-raising chorus of sympathy.

The guests who had been running around screaming in panic suddenly froze. The wolves weren't interested in them. They all turned to look at me.

The shield of green energy I'd created vanished, and I had no way to get it back. The bogle climbed halfway up my leg in fear and was hanging onto my garter belt, making the silk stocking on that leg fall

"Get out of there, Eva!" Duane called from the ballroom entrance.

I wanted to take such sound advice, but I had no place to go. The werewolves had me surrounded.

The wedding planner was a bawling heap on the floor, blocking the aisle until he scurried away to hide beneath a chair. Karolyne was helping her father to sling her unconscious mother over his shoulder. The four surviving EEP soldiers were tossing chairs aside, including the wedding planner's shelter, trying to find the elf leader's arm. The commandant was looking very pale and probably wouldn't make it.

Bell stood beside Duane. She seemed to have a mental inspiration and dug around in her pockets for something. She put a small, metal whistle to her lips and blew. I recognized the high pitch of a boson's whistle, the noise making the wolves growl discordantly as they covered their long ears in pain.

Bell was angering the werewolves, not a good thing, but their discomfort also made them pause long enough for me to step around Gypsum, grab Karolyne and her parents and lead them to the exit. The tax collector followed without me inviting him to come along.

The normal dwarves were running everywhere again, getting in the way. I looked for any I knew, but they were strangers. My friends—Bert, Reginald, Gypsum and Syla—had all turned into the bad guys. Now Jorg's campfire story made more sense to me. *Your dearest friend can become your direst enemy.*

"This way," Duane ordered, taking Karolyne's mother and slinging her over his shoulder. He took off towards engineering, the tax collector and Mister Frost following.

"Where's Wade?" Karolyne asked, looking around desperately.

"He's one of the werewolves," I told her. "Go."

Bell took a few quick breaths to keep up the whistling, but she was turning red, and the wolves kept moving towards us anyway, albeit more slowly, as they covered their ears. The sound seemed to be pissing them off more than anything now. I grabbed Bell, dragging her along with us.

I glanced back. Now that the whistle had stopped, the werewolves seemed joyful. Most snarled and swiped at each other and the guests, playing the way cats toyed with mice, but a group of them came right for us. Bell didn't need me dragging her anymore; she ran all out and was soon ahead of me. I rounded the corner and saw Duane holding the hatch to engineering open. I threw myself through it right after Bell, and he barred the door behind.

The werewolves scratched and banged on the thick metal. I didn't know if the hatch would hold, but then the sounds stopped. It was too quiet. I didn't feel like peeking my head out and seeing what they were up to, however.

I let out my breath and slowly took in the room around me. There was the double-decker cot I'd slept in last night, the machinery humming and clanging as before, but no sign of the engineers. Karolyne looked ashen, her parents on the floor at her feet, mother unconscious and father panting from exertion. The tax collector was cleaning his hands yet again, while Duane, Bell, and I looked at each other with wide-eyed expressions. That had been close.

"You hurt it," Duane said.

I hadn't realized I was still holding the silver dagger. Its edge was coated with something thick and black like boiled blood. I knew, because Nanny sometimes served something similar for breakfast. I squeezed the hilt tight, adrenaline still coursing through my veins.

"How did you know about the whistle?" I asked Bell.

"Animals with keen hearing are oversensitive to some sounds. Thought I'd give it a try. I read it in Kali's, I mean your, bookshop somewhere."

"I had no idea you took time to read whenever you came over to visit. You and Kali are usually up to other things when I walk in."

"Yeah, I really wish you'd stop walking in."

"How can you be so calm?" Karolyne shouted at the two of us. "Didn't you see what happened?"

"Is it legal to marry a werewolf?" I asked Duane.

"Why are you asking me?"

"I thought you'd be familiar with all Highcrowne laws, so you'd know which ones to break."

"I'm more familiar with tax law," the tax collector interjected, "but I do believe there is nothing in writing against interspecies marriage. In fact, I once found a tax precedent where a man had left his entire estate to the cow he was married to."

"That's disgustin'," Bell said.

"Are cows intelligent?" I asked. I'd never met one, but most people told me gralls were stupid, and I had believed them until I met Jorg.

"Did you hear me?" Karolyne shouted again. "There are werewolves!"

"We prefer humor to diffuse the situation," Bell said, "'Tis common after a fright like that. Nothing like running for your life to get the blood pumping."

I had to agree with her, and I was becoming far too familiar with the feeling.

I didn't have Gypsum there nagging me about my manners—I still hadn't digested that she was one of them, my best friend—but I still had another friend and her family to take care of, so I did what Gypsum would have wanted and checked on Mister and Missus Frost. Both seemed uninjured. I put a hand on the mother's forehead, which was clammy.

"We're fine, dear," Karolyne's father said. "I'm alive, and I'm glad my wife is out cold, so I don't have to listen to her along with my daughter. The two are almost identical." He laughed, which seemed to make Karolyne even angrier.

"Your father makes a good point," I told her. "We're alive and safe for the moment. That means we have time to figure out what's going on and how to get out of this mess."

"There's no escape parachutes left in here," Bell said, digging through hatches and thumping instruments. She spun a small wheel and picked up a wad of broken wires, frowning. "Looks like Kob and Vin bailed out after they sabotaged the backup steering. And the main steering. The cables up to the bridge are cut too. I assume it was them, as they did a high quality four-fingered job of it. I've no way of turning this ship around. Did you know we're headed east? We're way off course."

"We're headed to Solheim," I said. I could feel it in my bones, just as Bell had felt something wrong in the ship.

There was a moment of thoughtful silence all around.

Finally, I asked, "Are there any lifeboats?"

"If you mean escape balloons..." Bell shrugged. "Maybe we can reach one in the passenger section? There's also heaps up top."

"I won't abandon this fight," Duane said. "I want the werewolf who nearly killed me and Vicky."

"Hard to tell which one it is," I pointed out. "You should get Hilja and the others on this ship to safety."

"She's already going. You should go too."

"I want that wolf even more than you do. And I'm not leaving Rutgard's body behind, nor am I letting this ship reach Solheim." My paycheck was now a werewolf, but still ... if the Dead God wanted the Dwarf King's body, if that's why His minions had hijacked this ship, I wasn't about to let Him have it.

"What's this about a body?" Duane and Karolyne asked at once.

I told them a very short version of the story, and ended with, "We have to stop this ship no matter what. Crash it if need be."

"Crash *The Mathésis*? The pinnacle of human engineering?" Bell looked like she might cry at the thought.

"Didn't dwarves and Avians build it?" Duane said.

"Human-designed, and no credit for it. More propaganda to keep us down," Bell retorted.

I suddenly realized that, aside from the tax man, it was just us 'humans' here, and I wondered how the goblin doctor fared. And Conrad. Was he safe? I needed to know.

"I'm going to look for a route to the decks above," I said. "Bell, you do whatever you must to get this ship on the ground."

"I'll come with you," Duane said.

"Me too," Karolyne insisted.

"Shouldn't you look after your parents?" I told Karolyne.

"The best way for me to look after my parents is to help find an escape route." She hiked up her massive wedding skirts and headed for the ventilation shaft like she knew what she was doing.

A moment later, Karo had managed to detach the contraption Bell and the engineers had set up to collect air samples for the dynamite detector and swung open the grate. When she saw her skirts were too big, she dropped the dress frame and petticoats onto the heap of junk she'd removed from the wall and clambered inside the shaft. An echoing, tinny version of her voice called, "Are you coming?"

That was the friend I knew. "I'm right behind you."

"I shall remain here," the tax collector said. "This is obviously not an appropriate time to schedule a meeting, Miss Thorne, as I see you are genuinely busy."

"That's a relief." Hopefully we'd crash first.

Duane asked Bell, "What do you plan to do?"

"Bring this thing down gentle as I can. Still, you should find an escape balloon. Just in case, Boss."

"And miss all the fun?" He gave Bell a rakish grin and headed for the open grate. He paused, holding out his hand for me in the civilized way he'd held it out for his elf princess.

Duane, civilized? Did I know anyone in my life like I thought I did? They were all surprising or disappointing me at every turn.

And Gypsum was a werewolf.

"We're coming back," I told those staying behind. "We'll get you to safety. I promise."

"Not sure you should be promising impossible things," Bell said. "We're over the Ice Mountains, several miles shy of the Wall Fort and Solheim pass, so we'll be freezing once we land—if we're not too late and end up past the Wall and in enemy lands. Best you bring back some fancy furs from the royals' travelling wardrobe and some weapons too, in case of either eventuality. Something to fight werewolves, as we ended up dropping most of the silver in the panic." She held up a lone butter knife she'd managed to keep.

"Here, take this." I gave her my dagger. I knew it worked, and I was reluctant to part with it, but I was taking the vents to avoid the wolves, not fight them. "At least it's sharp."

Bell nodded, accepting it.

I headed for the ventilation shaft.

"Should you have given away our only weapon?" Duane asked.

"I'm sure you can steal more silverware. Or are you too civilized now?" I ignored his offered hand and crawled into the darkened tunnel.

"Karolyne?" I whispered.

"Come on," she insisted, somewhere up ahead.

"Where are the escape balloons?"

"All the way at the top," she said.

"How come everyone seems to know but me?"

"Did you read the safety sheet posted on the wall of your cabin?" Karolyne's tone indicated she already knew the answer.

"That would have spoiled all the fun," I grumbled, not that I'd had much time for reading.

I got moving and heard Duane clamber in behind me. Our movements made the shaft boom like thunder. So much for being stealthy.

"I don't know what you want from me, Eva." Duane said, almost shouting to be heard over the noise. "You call me a thief and say I'm trash..."

"I never said that, exactly."

"You think it. I see it in your eyes: I was never good enough to be Viktor's friend."

"I looked up to you both," I said, feeling uncomfortably exposed having this conversation with Duane staring at my behind and knowing Karolyne could hear us clearly, our voices amplified.

"Maybe once," he said, "but now you look down, and when I try to improve my station, and my manners, you ridicule me for it."

"Maybe I don't want you to change."

"You want me stealing the silverware forever?"

"Better than bigger crimes. Better than extortion or slavery."

"I'm no slaver."

"You're working with the biggest of them. The Elf King made it law when Highcrowne was established centuries ago and keeps the other Crowns from abandoning it now."

"Since when do you know about history and laws?"

"Gypsum is always..." I trailed off.

"Gypsum isn't what you thought she was. I'm not either. And this Elf King is not the same one who created slavery. Did you know Fharen is only four decades old? He had Hilja young and took the Crown even younger. His parents were assassinated by Darrub agents, back when Darrub was out to conquer the known world and before the Dead God appeared to show them how it's done. That's when my parents came to Highcrowne, shortly before I was born. Refugees. But they couldn't escape Darrub in the end; the old vendettas came along with them. They killed my family, not for a crown, but for a few coppers or bites of bread. Who knows? All I know was I was five and in the gutter, trying to survive. So, I know where Fharen's resentment comes from, how you can hate everyone for the crimes of a few. Still, he wasn't enslaving humans to get rid of us. Not exactly."

"You know what his plans are?"

"Were. He was conscripting refugees into his new army, training them to fight the Dead God with elvish magic, before you put a stop to it."

"You think I was wrong to save hundreds of innocent men, women and children from being hauled off to the Solhan border to die?"

"No. Of course not. But there's more than one side to every story. Fharen is egotistical and self-serving, but he's also the only one in Highcrowne lifting a finger to intervene in what's happening down south."

"Is that why you're helping him? Why you sold us all out?"

"Who is there to sell out? Your uncle? Both Ulric and your sister were working with him already. They sent me later to meet him as their cut out. Humanity? Fharen could help us take our lands back, and that's more beneficial to humanity than any amount of platitudes."

"Hating slavery is not a platitude."

"Fharen did what he did before I ever met him. I was helping you against the slavers. Remember?"

"I remember. Which makes you switching sides even more of a betrayal." We'd reached a junction of conduits. I spotted a ladder down a side duct, but Karolyne was headed straight ahead and the wrong way. "Go get her while I check this out," I told Duane. "I'd rather not be near you right now."

He made a frustrated sound. "Fine. You never listen to the full story anyway."

"Stories are all they are. How about some truth for a change?" I shot back before I turned the corner and fumed all the way to the access ladder.

We were already at the bottom of the ship, so the only way to go was up. I climbed, angrily, and realized I'd been climbing a long way with no more side conduits opening up to me. At least any large enough to crawl through. My bogle friend, wherever he'd disappeared to this time, could make it through some of them, but not me, no matter how tight I cinched my dress.

There was a very long section, which swayed as I climbed, and I fought off airsickness again. I finally reached the top and opened the hatch, carefully peeking over the rim. There was no one nearby, and no werewolf ripped my off head, so I climbed all the way up.

To my surprise, I was inside the balloon itself, the chamber more massive than anything I'd seen below. Metal struts crisscrossed the inside of the balloon, giving it structure. I was standing on a large platform covered with crates of cargo piled twice my height.

I took a step forward and froze when I spotted a black EEP uniform. The elf's back was to me, but he was blocking the path. I stepped around some crates to see if there was another way to go—and stopped dead in my tracks when I saw myself kissing the Elf King.

It was Ilsa, not me of course. Still, it was like looking into an evil mirror. She wore milky white lace and had her hair up, while I wore blood red and had my hair down, but we were otherwise identical.

Fharen was the surprise. Speak of the devil. He had his mask off and his glamour too, because he was no longer blonde but raven-haired like his daughter. He was halfway out of the floral suit I'd seen him in earlier, reclining on a crate, my sister astride him. He moaned, and she collapsed on top with a satisfied smirk. Seemed I'd arrived in time for the climax. *Yuck.*

I turned to look for another route, and maybe some werewolves or other nasties to get the hideous image of Ilsa and Fharen out of my brain, but then I stopped. I'd never have a more captive audience with the king.

I strode up to them. "You, hypocritical bastard."

Fharen did a double take when he saw me. I noted he looked decidedly half-elf, and a human or Solhan half at that, which explained Hilja's looks.

I went on before he or my sister had a chance to speak. "You enslave thousands of humans without even a slap on the wrist from the other Crowns, and now you have your Elven Protectorate minions spewing nonsense about elven superiority and purity while you're screwing a human? Of course, Ilsa barely counts as one on her good days, but that's beside the point. Plus, you don't look very pure to me. Is utter hypocrisy the latest elvish trend? Or will you go back to baby dragon hunting and bogle tossing as your usual past times soon?"

"Even if I were screwing a human," Fharen said calmly, "I'd be perfectly consistent in my policies don't you think?" He nudged Ilsa off him, and she let her dress fall back down as smoothly as though it were made for these kinds of liaisons. I got a good glimpse of the king's impressive endowment—seemed some people inherited everything, money, good looks ... too bad a heart wasn't usually included—and he didn't try to hide it, as he casually got dressed. "Instead," he continued, "I'm screwing a Solhan who stands to inherit Solheim once we defeat the Dead God."

"I'm older than Ilsa by about two minutes," I told Fharen. "And you won't be screwing me. Or my uncle for that matter, who is even closer to Solhan royalty, if there were such a thing. Solheim was ruled by a Council of Nine chosen for their power as much as their bloodlines. Which is all completely beside the point. The Dead God will kick your ass and all our asses now that you've messed with him and thrown away our neutrality. Highcrowne was safe, and now it's not. It's all your fault."

"Dear sister," Ilsa cooed, "you do get worked up about the most trivial things. You're still going on about those slaves? It's ancient history."

"You're older?" Fharen said, giving me an appraising look, lingering on my bodice region a little too long before he put that ridiculous mask back on and his glamour along with it. He was blonde and golden skinned again.

Ilsa glared at him. "The bargain is I teach you about Solheim and our magic, help you win, and I rule the old lands in your name. Don't be thinking my sister can substitute. She can't be trusted to help you or anyone. Besides, her health has been poor, and I don't think she has long to live."

I barely noticed Ilsa's threat on my life, as it was as commonplace as breathing for her. "None of you care about the werewolves?" I said, feeling like Karolyne must have earlier, ready to shake some fear into them.

"I was aware of a single werewolf," Fharen said, calmly straightening his jacket, "although it is most likely a troll, not that such creatures should be ignored either. Thus, we are in the process of making our exit. I had to do something to pass the time as the balloon was prepared."

"You really think you're untouchable, don't you?" I folded my arms in my favorite lecturing posture.

"I'm not averse to being touched by a beautiful woman," he flirted.

The Elf King was even worse than I imagined: he was a sleaze.

"I hope the dozen werewolves down below eat you both."

"A dozen?" The elf dressed quicker. Ilsa hastily put her veil back on, and the Elf King in his porcelain mask nodded ever so slightly to me. "A pleasure to meet you. You should join us next time so the pleasure can be yours."

"I'm not like my sister," I said. Of course, I couldn't help remembering my much more public encounter with Conrad earlier. Maybe I was like her. Still, I'd draw the line at sleeping with pure evil.

The King shrugged and joined the EEP soldier, who halted Ilsa from following.

"Royal guests only," the EEP said. Fharen did not even pause to tell Ilsa goodbye.

"Looks like you'll have to catch the next one," I told her with a bit too much delight in my voice.

The craft the King boarded could hold fifty people but was only carrying twenty. It resembled a giant woven basket held aloft by a bright yellow balloon, almost fully inflated now, and meant to be noticed by rescuers. I supposed parachutes were needed if you wanted to make a more rapid escape. I hated airships ... and spring and sisters and Elf Kings. My list was growing longer.

I could see the heads of everyone aboard peeking over the woven rim. Hilja was there, as well as Matriarch Kyln, but the rest were unknown courtiers, servants and EEP soldiers. Apparently, the king's mistress rated lower than all of them in an emergency.

The balloon was weighted and lacked the magic used to keep *The Mathésis* impossibly afloat, so as soon as it was untied and pushed to the edge of the platform by crewman it began to drop. I inched closer and noted there was an opening in *The Mathésis'* structure to allow the smaller vessel to exit. Three other escape balloons were being prepared, but it didn't look like enough for all the passengers. This must be first class only. I hoped the rest of us got something.

There was a line forming along the platform, fed by several walkways from the main vessel below. Looked like there were easier ways than crawling through ducts to get here. I hadn't heard any announcements, but people must have guessed it wise to leave because the royals were fleeing like rats.

Where was Duane and Karolyne? Had they gotten lost—or worse? I turned to fetch them, as well as Bell and the others, when Ilsa touched me between my shoulder blades.

It was like a cold knife had severed my spine, rooting me to the spot.

"I'll be taking the part of me you stole now," Ilsa said, "and maybe a bit more."

15 WHAT GOES UP

With Ilsa's touch paralyzing me, I had no weapon against her but my words, so I chose them carefully.

"You said the only way you know of to get your soul back is to kill me. Do you truly intend to murder your own sister?" I asked.

"I'd love to, Sugar. But our beloved Uncle Ulric insists he will kill me if I do such a thing, so I will try alternatives first. This is called the little death. Not as pleasurable as sex is it? Though they share the same nickname. This charm will bring you close to dying, bring your soul to the surface where I can snatch it, but your flesh will remain intact. Your heart will beat, your mind function even, although I know not how well. Still, Uncle should be mollified."

"Maybe your mind isn't functioning so well, because you cannot do this, Ilsa. Please."

"Ooh, I like you begging. Keep it up as I work."

I was stupid to turn my back on her; I should have known better. She was forever toying with dark magic, her jewelry and clothes stitched with charms and curses she could call upon at will. All I had was that weird glowing hand thing as Bell called it, and I was facing the wrong way to use it, even if I could summon it on demand.

I did have stubbornness. I gritted my teeth against the cold Ilsa had wedged into my spine and metaphorically wrapped my arms around my soul to clutch it to me. I could feel souls, even my own and the part of Ilsa inside me. I knew all Ilsa had left was a diminished spark, like a candle burned low and guttering out, trapped in that moment of faded light, and I felt sorry for her. I had stolen something I shouldn't have, but I had needed it to save all of us. I would give it back if I could. Although, I wasn't so repentant I'd let her steal mine if I could do anything about it.

I felt her efforts, like a dog gnawing at my boot heels. She seemed to be struggling in earnest, but nothing shifted. Her little death charm was not all she'd been promised. I often wondered where she got such things. Did she craft them from instructions in old books or purchase them from Solhan practitioners around Highcrowne? I had stayed determinedly away from those circles and paraphernalia because I did not want to be like her or Ulric. As soon as Ilsa realized she'd bought a dud spell, she might well try to shove a real dagger in my back, so I gritted my teeth harder and struggled to move.

I managed a step and then another.

Ilsa was gasping for breath behind me. "Stop. How…?"

The ice in my spine melted, and I pivoted around, knocking the charm she held to the ground. It was a black figurine of the Dead God, a forbidden symbol, on a bracelet of black beads. I kicked the robed and winged form across the metal grating and over the edge of the platform to fall somewhere far below us.

Ilsa's face was dotted with sweat, her chest heaving as though from physical exertion. She really had tried to yank the soul from my body and failed. I pulled the blade of my Ashur and held it between us.

"Stay away from me," I told her. "Board one of those balloons while you can. Find your way back to Highcrowne and Uncle's side; slip into the castle and screw the Elf King to your heart's content, but do not ever come near me again."

"Sugar…" she began sweetly.

"I mean it this time. The Solhan part of me that I don't like very much wants me to kill you right now. Try anything else, and I won't be able to stop it. I don't need baubles to rip out the last, pathetic scrap of your soul."

She glanced behind me, but I didn't dare take my eyes off her. "Very well. I'll go. For now."

It was a tactical retreat. I knew she intended to find some better charms before she sought me out again. I didn't want to kill her—actually, I wanted to very much—but I didn't want to give in to that desire. It would destroy me. Maybe that's how she'd win in the end, by forcing me to kill her.

Only when she had insinuated herself into the line for the next balloon, did I take a breath. It was a gasp, and I stood there gulping in air for a good long minute, my limbs shaking. Ilsa had come so close to ending me, but what disturbed me most was her determination. She was not even a little bit sorry.

I swear I caught a glimpse of iridescent skin and a tiny hand waving before the bogle vanished among the throng of fleeing passengers. Smart bogle.

I sensed someone standing behind me, and I snapped around, hoping to catch Duane sneaking up on me for once.

Gypsum was there. Not the werewolf, just ordinary Gypsum in her bridesmaid dress and a sheepish smile on her face.

"Now hear me out, Eva."

She knew me too well, because before she'd finished talking, I had my Ashur pointed at her eye.

"It's still me," Gypsum said.

"You were a werewolf all along and you never told me? You must have thought I was an idiot. I must have been to trust you. You, Duane ... you've all been lying to me."

"Duane's a werewolf?" she asked.

"No. He's an Elf King-loving traitor."

"I thought it would have been impossible, him being human, but I suppose he could have some dwarf in his lineage," she mused.

"What are you talking about? Only dwarves can be werewolves? I thought it was a curse or a bite or whatever Jorg's legends say?"

"That's a myth less frightening than the reality. It's magic of a kind, and a curse in a way," Gypsum said, "but it's not contagious. In fact, it's very hard to make new werewolves. Only certain dwarf lineages carry the trait, passed down to the descendants of the King's Guard.

"The Guard used to be much larger than it is now, all of them elite soldiers turned to wolves by the king and sent to fight the most brutal battles. This magic was their gift, their edge in war. How else does a four-foot-tall warrior defeat an army of ogres?

"Of course, once dwarves stopped fighting wars, the wolf lineages were more a danger than a help. Dwarves could sometimes turn in the heat of battle and be uncontrollable without a Dwarf King and his crown to command them. That's why children of those lines were given quiet jobs, like Reginald, or sent to the mountain borders to be unleashed against our enemies, like the current King's Guard. Until you pulled out that feather, I'd never turned into a werewolf in my entire life. I knew I was of one of the lineages, but I hadn't known I could turn."

"Okay," I said, my brain whirling. "That's a good story, but what else are you keeping from me? I know clients always lie, but this was a big one for you and Syla."

"It doesn't change the fact that there is a wolf or group of wolves responsible for the attacks in Highcrowne. All you know now is that your suspect needs to be a dwarf. I told you not to worry about Fharen. I tried to direct you to the best path without telling you. It is forbidden for the lineages to tell anyone, even other dwarves. The King's body is still key, and the motives you've surmised still apply: the suffragists want to derail the matriarchy by stealing the king, or someone wants to destabilize Highcrowne."

"I know it must be agents of the Dead God, else this ship wouldn't be headed to Solheim," I said. "So ... there are dwarf werewolves working for Him. Why?"

"The Dead God now rules Solheim. That should be reason enough. The ancient empire the dwarves once served was that of Solheim. It's Solheim's wars we once fought. King Rutgard and every Dwarf King before him once bent the knee to the Solhan Emperor."

"Nanny told me Solheim had a Council."

"Most recently it did, but I know my ancient history. There was an emperor and an empire for centuries before Solheim lost interest and let everything fall part. The Dead God is putting that empire back together."

That explained why He wanted Rutgard. "The Dwarf King's crown can control werewolves?"

"Yes. And create new lineages," Gypsum added. "At least, according to the ancient texts passed down to the matriarchy. Rutgard had it entombed with him so we could give up that past, give up war."

It was all becoming clear.

A werewolf army could take down Highcrowne from the inside and instill terror in the remaining unconquered nations. That's what the Dead God wanted. But He obviously didn't have control of them all now, only a few converts. I couldn't help thinking of Baroness Kiln, how her son and other suffragists had been praying to a statue of the Dead God. Bert, Reginald, even The Jerk had all been there. Any of them could be involved.

But Gypsum and a lot of other dwarves could turn into werewolves, without turning into bad guys. Seemed the wolf form was hungry for battle, but not intrinsically evil.

Okay. My knowledge of the world had taken a big shift to the left, but I could handle it. If not all gralls were dangerous, then not all potential werewolves were either.

I sheathed my sword. I wouldn't, couldn't trust her entirely again, but there was no reason to kill her.

"Thank you," she said.

"Don't thank me yet. Since you got me into this mess by recommending me to your sister, you're now going to help me get Rutgard's body off this ship. Where is Syla?"

"You found the body?" She hesitated. "I'm not sure where my sister is. I don't recall too clearly what happened when I was a wolf. I didn't hurt anyone did I?"

"Well, you're not covered in blood, so that's a good sign you stayed out of trouble. Unlike some. Where in all the hells did Duane go?" I headed back to the hatch to look for him. It popped open before I got there, and Karolyne stuck her head out.

"Eva. There you are." As though I was the one who had gotten lost. She spotted Gypsum behind me and her eyes widened. She started climbing back down.

"Wait," I told her. "It's alright. Gypsum explained everything, and not all werewolves are bad. It's only a thing that happens to some dwarf families. Rarely. It was the Avian feather that made them turn at the wedding."

Karolyne paused, thinking, and then climbed all the way up. "So, it's your fault my one and only wedding was ruined?"

"I wouldn't say ruined. The ceremony was finished; we missed out on the reception was all."

"And the speeches, and the dancing ... All the best parts!" Karo looked like she might manage what none of the wolves had and bite my head off.

"I'm sorry, but my priority was not your stupid wedding." I'd admitted it. It was a relief to have it out in the open.

"Hey!" Karolyne looked dangerous. "I was helping with the suffragist threat long before you came along. And doing a better job of it."

"Here's everyone," Duane said, making me jump. He was always sneaking up behind me. "Including the werewolf."

"Oh, it's not my fangs you need to worry about," Gypsum told him. "It's these two if we don't separate them soon, and the other wolves who don't know how to return to dwarf form, of course. You'd best get everyone on a balloon now."

"That was the plan." Duane gestured to the people climbing out the hatch behind him. I spotted Karolyne's parents, her mother, who was finally awake, and the tax collector. It looked like Missus Frost might faint again when she saw Gypsum, but Mister Frost got her on her feet.

"I'm not leaving until I have Rutgard," I reminded them. "The rest of you should get out of here now. Where's Bell?"

"Stupidly trying to bring the ship down like you asked, and I'm not leaving her, or you, behind," Duane said.

"I'm all grown up and don't need you to take care of me. So, go."

"Where's Wade?" Karolyne asked. "He is my husband, and I don't want anything bad to happen to him."

"He's one of the wolves running around confused, and you can't do anything for him right now. Eva and I will get everything sorted. Trust me." Gypsum had a convincing air of competence about her that I seemed to lack, because Karolyne didn't argue anymore. She took her mother's hand and led her parents to the ship.

"You too," I told the tax collector. "Get out while you can. What is your name anyway?"

"Liosh, my lady. Since we are to part company under uncertain circumstances, I think I can forgo the official channels for now and let you know you will be receiving written confirmation of my findings by courier—if you make it back to Highcrowne alive." I think there was almost a trace of humor in his otherwise humorless being.

I sighed. "How much do I owe?"

"You have it wrong, my lady. It is the Crowns who owe you for the erroneous tax payments made by your deceased brother. You see, I've been through all the precedents, and the high families of Solheim are exempt from taxes. Ancient law from the time of Empire, before the Kingdoms rebelled and built the Wall.

The laws were never expunged from the books, however, so they remain in force."

"I'm hearing a lot about the Solhan Empire today and it's all news to me."

"Crack a book once in a while," Gypsum interjected.

There might be obscure laws and annals hidden in the library of the Central City, where kings and tax collectors could read it, but there was nothing, absolutely nothing, anyplace else. I'd looked long and hard my whole life for more information on my birthplace than the tight-lipped survivors of Solheim's collapse would supply, and I'd inherited my brother's bookstore and touched every volume in there. It was not common knowledge, as much as Gypsum liked to pretend.

"Well, good day," the tax collector said, straightening his coat and heading for the nearest balloon.

"Thank you," I remembered to call after him. A refund. I guess all that running had been pointless. Stupid me.

I felt uncomfortable about all this special treatment for Solhans. Even King Fharen was enamored of us, or at least my sister. People were starting to worry. They wanted to be on the winning side of the Dead God's war. Not that I thought the god had any plan to treat exiled Solhans better than the rest of humanity, but maybe no one else but an exiled Solhan would know that.

A fight broke out around one of the escape balloons. There wasn't room for everyone, and orderly lines were quickly replaced by a frightened mob. Karolyne and the others hadn't yet made it through.

"Help them," I told Duane. "Knock a few heads if you have to but get Karolyne's family to safety."

"You have a bit of your uncle's commanding tone you know?" Duane said.

"Back to insults, are we?"

"I considered it a compliment."

"Why doesn't that surprise me?"

Duane winked and took off into the crowd. I had no idea how he'd do it, but he would get them aboard. He couldn't be trusted with anything of value, but he could be trusted with your life.

"Let's go," I told Gypsum. "You're a big, strong werewolf now, so you can help Conrad and I move the body."

"Where are we moving it to?"

"Another escape balloon. Or wherever Bell is. If she's crashing the ship, she'll make sure she's in the safest spot."

"Tell me again why we're crashing?" Gypsum asked, but she hiked up her skirts and followed even when I didn't answer.

I shoved elves out of my way, precipitating some rude looks. It was rough going against the current of people headed up the steps. The metal staircase was narrow and not much better than a ladder. It ran between the main hull and the balloon and was broken into sections, fitted together by hinges so the walkway could bend. The whole thing was enclosed by sheets of thin steel, with canvas joins that could flex in the wind.

I kept thinking about Gypsum's question. Crashing the ship would slow down the crazed werewolves running around and prevent Rutgard's body from reaching Solheim, but there was more.

I feared going to Solheim more than I feared anything. The place called to me in my dreams. The God of Death, all warmth and cinnamon smoke, whispered to me of sweet oblivion and beckoned. It was hard enough to resist in a dream, impossible if the dirigible carried me past the border and into the god's arms. It also wouldn't be good for everyone else left aboard— they would all be drafted into His army of the dead.

Yes, there were plenty of good reasons to risk smashing into a mountain. And it looked like we might. My ears popped, and I saw nearby peaks rising higher through a porthole we passed: we were losing altitude. Bell had succeeded in sabotaging the ship.

When Gypsum and I got past the crowds headed up, we emerged on a level I hadn't been to before, all utilitarian steel with bare walls and floors. We were in a service corridor above the grand ballroom. I could see crystal chandeliers through small glass panels set into the floor. It seemed a perfect place for the crew to laughingly watch the activities below—or for an enemy werewolf to watch the movements of his prey.

I grabbed the nearest speaking horn. "Bell?" I called. It was an intercom, and I heard my voice echo through the corridors. "Are you still in engineering? Where are you?"

After a moment, the horn in my hand crackled. Bell's voice said, "On my way up to the bridge."

"I know where it is. Follow me," Gypsum said. She must have studied the schematics when planning the wedding, because she didn't hesitate at any turn as she led the way.

We ran into Conrad going the other direction. Malcolm was with him, the red-haired dwarf limping and leaning against Conrad for support. Malcolm's shirt was torn by four parallel scratches, and he was bleeding, but not badly. It seemed his massive pectorals really were all muscle and not pumped up just for show.

"What happened to you?" Gypsum looked worried.

"Something damn stupid," Malcolm said. "I was caught unawares and nearly torn to bits. If I hadn't fallen down an open access shaft, I'd be dead instead of strikingly handsome."

"Where's Alum?" I asked.

"Busy," Conrad said. "King Rutgard and Doctor Ghunnan are safe. A wolf found us with the king's body, but he and Malcolm drove it off."

A wolf. Both Alum and Malcolm had to be were-wolves too. Gypsum had said all King's Guardsmen were, so that meant Verdis had been one, not that it had been enough to save him. Wolves fighting wolves. Why?

"Did you know about the werewolves?" I asked Conrad. He went quiet.

"Here, I'll take my nephew," Gypsum said, supporting Malcolm with ease. She was stronger than Conrad, and it was strange seeing this new side to my friend. What else had she hidden from me? What had Conrad?

"I know many things, Eva. And now that you know this, I don't want to lie to you anymore. I have no reason and no desire to. Ask me anything you want, and I will tell you." He took a breath and smiled at me as though he felt lighter, relieved.

"Get to the bridge!" Bell said, shooting past us.

"I wouldn't." Malcolm growled.

I felt a ghostly chill. Goosebumps like these along my neck and arms usually meant one thing: death.

"Where's your city guardsmen?" I asked Conrad.

"They were on the bridge."

'Were' didn't sound good. I reached out and touched Conrad's cheek. He seemed as surprised by the comforting gesture as I was. I didn't do comforting. He pressed his face against my hand, and I knew he had a world of worries on his shoulders he wanted nothing more than to lose for that moment. Then he shook off his languor and pulled my hand away, giving it a quick kiss to blunt the rejection. I understood. Sometimes you couldn't allow your burdens to drop for even a moment, else you'd never be able to pick them up again.

I followed Bell. She had stopped just outside the bridge, staring through the open door. I went inside and was surrounded by carnage.

I'd never been to an abattoir, but I imagined it looking something like the bridge did at that moment. Blood coated everything. Every inch of steel floor, every wall, the ceiling crisscrossed with pipes and cabling, every bolted down chair and table and mechanical instrument. There was more blood than one body could hold. Judging from the piles of them, I guessed a dozen. This was more than a murder—it was a war.

Bell vomited in the corridor. The stink of it added to the smell of offal and the sickly-sweet iron tang of blood.

I didn't need to look for clues, because a wolf had done this. Like Syla's bedchamber, claw marks were in the floors and walls. Wool from the stuffed leather chairs, now scratched to pieces, were scattered every-where and turning pink with spilled blood. Wood was shredded, brass dials grooved so deeply they might as well have been butter, and the crew and guardsmen were torn to pieces.

This is what had happened to all of Conrad's men. No wonder he seemed so desolate. I wished I could summon my usual ire. I was past stunned and moving quickly into the territory of shaken and terrified.

I spotted the helm. The brass wheel looked like it was taken straight from a sea vessel. I headed for it, noting the beautiful expanse of white cloud and blue sky barely visible through the red film of gore that coated the observation window.

I gripped the wheel with trembling hands and turned, not knowing which direction Highcrowne lay but certain I did not want to go east or into the mountain that was looming closer and closer.

I managed to spin the heavy wheel around a dozen times, but the horizon did not shift. It was broken, just as Bell had said, and there was no way to control where we landed. I ran out of the blood-soaked room to rejoin the others.

Bell looked as shaken and terrified as I felt. She grabbed the metal rungs of a crew ladder that led to a small access shaft and said, "Hold on to something, Eva!"

Malcolm copied her. Conrad grabbed hold of the banister of the nearest stairway, and I wrapped my arms around the railing next to him.

"She said hold on!" I told Gypsum, but she just stood there.

The room tilted thirty degrees, and an ear-piercing shriek of tearing metal joined in symphony with the groan and then crack of splintering wood. *Gypsum* tumbled down the stairs. Conrad and I slid down next, as the staircase and the entire floor collapsed into the grand ballroom.

The floor-to-ceiling windows in the ballroom showed we were at the snow line now. Escape balloons floated across the sky, gaining altitude as we lost it. Parachutes drifted like baby spiders on the wind.

I reached out to Gypsum. My old friend took my hand and then grabbed the railing with such force her fingers dug into the metal. Had she always been so strong, or had the transformation to werewolf changed her forever? What would keep her from changing next to me?

All I could see were mountains outside the huge windows, and it felt as though we had indeed hit one, but it didn't stop there. We slid, plummeting faster and faster as though the balloon holding us aloft had lost all power to sustain this monstrosity of opulence. In fact, I soon spotted the balloon portion of the dirigible drifting free of us. At least all those people vying for escape—and Duane and Karolyne if they had not made it aboard one of the other vessels—had been saved from the crash and were drifting away from the Solheim border. I hoped they made it down again safely. I hoped we did.

Whatever Bell had done to disable the ship must have ensured we hit as 'gently' as the world's largest dirigible could, but now the weight of *The Mathésis* gave us momentum. Our slide down the mountain was punctuated by sudden drops that put my stomach in my throat. I'd have been on the roof after each drop if it weren't for Gypsum. She held me with one hand, while the other wrapped the brass railing around her fist like a length of rope.

A black werewolf went skidding across the parquet floor, its claws scratching into the wood so deep splinters the size of my thumb went flying. It spotted us and came bounding our way, but another wolf wearing a top hat barreled into its side, the two of them rolling down the canted floor in a growling, yelping ball of fur and claws and fangs. They disappeared into a side corridor, the battle between them still undecided.

"Was the one in the hat the one who blew up the Market District?" I asked Gypsum.

She grunted when the ship dropped again, and when she could speak, she said, "Being a werewolf is new to me, and I'm not sure how to tell us apart, let alone tell you which one committed which crime."

I supposed being a member of a secret group of frightening creatures didn't give you special knowledge; I should know, as no one ever told me Thorne secrets. I had to learn everything from outsiders.

"Can we get off this thing yet?" I asked no one in particular. There were more jarring bumps that answered my question.

"You'll know when we hit—" Gypsum began, but she was cut off when the room righted itself and the ship found level ground.

The windows smashed, the sound adding to the grinding, moaning concert of the dying ship. The force of impact sent us flying up to the chandeliers, the brass railing Gypsum had hold of torn free and soaring with us.

Time seemed to stand still for a moment, and I saw Conrad. His expression was calm, accepting, and he smiled at me. I swear I could see a winged shadow looming over him. It was coming for me, for all of us.

What goes up must come down, and we came down onto the glass and splintered wood of the wrecked ballroom.

16 Logic and Reason

It felt like I'd fallen into a barrel of tacks. Tiny shards of glass stuck to my dress and hair and dug into the skin of my hands and arms. At least I'd avoided impalement on one of the ragged floorboards that were sticking up all around. Support pillars from the lower levels had pushed through the ballroom floor.

Conrad lay next to me. I touched his back, hesitating. He breathed deeply, and relief flooded over me. He climbed to his hands and knees, groaning.

"You're alive," I said.

"It appears so. A kiss would tell me for certain."

I didn't need to be asked twice. His cold lips quickly warmed against mine. The heat threatened to rise between us like it had on the stairwell, and we both pulled back.

I looked around and saw Gypsum had not landed as well as we had. She was bleeding from a wound in her side where a floorboard penetrated all the way through.

"Gypsum!" I reached out.

"Stand ... back," she said between pained gasps.

Ulric had healed Little Viktor. "Let me try something," I said, summoning the green glow, which made the blood on my palms look black.

She waved me away again, and her next gasp turned into a growl. I took a step back. Several steps, as much as the broken floor would allow me.

Her outline turned a translucent white first and then the rest of her followed. She was a wolf-shaped mist when she came toward me. The wolf shape started to solidify, the wound closing in the process, sealed up by mist that turned to flesh and fur. Glowing yellow eyes regarded me mercilessly, a mouth of fangs turned up into a sly smile.

Where was the dining silver when you needed it?

Then the wolf vanished into mist again, reshaping itself into my friend. Gypsum's red dress was torn where the wound had been, but no other sign of the injury remained.

"Most magic won't work on my kind, but we have other advantages," she explained.

"I wish I could do that," I said, pulling a pebble of glass from my forearm. The feeling of pain and pressure was replaced by a sharper sting as air hit the open wound. Only a few dozen more to go. "What happens to your clothes when you change?" I asked.

"They vanish into the mist along with the rest of my dwarf form and the wolf is pulled out in its place, plus whatever the wolf had hold of. Syla told me when she first changed into a werewolf, she'd donned a necklace and then lost it when she returned to her normal form, only to recover it recently. She thought she had misplaced it years ago."

"Wardrobe storage and fast healing? Sounds useful," I said.

"You would not like being a wolf." A bit of its growl remained in her voice. "You looked like easy prey to me. I could smell your blood, and it smelled good. It was an effort to change back again. Real effort."

"Okay," I said cautiously. "You go first, and we'll stay behind you. Downwind."

Conrad was on his feet now, Bell and Malcolm clambering down the debris to join us.

"Go where? The place is a wreck," Bell noted.

With the windows broken, we now had wide open doorways. I indicated them, shivering as an icy wind blew snow across our feet. It was nearly summer, but winter never lost its grip at this altitude.

"The cloakroom," I said, moving to the opposite end of the ballroom and digging through the piles of useless wraps and parasols until I found some fur coats. I put the thickest fur on, still not thick as I'd like, and handed the rest to the others. "Outside, now."

Gypsum raised an eyebrow. I didn't usually go around barking orders at my friend, but this dangerous chaos was my job, and werewolf Gypsum was now one of the most dangerous elements in it. I wanted her and Malcolm walking in front, where I could watch them. She clambered out a broken window and then helped her nephew through. I followed, Bell and Conrad behind me, pausing to pick a few more fragments of glass out of my arms. At least I'd instinctively shielded my face the whole time the ship was smashing around us.

The dirigible had been five stories tall, and now it was two, the levels collapsed into one another. We'd been fortunate to be on the top, for nothing could have survived on the lower decks. We descended where some of the broken boards had bowed out to form steps, or at least platforms we could jump between as we made our way down. I touched the snowy ground thankfully when I reached it.

Airships were an abomination I'd decided. They were not pretty: they were yet another way to kill you.

The balloon portion had floated harmlessly away, and Bell had shut down all the mechanical gizmos in engineering, so there were no explosions or fires. And now that the ship had settled in a depression between mountain peaks, even the groan of twisted wood and metal faded into a hollow whisper of wind through its cracked skeleton. *The Mathésis* died an eerily quiet and frozen death.

"Doctor Ghunnan?" I shouted. "Student? I mean, Katherine? Bert? Reginald? Syla?"

My voice froze in my throat. This was not what I'd envisioned when I asked Bell to bring the ship down. I had pictured a pinhole that let the air out like a child's inflatable toy slowly dying after a birthday party. This may have killed people, and I'd never wanted that. It may have killed everyone whose name I called.

The crash site was silent, the scattered wreckage interrupted by crags of rock with snow and ice piled in the crevices. The tree line was below us, the distance bridged by more fragments of the broken ship scattered like flotsam.

"I hear someone," Gypsum said.

I couldn't hear a thing through the wind in my ears.

She went around the side of the main wreckage, and I followed. The goblin and his student were both sitting on Rutgard's body like a park bench, an umbrella standing on legs of its own beside them to keep away the icy flakes of snow that had begun falling.

"My, what big ears you have," I told Gypsum, glad she'd found survivors.

"Have you seen any others?" I asked without even a 'good to see you'.

The goblin noticed Conrad and Bell who'd come up beside me. He said, "Miss Bell, you gave us dreadfully little warning over the speaker before you tried to kill us. My carry rig was destroyed, by the way. Sir Alum is trying to find something to aid me."

He gestured at a lump of wreckage, and I finally made out the King's Guardsman sifting through it. He had looked like a part of the strange outlines of the downed craft.

The crash site made an alien landscape all around, filled with once familiar objects that were now out of place, like chandeliers underneath beds, much of it twisted beyond recognition. Alum had a large canvas sack thrown over one shoulder that looked like a body bag. Not a good sign.

"I am glad to see you and King Rutgard are unharmed," Gypsum said.

"I am glad to see it as well," the goblin replied pithily. "Although it be through a crack in my glasses." He held up the broken spectacles to me with an accusing look, and I knew he blamed the whole uncomfortable circumstance on me. It was my fault, but I wasn't about to admit it.

"Yes, so glad you and Katherine are alright," I said, distracted, and went to Alum.

"Who is in there?" I asked, hoping horribly that it was not someone I knew.

"It's treasure left behind by the Elf King and his retinue, and it's mine, so hands off," Alum said.

"Fine. Crashing and nearly dying sure makes you touchy. Have you seen any other survivors?" I asked.

I answered my own question when I spotted a band of dwarves around the wrecked propeller. I was certain I'd seen a few of them at the wedding—as wolves. They must have found their self-control and turned back. For now.

I pulled Bell aside. "Gypsum is...."

"No longer a werewolf. Yeah, I spotted that. I ran across a few of the poor sods who turned from wolf to meek dwarf again once the engines failed and the ship, the poor ship, started to plummet. They were awful confused. You did a number on them with that spell of yours."

"I did not spell them. I only revealed they were wolves. Weren't you paying attention? The thing is, they—and we've more of them with us now—could turn back at any time, so hold on to that knife I gave you."

"Tis right here." She pulled it out of a makeshift sheath. "Even Gypsum?"

"Even her. I'm sure not all werewolves are working for the Dead God, but a real wolf isn't inherently evil when it eats your intestines either. Animal nature is what I'm worried about."

"Gotcha. I'll go stand by the goblin." She went to him and the med student. I wondered if that was wise, as goblins too were known to eat people when the opportunity arose.

Alum had constructed a travois from broken floor-boards, with which to carry Rutgard's body and the sack of loot he'd taken from the wreckage. He helped the goblin climb atop everything with his little motorized umbrella that shifted to shield his head from the snowfall. Alum was certainly a werewolf as well; else he would not be strong enough to carry everything he was piling on the stretcher.

I heard a howl more chilling than the wind. Not all werewolves had returned to a harmless form it seemed. There was still the wolf in the top hat somewhere, the one who had killed so many in Highcrowne. I doubted it had died in the crash.

"Let's..." I began, about to line everyone up and head as roughly west as we could, when a more commanding voice overrode mine.

"This way. Let's get moving now, before they come for us." It was Conrad. "We have to go," he told me more gently, real urgency in his voice.

I didn't argue, as that had been my plan too.

Conrad went ahead of the travois born by Alum, followed by Bell and Katherine, while I rounded up the five dwarf survivors I didn't know and hurried them along, Gypsum and Malcolm taking up the rear. We headed into the tree line.

"You must be on Wade's side of the family?" I asked the dwarves I was shepherding, trying to blunt the rudeness of having revealed their werewolf nature in front of the entire wedding party.

"Yes. We're his second, third or fourth cousins," one said. "Hope he's alright."

"I'm sure he is." I wasn't certain, but Wade was one of the wolves, and they tended to be hardy. Look how easily Gypsum had healed herself.

When we were on the move, I noted the direction of the lowering sun and went to Conrad at the front of the procession.

"We're still headed east. We need to turn west now."

"It would mean walking the entire mountain range back to Highcrowne," he argued. "There's a station this way, the last supply stop before the wall. We can get on a train and far away from the werewolves hunting us."

"You think they're hunting us?"

"I know they are. They slaughtered my men on the bridge."

"Good point."

I hurried my steps to keep up with Conrad. I used to complain about the treacherously uneven cobbles in Highcrowne, but it was even more treacherous walking without a path. Loose stones, patches of rock slicked with ice, drifts of snow not plowed aside by goblins each morning ... it took all my concentration to reach the tree line, where at least I could grab branches for support. Of course, the tree trunks were often gooey with sap, and I swear some sort of ice bug bit me when

I grabbed hold of a low-lying branch. I yipped and tripped in ankle deep snow.

Conrad glanced back but saw I wasn't hurt and kept clearing the path ahead for Alum, who was carrying the king's body and the goblin a lot faster than I could walk. The med student seemed to be enjoying herself, unburdened for once, and smelling the crisp air.

I was on my knees when Gypsum came back to me. "Don't get out of the city much?" she said.

"I never get out of the city. For good reason." I tried to wipe some of the sap and pine needles off my hands using snow, but all I did was freeze my fingers.

"Don't stay still too long," she warned. "Ice vipers are drawn out of their burrows by any trace of heat. Rest on solid rock only."

I jumped up as fast as I could, grabbing Gypsum for balance. Despite my limited experience with it, I hated the outdoors already.

"Gypsum," I began, "Conrad says werewolves are hunting us, but from what I've seen we'd be dead already if they were. Sure, I heard the howls, but maybe it's other survivors, dwarves surprised to be a wolf, like you, but unable to turn back? Maybe you could help them?"

"No. The only wolves on our side are right here," she said with certainty.

"What about Syla? Bert? Even Wade? What's happened to them all?"

"My sister told me how to change back to dwarf form. She already knew how, because she's changed before. She's not on our side," Gypsum said, speaking slowly so I'd understand.

"You think she was the one behind the attacks in Highcrowne all along? Why? I know she has no love for suffragists, but why would she attack her own people? Or work for the Dead God?"

My mind reeled. Syla? She didn't trust other matriarchs, she'd told me. Was that because she was jockeying for power? That could explain it. But not Bert and Reginald. How could they be part of this?

"What else do you know?" I demanded. "Why did another werewolf attack Syla at the wedding? And why would she kill the guardsmen on the bridge? Why hasn't she attacked us?"

"Because she's still my sister, that's why. I suspect she's gathering her forces right now, following from a distance, judging how best to strike—without killing me. Family bonds count for something. I'm sure she doesn't care if any of the rest of you die, though. All she wants is the King's body and to rise to power in Highcrowne."

"Then who stole the body to begin with? None of this makes any sense."

"I don't have all the answers. That's why you're here, isn't it?" She smiled, but I didn't think it was funny.

This case had become more complicated than I ever imagined, and along the way had made me doubt everyone I thought I knew.

Even Conrad was different from the naïve but well-meaning man I'd known. The new Conrad was far more interesting, and in his element. He looked like he was leading an army to battle rather than an amber coffin on a makeshift stretcher alongside a handful of crash survivors. He could take on both the mountain and the werewolves and win. I was a bit jealous that his attention wasn't on me at the moment, but I could understand his focus. We had a single silver dagger and a bunch of new werewolves as unpredictable as ice vipers. We had to run.

I let Gypsum herd Wade's cousins, while I joined Bell alongside the med student and the goblin. They were engaged in whispered conversation.

"What are you planning?" I asked when I caught up.

"Why do you think we're planning anything?" Bell asked innocently.

"You're always planning something."

"True, but your doctor friend here is not very helpful."

"How am I supposed to conjecture on tactics to defeat werewolves when they do not even exist?" the goblin said.

"Consider it a hypothetical," Bell said. "If there were such things as creatures that could turn to mist and switch between innocent little dwarf and terrifying battle beast at will? And it didn't like boson's whistles or silver much?"

"And it can heal completely when in mist form," I added, "not to mention travel that way faster than a person can run. In fact, the werewolf form moves so fast it's a blur."

"A hypothetical you say?" The goblin smirked, but said, "Very well. I will take you up on this little game to while away the travelling hours. Student, recite to me the properties of matter."

"Matter is composed of tiny bits of homogenous particles too small for the eye to see, which then are assembled into a set number of elements, which in turn assemble the infinite variety of chemical, mineral and other structures, as one assembles a house of bricks, on up until one builds heart, lungs ... an entire being. The ultimate of material complexity." It sounded like she'd memorized some textbook.

"And the laws of state change as it relates to matter?" he prompted.

"Matter can be a solid, liquid or gas depending on how much the particle components are compressed together. To change states between solid and liquid, for example, requires input of energy, typically heat, to allow the particles to move farther apart."

"There you have it," the goblin said. "To defeat your mist creatures, all we must do is prevent their transition between solid and gaseous states by preventing the required influx of energy. By freezing them."

"That's ridiculous," I began then stopped. "Would you call magic an energy, like heat? Hypothetically?"

"Hypothetically." It looked like the goblin's patience was being severely tried by the term 'magic'.

Perhaps there was a way to block the magic of the werewolves' transition? Or even compel it backwards?

I wished I had Ilsa's knowledge of charms. Then again, if the goblin's reasoning was sound, and he was pretty convincing, then some sort of ice magic might work? Of course, I had no idea how to do that either.

"I could build a box to freeze whatever's trapped inside it," Bell mused. "An ice trap. I'd need materials, though. Too many things we dunno got. Plus, it might only capture one wolf. Maybe."

"Back to the drawing board." I was feeling less clever and less hopeful with each passing moment.

Another howl carried down the mountain and sent shivers down my spine, not the pleasant kind of shivers I got with Conrad but the afraid-for-my-life kind. I began to feel like a fluffy, useless snow rabbit, one without even a burrow to hide in. I felt like prey. I didn't like that feeling.

"What are you doing?" Malcolm said, pulling the goblin's hand away from where it had been digging into the amber resin that encased King Rutgard. The over-muscled guardsman ripped the tool out of the doctor's grip and tossed it into a snow drift.

"How rude..." the doctor began.

"Keep your hands off the King or I'll toss you away too," the red-haired dwarf promised.

Malcolm hadn't flirted with me or the student once since the crash, so I suspected he was feeling a bit like prey as well, and a bit on edge to treat the goblin doctor so roughly.

"Am I to sit here uselessly when there is still so much to learn about the body?" the goblin argued. "How was it preserved? Why does it influence silver particles so strongly? Why—"

"—Why don't you be quiet?" Alum interjected. He looked to have as little patience for the goblin as Malcolm did.

"You're talking to two King's Guardsmen," I warned the doctor. "Their job is to protect the King, and you're never going to persuade them to let you desecrate him to satisfy your curiosity."

"There is more at stake than my curiosity. You know that."

I remembered his explanation of 'plague' research, but it never made sense to me that a learned doctor would trouble himself with something so far beyond his experience as the King of the Dwarves. Then again, perhaps the human plague was of more immediate concern to the goblins than to anyone, as they were on the border between the Three Kingdoms and the lands conquered by the Dead God. If not for the dense swamplands they dwelled in, they would have been overrun long ago.

The goblin swamps to the south, the wall to the east, the sea to the west, and Avian magic, were what I once assumed kept Highcrowne safe—until I learned of the Compact. Human sacrifice to appease the god had worked for most of my lifetime. Now things were changing. King Fharen was restless for war, centuries of stability in Highcrowne were threatened by suffragists and werewolf militants, and the Dead God was laughing at us all.

The pull I felt toward Solheim was always strong whenever I left the city, but this far to the east it was stronger than ever. I didn't like that we would have to go even closer before we reached the locomotive line and could turn back. If we made it that far.

Howls echoed on all sides of us now, and I caught glimpses of black forms racing through the trees. It felt like they were playing with us, running circles around us, when they could easily dart in and rip us to shreds. If Syla was their leader, we were lucky she cared for Gypsum more than I cared for my sister, or she for me.

"How can you not believe werewolves are hunting us now?" I asked the goblin. "See that there?" I pointed, but the shape was gone already.

"I see nothing." He was cleaning his spectacles, which explained that. "And I hear nothing but timber wolves. A worry for sure, but if these King's Guardsmen here are as willing to protect the rest of us as they are this ancient corpse, then we should have naught to be concerned about."

"Should we stop and make a fire?" Katherine asked.

"A superb idea," the goblin said. "Fire should frighten these creatures away."

"No," Alum ordered. "We keep moving."

I agreed with that tactic. Stopping might give Syla's wolf brain time to decide she didn't like her sister that much after all.

Despite the icy snow that crept down my boots, I was warm from exertion. We'd been headed downhill for an hour, and it took effort to maneuver over and around obstacles along the way. We were in thick forest, and at this rate it would take most of the remaining daylight to reach the valley. I didn't know if Alum could keep pace with his cargo for that long, but I knew I wouldn't last. Maybe I could hop atop the body for a time and be carried like the goblin?

It had gone quiet, and I hoped the wolves had tired too.

Never hope for the best.

In the silence, the sudden '*oompf* was loud. It was the sound of the wind being knocked out of someone.

Wade's relatives looked around dazed. There were wolf tracks in the snow near them.

"It took Sten!" one of them shouted, suddenly realizing what had happened.

And then there were seven dwarves.

17 FOR LOVE OF EMPIRE

Seven dwarves. Not counting the preserved king.

Plus, three humans and a goblin. That's all we had left.

I don't know why I chose that moment to do mathematics, but the mind does strange things when it's panicking.

"Why?" I asked, dumbly. At least I was out of the math loop.

I got a look from the dwarf who'd spoken that seemed to indicate I was being very rude and idiotic at the same time. "How should I know?" he said.

"I mean, the wolf butchered everyone on the ship's bridge. Why take Sten alive?" Even before the words were out of my mouth, the dark blurs of a pack of wolves passed by my vision like some sort of mirage.

Four more dwarves were gone. All of Wade's relatives. And now I was at the back of the line. The mathematical odds did not look good.

"Oh shit!" I shouted, back pedaling toward Gypsum and the stretcher so fast I stumbled and landed on my ass. Another blur passed overhead, and I knew my stumbling had saved me.

Alum dropped the stretcher, causing the goblin and his umbrella to tumble headfirst into the snow.

Before I could take a breath, both guardsmen and Gypsum had turned to white mist and then into naked werewolves. I thought losing all armor and weapons in the transformation seemed to be a drawback, until they unsheathed their claws. Each one was longer than the dagger I'd given Bell, which she'd pulled out and was now holding over me protectively. Conrad did not even bother to draw his sword. It wasn't silver and would be as useless as my Ashur.

When the next series of dark blurs attacked, Gypsum and the two King's Guardsmen were ready. They did not hold back, and blood sprayed across the white snow, forming melted, steaming canyons of red.

They'd killed two werewolves, who seemed to stop moving instantly and transformed in the process, dropping to the ground with a thud. The dead werewolves were both dwarves I recognized from the wedding, but I was relieved not to see Bert's or Reginald's faces.

Howls carried through the trees around us again. Sad, mournful howls that made my chest ache. Gypsum, Alum and Malcolm replied with howls of their own, short and sharp sounds that were defiant and challenging.

When the chill air quieted, Gypsum and the others turned back into their everyday forms, and I noted the defiant expression on Gypsum's face. "That should make them think twice," she said.

Bell helped me to my feet. I was shaking but not from the cold ground. "We lost five people in a heart-beat," I said. "And they lost two. Those are not good odds."

"Agreed," Bell said.

"What did I miss?" the goblin doctor asked, as he felt in the snow for his spectacles. His umbrella had righted itself and was following him around on tiny metal legs as he searched on his hands and knees.

The student found the spectacles first and gave them a wipe before she handed them to him, saying, "You missed werewolves."

He snorted and then gave her the most disappointed look when he saw she wasn't joking.

"It could have been a mass hallucination?" she added timidly.

"Keep moving," Conrad said in a way that broached no defiance.

Alum and Malcolm obeyed, both taking up the stretcher and moving forward faster than Alum had managed alone. The student scrambled to carry the goblin in her arms, and I hurried beside Bell through the churned up and bloody snow.

Gypsum assumed a defensive position at the rear, watching the trees. She had adapted well to life as a werewolf. She sniffed the air, as though searching for a scent. Had she really never turned before?

Only when we were well past the bloody scene of the attack did anyone speak again.

"Sorry Doctor," the student told the goblin, "but I'd like to have my arms free." She set him and his umbrella back atop King Rutgard's amber-encased form. The two King's guardsmen didn't seem to notice the extra weight.

Bell mumbled to herself and felt her pockets, taking stock of the resources she'd brought in her overalls. I knew she wanted to create some gadget that would fend off the werewolves when next they attacked—and we all knew they would attack again—but the silver dagger she held and the other wolves around us were the only reliable defense.

I knew it wasn't good enough.

I took a breath and doubled my pace, so I could catch up to Conrad at the front of the procession.

"You're calm," I noted. Even the werewolves among our group were on edge, watching the surroundings as they walked. "We lost five people."

"They weren't important."

I'd never seen Conrad not agonize over what he could have done better to carry out his duties for Highcrowne.

"I expected you to be a little bit more broken up about it," I said.

"I need to get you and the King onto a train and away from here, and that is all I'm thinking about right now. For once in my existence, I'm powerless to act in any way other than to keep us moving, so let's keep moving."

He swept me up in his arms and started carrying me. I might have been lagging a bit, but I felt stupid being cradled like an infant.

"Set me down!"

"No."

I struggled, but not too much. It really was a relief on my sore and freezing feet to be off them for a moment.

"You know, with me in your arms, you're completely defenseless," I argued.

"I am defenseless against you."

"I meant against the werewolves."

"They can kill me. They can kill all of us, but if I'm holding you, what better way is there to die?"

I could tell, even without his armor, the extra weight of me in his arms was tiring him.

"Okay, Mister Romance, I love the sentiment, but realistically you need to set me down. I can walk, and

I'd prefer there be no dying in anyone's arms. We may lack silver, but I have other weapons."

I showed him my hand, where a gem of green light was glowing in the center of the palm. It was like a tiny sun hovering a hairsbreadth above my skin, and it was itching like it was restless to do something.

"Do you know anything about your power?" he asked, and his tone wasn't accusing, more genuinely sad for me.

"No. But now is a perfect time to start learning. I may not be able to freeze a werewolf like Doctor Ghunnan suggests or stop the 'energy of transformation', but I feel souls, and werewolves have them. I'm wondering if there's a way to calm the soul within and shift the creature back into dwarf form. Gypsum mentioned the transformation is sometimes triggered in battle, which is why the Matriarchy has tried so hard to give affected males boring jobs or, alternatively, toss them onto the front lines far from civilization. Maybe I can drain the fight out of them."

"You can drain the very life from them," he said. "I know what happened with Erick."

"I don't...." I didn't want to think about Erick, the man who I had briefly loved, or at least lusted after, and who had betrayed me. The man I had killed. I couldn't forget him, but it wasn't like Conrad suggested. My knife had killed him; I only used necromancy to finish the job.

"It's not about what we want but what we need, Eva. You hesitate to kill, but death is your gift. No one should deny their gift." He set me down. "Practice on Gypsum."

"What? No! I won't practice killing on my best friend, or anyone for that matter."

"I meant practice calming her soul as you propose. Better now than when the other wolves come back," Conrad said.

"How about I practice on Malcolm?"

"Hey," Malcolm said. "I thought you liked me, or at least my body. I think it was my ass you said."

"I do like you. Not just your ass. Nothing personal, but...."

"Nothing personal," Conrad said, "but Malcolm and Alum are needed to carry the King. I'm not strong enough and neither is anyone else. Gypsum is the best candidate."

"No," I repeated.

"I'll do it," she said. "Tell me what you need."

"I don't know what I need." I'd only been thinking out loud about using my magic. Trying something right here and now on a real person was terrifying. I should keep my mouth shut when I'm thinking.

"I have a suggestion," Katherine said. "If magic and werewolves exist..." she was trying hard not to look at the goblin's dismayed expression over her betrayal of their stance against superstition "...and if it is akin to energy, whose properties we somewhat understand, I suggest you experiment scientifically. Practice on a control, a normal, like me, and then practice on Gypsum in her wolf form. You should be able to learn the differences in how the two 'souls', or as I would say 'energy states', behave and thus how best and most quickly to subdue the wolf form."

"Great idea," Bell said. "If it wasn't all about conjuring up a bunch of evil necromancy stuff that serves as a powerful bad temptation for Eva to start behavin' like certain other evil necromancers she's related to."

"I'm not like Ilsa," I said.

But the itch in my palm had become an itch in my mind, an overwhelming desire to play with the power I'd been denying for so long. It was like suppressing it had made the desire stronger, and now that the wolves had been a hairsbreadth away from killing me, my survival instinct had overridden the last arguments for suppressing it. Not that I planned to let go entirely. That way lay too much temptation, as Bell said, but a little bit couldn't hurt. Could it?

"Maybe Ilsa wasn't like Ilsa until she started playing with the dark," Bell said.

"Oh, enough naysaying and scientific reasoning. Here." Gypsum put my hand on her chest. "Give it a go. I'll try to turn wolf and you stop me."

"Wait..." I said, not even sure where to start, but Gypsum was already mist. She held that form while I thought about what to do.

Seeing souls was a bit like relaxing your eyes in the bathtub, becoming aware of the temperature and wetness on your skin, being aware of your own breath and your own heartbeat, your own soul. Once I could sense myself, it was easy enough to feel my 'control', Katherine, nearby, even Bell. Alum and Malcolm seemed no different from the humans, although I knew they were wolves. Conrad ... there was something different about Conrad, like he was so much brighter than all the others, more beautiful, vastly alluring. But I wasn't looking directly at him, was only aware of him in the periphery of my vision. He was a powerful distraction, so I made myself focus on Gypsum before me who, in her mist form, felt distinctly different from the other two dwarves.

Her soul felt a bit brighter as well, almost as though it were exposed and without flesh to hide inside. I sensed her in-between nature: part civilized mother of a dozen children and part animal. The animal part was hungry, not for meat or food, but for release, to run free and satiate every whim and desire. It was not at all like the souls of the skittish animals who hid in burrows in the winter soil below my feet or in the boles and branches of nearby trees. This was a beast without fetters or chains, without morality and without consequence.

Gypsum turned wolf before I could do anything about it, and that impression of her beastly soul was all the stronger. I felt her desire to shred my body with her claws, and I took a step backward. Bell and Katherine stepped even farther back.

I heard the goblin's jaw gape open so much there was a wet sound of saliva being sucked in. He had a massive mouth full of needle teeth like every goblin I'd seen before, but even those vicious things looked tame in comparison to the werewolf's gleaming fangs and claws like short swords. Gypsum's brown pelt was shiny and sleek. Her chest and arm muscles rippled with each deep breath she took. She sniffed the air, as though enjoying the scent of freshly baked bread. Only, I was the bread.

"I do not believe what I am seeing," the goblin said, wiping his spectacles, putting them back on, squinting, and then wiping them again. "It is not possible."

"Belfore's Theorem states that, when choosing among multiple hypotheses, the one requiring the fewest assumptions should be selected," Katherine pointed out.

"Then it is a hallucination," the goblin said.

"I was going to say I'd tend to believe my eyes," Katherine argued.

"You'd be wrong, my dear. The existence of werewolves and mist forms would require the existence of magic, which requires far too many assumptions and suspension of all scientific principles. Therefore, we must all be experiencing a mass hallucination brought on by the stress of the crash and psychological suggestion backed up by the nearby timber wolves who have been howling. Alternatively, I am unconscious at the crash site dreaming all of this. Yes, that sounds more probable. I will try to wake up now." Doctor Ghunnan shut his eyes as though that would help.

Gypsum and the rest of us didn't vanish. In fact, the werewolf took another step toward me, and my heart rate shot up. I was having difficulty staying calm enough to feel her soul, let alone calm enough to transform the beast.

"Again," Conrad commanded.

His voice seemed to work better than my magic, because Gypsum quickly dropped the wolf form and became Gypsum. There were a few beads of perspiration on her skin as she fought for self-control. The dark glint in her eye finally subsided, and she said, "Alright."

She became mist again, and I tried to pretend I was relaxing in the bath, but it wasn't working as well as the first time. The werewolf form had triggered an instinct to run. Don't pull my Ashur or taunt the creature like I did with most bad guys, simply run.

"I can't..." I began, before I was distracted by a strange snowfall.

Instead of delicate white flakes, about a dozen rope ladders dropped all around us. I looked up and saw a small dirigible drifting above the treetops. A swarm of goblins in midnight blue uniforms—rather than the mercenary leathers I was used to seeing around

Highcrowne—slid down. We were soon surrounded by an army of goblins, all aiming crossbows at our heads.

"No one move!" a soldier ordered.

Conrad and the King's Guard remained still; even Gypsum kept to her mist form.

A female goblin—who I could only tell was female because of the thick set of necklaces she wore and the fact she was in a dress instead of a uniform—made her way through the ranks to Doctor Ghunnan. The device she held in her hand squealed loudly when it came near the umbrella that had been with us since the crash, and she felt along the umbrella's handle until she found a switch. Once she flipped it, the electronic squeal stopped.

"Professor," she said. "Open your eyes, please. We tracked your signal. We're here to recue you. You have the body I see. Thank the Emperor."

"Miss Kissel?" Doctor Ghunnan said, finally becoming cognizant of his surroundings. "Miss Kissel! Thank the Emperor indeed for your arrival. We must secure the Dwarf King immediately."

"Doctor?" Katherine asked, shocked. "What are you doing?"

I felt sorry for the student; it did sting to be betrayed. I turned my glare back on, and it made me feel better. "You traitorous little bastard. I knew you couldn't be trusted."

"Then I am hardly a traitor," he said. "In fact, I am most loyal to my Emperor and to the Goblin Empire."

"Empire?" Bell snorted. "Ixia is a bunch of swamp hovels with a seaside trading fort on stilts. I've been there lookin' for parts and was never impressed."

"We like to keep outsiders unimpressed and incurious about what we're really up to," Ghunnan said.

"Quiet, Professor," Miss Kissel ordered. "Say too much and we'll have to kill all your friends here. We may have to regardless."

Now I was getting mad. I preferred that feeling. Instead of calming Gypsum's soul, I gave it a nudge to the beast form.

What must have appeared to the newly arrived goblins as a patch of fog was suddenly a slavering, hairy beast with claws the length of my forearm. Good thing there weren't any mirrors around, else Gypsum would be most embarrassed by her appearance with new guests to entertain. The wolf became a blur, knocking aside a rank of crossbow-wielding soldiers.

I slammed into Bell, making her take cover in the snow. There was a discordant *twang-flick-tung* sound, and a rush of air over our heads as a dozen crossbows fired at once. Gypsum howled piteously, and I looked up to see two bolts had hit her, one in her arm and one in her side, the flesh smoking and sizzling as though it were being burnt. They were using silver.

"Leave her alone," I said, climbing to my feet and rushing forward.

"Watch out," Conrad warned, and I was glad I listened, because an angry swipe of Gypsum's claws barely missed me.

"She needs help," I said, giving Miss Kissel an imploring look.

The doctor had closed his eyes again, trying to ignore the creature right in front of him.

"We can put her out of her misery," Miss Kissel offered.

"What do you hope to gain by taking the King's body?" Conrad asked calmly, ignoring the life and death situation before him as much as the doctor was ignoring evidence of magic. "Do you think you can sell it back to the Matriarchy? Or to the suffragists?"

"Syla and the Matriarchy won't be too pleased if you kill her sister," I pointed out, trying every argument I could think of to save my friend. "Leave Gypsum be."

"This is not about gold. We're not common thieves to be ransoming our hard-won trophy back to anyone," Miss Kissel snorted.

"This is about Crowns, and this one is not yours," Alum said, his lip curling into a snarl. I thought he looked a bit transparent, and I wondered if he was planning to transform. It hadn't done Gypsum much good.

"This operation could have been done simply, but I was most annoyed when the terrorist I armed as a distraction instead stole the King's body from the palace beneath my very nose," Miss Kissel said, scowling at the guardsman. "It complicated things. I kept my distance, let the good doctor work, and it has all turned out for the best. Of course, you will not live to see how this ends. Rest assured, we will use the Crown to best advantage of the Empire."

"Is angering the Dead God to your advantage?" Conrad's words had an ominous edge to them.

"You are making a big mistake, little goblins," Malcolm interjected. "The Dead God wants this body, and once you've carted it off to your swamp, he'll redirect His hordes, all of them, towards you. Why don't you run along and play soldier somewhere else? Leave this with us, else you might get hurt."

"We may yet broker a deal with the god," Miss Kissel said, "but that is for our Emperor to decide. I have my orders, which include determining the most logical actions to aid the completion of my mission. My apologies, but that means we must kill you all." She took Doctor Ghunnan aside so they'd both be out of the line of fire.

"My student," the doctor hesitated, looking at Katherine who was in the center of the killing field with the rest of us.

"You'll find another," Miss Kissel said. She raised her hand to give the signal.

I should have been paying attention when someone was about to order my execution, but there were distractions.

A cyclone of werewolves appeared all around us, growling and attacking the goblins from behind. The outer ranks were forced to turn and shoot to protect themselves, but there were too many wolves moving too quickly, and goblins began to die.

Alum and Malcolm transformed, attacking the inner rows of goblins, not without a few yowls of pain as bolts struck them. Bell pulled out one of her pocket bombs and gave it a backward toss into the midst of the fray.

It exploded, the sound making the wolves howl, and the choking cloud of powder hid the goblins in a haze of chaos. Bell rolled and grabbed Katherine. The two of them ducked behind the relative cover of the King's body. Conrad drew his sword and stood beside them. He held out his hand to me.

"Eva, come."

I pulled my Ashur. "Not until I make sure Gypsum's safe."

I made my way to her. My blade was useless against werewolves, but I'd worry about that when the time came. Steel worked just fine against goblins, and when one stumbled out of the haze of gas Bell had created, I gave him a slash across his hand, so he dropped his crossbow and had to feel about blindly for it.

No one else was near Gypsum, so I took a moment to sense her soul again. It was all pain and rage. I tried to calm her, but it was impossible to turn her back to mist or dwarf form. I think the silver was preventing it as much as her pain and my lack of knowledge. I did manage to soothe her enough for me to approach. I grabbed the first silver bolt and pulled hard, making sure I flung myself backward, so when the wave of pain made her strike at me, I was already out of reach. I turned on the calming aura again. It was a matter of making my own soul as calm as it could be and sharing that serenity with hers. Of course, my soul was as far from a saint's as could be, and there wasn't a whole lot of serenity to share. I couldn't get close enough to take out the second bolt in her side.

"Gypsum," I said, trying to reason with her. "Let me help you."

"You may not want to do that when you know what I know," Syla said. The baroness was standing beside me.

I swung my Ashur, meaning to wound and not kill, as there was still the possibility of getting paid. I had found the body as Syla instructed, but if she was working with the militants it might be better if I didn't hold back. I followed up with a jab of the silver bolt I'd taken from Gypsum's arm. My muscles had already made the decision to strike hard, when Syla became mist, and my Ashur passed right through her. The follow up with the silver worked much better, pinning the mist in place and forcing Syla to retake dwarf form.

"Eva, listen," she began.

I had every intention of listening now that she was immobilized, but I had only the one bolt, so, when three other misty wolf forms surrounded me, I couldn't do anything to stop them. Claws yanked the Ashur from my grip. Another set of hairy arms tightened around my upper body, trapping me, and a third wolf pulled the bolt out of Syla, growling with pain from touching the silver.

The smoke from Bell's bombs slowly dispersed, and I saw Conrad coming for me, sword drawn. "Eva," he called.

His voice was snatched away on the wind. The werewolf who had me carried me off so fast the world around became a blur. Oh, crap.

18   Utterly Reliable

When the world stopped moving, my stomach didn't, and I threw up all over the werewolf who had me. He transformed instantly into Bert, my little Bert from the café, and I threw up again. I couldn't help it. My head was swimming.

He looked down at his ruined shirt and breeches and said, "Just great, Eva. Now I have to take a snow bath and freeze my bollards off."

I didn't have much sympathy. "Then you shouldn't have kidnapped me if you were afraid for your bollards."

"He saved you," a too familiar voice said. It was Duane, a large gray wolf dead at his feet.

"That's not …?" I began.

"No. It's not anyone we know, not a werewolf," he said. "It's the local alpha timber wolf who was stalking the survivors. Bert killed it."

Wolves, the normal kind, were known to snatch stray children and wandering merchants, so it would have been attracted to the wounded, and its intentions would not have been kind.

"I suppose that makes me the local alpha now," Bert said proudly.

"Not with Baroness Syla around," Duane pointed out. "As far as I can tell, she's in charge."

Over a dozen survivors were milling about, mostly dwarves, with a few humans and elves among them, those not lucky enough to reach the escape balloons.

"What are you doing here?" I asked Duane. "I thought you got away with Karolyne."

"Was going to but figured I needed to save you first."

"I didn't need saving."

"You always need saving."

"And now the king's body requires saving," Syla said as she joined us.

"Bell first," Duane added. "Probably that tall red-headed girl too, but the rest of them are guilty as far as I can tell."

"What are you talking about?" I was confused, and still a bit nauseated from being dragged through the trees by Bert.

We were higher up the mountain, closer to the crash site. I could see the deflated remnants of the dirigible in the distance, like some white ghost gently swaying to unheard music.

"When the werewolf attacked me in my stateroom," Syla explained, "I fought him and killed him, which forced him back into dwarf form. I saw it was Verdis. The King's Guardsmen are supposed to protect the Matriarchy. I knew then I couldn't trust anyone."

"You killed him? That's why your face was scratched when the EEPs arrested you."

"I have more scars now." She showed me her shoulder, where huge bite marks were visible, red and sore. "Wounds inflicted by silver or other werewolves do not heal easily. After you used that damn Avian artifact at the wedding and I was forced to change, the wolf who ran into the chaos went after me. Once he'd killed the Elven Protectorate in his way of course. I recognized him. Malcolm. My own son."

"Wait. Your son bit you? He tried to kill you?"

"He didn't go for the jugular. He was angry about his friend's death and wanted to show his displeasure. When we were alone, he tried to convince me to join them."

"Them?" I asked, but Syla did not pause to answer.

"He took me to the ship's bridge," she said, "where we found Alum had already slaughtered the crew and redirected the ship to Solheim. I refused to help them."

There was a distant look in her eyes as she remembered, and I knew she wouldn't tell me everything that had transpired. She was hurting, and it wasn't from the flesh wound Malcolm had given her. His betrayal bit deepest.

"My son escaped," she continued, "as did Alum, but I killed Conrad's guardsmen. They too were wolves, although never turned before and untested. They would not let me correct the ship's course, so I had no choice."

"Must have been ten of them at least. You're one tough werewolf," Duane noted.

"I'm a matriarch," Syla said, as though that was explanation enough.

"Conrad's guards?" I repeated, dumbfounded.

Not again. I'd fallen for the bad guy—again? Syla had to be lying. Conrad was utterly reliable.

"There's more," Syla said, her words pained. "Gypsum was with them. She too tried to convince me to join them, to take the side of the Dead God, the 'victorious side', they said. I've been betrayed by my own sister, and my son."

"I feel pretty betrayed too," I said, "but, yes, it's probably worse for you. No offense, Baroness, but they all say you are the bad guy. I hardly know you, and I'm inclined to believe those I do know."

"You know me," Duane said. "I saw what Gypsum's brother, Alum, did to the fleeing passengers after you left."

"What? Is Karolyne alright?"

"She's fine. Her balloon got away in time, but Alum shifted into wolf form right before my eyes and killed his way through the crowd until he got to your sister."

"Ilsa?"

"She fought, but you can't beat werewolves with magic, and you can't fight mist. They stole her away," Duane said.

"Where is she then? She wasn't with us."

I suddenly remembered Alum's bag of 'treasure': Ilsa had been with us the whole time. I hadn't sensed her soul, because it was so diminished and obscured by the brightness of the wolves'.

"They wanted both of you for some reason," he said.

"What about the dwarves you just killed, Baroness? Wade's cousins. Whose side were they on?" I asked, my brain whirring as I tried to make sense of it all.

"No one's," Syla said. "They were oblivious to this conflict, as Bert and others were, and they are all alive. See for yourself." She indicated the gathering of survivors, and I spotted Sten and the other dwarves I thought had been killed. "I had to get them away from those vipers. The poor idiots were simply caught on the wrong side of the crash."

"You were the one searching my room, weren't you? You were the black wolf?" I said. The puzzle pieces were starting to fall into place, but I didn't like the picture they were forming. I needed to know every-thing.

"Yes. Apologies for knocking you down." Syla didn't appear too apologetic, but she had good matriarchal manners, which involved saying the right things even if she didn't mean them. "I was looking for the king's body."

She had spared me then when she could easily have killed me. Of course, I'd been working for her. "Why didn't you simply ask if I'd found the body and hidden it in my room?"

"I'm untrusting by nature, especially of new retainers like you, so I wanted to search your quarters myself. Only, that mutt was there, so I decided not to mince around about it and took wolf form. I searched other cabins for the body as well but couldn't find it. Verdis caught me at it and followed me to my room to kill me. I had to defend myself, and I knew then that at least one King's Guardsman was responsible for Rutgard's abduction."

Seemed Baroness Syla had done all the sleuthing without me. I felt quite left out and tried to contribute something.

"You couldn't find the body because Conrad's guards brought it aboard when they were supposedly searching the ship for suffragist threats," I said, no longer able to deny the truth. Too many little observations and deductions were pointing in a direction I didn't like. "That's why he was blatant about it, instead of being undercover as I'd asked. No one wants to hang around when the city guard is tearing through, so he had plenty of opportunity to secret the body unobserved. Of course, that means not only Conrad, but a significant portion of the Guard has been compromised and is working for the Dead God. We have far bigger worries than your missing king. Solheim has us in their sights, and the wall between us and them doesn't feel adequate anymore."

I spotted the 'mutt', as she'd called Jake the dog, frolicking in the snow with the other crash survivors and snuffling about. The bloodhound pulled an ice viper out of a burrow with its teeth and tossed it around like a chew toy. It gave me an idea.

"There is nowhere for Conrad and the others to hide," I said. "They are exposed, and their one goal will be to get to Solheim. Conrad told me he was headed to the train line. That may be true or not, but we can be certain he's headed east. He must have other guards at the wall who will let him through. I don't know why they are so keen on taking Rutgard with them, as it slows them down, but they went to a lot of trouble to get that body out of the city, which means we are obliged to stop them. It also means we can track them, whichever route they take.

"The dog has scented the resin that encases the King, and now that Malcolm isn't around to steer the dog in the wrong direction, we can stay close behind them. Then you can fight them, Baroness, with the help of all these other wolves we now have to back us up."

"It is hard to control myself in wolf form," she cautioned. "I don't want to kill my family, no matter that they've betrayed me, and so I won't risk fighting them again. I won't take on Gypsum, Alum and Malcolm. We need another way to subdue them."

"Can you snatch them like you did me and Wade's cousins?"

"They will fight and will not be so easily caught unaware."

I still had a hard time believing Gypsum and Conrad had betrayed Highcrowne and me, but, even if they had, it didn't mean everything they'd told me had to be distrusted. They had been right about my magic being something I could use.

"I may have a way," I said, "but I need werewolves to 'experiment' on."

Syla was a born leader. After listening to my plan, she quickly organized the band of survivors into two groups: those who were to stay behind and wait for help—a magic flare was released that the Highcrowne authorities were sure to detect—and the werewolves. She had the wolves tear down some saplings in order to build a wooden litter, and she put me and Reginald on it together, cross-legged, facing each other, while we headed down the mountain, Jake the dog leading the way. The mutt happily sniffed across the snow, and I hoped he was leading us in the right direction.

Duane walked beside me, shaking his head and smiling.

"What's so funny?" I asked. He wasn't helping the dwarves carry the litter, and he wasn't a werewolf or Syla's hired Private Eye like me, so he had no legitimate reason to come along.

"The way you always end up in the most dangerous situations imaginable. Only you would want to be trapped next to a werewolf as it shifts," he said.

"You'll be seeing it up close too if you don't step away. Besides, you're distracting me. I really need to focus here," I said.

"Why am I distracting you?"

"Because you talk too much."

"She's right. Shut up," Reginald told him in his usual surly tone. "This is an unprecedented request for self-control from me here, and I need to focus too. I might have more transformation experience than all this lot aside from the Baroness, but I was never good at the control side. There was a reason Gypsum kept threatening to send me back to the mines."

"Back?" I asked.

"Yes, 'tis where I spent a few years learning to control this little problem after it was first unleashed on the goblin front. I'd had military picket duty, and the first corpse that made its way past the goblins and into the Kingdoms triggered me wolfy reflex. The mines are too extreme a punishment, and I begged me aunt to get me out of there. Of course, I hadn't a known she would have set me to waiting tables at Karolyne's, else I might have asked to be sent back to the front instead."

"I see. Stay way back," I warned Duane again.

"I'm not sure I can let you do this," he said.

"No one *lets* me do anything. You certainly don't get a say."

"I'm only trying to look out for you," Duane persisted.

"Shift already," I told Reginald. "It's the only thing that will shut him up."

I wasn't prepared for how fast the dwarf obeyed. Between one heartbeat and the next, he was mist.

"Hold as long as you can," I said. I could feel Reginald's lack of control. Gypsum had been far more disciplined, which made it even clearer she'd lied about not knowing she was a wolf. How long had she been lying to me?

I stopped the mental dialogue. My thoughts tended to circle into a familiar pattern of regret and self-recrimination. From now on, I would be up against wolves who had slaughtered remorselessly, who had bombed Highcrowne, and who included King's Guardsmen and better fighters than me, even when they weren't in wolf form. I had no time for mind games; I needed power and a way to compel the wolves into dwarf form whenever I willed it.

I had no idea how my magic worked, but I didn't know how my heart worked either. It just did. So, I let the green glow in the palm of my hands wink its emerald eye open. Its raw power had been growing ever since I took a piece of Ilsa's soul and pulled Erick's soul out of the Dead God's grasp. Souls were what my power laid claim to, and I reached for Reginald's.

The dwarf looked surprised. No longer in mist form, he was simply the busboy from the restaurant again. It had worked!

Something was wrong though. His eyes continued to bulge, and he reached for me, scratching my forearm in the process with claws almost as long as a werewolf's. I gasped from the sharp sting of it and clamped my hand over the wound. Blood ran through my fingers in rivulets.

Reginald took a deep breath and said, "I'm sorry. You were hurting me."

Duane tied off my arm with a tourniquet. "I've got to stitch this up now, Eva, or you'll bleed out. I told you..." He was already off to grab the supplies he needed, while I continued to hold the wound and fight off shock. I felt a bit woozy.

"You almost killed me," I told Reginald.

"You almost killed me. I could feel me ... life. It felt like me very life being sucked away."

"It was your soul. I'm sorry. I have a hard time controlling myself too."

"Here." Duane was back already, and he pulled my arm out straight, stitching it as he walked slowly beside our litter. I had expected the needle and wiry thread he used to hurt more than it did, but the pain was dull in comparison to the wolf scratch. Reginald had cut into the vein but missed the artery at least, as far as I could tell. I was feeling a bit woozy again.

Duane slapped me and the fog faded from my brain. "Stay focused," he warned. "Shock can kill you."

"Here, smell this," the baroness said. She was beside us now too, and she held some tree fungus out to me. I took a whiff, and my eyes watered. It smelled like pure ammonia.

"That's awful." My sinuses burned. I put my good arm across my face.

"It is effective." Syla smiled. "My nursemaid was a battlefield medic in her youth. I learned some useful things growing up."

"I think we're done here," Reginald said, trying unartfully to clamber down from the swaying contraption we rode.

"No," I insisted. "We do it again. I want to be able to stop Gypsum without killing her."

"What's to stop her from killing you?" Duane said.

"She's my friend. Whatever reason she has for betraying Highcrowne, she's still Gypsum, and she's still your sister," I told the baroness. "We have to hear her out. Maybe she's been be-spelled?" Maybe Conrad had been too.

"Perhaps," Syla said. "My son as well? That is a comforting thought. I can only hope there is something we can do. I don't know what's happening or why."

"I know Highcrowne is at war and most people don't realize it yet," I said. "The Dead God has kidnapped one of the Three Crowns; the King's Guard and untold others have joined Him; they've been attacking Highcrowne at will with goblin-supplied bombs, encouraging the suffragists, sowing discord and distrust for humans and dwarves, and all of that means the elves will soon crack down and take more power, until they're running this war their way. The goblins want the Dwarf King too. Not sure what side they're on, or if they even know, but they're certainly agents of chaos."

"Okay," Syla said. "So maybe you do know what's happening. I thought this was simply misguided members of my family trying to gain an influential position on what they feel will be the winning side. The way you talk, I fear we've already lost."

"We might if we don't get Rutgard's body back. Anything our enemy wants that badly is something we should keep from him. That's why I'm going to try this again. Go Reginald. Change. I need to be able to do this without a moment's hesitation or thought."

"I don't..." Reginald stammered. He always seemed tough, but the way he'd wounded me really bothered him. No matter what anarchist group he joined, he couldn't lose his ingrained reverence for women.

"I'll dodge better next time. Don't hold back," I said, giving him my good glare, which was a challenge that usually sent the weak-willed scurrying for cover.

Reginald got the message and saw that I was a big girl. He took a breath and changed again.

Reginald didn't hold the mist form for long but went straight to werewolf. I wrapped his soul around my mental fist like I would the bloodhound's lead and gave it a good yank. Curtailing the soul, confining it, seemed to instantly reflect in Reginald's form because he was a dwarf again so fast I barely saw the shift. This time I tried to let go of the hold I had on him a bit quicker than last time. There was something too enticing about that warm glow of spirit within my grasp. It was too tempting to gobble it up like hot chocolate on a wintry day.

"There," I said, satisfied. "No one died."

I kept practicing with other wolves as we travelled, giving Reginald a break from my magic, as it seemed to be draining him. I'd worn Duane down from vocal protests to a disapproving look as he walked beside us.

For once, I had some control over my power, and it felt amazing. I felt like I could take on the Dead God Himself, and I started feeling guilty about the litter.

"We can ditch it," I told the dwarfs who had been roped into porter duty. They looked grateful to toss the thing aside.

I felt lighter too, as though I'd been unburdened from a weight that was holding me down. The green fire in my palm seemed to grow brighter, and I didn't hold it so tightly, which must be where the feeling of lightness came from. Part of me thought this new sensation was dangerous, but I tried not to listen to that part right now.

I hurried to the front of the procession beside Baroness Syla, Duane at my heels and Bert already there.

"I think we're getting close," Bert said. "The sniffing is gettin' more excited." He indicated the mutt who seemed to be in heaven as he tracked a scent across the frozen snow. I couldn't read the churned-up tracks well enough to know how many people had come through here.

"I didn't think we'd catch up so quickly," I said.

"They were burdened as well," Syla pointed out, "with the King's body and your sister."

The bloodhound had found something. It looked like another body. We'd already passed the battlefield where goblin commandos had been slaughtered by wolves. This body was intact, however. A green lump buried in the snow; a chunk of resin held triumphantly in an outstretched hand.

"It's Doctor Ghunnan," I said. "He's..." I was about to say dead and frozen solid, but I could see his soul without having to close my eyes. It burned brightly and with a fire of will I hadn't known he possessed.

The goblin brushed snow from his face and smiled. "I knew you'd find me as long as I had this," he said. The dog snuffled at the resin and the goblin doctor patted him happily.

"I'm surprised you're still alive," I said.

"As am I. When my compatriots met such an ignominious end, I was certain I would follow, but I hobbled into the woods in all the excitement and was overlooked. I quickly secluded myself here, hoping someone would find and rescue me. As the resin is quite odiferous, and as hounds are often employed on rescue missions, if not trolls as where I come from, then I was certain this resin would act as a beacon."

"What about your student?" I asked. "You ran off and left her behind?"

"Ah ... yes. Survival of the fittest, my dear."

"You don't look very fit to me."

"It is a bit of a tautological error in logic; the fittest is the one most suited to survive, but you don't know who that is until they survive do you? Easier to judge in hindsight."

"It's easy to see you're a coward. How could you let Miss Kissel execute everyone?"

"She did not, I should point out."

"Only because Gypsum and the other wolves spoiled her plans. You certainly did nothing to help. I'm of a mind to leave you here to freeze," I said.

"I can assist you with tracking them."

"We have the dog. And dangerous werewolves in a pinch, but as unpredictable as they are, you are predictably untrustworthy. We don't need you."

"Yes, very true. Then I can lend you my knowledge. From all appearances, the supposed 'god' of Solheim is behind this. I am quite learned in Solhan history and metaphysics."

"Isn't that convenient. How can you tell me anything useful about the Dead God when you don't even believe in Him?"

"I am a source of facts. What you believe is of no concern to me, but the facts may very well help you prevail against this conqueror."

"What about Bell?" Duane asked. I felt bad I hadn't asked about her, and a bit jealous Duane had. I shouldn't be jealous of Bell—Kali was more her type than Duane, and I didn't even want Duane—but she was the epitome of blonde cuteness I never could be.

"She was taken captive," the goblin said. "After the battle was over, I heard most distinctly that she would be used as bait. That guardsman...."

"Conrad?" I asked, a strange lump in my throat as I said his name.

"The golden one? Yes, I believe so. He said that he must get you back, and that you were certain to 'destroy mountains and putrefy rivers' if need be to return your friends to your side. He seemed to know you well and was certain you would come after them, as long as he held Bell ransom."

He did know me. I felt bad about being jealous of Bell, but I'd do anything for her. Or even Katherine who I hardly knew. They were innocents and deserved none of this mess. It was of my making. The god wanted me, and Conrad was working with him. Not as utterly reliable as I thought him to be. Could I trust my own judgement at all? Was it fatally flawed? Did I need new eyes? Did I need ... logic?

"I'll spare you, Doctor," I said, "but tell me everything, I mean everything, you know about Solheim."

19 Why Didn't I Know That?

It took an unbearably long time to see to the goblin's comfort before he'd share any shred of useful information. I almost asked Reginald to chuck him down the mountain at one point, which I'm sure Reginald would have been pleased to do. The dwarf was saddled like a prize pony, his bare shoulders were too sharp for the goblin's bony old behind, so a pillow was made from a wad of clothing. Next the doctor needed a back support.... Suffice it to say, I had given up on the goblin being any use and was focused on the dog sniffing the trail ahead of us, when he finally spoke anything besides complaints.

"So, this 'Dead God' seeks to restore the Solhan Empire?" the goblin said. "I believe that would indeed take someone able to raise the dead to achieve, if such nonsense were possible. The nation has been in its grave since the elves first stepped across the Void and settled here. Afore then, all this land was ruled by Avians, and when they went nearly extinct, the Solhans for a time and then the pawns of Solhans, especially the dwarves. Humans were an afterthought, come across the same Void the elves found, fleeing the Devourer of Worlds, and all the while this land's true peoples, we goblins, trolls, gralls and the like were never once thought of as its rightful inheritors."

"Solhans are from here and humans from the Void?" I asked, incredulous. And was this Devourer of Worlds the same god Solhans feared?

"From across the Void," he corrected. "Another land akin to this one most likely, but different and strange as it is similar. Such are the lands across the Void—places eerily similar, yet different."

"I'm not anything like a human at all am I?" I asked.

"Not at all. Although eerily similar, as I said."

"I thought you didn't believe in magic. How come you believe in the Void?" I asked.

"That is not magic—it is physics."

"Sounds like an incantation to me: fi-zix?"

"Do not attempt to impress your superstitious view of the world onto me. Physics is the study of the components of all things, be they energy or matter, and the Void is but the space between dimensions. It would take energy and devices beyond my comprehension to cross that Void, but naturally, at certain times and places, the Void shrinks upon itself, drawing two places, two dimensions close together so it is but a step through a wooded copse or across a threshold that carries humans or elves from their lands to ours and vice versa. The Void narrows at some places for centuries at a time, and superstitious folk such as yours built temples at such locations, believing them holy or divine. Solheim is rife with such corridors, the greatest of all on the Island of Fel. I do not doubt your 'god' comes from across the Void, but being foreign does not make him divine. He has less claim to this land than my kind do."

"Is that what the goblins are up to? Staking their claim in the bid for Empire?" I asked, remembering Miss Kissel and her commandos.

"We goblins have the right. We have stood by as Avians ruled, then Solhans, elves and dwarves ... but now all are on the brink of collapse and it is our time at last. We will lead this world out of darkness and to enlightenment. No more gods and superstition."

"Miss Kissel seemed to believe the Dead God's real enough to propose bargaining with Him for the King's body."

"I did not deny his existence, only clarify that he is not a god. Of course, I suppose someone who has obliterated the human lands can call himself anything he likes."

I didn't like the goblin's smirk, or his lack of empathy for all the lives lost in this war, not to mention his sacrilegious attitude. I wasn't as devout as my uncle, but even I felt uncomfortable when I heard gods disrespected.

"Well, we have now exhausted about ten minutes, and I don't see any more reason to keep you around," I said. I'd had to raise my voice, as the sound of rushing water from a nearby river grew louder. The mountain slope had leveled, and we were now in a broad valley below the snow line, densely forested as far as I could see.

Duane nodded his agreement. "Eva is too kind-hearted. People who betray me don't live this long."

"I have more useful information," the goblin said quickly. "Only, you won't know you need it until the situation presents itself. Consider me a walking tome, an encyclopedia of information on all things—within my area of specialty of course—but I do dabble in the other sciences and can take a stab at medicine for example. Or scalpel to it I mean. Ha, ha, ha..."

As pathetic as the old goblin was, I did kind of want to kill him, but those were bad thoughts. Bad, Eva, I told myself. Don't be like her. Don't listen to that part of her inside you.

"Did you see Ilsa with them?" I asked. "My twin?"

"There are two of you? Emperor save us," the goblin said.

I put a hand on my hip and cocked it dangerously.

"Now where to?" Baroness Syla asked loudly, having to shout over the noise of the rapids. It probably saved the goblin's life.

The bloodhound had led us to a wide river that tore over rocks and frothed white around a series of waterfalls. It was too treacherous to cross.

"Conrad said he was going to the train line, and I think he was telling me that much truth. Which way is it?" I asked.

"It runs parallel to the river, but on the other side," Syla said.

"Then we have to find a way across. Gypsum and the others must have managed it if they lost the hound," I reasoned.

Duane furrowed his brow. "Or they waded in far enough to wash away their scent but crossed elsewhere. They could have gone either direction. Baroness, take some of your people upstream, have some try to fjord here, while I take Jake down the bank a bit. I don't have your werewolf nose. Come on boy." He grabbed the dog's collar and took off.

I looked at Syla and the dwarven survivors and then back at Duane.

"Damn. I'm going with him," I said. "He needs someone to protect him this time, and I'm sure I can force any werewolf we see back into dwarf form."

"I'll send a runner if we find anything," Syla said. "I will need you to capture Gypsum alive."

I nodded before hiking up my skirt and setting off after Duane. I was not a good runner at the best of times; it was doubly hard with a dress and boot soles worn thin enough I could feel every rough stone and furrow I stepped on. I was panting worse than the dog when I caught up to them.

"Can we please walk?" I said. "The dog will track better if he's not running."

"Convenient argument," Duane said, but he slowed down. "Still following me everywhere I see."

I scowled. "I cannot believe you told that elf woman that."

"I tell Hilja everything."

Now I looked like the cynical street thug. "Really?"

"Okay, not everything, but enough to know it's real."

Duane in love. Why did that make me feel so lousy?

"It's spring fever you know," I told him. "It will wear off by winter."

"Like you and Conrad?"

I was about to tell him it was worn off already, but I'd be lying. I still thought Conrad and Gypsum were spelled somehow. Who knew what a god could do? And the Dead God was a god despite the goblin's idiotic arguments. Still ... my relationship with Conrad had been a bit tense of late, until after he stepped into that old temple in the suffragist hideout. If that's when he was spelled, then maybe it was the spelled version I liked. That complicated things. I fell in and out of love a lot, so there was always hope this too would pass soon.

"Uncharacteristically quiet," Duane said.

"Let's focus on finding them and getting the Dwarf King's body back."

"What if we have to kill that absurd guardsman or Gypsum in the process?" he asked.

"Do you enjoy tormenting me with what-ifs? Of course, I don't want to kill them, so let's not if we can avoid it. My plan doesn't have a lot of detail in it, but if we stop them from heading east, we'll call it a job done."

"I'm only saying that you have to think ahead, Eva. What do you do if Gypsum comes between you and stopping the Dead God?"

"I shove her aside. Wound her if I need to. I don't want any more killing. It...."

"What?"

"It feeds my soul and makes me feel different, Duane. You think I stick my nose up at you, but I don't. You kill because of practicalities that I can't condone, but I kill with ... pleasure, and that's even worse. I need you and everyone around me to keep me in check. I feel how close the loss of control is, how it felt to have Reginald's soul in my hands. You can't let me kill Gypsum or Conrad. I don't know if I can stop myself, so I need you to stop me. Promise me that."

"Why would I promise?"

"Because you owe Viktor."

"Yeah, I do."

He looked into my eyes and for a moment we shared a memory of my brother, of simpler times when we were all children in the streets playing at life and death instead of facing the real thing. I'd give anything to be back there again, to change things and stop my brother dying, stop myself from ever getting in a situation where I needed to kill, stop Duane from killing because he needed to survive. How hard would have it to been to bring Duane into Uncle's house, to feed him? Everything could have turned out differently. If only.

"I think Jake smells something." Duane looked away, and that moment in time was gone.

The dog snuffled frantically across the mossy stones and led us to a rocky, broad area in the river. A fjord.

"Go get Syla," I said.

"You get her."

"No, my feet are killing me. You have decent clothes on and can run back. I have a useless dress. I'll stay here, so we know where to cross."

"You're going to do something dangerous as soon as I'm gone," he said.

"I swear not to. Leave Jake. He'll keep me in line."

"No one can keep you in line, but...." He looked at how I stood on my sore feet, shifting from foot to foot, and a touch of pity crossed his features. "Okay. I'll be back before you know it."

He took off running and soon disappeared into the undergrowth. I looked at the fjord and fought the temptation to follow Conrad and the others on my own. For once, I would not be stupid. I sat down on a rock.

I waited patiently for what seemed like ages, until Jake started barking, and then I stood and drew my Ashur.

Apparently, trolls guarded fjords as they did bridges. This one had dropped down from a tree branch and now stood in the water, arms crossed, legs in a V-shape, and they were long legs. The creature was ten feet tall. It wasn't as bulky as a grall, but its limbs were covered in wiry muscle and green scales. Its huge nose was almost beak-like in shape, and large black eyes, like pools of oil, peered at me from beneath bushy brows and a mane of red hair.

"Listen," I told the troll, carefully re-sheathing my sword. It was tough when the sheath was on my back instead of my side, but I managed to do it while I kept talking. "I don't want any trouble. Name your price, and my friends will pay it when they're along in a few minutes. Any minute now really. I don't have my purse, but I'm sure someone has gold, trinkets, whatever you're looking for."

"Want meat."

That was not a good opening to the bargaining process. Trolls preferred intelligent meat, claiming it tasted better. Of course, the adage you are what you eat did not apply to them.

"Well … you like goblin meat?" I asked.

"Too small and bony."

Jake was still barking furiously, so I patted him and made hushing sounds.

"How about the noisy one for a snack, and then you I eat for dinner? Your friends can pass by safely after that." The troll sounded like he was being generous.

"How about not."

Now would be a really good time for Duane and the pack of werewolves that were on my side to show up. There was no sign of them though, and my hand drifted back to the handle of my Ashur. Trolls were highly successful extortionists because few survived them. I was likely to be eaten either way, but I'd prefer to go down fighting.

The troll saw what I was doing and narrowed its eyes. Its claws were dagger-length, but it retracted them and instead drew two swords longer than me from sheaths on its hips. I fumbled for my sword hilt and drew it as the troll bounded forward, each heavy footstep throwing up a geyser of water. I took a step back, but there was nowhere I could run fast enough.

The troll grunted, stopped and reached behind its back as though scratching an itch. It pulled out a silver bolt, looked at it curiously and then snapped it like a toothpick. Another bolt shot from across the river and lodged in one enormous black eye. That must have stung a bit, because the troll clutched his face and growled.

Conrad was on the opposite bank, smoothly loading and firing another shot from the goblin crossbow. He called to me, and despite the thunder of nearby rapids, I could hear him as clearly as if he were inside my head.

"Eva, take his soul. Pull it from his body and save yourself. Do it now."

I hesitated, tightening my grip on the handle of my Ashur. The troll could break my blade as easily as a crossbow bolt. Conrad fired continuously at the creature, but other than the wound to the eye, his attacks annoyed the troll as much as a swarm of mosquitoes might. I thought about running ... but all those thoughts were a desperate attempt to squirm away from the decision in front of me. As soon as Conrad had told me what to do, I desired it in a way that frightened me to my core.

As I stood and took a step forward, I felt elated. I lost all desire to fight the part of me that hesitated. I reached out, seeing the warm glow of the troll's soul without closing my eyes, and when I touched its scaly skin, I felt its thoughts and memories. I could taste the spicy human meat it had devoured mere days ago, a soldier who had deserted his post at the wall and wandered this way. I could feel the rumble in its belly for more, how Jake and I smelled wonderful to it, how it longed to gobble us up then return to its nest in the trees and sleep until the next travelers came along. I pulled all those feelings and troll-thoughts inside me, pulled in all that the creature was or ever would be, and my stomach felt full and warm, as though it were me devouring the troll and not the other way around. And I was devouring it. As the warmth inside me grew, its warmth diminished, the glow of its soul fading.

"No." I let go and took a step back. What had I done?

20   MEET THANE

The troll lay unconscious in the burbling water, the dimmest spark of soul remaining. I doubted it would recover or even wake before it starved, or some other creature came along and finished it off. I'd as good as killed it, but I couldn't bring myself to take that one morsel that remained. I'd already crossed a line I shouldn't have, and I knew deep down that there was an even worse line that could be crossed.

"*Eva*," Conrad called again, and it was like another warm touch inside me, as though his soul were speaking directly to mine. "*Come to me.*"

Then he was gone, vanished into the trees. Did he expect me to follow? I wanted to. The same part of me that had wanted to taste the troll's soul was the same part that wanted to chase after that connection with Conrad's, but not to devour. I wanted to coil myself around him, feel the warmth of him forever.... I took a step into the icy water, and the chill that spilled into my boot startled me awake.

No. I'd wait for the others and then go after the king's body. I wouldn't be lured alone into the woods or tempted. Must avoid temptation, I told myself.

I stroked Jake the Mutt over and over, trying to calm him as much as me. He kept barking at the downed troll in the water and wouldn't stop. Finally, Duane, Syla, and the dwarves showed. Syla was in wolf form, causing Jake to stick his tail between his legs and hide under my skirt with a yelp of fear. Syla bounded to the troll and gave it a sniff. With one snap of her jaws, she broke its neck and tore its head from its shoulders.

She retook dwarf form and spat blood. "It was riddled with silver and tasted awful. Trolls are impervious to everything but fire. How did you stop it?" she asked.

"There's no time," I said, looking only at Duane, as Syla's casual completion of the troll's murder disturbed me. I didn't want to talk about what I'd done. "I saw Conrad across the river, so the rest of them must be close. We need to keep moving."

I didn't stop to listen to more questions but bounded into the water, my feet and calves freezing.

Jake ran on ahead, sniffing the ground where Conrad had stood and wagging his tail excitedly, already recovered from the appearance of the werewolf. Wolf scents vanished as soon as they changed to dwarf form, so that probably helped the dog recover, that and his tiny brain.

When I reached the other side, Jake followed the scent along the ground, excited as could be, but he was heading the wrong way: west instead of east.

"No, Conrad went this way," I said, pointing downstream.

"Yet, the resin's trail heads off in this direction," the goblin said. He and the others were already across. The doctor was on Bert's shoulders instead of Reginald's now. Looked like they were playing 'share the annoying goblin lest I kill him' game.

"We go after the king," Syla insisted, directing everyone after the mutt.

"It's a trick. I saw...." I said.

"I know you probably saw what you saw, but Conrad is likely the distraction," Duane told me. "Don't fall for it."

If I'd known no one would have joined me, I would have gone after him on my own earlier. I was trying not to be stupid, but it seemed like that was impossible.

"I'm trusting my gut," I said. "I'm headed downstream. If it leads nowhere, I'll meet you at the train line."

Duane groaned. "We'll meet you at the train line," he told the Baroness.

"It's not wise to set off on your own," Syla called, but I wasn't listening.

I liked working alone. Of course, Duane wouldn't leave me in peace. I heard him close behind, so I dashed into some tangling bushes. By the time I emerged, I realized Duane, Bert, Reginald, and the goblin had all followed me. And they'd gone around the brambles.

Feeling stupid, I said, "I'm surprised to see you, Doctor. I thought you'd told us to believe the dog's nose and go with Baroness Syla?"

"I did, but I'm strapped to this dwarf here who has other ideas."

"Can't leave you alone in the forest," Bert said.

"Y'll get yerself killed," Reginald chimed in.

"I suppose you're following me because you think I'm incompetent too?" I asked Duane.

"No. I'm here to get Bell back, not some petrified dwarf. Conrad took her captive, so we go after him."

"Alright," I said, summoning a take charge tone. "This way."

"That leads us away from the riverbank," the goblin pointed out.

My direction sense sucked, and Conrad could have gone anywhere once he was out of my sight. Maybe this wasn't such a good idea.

"Lemme go first," Reginald said, moving in front. "I've some trackin' skill from me time in the army." He looked around for a bit, touched a broken twig ahead of us, rubbing sap against his fingertip, and then felt in the grassy prints left in the ground. "Boot-sized tracks, not animal. This way."

We followed Reginald, and I was extremely grateful he'd tagged along, not that I was going to say that out loud.

I was also grateful we'd left the snow line well behind, as my frozen feet wouldn't have lasted much longer. We moved quickly, Reginald following the trail, Duane behind me, and Bert taking up the rear, with the odd grunt and cry from the goblin riding piggyback as he got wacked by tree limbs and other things above Bert's height. I didn't feel a bit sorry for him.

Before long I heard a loud, metallic whistle.

"The train," Duane said.

I'd seen plenty of noisy, coughing and spluttering miniature locomotives in Highcrowne, but the full-sized trains never made it into the city proper. The nearest station outside Highcrowne was opposite the docks, where the mountain was less steep. Tracks led to the wall in the east and to the center of the dwarven and elven lands in the south and west. I'd only ever spotted its smoke from a distance when I was on a higher tier of the city. This locomotive sounded louder than any I'd heard before.

As we neared the tracks, the pounding of gears and pistons was thunderous, the screech of metal wheels on iron deafening. By the time the locomotive came into view, I saw that it was stopping. We'd found a station in the wilderness. The raucousness of the machine settled down to the hiss of steam and a *whuffle* like the sound of a giant beast coming to rest in an iron cradle.

The locomotive was about ten times the size of the ones that operated at the docks, but there wasn't as much bustle and activity here in the middle of a nowhere valley. This seemed to be a supply station, giant water towers filling up the steam engine's reserves, coal being shoveled aboard. The cargo cars behind the engine were crammed with crates of supplies for the soldiers at the wall. There were several soldiers on their way there, peering out the windows of the passenger car. A few got out to stretch their legs.

I spotted a familiar profile. Malcolm stepped onto the platform, bantering with the newly arrived dwarf soldiers. He offered them some dwarven snuff.

I hid behind trees and undergrowth, while Duane used the forest cover to creep closer. I wanted a closer look as well, even though I wasn't as stealthy. Duane glared when I rustled a few leaves, but the sighs and puffs of steam from the resting engine were far louder than me, so I kept moving until I could get a better view.

There was no sign of Bell, but Gypsum was there, hair combed and trying to look like she hadn't recently survived a dirigible crash. She climbed up the steps to the station, Conrad behind her. The dwarven stationmaster seemed surprised to find a female here. I could barely make out what they were saying.

"...passage to the wall and no questions..." Gypsum said. She handed him an official looking document with ribbons and wax seals and followed it up with a gold coin. "For your trouble. ...if you can help my servant?"

Conrad wasn't vacant eyed enough to pass for a slave, but a paid servant might be believed. He indicated a stack of large mail bags behind him. He and the stationmaster carried them to a barred security car behind the passenger car. There were three bags, each about the same size as the body bag of loot Malcolm had recovered from the crash. The squarish one had to be the king. That meant the other two held Ilsa and Bell—or Katherine. There weren't enough for all three women and the king's body, so someone had been left for dead, and I didn't think the med student was useful enough to them. I hadn't known her well, and I was sorry about that.

The rigid bag with the frozen king was smaller than I expected, so they must have exhumed him from the amber casing. I saw no sign of Alum, so he had probably taken the chipped off resin in a different direction, setting the false trail Syla and the rest of the wolves were now following.

We needed to stop them, but I didn't know how to do it without bloodshed. Malcolm had made friends with the soldiers on the train, and they were sure to come to his aid if we attacked. I didn't want Bert and Reginald changing and killing the soldiers who were innocent in all of this, and I needed to get close enough to touch to stop them from transforming. Malcolm and Gypsum wouldn't let us simply walk up to them. There had to be another way. I was trying to think of it when I spotted Duane slip onto a cargo car further down the line.

"Maybe we should be gettin' on too?" Reginald said.

I sighed. "Yeah, that looks like the plan."

I did not like locomotives, but Conrad was aboard now, following the mail bags into the security car, and Gypsum was climbing into the passenger car. Malcolm gave his new buddies a friendly slap on the back before they returned to the passenger cabin and Malcolm joined Conrad with the cargo. The engineer had finished loading coal, and the stationmaster turned off the water supply, so it looked like the train would be ready to leave any minute. Now or never.

I hurried to the train car where Duane had hidden himself, Bert and Reginald close behind me. I balked at the massive iron wheels. The car was higher off the ground than I expected, the floor about chest height on me. Reginald gave me a boost and then helped Bert and the goblin up, before he clambered after, using sheer arm strength to pull himself up.

The cargo car was open to the elements. Duane crouched behind some wooden crates, and we joined him. We were about three cars away from the one Conrad and Malcolm were in.

"Now what?" I asked, since Duane seemed to have some kind of plan.

"We wait until the train has moved away from the station, then we climb car to car until we reach the one with Bell. I've carried plenty of bodies in bags and know them when I see them. She must be unconscious and alive, else they wouldn't bother. I hope she's alive anyway. Then one of your dwarf friends here grows claws and tears his way past the bars. We kill the guardsmen—or seriously wound them if you prefer— then find a soft patch of bushes to toss the bags into and then jump after ourselves. I've done a train heist or two without a werewolf to help, so this should be easy as pie."

"Climb around on a moving train? Jump into a patch of bushes from a moving train? Are you crazy?" I spluttered.

"You want to wait until we get to the wall?" he asked.

"Let's go now, before the train starts." Everything jerked, knocking me back, and then we were moving, albeit slowly. "Or now," I said.

I hurried forward before the contraption could pick up any more speed. I jumped the gap to the next cargo car, but then we were already going faster than I preferred, so I climbed down to where the cars were linked. A small metal platform on each side made the gap easier to jump.

Only when I was nearly to the security car did I look back to see if anyone had followed me. They had. Duane was pulling out knives and other weapons from hidden pockets, while Reginald lowered the doctor down from Bert's shoulders.

"You wait here, little goblin," Bert said. "This could get messy."

I sensed Bert and Reginald trying to change form, and I reacted instantly, mentally putting a choke hold on their souls until they were forced to retain their dwarf form.

"Hey! Stop that," Reginald grumbled.

"If you're werewolves, how will you stop from killing Malcolm and Conrad?" I said.

"If we're not wolves, how will we keep them from killing us?" Bert retorted.

"I can do to Malcolm exactly what I did to you. Let's stick to fists and head knocking if possible." I brandished the heavy steel orb on the handle of my Ashur by way of illustration.

"How is you supposing we get through the bars, if none of us can turn wolf and rip them off?" Reginald asked, seemingly sad he wouldn't get to be destructive.

It was a good point.

"I have something most expedient for such situations, as I've had occasion to bypass certain security measures that interfered with the pursuit of science—and the desires of The Emperor." The goblin pulled some small jacks from an inner pocket, the objects indistinguishable from children's toys.

"Jacks?" I said, raising an eyebrow. "Stealing toys from children too? How do you find time between science, medicine, spying and betraying?"

"Where did you get those?" Duane asked, snatching one from the goblin's hand in a fluid movement almost too fast for me to see.

"These are not harmless playthings, I assure you," the goblin said, ignoring my criticism and a bit nervous at the casual way Duane was handling it.

"They're not," Duane chimed in. "They're very expensive burglary tools difficult to find on the black market."

"Although not difficult to make," the goblin said. "Not that I produced these ones myself."

"Goblin manufactured," I guessed. "What other weapons have you been manufacturing besides these and crossbows with the range to shoot heavy silver bolts across rivers? Did you manufacture the explosives your assistant gave to the wolf who blew up the marketplace and nearly killed my nephew?"

"I cannot directly comment on that, as my associate, Miss Kissel, has directives I am not aware of. My sole assignment was to obtain the king's body as a bargaining tool in this conflict."

"I think Miss Kissel learned the body was important because she was supplying the wolf with bombs and helping him stir up chaos," I said.

"Miss Kissel and I do not work for the Dead 'God'."

"No, but trouble in Highcrowne helps you too. You want to inherit this land, don't you? That means you deliberately helped the wolf sow chaos. I bet you can point out which one is responsible for the bombings. Was it Wade? Alum? Who is the wolf in the top hat who nearly blew Duane and Little Viktor to smithereens?"

"I told you that Miss Kissel—"

"—Yes, you protest innocence, but you know where Miss Kissel is. You don't talk about her in the past tense, and I did not see her body among the dead commandos, so she must still be alive, and you know where she's gone."

The goblin went quiet.

"First things first," Duane pointed out. "We have a train to hijack. I want the guilty wolf too, but the goblin isn't going anywhere right now. We're picking up speed by the way."

Duane was right, even though it was against my personal code to tell him that. "Then use those jacks or whatever they are and get us in there. I'm as ready as I'll ever be."

"No claws, no weapons," Reginald grumbled as he pulled a plank from one of the crates to use as a bludgeon.

Duane leaped across to the security car and quickly set an explosive on the door. He jumped back and counted under his breath until it blew. After the ear buzzing bang of the explosion, the door dropped like lead and vanished beneath the train, which was now going a lot faster than any reasonable mode of transport should.

There was too much smoke to see Conrad or anyone within, but I knew this was our only moment of surprise. Duane and I leaped across almost at the same time and crowded each other going through the door. We both rolled once we were in, going to opposite sides of the car, him a bit more graceful about it than me. I heard the dwarves' curses as they followed; they offered another distraction while I crouched, looking for recognizable figures in the haze.

Malcolm's finely-toned ass was in my face. I needed to stand up if I was going to brain him, although I suspected I was in the general vicinity of his real brain already. I swung the hilt of my Ashur, but it passed through mist. Malcolm was shifting.

I felt for his soul, ready to choke it back into dwarf form as I'd learned to do so easily with Bert and Reginald, but it was slippery, evading my mental grip. There was something very different about Malcolm. I didn't know if it was because he was a King's Guardsman or if it had something to do with his alliance with the Dead God, all I knew was that I couldn't catch him let alone hold him, and he shifted.

I felt his fury, the animal side of him desiring my death, and I was already rolling, but then Conrad was there. He stood between me and the werewolf.

"Stay away from her," he commanded, and Malcolm obeyed, swiping at the clearing air where I could see Duane and the two dwarves trying to swing their makeshift weapons.

When I felt Bert and Reginald's urge to change, I didn't stop them this time. They were the only ones who could beat Malcolm now. If that meant killing him, I'd have to apologize to Syla later.

Conrad and the enemy werewolf were between me and the others. I saw Duane's calculating gaze assessing the scene, and then he dropped a smoke bomb. The acrid stench made Conrad and I cough and cover our mouths. My eyes watered uncontrollably, and when I could see again Duane was gone. The three werewolves were rubbing their muzzles and whining. I had no idea what Duane was up to, but I hoped he did it soon.

"Eva," Conrad said, reaching for me.

I took a step back and ran into the mail bags stacked like cord wood behind me. I dropped down beneath the smoke and reached inside one, searching blindly. I recognized the braided leather Bell wore as a bracelet and felt her wrist. Her heart still beat.

"How are you keeping them knocked out?" I asked. "I assume you have Ilsa along with Bell in there. Rutgard's body too?"

"Yes, and they're alive. If you come with me willingly, I will set Bell free." Conrad crouched beside me.

The smoke was almost gone now, sucked out by the wind rushing past the open door. My hair was caught in tiny whirlwinds, whipping around my face and catching in my mouth. I pulled the strands free.

"What about Katherine?" I asked. "Did you treat her so well?"

"She is already free, escaped with the surviving goblins. I do not kill without reason." He made it sound like he should be congratulated for that.

"So, you had good reason then for killing the dirigible crew and who knows how many others as part of this little plan?"

He frowned. "I am ultimately responsible."

I shook my head. "Why are you doing this, Conrad? Go with you to where?"

"To Solheim."

He had not drawn his weapon, while I had my Ashur. I could kill him, or at least brain him to ask questions later, but looking into the deep blue wells of his eyes, I felt compelled to reach out instead.

I took him by the shoulders and said, "Fight whatever's happening to you. This isn't you."

"No, it is not. I am not Conrad at all. My name is Thane."

"You haven't replaced Karolyne's cousin like some doppelganger and been lying to me for the past year, have you?"

I had been blind to a lot of betrayals lately, and I wouldn't be surprised if this one had been set up a while ago. I'd begun to realize I was incredibly unobservant, easily fooled, and tended to fall for the bad guy. All things that made me likely to fail in my newly chosen profession, and which explained why finding missing pets was all I had managed with middling success. I was definitely out of my league when it came to thwarting enemy plots and dealing with missing kings and affairs of state.

"Erick was a believable liar," Conrad—or Thane— said, homing in on my real doubt. Did he know me so well? "Because I helped. It was I who spoke through his lips when he said he loved you. Don't blame yourself, for his actions too are ultimately my respon- sibility. I allowed him to take his vengeance, to attempt to retrieve Ulric's power, as long as he brought you to me by whatever means necessary."

"You were Erick's boss?" It was as bad as I feared. Stupid, Eva. Stupid. I wanted to take my hands off his shoulders, but I couldn't move.

I could feel the warmth of his soul beneath my fingers, and it was stronger than the troll's had been, stronger than a werewolf's. It seemed to grow stronger as he spoke, as though he'd been hiding it along with his true name. The stronger the glow of his soul grew, the more I was drawn to him.

He kissed me, and still I didn't move. I was vaguely aware the werewolves had recovered and were fighting each other only steps away from us. I was aware that Duane was still gone and part of me wondered where, wanted him to hurry back and help. But the greatest part of me fell into the kiss.

It felt like I was on fire, in the heart of the sun. The heat was intense, but I felt no pain. The opposite. Every nerve in my body tingled with life. The brush of his hand against my cheek, the sharp stubble pressed into my chin, a soft wet tongue against mine ... each sensation brought me to the brink. I had never wanted anything more deeply than I wanted him. So, when he pulled away to take a breath, I almost sobbed with disappointment.

"You see, Eva. Before I felt what it was like to touch you like that, to taste you, to have your scent wash over me, I was content to have you alive or dead. I did not know what 'alive' was. Not until recently. I want what this body offers. I want to experience life, to hold your life precious, as long as I can. We can have eternity together after death, but this time should be treasured. I won't kill you, but I need you to come with me. Be with me."

I wanted that too, and I almost breathed 'yes' before my brain could function again, but it was functioning, and it had been listening even if the rest of me hadn't.

"Wait," my brain said, and I wanted to kick it. "This body? Eternity together after death? ... Why do we have to go to Solheim?"

"You know who I am, Eva."

I smelled it then: the scent of cinnamon smoke. His soul had grown bright and beautiful, and I was drawn to it exactly as a moth to a flame. I didn't know if I could pull away. I would burn.

Then the train car jerked, knocking us all to the floor, and I crawled away from Conrad-Thane. The open doorway was in front of me, and Duane was there.

"Laying down on the job, Eva?" he said, before he tossed Bell's mail bag over his shoulder and leaped back to the cargo car. He was back again by the time I regained my feet.

Malcolm paused in his fight against Bert and Reginald—who were nipping at his heels and taking turns attacking him from the back and front—and swiped at Duane. He dodged, but the werewolf's reach was long and powerful, and Duane was knocked down. He'd been slashed from shoulder to elbow and lay huddled, looking somehow like a wounded bird, smaller and more fragile than I'd ever seen him.

I ran to him and clamped a hand over the wound. "The..." I began, but the words wouldn't come. "...He's here. We need to leave!"

I dragged Duane to the gap we'd jumped across earlier. The train was slowing down, and I guessed Duane must have uncoupled us from the engine. I spied the goblin on the other car, sitting atop Bell's mail bag like he was relaxing comfortably on a ride through the country.

"Bert," I called, not that I could tell which wolf he was, "help me get Duane out of here. Run now. The Dead God is ... He's here!"

21 Not Again

The Dead God is here.

Saying it aloud gave me a chill of terror, and I looked at Him—with the face of Conrad—and my mind boggled. The god had always seemed a distant, nameless dread, but He was incredibly real, and His name was Thane.

"Eva," he spoke in that way that seemed to touch my soul rather than my ears. "Stay."

I took a step toward Him, forgetting Duane and the rest of the world, but Reginald swept me up, and in an instant, we were on the cargo car with the goblin. Bert followed with Duane a heartbeat later.

Malcolm followed too.

Reginald dropped me and resumed his match with Malcolm right above me, claws ripping the air in a blur too fast for me to see, their growls vibrating through my skull and drool dripping onto my hair. Trying to avoid being stepped on, I crawled to the goblin.

"Do you have more of those jacks?" I demanded, holding out my hand.

The goblin seemed to be studiously ignoring the existence of the werewolves, so he calmly retrieved a few more of the small explosives from his jacket pocket and handed them to me.

"Activate them by pressing the studs," he said. "But do keep them a minimum of ten feet away after you do so."

I judged the distance. "We've got five feet, so take cover."

I secured Bell as best I could. Everything was tied down with ropes, and I found a small triangular gap between the bottom crate nearest me and the metal loop the rope was tied through. I wedged her in there. Bert was still tending to Duane.

"Hold on to something," I warned them. I pressed the studs on about half a dozen of the jack bombs and tossed them at the security car. A few rolled inside at Thane's feet, but the others tumbled onto the small platform between the cars.

I had just killed Conrad. If he wasn't already dead. Ilsa too.

Thane's gaze was calm, entreating. He didn't seem to notice His stolen body was about to be blown apart.

An overwhelming, choking regret passed through me, and I shouted, "Get back!"

He seemed to finally notice the bombs at His feet, and He gave them a kick, dislodging them from the floorboards so they rolled into the gap.

"Find me, Eva."

Reginald threw Malcolm at Thane—an impressive feat, sending a snarling, biting, thrashing werewolf hurtling through the air—and then the bombs exploded.

I hadn't taken my own advice and had no cover. The world spun around me; I was flying, my ears deafened. I hit ground. There may have been some foliage to break my fall, but it felt exactly like slamming into solid rock, and all the wind went out of me. Something cracked, and it wasn't a tree branch. Blinding pain shot across my neck and shoulder. I wished I could pass out.

The sound of screeching metal and the boom of something heavier than me hitting the ground told me the train cars must have derailed. With my luck, I expected one to land on top of me, but soon the sounds died.

I realized I was lying face first in a field of wildflowers, a few of them in my mouth. Birds started to chirp excitedly, disturbed by all the ruckus.

I tried to push myself up, but one of my arms wouldn't move and using the other sent a burning pain across my chest and shoulder. Dropping back down caused the same blinding pain, so I rolled onto my back, gasping for breath. I waited for the agony to dull to merely excruciating.

The blue sky had wispy, feather-shaped clouds, I noted. A moment later my view was obscured by a large head with salt and pepper beard, swarthy skin, and eyes like glowing orbs of lapis lazuli. It was Reginald, only I'd never been so close to his face or seen him at this angle before, and I had a new appreciation for his striking mixture of handsomeness and homeliness. The top half was handsome, the bottom half homely, especially when he smiled, revealing crooked yellow teeth and breath like wet dog fur.

"Go away," I begged. "Let me die in peace."

"None of that. Yer not dying, and yer not goin' to git to lie down on the job neither," Reginald said. "I spied ye many a days relaxin' at the café while I was a sweatin' and a toilin'. Yer turn to suck it up. 'Tis only a broken collarbone looks like."

"Only...?" I began, but it turned into an ear-splitting shriek when Reginald hoisted me to my feet by my 'good' arm.

"They can sting a bit sometimes," he admitted, shaking his earlobe where I'd deafened him.

It did feel better now that I was standing, but as soon as I tried to look down, the pain threated to come back, so I stared straight ahead at the wreckage.

There were about five cargo cars spread across the meadow; a few had rolled further and toppled some of the surrounding trees. There was no sign of the security car where Thane, Ilsa, and the Dwarf King had been, but then I spotted it some distance along the track, still upright but so far away it seemed the explosion had propelled it forward instead of derailing it like the rest.

Bert was tending to Duane and the goblin doctor, who looked pretty scraped up. I spotted the mail bag holding Bell still wedged where I'd left her, but the whole cargo car was lying on its side, on end.

My second crash in one day. I was certain I liked locomotives even less than I liked dirigibles.

I started towards Bell at a run but switched to a sedate walk when the bouncing caused fiery tendrils of pain to shoot along my chest and shoulder. When I reached her, I realized there was no way I could climb up, let alone disentangle her without passing out. Fortunately, Reginald was there and had her down in moments, revealing the werewolf speed he'd never used even once when working at Karolyne's.

When Bell was out of the bag, I used my good hand to feel her pulse again. Even more reliably, I could see her soul still bright and strong and tightly tethered to her body.

There was no visible sign of breaks or even bruises, but I called to the goblin, "Get over here, Doctor. Find out why she's not waking up."

"I may have some internal bleeding, and my legs don't function, remember?" he replied.

"Quit making excuses. Reginald, can you help him?"

The dwarf immediately adopted the lazy, distant, 'I'm not listening' gaze which I was more familiar with.

"Here you go," Bert said, giving one last test of the makeshift bandage he'd placed on Duane's arm, before scooping up the goblin and carting him over on his shoulders. The goblin was wincing and feeling his ribcage, so I wondered if he hadn't been exaggerating about the internal bleeding.

The goblin examined Bell using an array of strange devices drawn from a myriad of tiny pockets sewn into the inside of his jacket. There was a set of pincers to measure the width of her head, nose, mouth, even the separation of her eyes. He had a vial of mercury in water, the silver drop floating at the meniscuses, to which he added a sample of her saliva. He squinted at it through a magnifying glass, then grunted and stoppered the vial. Next was a rack of more stoppered test tubes, filled with brown, yellow, or clear crystals.

"How much longer will this take?" I asked. I knew we should investigate the train crash to see what had happened to Conrad ... no, Thane, and the others.

"A drop of her blood please," he said, ignoring the question.

Bert and Reginald looked at me, and I looked at them. "My Ashur is better at taking a finger than a drop. Don't you have anything?"

"I have claws," Reginald said. A bit less precise those.

"And I have a log," Bert said, brandishing his.

"Her dagger," Duane said through gritted teeth.

I was relieved to see him sitting up, but the blood already seeping into the bandages worried me. He looked ill, his normally bronze skin a shade of yellow.

"Duane first," I told the goblin. "He needs stitches and something for the pain."

"I'm fine. Bell first."

He didn't look fine.

"You heard me," I said, and the note of authority in my voice was a match for my uncle's. It broached no argument.

"Here, there, here again.... My own wound may kill me in the interim," the goblin said, his complaints falling on unsympathetic ears, as Bert carried him to Duane's side.

The doctor had a sewing kit in his many pockets and set about stitching the long wound in Duane's shoulder as meticulously as a practiced tailor, not caring that Duane paled even more from the pain.

"Don't let him go into shock," I warned, remembering all Duane and Syla had done for me.

What had that weed looked like that she gave me? I kicked at the plants nearby, but there was nothing but grass and yellow wildflowers.

The goblin presented a glass phial and eye dropper and said, "Stick out your tongue."

Duane obeyed, and the goblin sprinkled a few drops. Duane swallowed and visibly relaxed, his expression dreamy.

"You've kept a treasure hidden," Duane told the doctor. "We could make a fortune with that potion."

"Not when I have so little and it takes months to procure more of the essential ingredients." The goblin chuckled. "If only I cared about fortunes, I'd have made mine long ago and not be in this wretched place. Alas, duty is a stronger force, is it not so, young thief?"

"I don't know what you're talking about."

"It does dull the processing of signals within the brain," the goblin said, "so let me clarify. I mean you are a creature of material concerns, a criminal lord fighting ceaselessly to maintain control of a small fiefdom of other criminals, all for the benefits of wealth and comfort, which you can hardly enjoy because of the grasping natures of your compatriots, who would see you dead and replaced at the first sign of weakness. Yet, despite these facts of your existence, you choose to set out on a voyage, leaving your criminal kingdom unattended, possibly stolen by whichever lieutenant you left in charge, all to pursue a woman."

I hadn't realized how precarious Duane's current position was, not until the goblin spelled it out in analytical terms, as he might the habits of a rare breed of animal.

"My 'fiefdom' is just fine, don't you worry," Duane said.

"Studies of the underbelly of various societies throughout history and in the current time, before the disturbances of the recent war of course, have always revealed otherwise," the goblin said. "It is for such astute observations the Emperor relies on me, even more so than my scientific endeavors, so I am quite certain you have taken a great risk and likely know it."

"Hilja must be pretty special," I said.

"It wasn't for her." His green eyes were dark now that the doctor's miracle drug had relaxed the pupils. He pinned me with his gaze, and it was as though I could truly see him for the first time.

Despite everything we'd been through, everything he'd endured his whole life, he was still full of sharp, aching life. I couldn't help but compare the intensity of him to the brightness of Thane's soul. He lacked the raw power, the irresistible pull to succumb, to give in to the peace of death. Instead, Duane's soul reached out like the steadying hand that catches you when you are about to fall, but then shoves you forward when you need it, that does not let you rest securely when there is a fear to confront. He was so alive and so much the opposite of peace.

"What woman were you pursing?" I asked.

"...Bell. Who else? I'm responsible for her."

I knew he was lying.

But the truth I saw beneath the surface frightened me. The fierceness of the feelings he couldn't hide from this new, soul-seeing gaze of mine were too much. I turned away, grateful for the sudden clarity of pain from my broken collarbone. Looking into his eyes made me uncomfortable, as though my own soul were wriggling beneath my skin, like an ice serpent trying to escape the light.

When Duane was stitched up and a fresh bandage applied, I allowed the goblin some time to examine his own injuries.

"I've been thinking about this coma Bell's in," I said aloud, already breaking my earlier resolution to stop thinking so vocally, "Thane, the Dead God, is not only God of Death but also of the Little Death."

"What does sex have to do with it?" Duane asked.

I laughed. That was the Duane I knew. Easier to ignore than what I'd seen in his eyes.

"Sex..." I began, blushing. I could hear Nanny's admonishments about what ladies should and should not discuss in the company of men buzzing about in my ear like a gnat. "...Sex is the Little Death, but so is sleep. Perhaps the god has put some sort of sleep spell on her?"

The goblin sighed, taking out his equipment again. "Let us not talk of spells until I have at least completed my examination. I still need a drop of her blood."

I knew the goblin would say that, but even Duane and the dwarves seemed to prefer the change of topic. The thought that the God of Death had been with us on that train was too frightening to contemplate. I knew how they felt. Once again, I looked at the distant security car, knowing I should investigate but unwilling to take another step toward it.

I retrieved the silver dagger I'd given Bell and used the tip to prick her finger. Only I couldn't. I saw the flesh indent, but the skin wouldn't break, and I couldn't get any blood.

"Something's wrong," I said.

"Give it here." Reginald took the knife, careful to keep his fingers on the leather-wrapped sheath and avoid touching the silver blade.

He couldn't cut her either. I could tell from the way he paled that he was thinking the same thing as me. He even went so far as to cut across her forearm before I could stop him, but the blade did not penetrate the skin there either.

"Is she dead?" Bert asked. "Do we have to burn her before it's too late?"

"She's not dead," Duane and I said at the same time. Duane's comment might be wishful thinking, but I could see her soul and it was very different from the way the souls of the risen dead were trapped inside their corpses. Besides, I'd seen a corpse before it rose, and the skin was hard as marble when it could no longer be cut. This seemed like something else, almost a protection on the sleeper.

"It must be Thane," I said. "When we catch up to him, we'll make him release her from this state."

"Catch up? Make?" Reginald said, incredulous. "He's not that annoying cousin of Karolyne's who can't find his shield for his ass—it's a..." he trailed off.

"So, you were paying attention during your fight with Malcolm."

"Werewolf ears are keen," he pointed out. "It's a freakin' *god*, Eva, and we is a stone's throw from the wall and the center of His power. We need to get the hell out of 'ere and back to Highcrowne."

"I know what He is," I said, slowly growing more comfortable with the reality of the situation. A god had kissed me, wanted me. What girl wouldn't be flattered? If only He didn't want to own my soul and keep it in the halls of death with Him for all eternity— once His dalliance with living lost its charms. "It doesn't change what we have to do, which is keep Him from taking the Dwarf King and even, I hate to say it, my sister. We must stop whatever He has planned. It's either that or give up now, because if we don't stop Him, no one we care about in Highcrowne will be safe, and there'll be no point going back there."

"She's right," Duane said, without any of his usual admonishments about my rashness and stupidity.

I planned to take off dramatically, but the non-werewolves were seriously wounded, including me, and even Bert and Reginald had a few unhealed scratches from their bout with Malcolm. So, there were no dramatics, just a slow migration toward that dreaded railway car.

"There is a rational explanation for this Thane person," the goblin mused. I thought he hadn't been listening, keeping his ears closed to our 'superstitious nonsense', but he must have been thinking. "Several explanations, actually. The most mundane being a disturbed personality. The other is possession by a being from the Void. I've heard of such instances, although I've not encountered such an affliction myself."

"How is that not magic?" I exclaimed for what felt like the hundredth time.

"It is not," he insisted, wincing as he examined his own injuries. "The laws of physics can ... differ in the Void and in other realms."

I didn't want to repeat myself.

Once the doctor assured himself he was not dying from internal injuries as originally feared, he tore a piece from my beautiful dress to make a sling for Duane's arm and a bandage for himself.

"There's little I can do about your injury, my dear. Try not to move around too much until it is healed," he admonished. I didn't see how I'd manage that.

Bert and Reginald tossed a coin, both vying for the chance of carrying the pretty girl. Reginald got Bell, and the normally smooth-tempered Bert cursed about getting the goblin.

It was a pathetic group that set off: Duane wielding the silver dagger one-handed, me unable to swing my Ashur without crippling agony, and the two dwarfs who could fight carrying the two who couldn't even walk.

So, when we reached the derailed security car and there was no sign of Thane—I'd decided not to think of him as Conrad right now—I was a tiny bit relieved. I had no idea how to stop a god. Malcolm and the bags with the king and Ilsa were gone too.

"Now what?" Reginald grumbled.

"Use your nose," I said. "You're better than a bloodhound. Help us track them down."

Reginald had to turn wolf for a few moments to find it, but there was a trail. Hope grew in me.

There were drawbacks to using the body He had hijacked. Thane wasn't in a rush to give up the sensations of being alive, but that also meant He had to take trains and dirigibles and walk on two feet rather that misting about or whatever it was gods normally did to travel. Because of Highcrowne's magical protections, the Compact among them, He probably couldn't even be here if He weren't hiding inside Conrad. All of which meant He was limited, and that meant it was possible to at least drive Him off.

Reginald stopped often to check we were still on the trail. I stumbled after him through the woods, gasping painfully each time I accidentally bumped against a branch. The others cursed and complained as well. There had to be a better way.

"Let's stop a minute and think," I said. "This is stupid with so many wounded. Bert, please use your werewolf speed and go back to find Baroness Syla and the others. We need reinforcements. Doctor Ghunnan, you stay here with Duane and Bell until they arrive. Meanwhile, Reginald and I will follow the trail and mark the path with..." I looked around for something and reluctantly tore another bit of red cloth from the sleeve of my dress "...this. Should be easy to spot even without werewolf nostrils to smell us."

"Eva, you should stay. You're worse off than me," Duane said, sounding logical.

"And miss out on the pain? I'd love to, but even if we get Syla's help, I may be the only one who can do anything. Thane wants me."

"Which is why we don't give you to him," Duane argued.

"He wants me, but He also doesn't want to harm me. That rule doesn't apply to the rest of you. I'll wait for reinforcements, but if need be Reginald can deal with Malcolm—I hope—and I can keep Thane distracted long enough for them to arrive."

"If I didn't know better, I'd think you wanted to be captured. With a suicidal plan like that," Duane said.

I was about to argue, but then I wondered myself. I felt drawn to Thane as much as to Solheim. Was I being drawn now?

"There is an alternative," the goblin said. "We know where they are going. The wall. Why not get there before them?"

"How?"

"I know a shortcut near here. A mere step across the Void."

"How do you know that?" I asked, suspicious as usual, but with good reason I reckoned in this case.

"Let us say that it is not a simple matter to traverse the goblin swamps and penetrate the Kingdoms' defenses to the north, or the Dead God's hordes to the south, to retrieve useful information on the key players of this war, or to investigate various natural laws and trends in modern medicine as suits my interests. To clarify—"

"—You're a spy," I said.

"Er ... a collector of knowledge, let us say. In any event, I know well the usefulness of the thresholds between worlds. I have extensive experience of which ones to avoid, as they lead only to the Void. Ha, ha. Which ones lead to worlds we care not to make aware of our existence, and which ones remain anchored to this physical realm. It may well be that the portal of which I speak is the very passage our quarry seeks as well, for it passes from this valley to the lee side of the wall. The Solheim side I should add."

"What?" I gaped. "Are you saying there's a—we'll call it a tunnel as I don't entirely understand this portal business—that bypasses the wall entirely? The wall the ancient elves built and have maintained for centuries, where most of The Kingdoms' soldiers are stationed should the Dead God's armies turn this way? You're saying they shouldn't have bothered, because the enemy could come through at any time?"

"Not with an army. The portal is small and a tad unpredictable. I find that when a portal is overly traversed it seems to disturb the energy patterns that tether it, and at times it can drift deeper into the Void. Thus, I always stick my monocular through first before I take a step myself, to get the lay of the land as it were." He pulled a small telescope from one of his inner pockets and extended it a good three feet.

"Quite the compact telescope," Duane noted with some admiration for the gadget.

"Monocular. The lenses are not shaped to magnify, beyond compensating for the light waves scattered as they travel the length of the shaft. It is quite like extending your eyeball several steps ahead of yourself. An interesting sensation. Would you like to try it?"

"No thanks." I said, stepping between Duane and the goblin before they could get us further side-tracked.

"Time's a wastin'. Where's this hidey hole yer speakin' of?" Reginald asked, as impatient as me.

"A short distance almost due east of here. It lies in the ruins of an abandoned temple overgrown with white morning glory of a distinctive variety whose seeds when dried and ground into a powder have many medicinal uses. If the alkaloids are extracted, a more powerful hallucinogenic solution can be obtained, which my poor dear student described as most entertaining."

"I'll find it. Bert can stay here to deal with all yer chit chat while I fetch Baroness Syla. I'll be back in time to rescue you all." Reginald shifted into wolf form and took off so fast he seemed to instantly vanish.

The goblin's eyes were squeezed tightly shut, as though he were trying to un-see Reginald's werewolf form. He must have failed to come up with a rational explanation for it.

"What happened to Katherine?" I asked. Thane must have lied about setting her free. "Why did you call her 'poor'?"

"Oh, no need for that glum look; she's not dead," he said, opening his eyes again. "That overly muscled dwarf attempted to carry her off with the others but could not manage it with three bodies already to juggle between them, one of them embedded in several hundred pounds of resin at that time. He released her in the woods, and I dared not move from my position of concealment to hail her to me. I know not where she went, but I believed it best for her to continue away from this place and to whatever safety she could find.

She did well to avoid all the insanity that has transpired and affected us so far."

My aching collarbone agreed with him on that point.

"You've always treated her like crap. Why so kind-hearted now?" I asked.

"There are certain proprieties of rank and duty that must be maintained with a student, but as she is now released from my care, I can view her once more as a private individual rather than a lump of clay to be pounded into useable shape."

"I wish we were all in more useable shape," Duane said, adjusting his bandages with a wince. "I can tell by that twitch in your lip, Eva, how eager you are to head off after more than you can handle, but the dwarf will be back soon. Wait here."

Duane ordering me around always had the opposite effect. The indecision that had held me in place, willing to listen to 'chit chat' from the goblin of all people suddenly evaporated.

"I can't." I grabbed the monocular with my good hand and started walking. "I'd prefer not to finish this fight on the other side of the wall where the god can call on His reinforcements. You do remember what's on the other side? I can delay Him at the ruins. You stay with Bell. Come on Bert. And bring the doctor, so we can find his magical doorway."

"It's physics not magic," the goblin grumbled under his breath.

Bert swung the doctor onto his shoulders and followed me.

Duane was in a quandary. He tried to scoop up Bell, but his arm gave out. "Eva. Wait."

I walked backwards, glancing down to make sure I didn't trip on a stick while I was making my point to Duane, and said, "You need to look after her."

"I want to look after you too."

"Because of your duty to Viktor? You have a greater duty to the living, especially Bell who admires you for reasons I can't fathom. Watch over her or you'll disappoint me more than every other reprehensible act in your life ever has."

"What if I don't care if you're disappointed?" he shot back.

I had to shout to be heard now. "You do. Else you'd be following me already."

"Take care of her, Bert," Duane said in a tone that threatened violence.

"She took down a troll," he said. "I think I need her to protect me."

By then we were deep into the woods, and I couldn't see Duane anymore. Bert's last comment rang in my ears, and I remembered the sweet taste of the soul I'd nearly devoured. I picked on Duane a lot, mostly because it was fun, but I was beginning to fear that I was the bigger monster. No. It was past that. I knew I was the bigger monster. Duane hadn't seemed to catch on yet: I wasn't Viktor's little sister anymore, or even whatever it was he saw me as, whatever I'd glimpsed when I looked into his soul.

I didn't know what I was—and Thane did. I wanted to stop Him, but I also wanted answers.

22   DESTINY

It was quiet in the forest. Having been raised in the city with all its chaos, it was soothing whenever we noisily crashed through a thicket or patch of undergrowth. I let Bert and the goblin go ahead to break the trail and save my collarbone from pain, but we paused often to check the goblin's compass. The device helped him spot 'portals' or 'doorways' as he referred to them.

"A mere matter of detecting distortions in the magnetic fields that run along..." he said, but I wasn't listening to him.

I was listening to the quiet of the woods. That silence was like death. Like the gap between thought and darkness. I knew there should be birdsong, the chirping of insects and other sounds; the forest earlier had been as loud as the city in its own way. All too quiet now.

"I think we've found the place," I said.

"I'm more familiar with this instrument, my dear, and I must say it is acting up quite a bit. It's very hard to compensate without—"

"—She's right," Bert cut in. "I see the top of some ruined tower over there."

I looked where he pointed and saw it too. "What was this place?" I asked.

"A haven of superstition and wastefulness," the goblin said. "People spending all day chanting, giving offerings, and killing each other over arguments about the sacredness of the place and the gods they listened too. All nonsense. The voice of their gods was nothing but the babbling of voices from across the Void. None worthy of worship, I assure you."

"One person's babble is another's profundity," Bert said sagely.

"Not in a world of facts. In the real world, some ideas are correct, and some are simply idiotic. The difference can easily be determined through observation, measurement, and testing," the goblin pronounced.

"Unless you close your eyes and refuse to observe what you don't like," I said, thinking of the clever goblin's very idiotic refusal to contemplate the existence of werewolves or magic. I saw no reason to exclude them from the universe. Nor did I have any difficulty calling a being, capable of controlling the souls of the dead, a god. What did that make me?

Whoa, Eva. I stopped myself. I was getting a swelled head. Something about this place made the blood surge through my veins and the green glow in my palms grow brighter and hungrier. I felt like I could take on anything, and I made straight for the ruins, not even caring if Bert followed. What were werewolf claws compared to the power within me?

The ruins were not as large as I expected. Not a city or even a small town, only a single, tumbled-down tower with stairs leading nowhere. There was a darkened doorway at the base with more steps going down, and I felt drawn in that direction.

"There are caverns beneath," the goblin said, confirming my instinct to head underground.

Bert with the goblin atop his shoulders was the same height as me, and we all had to stoop to make it through the doorway. Carved into the lintel above us was an image of a winged skull, the symbol of the Dead God.

"I have it," the goblin exclaimed. "These werewolves are some dwarf variant from a land beyond the Void. As unlike our dwarves as humans are unlike Solhans. Beings of vapor perhaps, able to reassemble their component pieces just as we would mold clay or wetted sand. That's a relief." He looked content now that he'd made up a theory he liked.

I envied him his delusions.

I led the way, my Solhan night vision allowing me to see the steps clearly, but Bert cursed and stopped as he and the goblin got caught on a warped piece of rusted metal that might once have been a portcullis or gate. I kept going, hearing them call my name but not registering their voices.

Another call reached into my soul, compelling me onward, and soon I was in the chamber beneath the ruins. It was a large, natural cavern thick with stalagmites and stalactites—I never knew which was which—many fused to form floor-to-ceiling columns of limestone. The natural pillars were carved with symbols in a language I didn't recognize. Little shelves had been cut into them as well, some holding figurines of winged death, others holding candles that had burned out long ago.

The flicker of light from living candles drew me deeper toward the center of the chamber. Shadows shifted as people moved in front of the light. I made my way toward them, a part of me thinking it was time to draw my Ashur, but even as my hand twitched toward it, pain shot across my shoulder, and I knew I couldn't wield it if I tried.

The plan had been to stall until Baroness Syla and her pack of wolves arrived to save the day, but there was no way anyone could save me. This inexorable pull on my soul called me deeper into the darkness.

I saw the king's body first, no longer hidden in a mail bag. It was obvious where the resin had been roughly hewn away, the remaining layer making the dwarf appear to be covered in honey. The silver crown was clearly visible, and, likewise, his soul felt closer to the surface. At least I could feel it more than before, and it was fighting, like a dreamer trying to wake from a nightmare. It had been trapped between life and death for centuries, but it sensed something had changed and was afraid.

"He believed he had struck the final blow to the Solhan Empire," Thane said, as if we were continuing an earlier conversation. "He was clever, locking away the crown that controlled the dwarven fighters, along with the ability to create more. He sought to escape me—or more rightly the Solhans who wielded my power, as he did not know then that I would come for him—but even a king cannot hide from Death forever."

Malcolm was wriggling Ilsa's inert form out of the mail bag that held her, humming while he worked, and it was disturbing watching him handle my double.

He gave me a wink and said, "Hey there, Eva. Finally catching up? Weren't sure how long we'd have to wait. I said you were too tough to give in to 'love's pull' or whatever, but I guess there's no winning a bet against a god. Suppose that's why He's running things."

"Love?" I snorted. "I'm as sick of love as I am spring. Love did not pull me here. Danger and the certainty that I would find it are the more likely culprits. I'm self-destructive that way. I'm also here to stop you. You can start by letting my sister go." I tried pulling my sword and failed miserably, as I couldn't even lift an arm without passing out from the pain.

Malcolm smiled and shook his head. He had Ilsa out now and was laying her on an altar in the center of the chamber. It was limestone like the rest of the place, and the air nearby was heavy with the same stillness I'd felt in the forest. The doorway the goblin had spoken of must be near.

Altars were never a good sign.

"Stop whatever you're doing," I ordered.

Malcolm ignored me and kept working. "Boss needs the Dwarf King's body—and his crown—if he's to command the dwarves. Just doing as I'm told."

"You stole Conrad's body, why not the king's if you want it so badly?" I asked Thane.

"Rutgard is near dead," Thane said. "I have to resurrect him first, and that's not easy for Death, as we're more familiar with the other direction." He smiled like death and resurrection were common occurrences.

I wished I had Syla's army of wolves behind me after all. I couldn't even summon the fear that had let me stand against the troll. My hands were glowing bright enough to transform the light around us from the orange of flame to the green of magic, but I couldn't summon the will to direct it anywhere. I was standing almost as still as Ilsa.

"Our power is stronger here; that is why you were drawn," Thane said, as though I'd asked him a question.

His voice suddenly took on the distant echo I'd first heard from a risen corpse, a sound like a voice in a heavy wind, but the voice was stronger now. It said: "This body cannot contain me. This world cannot contain me, and I am forever diminishing myself. Only a portion of my being came through at the call of your Solhan priests before the ritual was interrupted, else this world would have perished in an instant, and only a portion of that portion resides within this flesh. But all of me is here ... but a step away, locked in the Void. Only it is vast enough to be worthy of me."

I thought Thane had sounded alien, but the voice of the Dead God Himself, the full version, was like a raging storm, a force of nature. He was so vast and powerful I couldn't comprehend Him. Not really. That's probably why I said the next stupid thing that came to mind.

"I'm starting to like the goblin's theory. You're not a god—just an asshole." Cockiness was not attractive, unless I was doing it.

"Why do you force me to endure such limitation? You are the key, and it pains me to be confined, waiting for the key to turn. Each moment is agony ... I cannot bear to speak through this form, for the pain is worsened." A shadow crossed Thane's face, and his expression relaxed.

"Conrad?" I asked.

"Would that make you happy? I chose him for you."

"Thane," I said. At least the creepy voice was gone, leaving Conrad's voice in its place.

"I am not Conrad, and I am not a god, Eva, but the rest of me is. I must be separate from Him to avoid breaking the Compact. I can do what He cannot. You heard how He is trapped, and so you know now why He wants you."

"I don't know. Not really. And I don't know how you can talk about Him as separate from you. Are you or are you not the Dead God? This does my head in."

"I am the part that is yours. I have been separate for a long time, waiting for you to be ready, thinking only of you. Most of me, of the Dead God, is trapped in the Void, while yet another portion commands His armies, raising the fallen to do battle against all the lands of this world that once belonged to Solheim. That was the bargain for bringing us through, the request the Nine made, before they realized that once the door was open ... all of me, of Him, could come through, and nothing would survive. They stopped the ritual and took you from us. Come back to me, Eva."

"Give Conrad his body back. Tell the Dead God to go home and give this world back." I could make requests too.

"Do you truly want me gone?"

I shouldn't have paused so long. Poor Conrad. I wanted him freed, I did, but there was something so mesmerizing about the scene before me, the pull that had drawn me to this cavern. A pull that I knew led to worlds beyond imagining.

"Possessing two bodies is a bit greedy, isn't it?" he said, suddenly smiling in a way that was utterly disarming and so at odds with the scene. "I can't help wanting to stay here, though. You've made me weak, a weakness I cannot resist. I want to touch you ... But I also need Highcrowne and all the dwarves to be mine, to sweep the last who oppose me ... us ... Him away."

He seemed to find it difficult reconciling his identities. Even his body language was torn between reaching out to me and moving toward the altar.

"I am required to give Him Highcrowne," Thane said, "without breaking the Compact of course. Rules are rules."

"Rules? I didn't think you were the type to obey those." I couldn't keep a flirtatious note out of my voice. It was because of Conrad's gorgeous good looks I told myself, but there was something more behind Thane's eyes, a fire and cunning that sent a shiver along my spine.

"Death is the ultimate rule," he said in a way that made it appealing ... and chilling.

"Enough foreplay." I instinctively reached for my Ashur again, and froze with agony from my broken collarbone before inching my hand back to my side. Through gritted teeth, I said, "I can't let you."

"There's only one way to stop me … Him," Thane said.

"How do I kill Death?"

"You don't. Embrace it." He stepped closer, and I took a step back.

"Don't tell me what to do," I warned. Nothing like my stubborn instinct to override my self-destructive impulses.

"Then don't tell me," he warned.

Seemed we were at an impasse. There was one wounded pet detective against one god and one were-wolf. Hardly fair odds. I vaguely remembered having left my own werewolf and lame goblin somewhere. I took a few more steps away from Thane, moving closer to the altar. This was usually the time I started mentally replaying all the stupid decisions I'd made to wind up where I was.

I decided not to play that game with myself and try something new.

I felt for the cold poison glow of power that pooled in my bones these days and overflowed into my palms, threatening to spill out like blood from my veins at any opportunity if not for the stubborn control I sought over it. I let go and let green fire come.

Malcolm turned furry and grew claws. I grew my own long, lightning tendrils of green that reached out with sharp death, and I barely needed to swing my arm for the swipe of power to cut across Malcolm's chest

He growled and shot toward me like true lightning.

"Stop," Thane commanded, and Malcolm turned in midair, careening into a stalactite.

"Cramping my style, Boss," the werewolf growled, wiping away blood from a split lip. The skin where I'd scratched him was unbroken. That's all I'd managed? I forgot werewolves were pretty much immune to magic, and Malcolm resisted when I tried to grab his soul before. Not good.

I was between them and Ilsa now at least. The chasm of the Void felt like a cold wind at my back. Nothing was visible with my eyes, but I could feel it with my soul, which felt like it was clinging to my body by its fingernails.

The voice of the god rolled out like an ocean wave behind me, making me spin to face the greater enemy I'd inadvertently forgotten. The physical danger Malcolm represented seemed the lesser threat now.

"Eva," the God's voice said, and I felt ready to fall to my knees. "Do not defy me. You are mine."

It felt like I was being pushed back by a wind I couldn't breathe through, but I stood my ground. "You keep saying that."

"You were promised to me," the voice said, the one I wasn't liking so much for the way it was trying to pulverize me. I hadn't noticed Thane behind me until he had his lips to my ear.

Thane whispered in his Conrad voice, and I heard him more clearly than I did the god, booming his words across the Void. "You were promised before you were born, Eva. You see, I want you to be with me. Not He who is cold and ambitious, but with me who has tasted your lips, felt your body hot against mine..." As he spoke, I remembered the feel of him, how good it had been to be in his arms back on the airship. "...I want you. You are mine, promised to me before you were born. You are my wife."

I was nothing for a long moment. It seemed there was no time, no thought, and no existence. I was lost in those words. His. And I was no more. That loss of self was a pure existence without regret or worry, eternal ... and then I breathed deeply and reminded myself I was not dead. And I was not married. Not by my choice.

That's why my mother had left me behind in Solheim.

I felt relief. I was not unworthy or weaker than Ilsa. I was chosen. I was special. And I would not lose myself, because I was stronger than her or anyone.

"I don't believe in betrothals or child brides," I said, standing up. "I don't like you manipulating my feelings, either, or invading my dreams ... Win my love if you want it."

I pushed him back with power, as my shoulder was too weak to give any strength to the simultaneous shove I gave him with my good arm. I was surprised when he flew through the air and almost smacked into the same stalactite that Malcolm had crashed into earlier.

I wanted to run to him to see if he was okay. What was wrong with me?

"Finish him," Bert called, stepping from the shadows.

Bert swung the goblin off his back, dropped him to the floor with a grunt, and then transformed into a werewolf just in time to face off against Malcolm.

Thane looked at me in such a way my heart felt torn from my chest. *He's the bad guy, Eva*, I kept reminding myself.

"Don't," Thane said holding out a shielding hand. "I don't want to go."

He wasn't as resistant to my magic as the werewolf had been. I could kill him, kill the body he inhabited anyway. Kill Conrad. I couldn't do it. Besides, there was still the Dwarf King and plenty of other bodies around he could take, so there was no point. Death didn't have the same rules for him.

"Let Conrad go," I commanded.

"Then give me Ilsa and Rutgard," he said in the distant and far off voice of a God. "And you. I need you most of all."

"This isn't the marketplace where we can haggle. This is me telling you to go back to the Void and leave us mortals alone. We never asked for you to build the Solhan Empire all over again."

"Your family did. Shall you ask your mother? She waits for us in Solheim, waits to give you to me."

"My mother?" I shouldn't care, shouldn't listen to anything He had to say, but there is always something missing when you've never known a mother, and I couldn't help asking: "What happened to her?".

"Nothing she did not want. Your mother is one of us, as is Malcolm, as is Alum, and even your Gypsum."

"Because you did something to them."

"It is of their own free will they serve Him," it was Thane talking again and not the voice from the Void. The two of them, one luscious and tempting as cinnamon smoke, the other vast and dark and alluring in that kiss of death kind of way, were doing my head in. They kept whipping back and forth, working very hard to convince me—and not kill me.

"You need me. You've said it many times before, and I know you don't mean in the physical kind of way. You need me for something that Rutgard, Gypsum, my mother, not even Ilsa can give you. What do you really want?"

Silence speaks volumes.

"Not something I'm going to like. Let me guess, end of the world kind of thing?"

"It is glorious and inevitable," the voice from the Void said as though that were compensation.

"We can have lifetimes together," Thane said. "The end will not be quick." That sounded less than reassuring. It sounded painful for everyone else except we chosen few in our deep Solhan tombs, sealed and safe from the deaths of countless innocents.

"I'm not the God of Death," I said. "I don't have a quota for those I kill, and I'm happy to keep it down to one if possible." Or was it two now? More? Was I losing count? Not good, Eva.

"The deal is sealed," Malcolm said. "Accept it, Eva. I tried to give you one last tumble before you knew you were a married woman, but too late now. Your husbands are here." He stood face to face with Bert, patiently waiting. For what? Me to choose?

"What do you get, Malcolm?" I asked. "If I get an empire of death, what's in this for you and Gypsum? What payment is worth it all?"

"Immortality. This isn't the only world, Eva. Lots of other places to enjoy before their time runs out too. On to the next, one lady love after another for all eternity. Sounds good to me."

"I can see your hedonism knows no bounds, but why would Gypsum do this?" That's what I really wanted to know. She was a mother, wife, friend, and she had betrayed us all, betrayed Highcrowne and her home.

"Can't say. She recruited me and the others and didn't have to mention more than service to the once and future Solhan Empire and that immortality bit before I was won over. But I do know she's smart. I'm sure that's why she made the right decision. So, should you."

"I'm not one for smart," I said. Bert looked calm, staring down his fellow wolf, and I asked him, "So are they here yet? I think I've stalled as long as I can."

"Should be. I scented Matriarch Syla just before I came in to see if you were still alive. Surprised to find you holding your own."

"I do surprise a lot."

More Surprises

Thane stood and said, "Time is running out, my love."

The way he said it reminded me of how Erick had spoken, and I wondered if Thane had possessed him then. Had it been Thane who seduced me before? I was proud I'd resisted a bit better this time around. A bit.

"Your sister and Rutgard will be useful," Thane continued, "but they were never more than bait to lure you from the protections of Highcrowne. You are the one I desire." He looked to Malcolm then. "Take her."

I guessed there would be no real choice in the matter. I summoned my magical green claws to stave him off, but Bert interceded on my behalf, knocking

Malcolm aside, and I had to change my aim, obliterating another stalactite.

"*Tsk, tsk*, none of that," Alum clucked, stepping into the circle around the altar and grabbing Bert by his scruff like a kitten. "Malcolm wants to stay pretty for eternity. It matters less to me."

Alum's golden, King's Guard uniform suddenly faded into mist, as did the rest of him, and a moment later the wolf stood there—a wolf in a black suit and top hat, smiling as only wolves do, tongue lolling out the side of its mouth. "Well, I like to be a tad pretty." The words were snarled, the drool dripping from his jagged teeth incongruous with his fashionable attire.

It was Alum, Gypsum's brother. He was the wolf. The one I wanted dead more than any other. He had smiled like that just before he tried to kill Little Viktor and Duane, just before he killed dozens in the market-place.

Bert slashed at him, but Alum's reach was far longer. He was also a lot stronger than any werewolf I'd seen, because he casually tossed Bert over his shoulder. Bert went flying until he struck the wall beside the cavern entrance. I could see the silhouette of his crumpled form in the faint light pouring in from outside.

"I hope you didn't kill him," Malcolm said, glaring at Alum and popping his knuckles. "Bert's my second cousin."

"And I'm your uncle," Alum pointed out.

"Yeah, but I like him," Malcolm said.

I suddenly realized Malcolm had been holding back when we fought on the train. He was probably as strong as Alum, but he hadn't wanted to hurt Bert or me.

I was really screwed this time: No hope of fighting against werewolves like these or of using magic. I couldn't even summon any scathing words or witty insults, because Alum made me furious—and frightened.

"Syla and the others here? You were supposed to lead them away with the scent of the Dwarf King," Thane said, admonishing.

"I led my sister a merry chase as you asked, but Cousin Reginald has put her on the right track again. Kind of. They are wasting time out there looking for these two."

Alum stepped back into the darkness of the cavern and dragged out an unconscious Bell and an even more wounded Duane. Duane looked as crumpled and broken as Bert, and I would have thought him dead if not for the whimper of pain he made.

"Duane," I whispered. I felt paralyzed with fear for him and Bell. Alum was like some child's story villain come to life, the kind of stories Nanny used to tell where the monster always won, and I went to bed crying and shivering in the dark with Ilsa laughing at me. Hiding under a tear-soaked pillow wouldn't work this time.

"You want them dead or alive?" Alum asked, as though it made no difference.

"Will you obey if I tell you? You have not obeyed well of late," Thane said, angry.

"Because you've been acting loopy of late. It grows worse the longer you're in human bodies. The lord I vowed to serve would have wanted all of Highcrowne dead, not abandoned warehouses blown up. Instead, you admonish me for wielding death as is our right, and you have us run away, hiding our strength, leaving the airship intact instead of blowing it apart, although others destroyed it for us, all the while you grow weaker and speak only of Eva."

"Do not cross me. I am your god, and she is the missing key," Thane said.

"A key that serves as well dead—the god only needs her soul—and I've started to doubt you are my god at all. You are the palest shadow of Him."

"I am Death, believe me. Even confined and human, I have power enough to make those of you bound to Him feel the burning reserved for transgressors." Thane raised his hand, and Alum grit his teeth, perspiration beading on his forehead. Some invisible compulsion overwhelmed him, and the wolf dropped his prisoners before howling in pain.

As the sound echoed through the cavern, I realized Thane was my key.

"You want me?" I said. "Then I want you to send your big bad wolves away. Wake Bell. Heal Duane. Give me all I desire, and I can be all you desire."

I wasn't as good at playing the femme fatale as my sister, but I had seen her do it enough that I could fake it. I went all languid with my pose, and the few steps I took to reach him were slow and deliberate, my gaze meeting his with intensity.

I stumbled when I looked deep into his eyes, for my soul sense was strong; it had grown since using it to control the lesser werewolves' transformations. All the different souls around me were like colored lights: the orange embers of wounded Bert; the sharp white flame of the goblin deeper in the cavern, the pale blue of Bell sleeping away her life like some enchanted princess; yellow columns of flames for Malcolm and Alum, dangerous fires poised to burn and consume all they could if left unchecked; the red warmth of Duane, strong and unflinching, even as his wounds continued to weaken the tether between his soul and his body; and Thane.... Thane was like looking into the heart of the sun. His brightness was a stark contrast to the black of the Void which held the greater extent of the God. My soul sight flinched from that vast darkness. It was incomprehensible. But Thane pulled me in.

I circled him, like a moon in his orbit, and he turned to face me as I went around and round, the room spinning into a blur, so it felt like we were the only two beings in existence. I pressed myself against him, and he steadied me, else I might have toppled over. I wrapped my arms around his neck and kissed him.

I wasn't kissing Conrad. I was kissing Thane, and he felt it. His light reached out for me, and mine reached out for his, the bodies between us getting in the way. I wanted him more than physically. I wanted … resisting him was so much harder this time, but I stepped back.

It was like stepping into the grave when I had been dancing in the light of midday.

"Wake her. Heal him. Send your wolves away," I said, repeating my demands. I should have asked him to wake Ilsa as well, but I didn't want to hear my sister's ridicule. She would criticize my acting; she would know it was weakness and not an act at all. I wanted Thane. I couldn't help it. Fortunately, my desire to save my friends was stronger than my desire to destroy myself.

"Eva," he whispered, reaching for me. I took a step back, and it was agony.

Thane went to Bell's side, and with a touch she woke. She gulped air, choked and coughed, and then rolled onto her side, recovering.

One demand met.

"I can't help Duane," Thane said. "Healing is not within my power."

"Then send Alum and Malcolm away at least."

"Go ..." Thane began, but we all turned at a noise from the cavern entrance.

More silhouettes blocked the light. Lots of them. My backup had finally arrived.

"Stop," Alum, shouted in warning. "Come any closer, Syla, and this whole cavern comes down on our heads. I don't care that you're my sister. I will kill you."

Alum shrugged off his outer coat and undid his silk waistcoat, revealing a furry brown wolf chest and a large belt of dynamite strapped to it.

Werewolves must have keen sight, because I couldn't make out any of the silhouettes in the distance, but I heard Syla's wolf voice say, "Don't be foolish, Alum. You'll kill yourself and all of us. For what?"

"For my God," he said. "I will go to Him, but when I bring His enemies with me my reward will be great. Paradise for eternity."

"Isn't that what we're all supposed to expect anyway?" Syla argued.

"Yes," Thane cut in. "There is no reason to resist. Join us, Baroness, and you'll see that we offer this world peace. Stop these threats, Alum. This is not what I wish."

"What *you* wish or the Dead God? Speak to me, Lord, and tell me your true wishes," Alum called toward the Void at my back.

The voice like a hurricane pressed against me as He said, "I want to be free."

Not very detailed instructions, and I felt the god was leaving a bit too much to individual interpretation. Most irresponsible of Him.

"Knock this off, you idiot. I was promised eternity in the flesh," Malcolm said, "not in some wispy other-world. I want meat and good mead and women. There are not enough fine dwarf women or otherwise, not for one lifetime. Don't you be killing us all and robbing me of my reward."

"If he be movin' about too much, he's likely to kill us all accidental if not intentional," Bell said, fully awake now. "That dynamite is not stable. I see it sweating."

"You are all pathetic," Alum said. "Death is to be embraced."

Death wanted to embrace me, and I had no intention of letting Him.

Bell had caught my attention when she spoke, and I saw Duane next to her. He had the silver dagger half hidden beneath his palm, but he was too weak to move, let alone stand up and use it. He nodded to me.

I crouched down beside my friends. "All you have to do is let Bell and Duane go," I told Alum. "I'll come along and no one has to die right now. You don't want to piss Malcolm off. I think he'd hunt you down in this world or the next." When Alum glanced at his nephew, I grabbed the silver dagger.

I lunged upward, shoving the dagger into Alum's furry wolf throat, which spurt boiled blood, steam rising from the wound. His top hat went flying, and he stumbled backwards, tripping over the goblin who had crawled up behind the wolf with his umbrella. The pointed end of the umbrella sprung open to reveal a thin blade, and the wolf impaled himself on it as the goblin rolled aside.

"Get back," Bell warned, dragging Duane with her toward the altar.

I snatched the goblin by one shriveled leg and pulled him back as well.

Alum wasn't dead yet. He didn't bother to pull the umbrella sword out of his back or the dagger out of his throat. The silver blade was visible when he opened his maw in another wolfish grin. He couldn't speak, but he didn't need to. The satisfied sparkle of joy in his eyes told me all I needed to. He pulled a mechanical sparker from the pocket of his waistcoat and lighted it.

My instinct was faster than my wits. I raised my hand, and what I could only call a curtain of green fire rose before me. Malcolm was running toward me, and he hit it with a yelp, falling to the floor like he'd run into the side of a mountain. Syla was on him before he could regain his feet, and once again a snarling ball of werewolf fought only steps away from me.

The magical barrier I'd erected on instinct widened, encompassing Bell and Duane, spreading around me like a curtain being drawn closed. Thane walked the edge, trying to step inside it, but the shield was too fast for him. His eyes were on me the whole time, and when the shield was complete, we looked at each other through fiery green glass. I felt a pang. Once again, my instinct was faster than my wits, and I widened the circle, enveloping Thane just as Alum's dynamite went off.

My shield blocked everything, even sound, and so it was a surreal sight as destructive force shot outward from Alum's death, the grin still on his wolf face before he died.

Syla and Malcolm had rolled, fighting, back to the entrance to the cavern, and I wondered if Syla had been dragging her son to safety all along. I hoped she and the other wolves made it out, but I couldn't tell.

Dirt and limestone, stalactites and stalagmites, the cavern roof, and stone blocks from the tower above ... everything crashed down on us. The explosion and the rain of debris afterwards happened in silence. My shield had protected our heads too; dirt and stone pressed against it to form a dome over us. We were entombed.

I was afraid to let the shield drop, because I didn't know how I'd created it in the first place. I took a breath to calm myself. The Void and the altar were at my back, and I felt the Dead God on the other side, a pool of gravity drawing me in. My gaze went to Thane.

"Thank you," he said.

I saw him in double vision: one the golden Conrad, the other the bright soul of Thane.

The goblin checked Duane over. "He'll live."

"I want to stand," Duane said. Bell helped him regain his feet, and I saw he was covered in bruises.

Bell shot me a wild grin, like the one we'd shared after running from werewolves on *The Mathésis*, but I couldn't share this one. I wasn't relieved or giddy, because this wasn't over. A cold iron knot lodged in my stomach.

I went to the altar.

My twin was a mirror of me when she slept, without her cruel smile or piercing eyes which bore into me when she was awake. She looked so vulnerable laying on the slab of stone next to the still-cocooned form of King Rutgard.

The Dwarf King too appeared fragile, half my sister's size, frozen and staring at me helplessly. I could feel the agony of his soul, so close to waking, so close to death. Poised between with no hope of surcease. I could feel my sister's small soul too, slumbering inside her like a serpent in its burrow through the deep cold of winter.

"Wake up, Ilsa," I said, sounding like a child myself, with my voice small and terrified.

She had always been the bogeyman, but the real one lurked nearby. Ilsa and the king lay in darkness's lap, and I was afraid to reach out and touch her for fear of touching Him, a mere step away through one of the goblin's doorways.

"Ilsa..." This time I dared a touch, and to my surprise her eyes immediately sprung open. I took a step back.

"Come closer, Eva." The voice was that of the Dead God. She was a shadow puppet for that unseen force.

"You think you have me trapped, all the prizes you dream of within your grasp?" I said. "You think you've won? Think again. I won't give you anything."

I sidestepped Ilsa and touched the warm resin encasing the Dwarf King.

I can't explain how well I know some souls for the moments I'm touching them. It's like being inside another person's life in your dreams, when you know all their past and their confused desires for the future. So real, this dream, but this was a man's life. No life at all. He wanted to give up his watch over the crown, wanted to join Death as a soul should. Wanted to give up.

I couldn't give in like that, but I could let him.

"Rutgard, you did well. You saved the dwarves from war for centuries and now it's time someone saved you."

I touched his soul and pulled it from his body, but not into me. I wasn't hungry for it as I'd been for the troll's. It was like pulling a thread until the whole tapestry unraveled, revealing a long, shining strand without form but with infinite potential.

Rutgard's voice inside my mind was pleased. *Thank you.*

There could be no resurrection now, no living king for Thane to possess. Rutgard's soul travelled into the Void. This was not the disappearance of souls I'd witnessed at the marketplace, vanishing to somewhere unknowable. I could see where this soul had gone because I was at the threshold. A black line appeared before me, infinitely wide when looked at a certain way and barely visible when looked at another. Rutgard's soul fled into it, but the opening remained.

Eyes like suns, large and vast and far away burned on the other side, looking into me. "Come to me."

I was moving before I knew what I was doing. I clutched the corpse of the king to stop my forward momentum and pushed it in front of me. The green fire in my hands spread to the corpse, consuming it, melting resin and flesh. I shoved the burning body into the Void.

"Take your king and crown, in ashes, and you'll have no Thorne today," I said.

The body vanished into the dark line, which was suddenly wide enough to contain it. The line grew wider and closer, like a mouth opening for me, those sun-like eyes inside it burning in the darkness.

That was Thane's other half inside the Void, a deeper blackness, robed in darkness instead of cloth, with massive wings that stretched above and below, like feathers, like a bat's, but neither, more like tendrils stretching out and casting their shadow across all the world, across all souls. The darkness had a chill, and it seemed all the cinnamon warmth that had been alluring before was only contained within Thane, while all that remained in the Void was as cold and lifeless as the grave.

A sound like a knock on a window caught my attention and broke the spell. The Void closed, and I looked back to see the little goblin tapping at the shield I'd erected.

"Don't mess with that," I said.

"I say, we should try to make our exit from this ... whatever it is collapses," the goblin said, ignoring me.

As I feared, the green shield suddenly vanished. I held my breath, expecting to be crushed, but nothing happened other than a few streams of loose dirt falling to the ground like rain. The rest of the rocks held, forming a smaller cavern around us. With the barrier gone, I now heard digging on the other side.

A short time later Syla's voice carried, distant and muffled, "We're coming."

"We're saved!" Bell hugged Duane. He winced but hugged her back.

I leaned against the altar, sagging with relief. I tried very hard not to look at Thane. I had no idea what I was going to do with him.

"You'd best step away from that threshold," the goblin warned me. "As I mentioned before, whenever a portal is approached in the right way, it acts as a physical bridge between points in space, allowing travel within this realm as well as to the Void between. This is the path to the other side of the wall, remember? Oh, and the door opens both ways."

I was still registering what he was saying when arms appeared out of the air and grabbed Ilsa. I could no longer see the black of the Void; the threshold was invisible, and when they pulled her through, she vanished. More arms reached for me. Dead white, corpse-like arms. The hairs on my neck rose. The other side of the wall....

A small woman stepped through the unseen doorway next, purple eyes like amethysts. Gypsum, calm as could be.

"I knew you'd end up in the thick of trouble, Eva. You always do. Come along now. Your mother sent me to fetch you." She smiled.

"Keep away from her," Duane said. I could tell he was looking for a weapon, but our only silver dagger was buried along with Alum.

"How could you...?" I began.

"What? Betray you? There are more important things than you, Eva, believe it or not. We dwarves once served a great empire, and when the Dead God called, I chose to serve again, not without thought or hesitation, but because, as I said, I want to keep my sons and husbands safe from war. The Dead God will win this war, and my family will live, eternal. If I serve the winning side." She shook her head like I was the most obtuse of her children. "You never thought it strange a Solhan girl and noble dwarf would become such fast friends? You never questioned why I, with my titles and station—or Syla's title anyway and my bloodline—why I'd care a wit about a refugee like you? It was my job all along to watch and wait until it was time to bring you to your destiny. Well, here it is."

Behind her, like an image on a dark pond coming into focus, I could now see the other side of the doorway. The plains of Solheim bathed in the orange of sunset, vast and frightening ... and the army of dead.

Gypsum turned to wolf form between one eye blink and the next. She yanked me the few steps it took to cross to the other side.

"Welcome home," Gypsum said, in that growl that was a rougher, more terrifying version of her voice.

I wanted to retreat but cold, marble-like hands held me in their grip. Risen corpses surrounded me, each as fast and strong as the old man it had taken a squad of city guard to defeat in the marketplace. They held my arms and ankles, and I couldn't call the green fire. I was too terrified.

Ilsa was already there, unconscious on the ground beside me. I whipped my head around and saw through the open portal to the darkened cave. The goblin gaped in astonishment; the others were horrorstruck. They stared out at me from a small tear in the world that hung in mid-air like a painting without a wall to support it.

To either side of the opening was the mountain range we'd been in, bypassed in a single step, and in the distance was the ancient, stone wall that blocked the only pass into the Three Kingdoms. I was on the wrong side of it. Highcrowne soldiers manning it were small, black shapes along the top, too far away for me to see their faces, but there were a lot of them up there, likely disturbed by this gathering of the God's soldiers.

Thane stepped across the threshold next, and he looked at me with gentle understanding. "You only fear what you do not know. This is where you were meant to be, Eva. With me."

Why am I such a catch? I wondered. Because I'm the key? The lock turns both ways, that strange creature, No-Thing, had said. My brain whirled faster than a locomotive's wheels, spinning in place with no idea what to do now.

Thane reached for me, and I wanted to scream. All I said was, "Help me."

"I will..." he began, but he was cut short by a scream more powerful than mine would have been, assuming I could work my throat. It was a bone shattering screech, angry and threatening.

A shadow passed over the sunlit plain, and that shriek split the air again. The dead did not respond to it, but Gypsum, Thane, and I looked up to see the dragon, scales glinting golden orange in the fading light.

I was sure it was the same one I had spotted from *The Mathésis.* You didn't see many dragons. This one landed atop a group of risen corpses, smashing them into the golden grass. It bounded forward in two great steps, looming over us, and buried its maw, full of jagged white teeth, into a dead neck. It bit the head off one of the things holding me.

The dragon looked at me with cream-colored eyes, and I swear it smiled as it said, "Silly girl."

The dragon swiped Thane aside, while Gypsum stepped back of her own accord. Massive talons grabbed me, squeezing harder than the vice-like grip of the corpses holding my ankles. It lifted me and flicked the last corpses away like annoying fleas. I looked down at Thane, Conrad, whoever he was, and for the first time he had real fear in his eyes.

I couldn't breathe, couldn't call or beg for help, not with giant claws clenched around my ribs and causing my broken collarbone to burn with fiery agony.

Those massive yellow eyes appraised me closely. "Is it you? Or her I need to worry about?" the beast asked, looking first at me and then down at Ilsa's prone form. The dragon snatched her up with the other talon. A moment later, I heard the snap of sheet-like wings and felt a rush of wind pull at my hair and clothes. We were airborne.

I was flying.

UNTIL NEXT TIME...

Find out what happens next in Eva Thorne Book Three, "Blood & Thorne", out now.

Subscribe at http://www.lorelclayton.com for updates from Author Lorel Clayton.

ABOUT THE AUTHORS

Lorel and Clayton were both born and raised in
the Western United States and were teen
sweethearts, brought together by a fierce love of
books and hormones, of course. They traveled to
Australia in 1997 and never left, finding the
sunshine and beaches of "Oz" too irresistible.

Lorel has a PhD in Pathology and Once Upon a Time did cancer research before turning to marketing. Clayton has a Master's Degree in Visual Art and prefers Expressionist painting in acrylics but has recently tackled digital painting, mostly because there's a hyperactive eight-year-old boy running around the house (their gorgeous son, in case you were wondering if that's normal). Despite having been married for thirty years, they are still madly in love and still writing! As writing partners, they meld logic and creativity, as well as genres. Fantasy, science-fiction, mystery, horror, steampunk, thriller, romance, and the classics—they read them all, and if they can mix them, they will.

Connect with Lorel Clayton

Website: lorelclayton.com
Twitter: @lorelclayton
Facebook:
https://www.facebook.com/AuthorLorelClayton/